SOMETHING STRANGE

The thing lay on a stretch of gravel shoulder along the deserted highway near a sixty-five miles per hour sign. The shape was vaguely round, the size of a small beach ball.

Jamie squatted beside the nasty thing and used a branch to poke at what appeared to be a dark crust covering it. There were bits of white throughout and she dug deeper, then pried a small section loose.

Something broke free and dropped near the scuffed toe of her right boot. A tooth, a human molar with a tarnished silver filling at the center.

She'd seen a lot of death over the last few years, but nothing came close to this. Man was a genius when it came to devising unique ways of killing his fellow man . . .

SUMMERLAND

L. DEAN JAMES

AVON BOOKS • NEW YORK

SUMMERLAND is an original publication of Avon Books. This work has never before appeared in book form. This work is a novel. Any similarity to actual persons or events is purely coincidental.

AVON BOOKS
A division of
The Hearst Corporation
1350 Avenue of the Americas
New York, New York 10019

Copyright © 1994 by L. Dean James
Published by arrangement with the author
Library of Congress Catalog Card Number: 93-91639
ISBN: 0–380–77325–2

First AvoNova Printing: January 1994

AVONOVA TRADEMARK REG. U.S. PAT. OFF. AND IN OTHER COUNTRIES, MARCA REGISTRADA, HECHO EN U.S.A.

Printed in the U.S.A.

RA 10 9 8 7 6 5 4 3 2 1

For Vickie Hamilton Lockard,
whose entire life held cruelty and abuse
and far more misery than joy.
And yet, whose heart was so pure
that any unicorn would gladly
have laid his head upon her lap.
Who will I read my stories to, now?

THE SOUNDS OF the crowd, their angry shouts and shrieks, faded slowly with distance. All that could be heard now was the rustle and crackle of flames from the house across the street.

"Jamie?" A soft voice found her in the dark, and she pushed herself back deeper in the closet. "Jamie!" The whispered word grew harsh with urgency. The door slid back and, by firelight through the shattered bedroom window, the girl saw his face and knew him.

Sick with horror and misery, she felt Will Weston's hands grip her wrists and pull her from the safety of the darkness, then his arms were around her, offering comfort. This was the father she hadn't seen in nearly four months, who'd left his small family to face the insanity of the food riots alone. But he was here now. In his embrace, Jamie broke down.

"Daddy," she sobbed against his chest, "they're dead. Mommy and Robbie are dead."

The tall man stroked her tangled brown hair. "I know, baby. I'm so sorry." He pushed her back far enough to look into her face. "But are you all right?"

"I hid." That confession brought a pain so intense it nearly doubled her over. "They were screaming, and I didn't even try to help them. I just hid." The sobs racked her body.

"Shhh . . ." Will shook her gently. "You couldn't have done anything. They would have killed you, too. You did what you had to." He paused, gazing out through the broken window. "The wind will spread the fire. There isn't much time." The man drew her into the master bathroom,

1

and dug through the drawers until the scissors were found. "Sit!"

Jamie sat slumped on the toilet seat while her father cut handfuls of her long brown hair, dropping them to the floor. The insanity of what he was doing hardly touched her.

"You have to survive," Will Weston said as he worked. "The earth is dying, baby, and you're the only one who can save it." He took a comb and continued the haircut with quick, sure snips of the scissors. "You'll have to dress in Robbie's clothes. They'll be large, but they'll do. No one must know you're a girl, Jamie. No one. Go to the Nelsons. They have a car and can get you clear of the city. Get as far from here as you possibly can."

A whiff of smoke, sharp and pungent, drifted in through the doorway. The scissors hit the tile counter with a clatter, and Jamie, chest tight, eyes still streaming tears, looked up.

"Daddy, you're coming with me . . ."

"No, honey. I can't . . ."

She grabbed one of his big hands in both of hers and gripped it as tight as she could. "Don't leave me!"

"Jamie, listen. You've got to find the rain and bring it back." He pulled loose, then took something from the pocket of his worn Levi's and held it out to her. An oval piece of clear glass lay on his palm, glinting in the fire-light. "This is your guide stone. Keep it with you always; guard it well. When the time comes, the stone will lead you." Will pressed the piece of glass, small but heavy, into her right hand.

Find the rain? The uncontrollable sobs began again. None of what her father said made any sense. She was fourteen years old, her mother and brother lay dead in the living room of their ruined upper-class tract home, and there was no one left to turn to except Will.

"But where are you going?" Jamie cried brokenly, on the verge of hysteria.

"Far away, baby. Farther than you can ever imagine."

"No! Please . . ."

The flickering orange light brightened. Across the road

the houses on either side of the first were burning now, and she saw something close to desperation in her father's face, then his expression softened with pity.

"Jamie, there are worse things to come—much worse. Such danger and heartache. But you won't be alone. Let the guide stone lead you to the ones who can help you most. Just be strong. You must be strong. Don't let Earth become another Summerland." Will Weston leaned to brush his lips to hers. "I love you, baby. I'll always love you, no matter what." He stepped back. "Put the stone to your forehead."

Jamie only stared at him in confusion.

"Do it!" her father snapped.

Slowly, she brought the glass oval up and touched it to her skin. For just an instant the guide stone seemed to turn to ice, then hot white light fired into her skull. A jumble of images flowed swiftly behind her eyes, alien and beyond understanding, and with a gasp, Jamie jerked the stone away, momentarily blinded.

She groped the air before her. "Daddy!"

"The guide is keyed to you now, baby. And you to it."

"Daddy!" Her sight returned, but Will had left the bathroom. The bedroom was also empty. She stood with the glass stone in her hand, somehow certain that her father was no longer in the house, no longer anywhere within reach.

There was no time for tears. A sudden anger replaced her desolation. Will Weston had left her again just as he had all her life. Bastard. She'd survive, all right, but not to follow some crazy scheme of his. The guide stone was thrown on the floor. Beyond the window the flames leaped, pouring black smoke into the night sky. Jamie ran to Robbie's room to find the clothes she'd need, then dressed quickly and took her brother's Buck knife in its sheath from his dresser drawer—a Christmas gift from Will to his sixteen-year-old son the year before. Hers now.

At the patio door, Jamie turned and went back through the ruined house to the master bedroom to retrieve the glass stone from under the dresser. Somehow, she couldn't leave the thing behind. Flames began to crackle on the roof as Jamie slipped out into the backyard. There would be no fire engines to wail down this deserted suburban street tonight, because there was no water to fight the fire. Not now, and maybe never again.

Chapter One

HARRY ARRIVED AT the north gate near the bottom of Laurel Canyon around midmorning. The L.A. haze lay thick in the barren foothills around him, clogging the nose and stinging the eyes. Overhead, a very few birds—mud-brown sparrows—made their way from one leafless tree to another. Before him, the line of refugees was already long and slow moving, and the winter sun had enough strength to make the wait an uncomfortable one. But Harry was used to discomfort. Most Americans were, nowadays.

He passed the time observing the world around him. The L.A. wall zigged and zagged its way into the distance in either direction, a crazy quilt of mismatched materials; brick, concrete, and plaster over a sturdy frame constructed of dismantled tract houses from the outlying suburbs. It would never make it into the history books, this wall. It could not be observed with the naked eye by someone standing on the moon, but at twenty feet high and topped with broken glass and razor wire, it served its purpose well.

Harry understood that purpose and respected what the wall represented—survival. He'd helped to build it nearly seven years ago during the worst of the drought chaos, then arbitrarily chosen to live outside its protection.

A row of spikes lined the top of the wall a short way on either side of the gate. Human heads in various degrees of decay were impaled there, mostly male, but a few female—a grim reminder that justice was simple and swift now. To steal food or water was the same as murder when people had so little of either. The city-state of Los Angeles had no prisons, no public assistance, and what might have

5

been considered cruel ten years ago was a matter of preservation today. Harry didn't dwell overlong on the subject or spend much time viewing the grisly rotting flesh on the wall. He'd seen all too much of that.

The gatekeepers were turning away over half of the applicants. Very few complained. The rare one who did regretted it instantly, painfully. Harry dragged the motor scooter and cart forward over the broken sandy pavement each time the line moved. No sense in wasting gas. He'd long since shed his jacket, but the long-sleeved green flannel shirt, neatly patched in many places with as many different colors, caused the sweat to prickle on his forehead and under his arms.

Three spaces ahead of him a woman with three small children clinging to her skirts finally arrived at the gate. Harry listened to the exchange, though the woman's voice was almost too low to hear. The two gatekeepers, the black man in his booth and the other, a Caucasian standing in the road, were nasty and coarse and unsympathetic. Head bowed, she led the children away, tears streaming down her narrow fleshless face.

Harry caught her ragged sleeve as she passed by and asked, "Where you from?"

"Lancaster," she said, voice catching. "But we can't go back."

"You have to. There's nothing better for you here. Nothing better anywhere. Believe me. Right now, you need to stick to the areas you know, to the people you know. The kids need that. Have you got a way home? Any money?"

She shook her head, no, to both questions.

Harry, you asshole, he thought bitterly and dug deep in a pocket. Most times he hardened himself to the poverty around him, but at the moment there was a little cash in his pocket and a lot of trade goods in the cart. He pushed a worn twenty-dollar bill, old U.S. currency, into her hand. Not worth a lot, but it'd get them a small meal and home safely.

When she tried to thank him, he shrugged it off gruffly. "Did you get water?"

"What?"

"Did you ask for water? By law, they have to give it to anyone they turn away. Eight ounces apiece. It's not much, but it's free."

She tried to smile while the children shuffled beside her. "I didn't know."

"Go on back and ask for it. You don't have to wait in line. Then you'll go home, right?"

"Yes." The misery returned to her plain brown eyes.

Harry watched her go back to the gatehouse, a canteen in her thin hands. Grumbling, the gatekeeper provided the water, pouring the precious liquid carefully into her container, but when the woman turned back to Harry, he looked away, embarrassed by his own kindness. She took the barefoot, silent children with her to the outbound gate with its light stream of pedestrian and vehicular traffic. There, they would eventually find transportation east.

Harry waited patiently for the line to move again. His turn was next.

"Name?" the man in the booth demanded as Harry dragged the scooter and cart to the gate.

"Harry I. Roswell." Harry pulled out his tattered driver's license, long expired.

"Says you're thirty-eight."

"That's right."

The guy eyed him long and hard, then checked a list on the desk before him, probably a list of undesirables.

"Occupation?"

"Dentist."

The balding man in the road beside him laughed, revealing a great gap between his front teeth. "The last thing we need in L.A. is another fucking dentist."

"I don't want to immigrate. I just need a three-day pass." Harry held his temper in check. The gatekeepers were necessarily big men and mean.

"What's your business in L.A.?" the black man asked.

"I need supplies."

"You got a sponsor?"

"Jeffery Cummings, M.D."

"Oh, yeah? Some kinda hotshot, huh? But it's easy

enough to check." The guy in the booth took down the handpiece from a wall phone.

Harry watched in wonder. "You've got phones again?"

"Once in a while," the balding man snorted.

"Wants to talk to you," the other one grunted a moment later.

The receiver was handed out through the door, and Harry took it.

"Hey, Harry, old buddy!" Jeff hollered over the static. "You're still alive!"

"Mostly. You've got phones."

"Sure. All the conveniences of modern living. Got electricity to most of the city now, too. Look, I gave those jerks the okay. Get your sorry ass into Brentwood. I'm at Mount Sinai, but I'll be home before dark. Water allotments are up enough so you can even take a shower."

"Shit." The thought of wasting that much water didn't sit right, but to be clean all over . . .

"Oh, and Harry—" Jeff's voice faded, and the line went dead.

Harry handed the phone back.

The black man hung it up, then sneered. "You ain't cleared yet, chump. Minimum requirement for a three-day stay is $150 L.A. scrip or equivalent value." Now he was quoting right from the book.

"It's gone up."

"Do you have it or not?"

Harry pulled the corner of the tarp loose on the cart and dug into his belongings, brought up a small cloth pouch. The contents were spilled into his palm. Gold, a handful of tiny irregular lumps. Two of similar size were placed on the desk in the booth, purposefully ignored by them all while Harry poured the rest onto the metal plate of a battered triple beam balance. Baksheesh was a way of life here, and the gatekeepers' attitudes altered immediately, grew more friendly.

As jobs went, the gatekeepers had it pretty good. They, along with their brethren at the other four gates into L.A., were witness to all the comings and goings, privy to all the latest gossip. And bribery, while highly illegal, was widely practiced. But beyond that, they had the power of life and death over nearly everyone who stood before the gates. Hunger and thirst would claim many of those they turned away.

"Hundred and eighty bucks worth. Cutting it close, fella." The black man opened a small floor safe under his desk and dropped the gold in, took out a sheaf of paper bills. He counted Harry's share three times before handing it over. The money was ugly and newly printed, with city hall on one side and Mayor Bradley on the other.

"You got any weapons?" The bald one again, already poking through the cart.

"Just my knife. And the scalpels in my medical bag."

Harry watched the man without too much concern. His rifle lay snug in the cart's false bottom. L.A. practiced strict gun control, and he risked losing his own head by taking a weapon inside the gate, but if he left the Ruger with the gatekeepers, it was sure to disappear. His complaint would only be filed and just as quickly lost.

Baldy got down on one knee and gave the underside of the cart a cursory glance, then stood up with a groan.

"He's clean."

"Have a nice stay." The man in the booth gave him a lifeless smile along with the official three-day pass. The two nuggets had vanished from the desk.

Harry fired up the scooter and started out slowly to take up the slack on the hitch. The little bike motor bogged a bit under the drag of the cart, then puttered them off down Laurel Canyon Road toward the city. The dry wind felt good against his face. He'd been sweating as much from nerves as the heat. It hadn't been so bad really. A year ago, one of the gate men had broken Harry's right hand for him. Maybe the bribe hadn't been as big as he felt it should be, or maybe he'd had a fight with his wife. Now *that* had been bad. But Jeff had set the bones, and except for a little pain and stiffness on cold mornings, Harry really couldn't complain. It had sure slowed him down for a while. No, this gate passage had gone rather well.

There were a few cars out on the streets, not many, and Harry tried to remember the time before the drought. Hollywood had been a busy place then. Now the shops along Hollywood and Sunset Boulevards were low-rent housing, the streets dirty and squalid. Smoke drifted from the cookfires on the sidewalks, the Walk of the Stars buried under ashes. This new smog was somehow worse than the old.

But Harry also remembered his mother telling him that the local Southern California tribes had called this basin the Valley of the Smokes long before the Spaniards arrived. Ten million people had lived here not ten years ago. Now there were a mere one hundred thousand walled into a twenty-square-mile area. The rest had migrated, flooded north to Canada or south to Mexico until those borders were closed. And too many had died. But not just on the West Coast—all across the continental United States. The drought had started here and spread. It continued to spread, Europe and Africa and Asia all caught up in the cycle, angry because they believed the U.S. responsible somehow through weather control experimentation. But that was just an excuse to turn their backs on the nation that had always been so quick to come to their rescue. And that was only Harry's bitter opinion.

No one really knew for certain why the earth was dying. All the theories about the Greenhouse Effect, the heating trend, the coming of a new ice age, were meaningless. Without water, the crops had died in the fields. Without food, the people had died. The very old, the very young, the weak—they were the first to go. Then the riots took their toll. And a lot of good people did a lot of horrible things to survive.

Harry cut that line of thinking abruptly. It served no purpose other than to make him feel sick in the pit of his stomach. The madness had passed; life went on. What was left of it. He'd turned west on Sunset without realizing it, found himself cruising past mansions landscaped with raw dirt for lawns and skeletal trees. Some were lived in, some were gutted shells. A car slowed beside him, blue and white and official. The emblem on the door read Beverly Hills Security, a private little police force for the wealthy. Harry kept his eyes straight ahead, and eventually they pulled in front, went on. He was sweating again. God, he hated L.A. But the cool, faintly moist breeze off the ocean found him, lightened his mood. At San Vicente, he turned right, watching for Jeff's street, then followed it up into the hills. Each neatly kept house had a car, an expensive one, parked in the drive, and each had the same arid gardener to keep its yard. The memory of green growing things brought a small ache. Up north, in Oregon and Washington, some of the older trees still survived, but they were dying, too. And once the trees were gone from the world, Harry figured the air supply would follow.

Jeff's house was little different from the others. Harry drove the scooter to the wide gate in the fence and pulled through to the backyard. The dry swimming pool had been two-thirds filled with soil. Cheesecloth, tacked to the edges with rocks, fluttered in the wind, and underneath he could see plants, stunted spindly vegetables—radishes, lettuce, spinach. A piece of white plastic pipe crossed the cement from kitchen to pool, possibly runoff from the sink.

Harry parked the scooter and cart on the patio, pressed his thumb to the electronic security system on the back door. The lock clicked, and the house let him in. It was a time machine, an unsettling look into the past with its Oriental rugs and tasteful furnishings. It affected him this way every time, all the genteel wealth. The refrigerator hummed quietly in the kitchen. He opened it. Except for a bottle of water and some limp greens in the crisper, it was empty. No butter, no jam. No caviar, cheese, or fancy wines. Reality in the fridge, if nowhere else.

He unpacked the cart and brought everything inside, stacking it in the dining room, even the empty gas cans. The trip down from Portland had taken almost two days of straight driving and he was beginning to feel it. Top speed for the ten-year-old Riva was forty-five and, with the cart and the bad roads, he never took it over thirty-five. He figured both he and the scooter would live longer that way.

He wandered through the empty house for a while, then, curious, tried the television in the den. Only one station was broadcasting, but that was one more than the last time he'd visited. Reruns, of course. "The Love Boat." What an odd selection. The commercial breaks were even more bizarre, amateurish and simpleminded, but starved for any kind of input, Harry settled on the couch and blitzed out through the next four shows, mostly black and white "I Love Lucy"s. Only for some reason, the humor escaped him.

"Harry!"

The shout startled him out of his trance.

"Harry! Where the hell are you?"

He heard the heavy door that led from garage to kitchen thump closed and roused himself from the couch, heading toward the back of the house. Jeff Cummings, M.D., slightly pudgy and round faced, stood with the refrigerator door open, dumping white butcher paper–wrapped packages onto the shelves.

"Fish for dinner," he said over his shoulder. "As usual." He turned and grinned, suddenly boyish. A lock of thinning blond hair fell into watery blue eyes, and he brushed it aside. "God, it's good to see you. Did you take a shower?"

"No." Harry grinned back. "But I've got something to go with the meal."

He made a quick trip into the dining room and rummaged in a bag full of dirty clothes.

"Wine!" Jeff cried when Harry returned with the bottle.

"But it's red, and a bit shook up from the trip. Sorry."

"Who gives a shit? Where the hell did you find it?"

"I got it in trade for three stitches and some salve in Bend."

"Well, we can't drink it. I know a few people who'd give you a thousand bucks for a bottle of good wine."

Harry shrugged. "I don't know how good it is. Besides, it's for dinner, for you."

"Got any more?"

"No."

"Too bad," Jeff sighed, then perked up. "Well, open the sucker up and let it breathe." He held out a cork puller. "Besides, I'll bet you've got a lot of other goodies. It's like Christmas when you come for a visit. Sit down while I cook the food. Oh, wait! I've got something for *you.*" He pulled a drawer out from under the counter and tossed Harry a small but heavy cardboard box. "Shells for the Ruger. .223, right? You're not the only one on the barter system. Except I got a whole reloading setup and a fifty-five-gallon drum of gas for a gallbladder operation." He raised a faded brow. "Pretty good, huh?"

Harry nodded, staring at the rows of neat brass shells. This gift was far more precious than a bottle of wine.

"You got the spent casings? I can reload them before you leave. Doesn't take long. Look, running water." Jeff turned the tap and, sure enough, a thin trickle of clear water splashed over the fish he'd just dumped in the sink. "They built another salt water–processing plant. Over in Hermosa Beach this time. Of course, the wealthy neighborhoods are the only ones that get it through the pipes. The rest still have to wait for the water trucks. But it's a start." He slid the fish on a blackened cookie sheet under the glowing coils of the broiler and closed the oven door. They began to sizzle immediately. "Fish and salad and wine. An incredible meal."

He continued to talk while he fixed the salad, which included some of the unknown limp greens from the fridge. "You think you'd get sick of fish, day after day, but it tastes damn good when you're hungry. And we're damn lucky to have it."

"Sea level still dropping?" Harry asked quietly.

Jeff frowned. "Yeah. Little over a foot a year now, and it's accelerating, they say." The fish fillets were done. He brought them to the breakfast counter, where Harry sat on one of the stools.

"I think you better enjoy the fish while you can," Harry said. "I'm no scientist, but it seems to me when the salinity finally goes high enough, there won't be any fish at all."

"Jesus, Harry, don't tell me that, okay?" Jeff poured the wine into their glasses.

"Also seems like the lease on this planet is just about up."

"Don't be a downer. Just eat the fish and be grateful."

He did and was. He'd decided long ago to be a survivor

no matter how hopeless the situation. The wine helped to lift his mood, at least a little. Jeff got downright silly, but then he drank the most. Harry ate slowly, savoring every morsel, and enjoyed his friend's company, his medical tales. In between he added tales of his own, tales of the road and the desolate American countryside.

"So when are you going to stop roaming around the West Coast and come home?" Jeff peered at him over his glass.

It was the opening gambit of an ongoing argument.

Harry sipped his wine. "L.A. isn't my home anymore. Police states make me nervous."

"Oh, come off it. It's a fuck of a lot better than you'll find in the outback. We could really use you here."

"Here I'm just a dentist. . . ."

"And out there you're Harry Roswell, dentist, barber-surgeon, and all-around witch doctor."

"They've got no one, Jeff. All the real doctors are sitting on their fat secure asses inside this wall."

Silence now. Harry looked out the windows at the dry winter dusk. They'd gone into premed together at UCLA, he and Jeff, but Harry's mother was dying of cancer at the time and he'd watched her life, her death, her pain prolonged by the wonders of medical science. While still lucid she begged him to let her die. Only he loved her too much to let her go, and then later the ethics of medicine and law kept her tied to the machines. Death finally came in slow increments. He'd finished premed and gone into dentistry, leaving Jeff, his closest friend, to go on to medical school alone.

"I didn't mean that," Harry said gently into the quiet kitchen.

Jeff smiled. "But it's true. Maybe I'm a little jealous of your freedom. Only I don't think I could handle living on the road—all the dangers, all the deprivations. I know they need you. I'm just being selfish. I don't want you murdered for your food and water. I don't want to look up some year and realize you never made it back . . . that you're never coming back."

"You need some more wine," Harry said and poured the last of it into his friend's glass.

"Hey, Anheuser-Busch is reopening its brewery. I don't know what the hell they're gonna make it out of. Seaweed, probably. But we should have beer in another couple of months." Jeff widened his eyes, hopeful, then chuckled. "What's it going to take to entice you back to L.A.?"

"Rain."

"Well, we never had much of that anyway." He cleared the dishes away, setting them neatly in the sink, and returned with a pad of paper and a pen. "So, what's the shopping list this time? And what have you got to trade?"

Harry'd been considering that the whole trip south. "I need antibiotics bad. Penicillin, ampicillin, erythromycin. As much as you can get your hands on. Antibiotic salves, too. Local anesthetics, syringes, scalpel blades and sutures and ether. I could use more iodine and cold disinfectant. And surgical gloves and—"

"You want to pack a hospital in that cart of yours." Jeff tossed the pad in front of him. "Write it down. And I hope you've got plenty of trade goods, 'cause none of this comes cheap. You used to be happy with a sterile needle and thread."

"Not anymore. I've got a lot of gold."

Jeff groaned. "You're still melting down gold crowns into those things you call nuggets. Doesn't it give you the creeps digging the teeth out of skulls?"

"The dead don't need to eat, Jeff."

But it did bother Harry. So many had died of hunger, thirst, disease. There hadn't been time or even people well enough to bury the bodies. They littered the countryside, the bones picked clean by scavengers. Many had been heaped together and burned in common funeral pyres, sometimes hundreds of them at a time. In the ashes of one, he'd found his first "nugget" and realized that gold would be far more negotiable than paper currency, good in any of the settlements or the few surviving cities.

Dread and superstition kept most of the remains from being disturbed. Only Harry had the audacity to take what little the dead had left and use it to serve the living. Jeff was right, though. Harry I. Roswell, D.D.S., was nothing more than a witch doctor.

"Harry? You're spacing out on me, buddy. It doesn't really matter where the gold comes from. But come on, show me the rest of it, so I'll know what to offer to whomever for whatever you need." Jeff grinned in anticipation now.

Harry led him into the dining room and turned on the light, then began to dump items on the polished Chippendale table.

"Oh, dear God," Jeff muttered. "Where'd you get these?" He held out a worn plastic bag filled with dried apricots.

"Up in Humboldt County, a little place called Pepperwood. Some old geezer's got a magic spring that hasn't dried up yet. He's managed to keep about a dozen people and half a dozen fruit trees alive. They've even got a garden, some chickens, and a milk goat. I delivered a baby, would you believe that? The honey came from them, too."

"Honey?" Now there was awe in Jeff's voice. "Harry, I think you must be the greatest horse trader ever came down the pike."

"I never take more than they can spare."

"Of course you don't. What's this?" Another, smaller plastic sack was held up.

"Vanilla beans. They're pretty old, but I figured someone would get some use out of them."

"I know just the someone. Hell, Harry, by the looks of this stuff, I don't think you're going to have any problem getting your supplies. You've outdone yourself this time."

Harry settled on the floor beside his belongings. "I don't want to get anyone in trouble. Most especially me and you."

"No problem. I know my way around the black market pretty well, by now. How do you think we keep the hospitals running? It's getting better, though, with trade opening up along the coast. We've got our own cargo ships, our own oil sources and refineries. We're even getting shipments from British Columbia, and they're talking about trying for the Panama Canal in the spring."

"That's great," Harry said without much enthusiasm.

"Give me a break, old buddy. After ten years of hell, things are looking up. L.A.'s got a future."

I wish I could believe that, thought Harry; instead he said, "I need some sleep, Jeff."

"Oh ... yeah. Take a shower first, okay? You're just a little ripe, friend, and it saves the sheets. The guest room's ready, and there're towels in the bathroom. I can do some laundry, too."

Christ. A clean body and clean clothes. These were luxuries he didn't want to get used to. And it dug at him a little to know that most of the citizens in this fine city with a future would go to bed dirty tonight, and probably hungry. Jeff was still speaking, and Harry tried to concentrate on the words.

". . . early rounds tomorrow. If you come along, we can start making contacts, grease a few palms."

Harry blinked. "Okay. I need some parts for the Riva, too. And a tire. And gas."

"Gas is no problem, I've got more than you can haul. And we'll hit the junkyards on the way home tomorrow. Not to worry, old friend, I've got everything under control. Go on to bed. I'll see you in the morning."

Somehow, he made it to his feet, made it to the other end of the house. The place was huge, and he wondered if Jeff ever got lonely, if he had anybody to bring home to share his bed and his life. But everything was too neat, too perfect, too unlived-in for that. Electric lights instead of candlelight and firelight. Running water, hot water. He stood in the shower, bewildered by it all. This happened whenever he came to town—once, sometimes twice, a year. They used to call it culture shock. Each time, there were new marvels to behold. It almost had to be another planet.

Hair clean and wet, Harry laid his head on a real pillow and dropped off into uneasy sleep. His last conscious thought was the same as always—where had all the rain gone?

II

Two days west of San Antonio, Texas, Jamie Weston found something strange along the deserted highway. An afternoon wind had brought her the stench long before— the foul sweetness of death and something more, something worse and unidentifiable. The thing itself lay on a stretch of gravel shoulder near a sixty-five miles per hour sign. The shape was vaguely round, the size of a small beach ball, and, at close range, the smell offended her stomach as well as her nose.

She walked a short distance into the brittle scrub brush and gathered a long sturdy stick, bleached white by the sun. Every instinct told her to pass this object by, but curiosity brought her back to it, one hand over nose and mouth to filter the air. Porcupine and opossum might curl into such a shape to die, but this was far too large. Jamie squatted beside the nasty thing and used the branch to poke at what appeared to be a dry dark crust covering it. There were bits of white throughout, and she dug deeper, then pried a small section loose.

It crumbled, revealing bone, some pieces in small chips, others nearly whole. Something broke free and dropped near the scruffed toe of her right boot. She turned it over carefully. A tooth, a human molar with a tarnished silver filling at the center. Her stomach made an uneasy roll, but she leaned closer to the ball. Hair and skin and bone, all twisted together with ropes of drying intestines. There were no tracks in the sand around it.

She scuttled back several feet before standing, then turned slowly, eyes on the distant horizon. Whatever had done this might still be close. The thought caused her heart to thump in her chest. Sweet Jesus! She'd seen a lot of death over the last few years and some of it had been fairly gruesome. Man was a genius when it came to devising unique ways of killing his fellowman, but nothing came close to this.

Her Buck knife was in her hand, nine inches of razor-sharp steel. She'd drawn it without realizing. Best to put as much distance between herself and that thing as quickly as possible. The knife still ready, she dogtrotted down the asphalt until her mouth was dry and her side ached. Stupid. A waste of water and energy. She sipped lightly from the smaller canteen and slowed to a walk, then finally sheathed the knife.

The sky, far too dark a blue for winter, stretched high above her, an upended azure bowl without mountains to crowd it on any side. No clouds anywhere, as if they'd been sucked away. Their absence made the dry wind all the more ominous. Each morning, when she first opened her eyes, she hoped that they would be there, great rounded masses heavy with rain. And each dawn brought clear, empty skies.

Ten years ago, Will Weston had given her the small piece of glass that he'd called a guide stone. She'd carried it ever since in a little medicine bag tied around her neck. It had become a part of her, as unnoticed as a mole or a birthmark. Until two weeks ago. That morning, Jamie had awakened under a Virginia overpass near Richmond with the strong urge to open the medicine bag and look at the stone. The moment her fingers touched the glass, a tiny blue light had winked to life in the very center. The flash of blue had changed rhythm with each move she made. The light blinked most urgently when pointed west, and Jamie had had to follow it.

Everything her father had said and done that night ten years ago was burned into her mind—her brilliant, unreliable, scientist father, who had been a renegade even among his friends and associates. Part of her wanted to believe that his words that night were only madness, but she knew that the drought itself was madness, and that the earth was truly dying. Will had told her to bring the rain back. He'd asked the impossible and yet, here she stood on a lonely, deserted highway headed west, obeying the guide stone.

The wind scattered grit in her face, and the road dwindled in the distance, shimmering in the heat. Creosote-soaked telephone poles paralleled it, bare of wires mostly, and occasionally a pole lay across the pavement. Jamie continued to walk, a long, loose-jointed stride that covered ground quickly without tiring her. The bigger canteen chafed, and she shifted the weight to her left side. She carried very little, had few possessions—the Buck knife and another sharp blade hidden in her right boot; the two canteens; and a leather satchel with a long shoulder strap that held a small amount of food, a few clothes, some personal items, and several letters she'd been entrusted with to deliver along her way. And the medicine bag on its thong around her neck, usually hidden, like now, inside her oversized shirt.

The sun drifted toward the west, dropped low enough to glare in her eyes. She dug the wire-rimmed sunglasses from her pouch and donned them, denying herself another drink from the canteen. Going into the wind, she failed to hear the vehicle until it was already upon her. It swung past, a battered red pickup, dust covered and missing on one cylinder. The back was covered with a tarp and heavily loaded, bottomed out on its springs. Blue smoke poured from the tail pipe in a wispy corkscrew before the back draft tore it apart. Except for the man behind the wheel, there appeared to be no one else in the cab. She had just enough time to stick out a thumb. The truck rattled another twenty yards down the road, then slowed and stopped.

The driver leaned across to push the passenger door open, and Jamie ran the short distance.

"Hello there, young man. In need of a ride?"

She nodded as she climbed in. The man behind the wheel was an elderly Hispanic gentleman, white-haired and neatly dressed. His cologne smelled pleasant. Old Spice. Jamie clamped her arms down. She used sand to bathe with, scrubbing away the worst of the grime. That even worked on her hair, removing the natural oils, but it had little effect on body odor.

"I am Carlos Guerrerra. And you?" He held out a dark, weathered hand.

"Jamie Weston." She took the hand firmly.

"Your grip is strong, but the skin is soft, Jamie Weston. How do you survive in such a harsh world? Are you a thief?"

No rancor in that question. Jamie laughed. "No. Thieves have to work too hard. I'm a storyteller."

"A storyteller!" Carlos returned her laugh. "An old profession." He put the truck in gear and sent it down the road again. "But an honorable one. I thought it had died out among the Anglos long before the drought."

"Not entirely. It just got lost behind all the books and TV and movies. There're quite a few of us now on the East Coast."

Carlos turned deep brown eyes on her. "You've come a long way, and all by yourself?"

"Mostly."

"Without trouble?"

"Hardly. But I run fast."

"And use your knife."

"If I have to."

She liked his open smile, his laughter, and felt no threat from him as she settled back on the lumpy bench seat.

"So, where are you headed, youngster?"

"Just going west."

"At Fort Stockton I'm heading north, up into New Mexico. It would be safer for you to come with me. El Paso is a dangerous place, especially when you're only passing through. You can cross into Arizona just past Gallup. I'm going to the Laguna Indian reservation. That's my home."

"You have water then."

"Some. Enough."

"Are you . . . ?"

"No, I'm not Laguna. I have some Yaqui blood, not that it matters. There's a new tribe on the Laguna reservation—the tribe of man. Our survival depended on our banding together and skin color means nothing to us anymore. You'd be welcome there. We have our own storytellers, of course, but I have a feeling your tales would be very different. Are you a hard worker?"

"When I have to be. And if this is an invitation, I'll take you up on it. For a little while, at least. Why did you leave the reservation?"

The old man was silent for a long moment, then, "I had a son in Navasota. But he's dead and so is the town."

"I'm sorry."

"Oh, he was a worthless fool, but I thought maybe ... Good still came of it. I found tools and nails and salt—a lot of things we need, all left behind by the others. And there's plenty of gas in the abandoned cars. I may go back again someday."

They drove in silence then, and Jamie stared out past the windshield at the unchanging landscape. Only the sun moved, slipping closer to the earth. The truck rode hard, and the seat jounced over the cracks in the pavement, the deep potholes. Jamie endured, grateful to have the ground pass beneath her without any effort on her part.

A recent memory crowded into the lethargy, and she glanced at Carlos.

"Do you know of any predator that eats its prey whole, then vomits up what it can't digest? Like bones and hair."

"Sounds like an owl. They're rare, but they're around. Did you see it?"

"I saw what it left behind." The rest of her thoughts she kept to herself. If it was an owl, it had to be the biggest damned owl in history.

Dusky buildings appeared in the distance, unlit despite the growing twilight. Fort Stockton. The air cooled and Jamie rolled the window up. It would only go halfway. She pulled her jacket from the pouch and put it on while Carlos took the off ramp, putting them on the surface streets. The town was long deceased. Scattered bones on the sidewalk in front of a gutted supermarket might be human. She didn't look hard enough to find out. Sand had drifted into the doorways, along the walls, against the tires of abandoned cars. Carlos ignored the stop signs and the dead streetlights, never slowing.

"Nothing here," he muttered. "It was looted long time back."

They passed under the freeway, heading in a northwesterly direction. Carlos turned on the headlights. The beams were walleyed and lit nearly everything but the road.

"Can you drive?" Carlos asked.

Jamie stuck her hands in her jacket pockets. "No. Things fell apart before I was old enough to learn."

"Too bad. We've got another eight hours of driving. Maybe tonight I could teach you."

"Sure," she said, doubtful.

"At least you won't have to worry about traffic."

Too true. The night closed in, the truck rattled on, and Jamie closed her eyes.

Chapter Two

"LILA ANNE, GO to bed."

In the kitchen of the three-room clapboard house, which also served as the children's bedroom, Lila Anne sat at the table, nose deep in the insect-chewed pages of a book. Vaguely, she heard ten-year-old Martha's imperious command, but was so far gone in another world that she couldn't obey.

Lila Anne had already been learning to read when she was just three years old. Then the drought came and everything changed. Her mother went out one night to find food and never came back, and Lila Anne spent over a week alone in a Phoenix apartment. Or so her Aunt Nonnie told her after she found her there, sick, starving, and filthy, and took her home to Winona, a little town just east of Flagstaff, Arizona. They had taken her in out of kindness.

Kindness. Aunt Nonnie's definition of the word was far different from Lila Anne's. To Lila Anne, kindness meant gentleness, caring, maybe even love—things she had never found in her aunt's family. No one read to her like her mother had, but she had already gained the basics and taught herself as best she could, hoarding books when she came across them. The printed word fascinated her and brought her what little joy she found in life.

It also made her vulnerable. Out of petty cruelty, Aunt Nonnie or her husband, Joe, used the books to punish her. As often as not, they were used to start the cookfire, the pages torn and crumpled and thrown into the stove while Lila Anne watched in helpless fury. That hurt far worse than the beatings with Joe's leather belt.

"Put the lamp out, Lila Anne. Right now."

"Shut up, Martha," she snapped without thinking.

"I'm gonna tell Mama!" The child in the loft above her imitated her mother's screech perfectly.

"Hush. You'll wake the baby."

Lila Anne closed the book—a hardcover copy of *Downward to the Earth* by Robert Silverberg—and placed it carefully under her makeshift pillow before checking tiny Mary, asleep in her crib by the kitchen door. This baby was too good, too quiet, and Lila Anne worried about her. Aunt Nonnie, approaching middle age, should never have had another child. Her labor had taken two long days, and the birth had been difficult.

"Lila Anne!"

She returned to the table and reluctantly cupped a hand over the lamp chimney to blow out the flame, then scrambled into her bed on the floor, pulling the blankets to her chin. They were her only protection against the dark.

All her short life, the dark had terrified her. They were two separate worlds, day and night. In the absence of light, things changed. A door was no longer a passage between rooms; a chair became something monstrous and moved noiselessly from place to place in search of the unprotected. Joe told her over and over that there was nothing in the dark to harm her. But he was wrong and stupid and some night some thing would find him in the dark and then he'd know—too late.

Eyes squeezed tight, she lay stiff and shivering, ashamed of her fear, her bad thoughts. She wished her Uncle Joe dead, and his awful friend, Bonner, though it was a sin. But it didn't matter now. Her soul was already lost. Jesus would never come to take her to heaven with him anyway. Aunt Nonnie said an evil thought was as bad as the deed, and hatred was the biggest sin of all.

Lila Anne hated Bonner, had hated him from the first time he'd trapped her alone in the shed when she was five, his hands delving under her clothes, his tongue pushing into her mouth. Joe had only laughed when she complained, telling her she'd grow to like it one day. Never! The thought made her want to puke.

And now, after years of dodging Bonner's attentions, the very worst thing was going to happen. In three months, on her thirteenth birthday, Lila Anne would be given to Bonner in marriage.

According to Aunt Nonnie, she was a useless, foolish child, and they could no longer afford to feed her. Let Bonner do that if he was so inclined. Only Lila Anne would sooner die. Perhaps she should let the night have her so they could find her broken, twisted body in the morning and weep. Except no one would really care. She wriggled deeper into the dusty, dirty blankets. There was no sense in praying to Jesus. He wouldn't listen. If there was a way out, Lila Anne would have to find it herself. And she had just three months to do it.

II

The sounds of feminine giggles woke Jamie late in the afternoon. Sunlight through the deep windowsills washed the adobe walls of the room with a rich gold. The floor, swept clean, was also dried packed mud.

"He's awake," someone whispered from the doorway.

More giggles and a quick glimpse of woolen skirts as the girls fled. Their voices and laughter were pleasant, which spoke well of the environment they lived in. Jamie pushed back the blankets and climbed from the cot, found the broken-toothed comb in her satchel. The tangles in her short-cropped hair were easily dealt with, though the cowlick in the back refused to lie right. Toothbrush next, in far worse shape than the comb. Brushing without water was a pain, but she'd had plenty of time to get used to it.

She remembered little of their arrival last night. Too damn dog tired after driving the last five hours alone. Carlos, obviously exhausted, had fallen asleep as soon as he trusted her to keep the old pickup on the road and not grind the gears too badly. Trial by fire, that drive, but there was a deep satisfaction that came with learning a new skill.

There were rooms beyond this one, not so brightly lit, but just as clean, just as neatly kept. In the kitchen, a young woman looked up from her work at the table with a smile. Warmth radiated from a big cast iron cookstove.

"Are you hungry?" she asked. "Jamie Weston."

Jamie nodded, cleared her throat. "Yes, thank you."

But the woman was already in motion as she patted out small lumps of dough into tortillas and dropped them onto the hot surface of the stove. She dished out beans from a huge pot into a bowl and set it on the table.

"Sit. Please."

Jamie pulled out a chair across from hers, accepting the food. Real food. Far better and far more than she'd had in a very long time. The thought halted her in midbite.

"This isn't . . . I mean, you aren't . . ." Flustered, she set her spoon down. "I don't want anyone to go without in order to feed me."

"Eat, Jamie Weston," the young woman said gently. "We've been luckier than most, or maybe unluckier. The water flowed well enough for our small crops last season, but we lost nearly half our people to sickness this winter, so there's extra."

"I'm sorry."

"Don't be." But her dark eyes glistened. "Carlos hopes, we all hope, you'll decide to stay with us. We have many young ladies of marriageable age and very few young men."

Jamie choked on a mouthful of tortilla, then reached for the water the woman brought in a chipped coffee mug. She'd been traveling as a boy since the night Will had cut her hair. Far safer on the roads alone, though not always as safe as she would've liked. She'd studied male behavior carefully, imitated their long, sure stride, their uninhibited mannerisms. Her above-average height and voice, a natural contralto, helped the image. And she kept to herself, shunning friendships from either sex, always moving on before anyone could grow too familiar with her.

She ate with her eyes on the food, aware of the young woman's scrutiny. "You haven't told me your name," Jamie said finally.

"Irene Guerrerra."

"Carlos is your father?"

"My husband."

Oh. "How many live here?"

"Seventeen now, including the four babies, but some of them will not survive the winter. Carlos speaks well of you and he doesn't often take to strangers. We know there are some who would take what we have here by force, if they could find it."

Find it, indeed. Carlos had driven the last twenty miles down dirt roads that were all but invisible. Jamie would never find her way back to the highway alone and that made her a little uneasy. The giggles returned, this time from the yard beyond the kitchen door. Round faces, pretty and dark, peered in at them. Irene shooed the girls away, speaking in Spanish.

"I promised them you would tell a story tonight."

"I'd be happy to."

"Would you like some more food?" When Jamie shook her head, Irene retrieved the empty bowl. "Carlos is with the men digging our new well. One of the children will take you there if you like."

Paco elected to take their guest to the site. The boy was six and mixed his English and Spanish with great enthusiasm. Jamie followed him, if not the conversation, along a well-beaten path through the small dormant fields laid out along the southern base of a high stone mesa. She'd nearly slept through the day, and the warm sunlight gave way already to an evening chill. At the top of a long gentle slope, the swarthy, mostly older men greeted her with friendly claps on the shoulder, cautioning her to steer clear of their excavation. They were mud encrusted, but happy. Carlos climbed the ladder last. His shoes were wet.

"God is good to us," he said. "With his blessing there'll be water enough for a new field, more maize."

He introduced Jamie around, and she filed the names in her storyteller's memory. Roland, she remembered vaguely from the night before. A Laguna Indian, he was ancient and beautiful, and the deep lines on his face were a map of his life. He spoke with a lisp, his front teeth long gone. Jamie felt somehow drawn to him and let him keep her back to the rear as they returned to the little group of houses.

"I have thought long and hard on your dreams last night, Jamie Weston," he said, his voice as old as his body.

"My dreams?"

"The dreams you sent me." He cackled. "You make a fine boy, but an even better girl, I think." When she stopped dead in the path, he hooked her elbow and drew her along. "These dreams—you won't find what you look for here. He's of another tribe, this warrior. There are others, too, that you'll need, but I don't see them so clear.

"There's an old, old story among the Southwest tribes, told long before the Anglos came—'bout the end of the world and how a new tribe would come together with men of all skin colors fighting side by side."

The old man fell silent. They walked in fading light, the men ahead laughed and joked.

"Do they win their fight?" Jamie asked after a while.

"No," Roland said firmly. "But that don't mean you shouldn't try, Jamie Weston, Girl Who Walks Like a Man." He cackled again, pleased with himself and her obvious alarm. "I won't tell. It's a fine joke on the others. Can you pee standing up?" The cackle turned to hoarse laughter. "All our young women will be making moon eyes at you, but it don't really matter, 'cause I like you, kid. You got chutzpah."

It was Jamie's turn to laugh.

III

Trey Sweetwater woke at sunrise, and opened his eyes on a high western horizon where a few faint stars still glittered behind the trees. Cold. Too damn cold to sleep any longer. Teeth chattering, he crawled from the blankets to stir the live coals buried deep in the ashes of the campfire. With brittle pine needles and warm breath, he coaxed a flame into existence, then fed it larger pieces of wood until the fire crackled and smoked in the small, sandy pit. It felt good, the warmth seeping slowly back into his bones.

But the chill air at his back made him retrieve one of the blankets and drape it over his shoulders before returning to sit cross-legged as near to the fire as possible. His stomach ached from hunger, sharp insistent pains. Three days now without food, due mostly to his half-assed hunting skills, though the scarcity of game hadn't helped. He knew eventually the pain would leave, replaced by a calm lethargy. You could live a long time without food, the body slowly devouring itself. But not without water. And that was running dangerously low.

To the south, where the mountains gave way to the desert, a form bobbed toward him in the early light with a rhythmic swaying gait. Her. He wondered briefly if she'd had any luck finding water or nourishment on her nightly sojourn. Her needs were more basic than his, but greater. The fact that she had come back to him at all no longer surprised him. They were inexplicably tied somehow, man and animal. An ersatz cowboy and his horse.

She arrived without greeting, and went immediately to nose through his gear, searching for something, anything, edible. By the looks of her sunken flanks she'd found no water and little, if any, graze. He tossed a pebble at her when she started to chew on the saddle skirts, and, insulted, she dodged away.

He watched her, admiring the animal grace of her movements. She was a small rangy beast, an Oregon dun, a descendant of the shaggy steppe ponies of northeastern Europe. As well as the dark buckskin coloring, the backs of her forelegs were marked with a distinct and delicate zebra striping. At the moment, her thick winter coat did nothing to hide the sunken hips, the stark outline of ribs.

They were both half-starved, Trey and the dun. He left the fire to groom her, brushing the dirt from her back carefully. She enjoyed this part of their relationship at least, standing quietly even while he slipped the bosal of the hackamore over her nose. But when he settled the saddle blankets in place, she turned her head and bared large yellow teeth, ears flat to her skull.

Trey slapped her nose. "Don't even think about it!" There were already several nasty bruises on his body from their disputes. "Somebody's got to carry the gear, and you just happened to be born the horse. And I wouldn't need half this shit if it wasn't for you."

He dropped the saddle into place, dodging a well-aimed cowkick when the cinch was tightened. She bared her teeth again, and he wondered briefly if she might be considering carnivorousness. He'd certainly eyed her a time or two when the hunger gnawed at him bad. But no. Their symbiotic love-hate relationship had kept them both alive this long.

Trey tied the two near-empty five-gallon plastic water jugs on either side of the cantle, used their flat backs to stack the remaining equipment with the blankets, and lashed it all down.

He hated to add his weight to her burden, but the simple process of saddling her had exhausted his small reserve of energy. First the fire needed to be smothered with sandy loam. The trees around the camp were tinder dry, and a flash fire would bring complete ruin to Oregon's Malheur National Forest. Here, one in every three trees was already dead, the color and life leeched out of them. Another third were nearly gone, dying slowly of thirst. A few whose roots ran exceptionally deep still clung to life. For how long, Trey had no way of knowing. After so much time, he'd given up hope of rain. Now he cared only about surviving day by bitter day.

When he gathered the rope reins and put a foot in the stirrup, the mare sidled away and dragged him hopping on one foot after her.

"Bitch," he said almost lovingly and swung a leg over the saddle, expecting her to bog her head, crow-hop a step or two. But she had no more energy for such foolishness than he.

So he gave her her head, let her choose their way. She went south first, down out of the forest again, then southwest, skirting the BLM land, but keeping to the open arid countryside. Horses, Trey knew, had three priorities— food, water, and other horses. Not necessarily in that order. The Oregon dun hunted water now and moved, nostrils flared, head swinging with deliberate care.

Trey pulled the Winchester from its scabbard, just in case they accidentally scared up a rabbit from the grease-wood. Or even a snake. The thoughts caused his mouth to water painfully. The sun grew in strength, climbing into the midheavens, and Trey, rifle cradled in his arms, caught himself dozing, lulled by the mare's plodding pace.

Somewhere near the wide depression that had once been Malheur Lake, she halted a moment, testing the air, then turned suddenly and went north, across the flats and up a steep incline. Trey replaced the rifle on the saddle and stepped off, scrambling up the slope beside her. In a sparsely shaded gully, she stopped once more, sides heaving. Dark sweat matted the hair on her neck and flanks. Trey searched the area visually first and found only a hint of green among some rocks at the far end. He pried them loose, one by one, and let them roll to the gully floor. Centipedes and scorpions scuttled for cover. Finally, under one, a damp stain darkened the earth. He dug into it with bare hands, elated, hopeful. There were four two-foot sections of half-inch steel pipe in the pack. He collected them, along with a small sledgehammer and wooden block.

It paid to be a rancher's stepson. Most of his heritage as an Umatilla Indian may have been lost, but his stepfather had given him a knowledge of the land perhaps almost as valuable. And that train of thought led in unhappy directions. He concentrated on the task at hand, driving the pipe into the ground horizontally with the wood block to protect the threaded ends. The second section was screwed on to the first and both hammered deeper into the damp soil. But a little more than three feet in, he hit something solid—stone maybe.

Trey squatted on his heels and waited, watching the mouth of the pipe intently. At last moisture glistened there, began a steady drip-drip of brown water. He grabbed the dented pot from his gear and placed it underneath, then began to suck on the pipe, encouraging the flow. A gush of muddy liquid flooded his mouth, and he spit it out. The mare muscled him aside, got her prehensile lips into the tiny pot, and began to suck noisily. The thin stream from the pipe splashed over her nose.

"Greedy gut," Trey muttered and repositioned the pan, then held her back until it was mostly filled.

She drank a long time, the flow slow enough to keep her from getting a bellyache. Eventually, her gaunted sides filled out, and she backed away, began to browse while Trey filled the water tanks and his canteen, a tedious process. Now he'd definitely have to walk, with her packing eighty extra pounds with all the gear. The water ran clean finally, but the stream had dwindled again to a slow drip. All tapped out.

He wiggled the pipe loose and drew it free, packed dirt into the hole. Above the gully, the mare blundered into dry brush. An angry buzzing started. Rattlesnake. Good fortune had decided to smile on them twice today. Trey brought the sledge with him and climbed out of the gully on the uphill side. The horse had danced out of range and stood, head high, eyes rolling. Coiled at the base of a pine, the snake continued its shrill warning.

"Brother Snake," Trey said gently. "I'm very sorry about this, but I'm hungry."

It had nothing conscious to do with his Indian blood; it only seemed a proper thing to say. He considered the aim with care, brought the three-pound sledge to shoulder level, and tossed. The hammer turned end over end on its flight, and caught the rattler square on the head, smashing it against the tree bole.

"Gotcha!" Trey shouted and startled the mare. With a boot on the reptile's triangular head, he used his hunting knife to saw the body free. Only a three-footer, this one, but big enough. "Thank you," he said to whatever, whoever might be listening.

The water gathering had been a long slow process, and he realized the day was spent, winter dusk fast approaching. The gully, while small, would afford shelter from the chill night wind, and there were plenty of dry tree limbs scattered about for a fire. Part of him felt anxious to be on their way—to where, he had no idea. He only wanted to put as much distance as possible between himself and the Wallen Ranch. In three days, he and the horse had managed to cover maybe twenty miles. Not near enough to his way of thinking, but the search for food and water consumed so much of their time. So far there were no signs of their being followed.

The biggest reason to make camp here and now, he held in his hand, blood dripping at his feet. Food. The blood scent made his stomach clench and growl. He caught the mare and unsaddled her, stacking their belongings in the gully, then went to gather wood. His hands shook slightly and the weakness was more pronounced, but he got the fire going. While it burned down to coals, he gutted the snake, slit the skin, and peeled it off. The meat was cut into several four-inch sections before being thrown in the hot frying pan. He resisted the urge to lick the blood from his fingers, wiping them in the dirt instead.

But the first piece was still near-rare when he picked it out of the pan, sank his teeth into the flesh. The taste was reminiscent of greasy chicken, only infinitely better. Mustn't gobble, mustn't make himself sick. He ate slowly, with total concentration, and finished it all even though his shrunken stomach complained, then carried the remains a distance from the camp before burying it. Food scraps would attract unwanted wild company in the night.

The mare was gone. He returned to the fire and allowed himself a cup of unsweetened weak tea from a previously used tea bag. There were seven left in their faded paper wrappers from his mother's stash, hoarded all these years. In the midst of the blood and gore, he'd calmly picked a little of this and a little of that from the house for the run south.

He'd come back that day from hunting water up on Rabbit Mountain in the jeep and found the ranch house quiet. Too quiet. His mother's nude body was strung by the Achilles tendons from the open rafters in the living room. Her throat had been cut and blood jellied on the hardwood floor under her. She'd been gutted, her internal organs caught in a galvanized washtub, all but the liver, heart, and kidneys, which were missing.

With a sharp knife, someone had taken only the choicest cuts, as though she were a carcass—the hams filleted from the thigh bones, the tenderloin and rump roasts likewise removed. They'd done the same to his stepfather in the kitchen, then ransacked the place. Every bit of food was gone except his mother's tea and a little salt she'd put by for even worse times, hidden behind the stove.

Trey had considered burying them, then considered the return of the people who had done this. He left the butchered carcasses and went to the barn, the horror suppressed by the need to escape. The last of their livestock had been taken, too: a few old hens, a cow and heifer, and his stepdad's saddle horse, all hauled away in a truck by the look of the dual tire tracks in the road. But the tools and harness hadn't been worth their bother.

Carefully, he chose what he might need to survive, bringing it all out to the jeep, but the jeep had little gas left, and the killers had emptied the last from their storage tank. That was when the Oregon dun had returned—his stepfather's pride and joy. She'd somehow gotten away. And it took nearly an hour to catch her, the bitch, while she raced around him in circles as if it were some game. When he'd finally given up, turned away in disgust, she came to him, allowed him to saddle her and pack the water and equipment.

Now, sitting here by the fire with darkness all around, he also considered the possibility of the Oregon dun's failing to return from one of her nightly forages. There was always the chance she might find other horses or somehow be killed—he couldn't be the only hunter in these mountains. Then he'd be forced to leave most of the gear behind. To the northwest lay Bend and beyond that Eugene, and a number of small communities that had so far survived the drought. There, he might find refuge . . . or a butcher knife.

The thought of being another man's meal made the hair prickle on his arms and neck. Intellectually, it shouldn't bother him. Dead was dead and meat was meat. Or so he told himself. Uh-uh. No way. Better to die out here, feed the wild things, than be served up on somebody's fucking dinner plate.

And he'd done enough thinking for the evening. His belly was full, they had water enough for another couple of days. What more could he want? A softer bed maybe. He cleared a spot a little way from the fire, making small depressions in the soft soil for hips and shoulders, and laid out his blankets. Silent night. The insect world suffered from the drought, too. The wind soughed in the dead tree branches, the Milky Way stretched far above him, and he settled back on his bed with the rifle beside him, staring into the depths of the galaxy. *We were going to go there,* he thought, *only we never even made it to Mars. Big dreams for such infinitesimal specks on a galactic scale. Now we know nature's the real boss, and it's too late.*

Sleep took him to unpleasant places, back to the ranch house to talk with his mother, her long black hair hiding the cut in her throat. But nothing could hide the open empty rib cage, the bared bones, and he kept staring impolitely at them. Her annoyance grew at his inattentiveness.

Something dark and smothering settled over him, denying him air. The weight crushed him down, down. Then he felt a prick that became a deep stabbing pain and it wasn't a dream anymore. Panic tore a muffled scream from his throat, and he tried to fight, only his arms and legs were pinned to the blankets.

Something sharp ripped into his shoulder, and he screamed again, was answered immediately by a high-pitched squeal of inhuman rage. The weight holding him shuddered, once, twice, then he was dragged bodily up from the ground several feet, airborne for an instant, and dropped.

The collision with the earth stunned him. Dazed, he saw a familiar shadow standing over him, smelled her sweat, and heard the air exploding from her lungs. *God, don't step on me,* he thought, the panic returning, but she stood steady, unmoving, then finally dropped her head to blow hot equine breath in his face. She snuffled him all over before giving a chuff of seeming satisfaction, and stepped carefully away.

The pain in his shoulder was acute, and he touched it gingerly, found the flannel-lined jean jacket and shirt both torn, felt a sticky wetness. Blood. What in Christ's name had attacked him? Something large, a mountain lion maybe. Only a cougar couldn't pick a grown man up, not four feet off the ground. Whatever it was, the mare had driven it off.

She hovered near while he rebuilt the fire, the rifle in one hand the whole time. The wound had to be cauterized and quick. He couldn't afford infection. A flap of skin had been laid open to the collarbone on his right shoulder, a long six-inch slash as if from a knife. At least it bled well—maybe too well.

He stuck the blade of his hunting knife into the coals, waited till the metal glowed cherry, then slipped it into the wound. The pain and the stench and the sound nearly put him out, made him grit his teeth to keep from yelping. Christ! It had seemed like a good idea at the time.

The knife fell smoking to the ground. Seated there beside the fire, he swayed and fought to keep his dinner down. The bleeding stopped, but try as he might, he couldn't get a bandage tied over the shoulder with his left hand. He gave up finally, content to cover it and himself with a fresh shirt from his pack. The remainder of the night was spent sitting before a blazing fire with the rifle in his lap and the mare standing close beside him.

IV

Three days in L.A. was just about all Harry could handle. Too easy to hang out in upper-class Brentwood enjoying Jeff's company and comparatively luxurious lifestyle. But still not so easy that he could ignore the absolute poverty in the other areas of the city. Guilt gnawed at him, knowing he could, at the very least, provide the poor with a minimum of medical help and knowing his head would end up on a gate spike if he tried.

"Just keep your mouth shut and pay attention," Jeff said

as he pulled the older model Jaguar XKE into the near-empty hospital parking lot.

It was 6:00 A.M. and winter dark. Surgery was still a predawn affair.

"What month is this?" Harry asked.

"You're kidding." Jeff stared at him, then looked away. "It's the end of January. Tuesday the—"

"Thanks, the month's enough."

His friend put the car in the stall marked J. Cummings, M.D., Chief of Surgery.

"Kind of young for Chief of Surgery," Harry commented, pushing the car door open.

"Yeah, well, the last bout of influenza left me the oldest surgeon on staff." He led Harry in through the E.R. "Remember—"

"Keep my mouth shut," Harry finished for him.

They went to the storage rooms first, just off the doctors' lounge. From a locker, Jeff handed him a white coat with a visitor's pass clipped to the pocket, then donned his own.

"The stuff's over here."

Four medium boxes stood in a far corner of the room—Harry's, by right of some fast wheeling and dealing.

"Nearly everything on the list, and a little something extra." Jeff opened the top carton and held up a small unmarked pill bottle. "Codeine. I could only get a few, so save them for emergencies."

"They're all emergencies, Jeff."

"Then save them for yourself. Witch doctors have accidents, too."

"What about the stronger stuff?"

"Couldn't do it, Harry. Sorry. You'll have to get along without. You have so far."

Harry glanced down at the floor. "I've got a terminal cancer patient in Bend. I was hoping . . ."

"God, I'd never be able to get you enough to keep a cancer patient comfortable. They can take a long time dying . . ." He paused when Harry looked up, met his gaze. "Oh, no, Harry. You can't do that. It's professionally, ethically, and morally wrong."

"I'm just a witch doctor, remember? I don't feel bound by your ethics. And I certainly don't agree with your morals. Cancer research, all research, is over. As far as I'm concerned, to prolong suffering is morally wrong. We'd never let an animal suffer like that. There's got to be some dignity in death if possible."

Jeff grabbed the lapels of Harry's white coat. "You stupid softhearted jackass. What about using the ether?"

"That's almost as tough to get ahold of, and I need it for anesthesia."

"Yeah." Jeff released him. "I'll see if I can get my hands on some sodium Pentothal. Somehow. But for God's sake, I hope you know what you're doing." He checked his Rolex. "Shit! We've got to scrub. The cesarean is scheduled for seven. And you can stand in on the appendectomy at nine, too. I figure those'll be the handiest procedures to take back on the road with you. They're fairly straightforward for life-saving surgeries. And you've already got the basics. I've told them you're a visiting medical student from Portland."

"Portland doesn't have any hospitals, anymore. Or doctors."

"So? Who's going to know? Of course, they think it's an exchange program. Won't they be surprised?"

"There's another slight problem. I don't have most of the instruments for those kinds of procedures."

"Yes, you do. I've got them at home. They're a bit old-fashioned, but that's the kind of surgery you'll be performing, anyway. Come on, we'll walk and talk." Jeff took him back into the quiet corridor. "I want you here in L.A., I admit. But I approve of what you're doing. I'm glad you're doing it. Better you than me, buddy." At the wide double doors marked Surgery, Jeff paused. "Harry, I know you've got to lose a lot of patients with the odds so against you. How do you handle it? I mean, when they die despite everything you do, do you feel responsible?"

"Do you?" Harry leaned against the right-hand door and it swung open.

Chapter Three

AT CARLOS'S INSISTENCE, Jamie stayed another day in the Laguna settlement. She worked with the men, drawing heavy buckets filled with wet dirt from the bottom of the new well until her arms and shoulders ached, and she was covered head to toe with drying mud. The noon meal brought to them consisted of more tortillas and beans, and she squatted on her heels with the rest of the group in the sparse shade of a cottonwood near the well, dipping into the common pot.

Aches aside, she enjoyed the company and the work. The problem came later, at the end of the day, when she was invited to bathe with the laborers, a simple enough procedure involving a galvanized laundry tub set up in one of the empty buildings that lined the small plaza. Each man in his turn stripped, stepped into the tub, and using a small amount of water, scrubbed and rinsed. The soapy water was carted out to the winter garden between baths.

Jamie had declined going first and waited, uneasy, trying to think of some excuse to avoid her own bath. Nude male bodies didn't disturb her. She'd grown used to the uninhibited nature of men during her years of travel, and this wasn't the first time she'd been caught in a sticky situation.

Roland came to her rescue at the last moment, sending the others off, though Carlos's expression was filled with concern and curiosity.

"I told them you're a shy youngster and needed privacy." Roland grinned. "I told them I would help you rinse."

"Thanks, but I can manage alone."

Roland brought a bucket near. "I'm an old, old man, Jamie Weston, and I haven't seen a naked woman in more time than you've been alive. Before I die, I'd like the pleasure of washing your back. I'm feeble and harmless."

"I doubt that." Jamie, lips pursed, unbuttoned her oversize shirt and took it off, baring small round breasts, then stepped out of her muddy jeans.

"Ahhh," Roland murmured. "Just as I thought—you make a pretty boy, but a much more beautiful girl." He handed her a soapy sponge when she stepped into the tub. "You sent me dreams again last night and in them I saw this medicine bag you wear. I saw also the clear stone with its blue light that guides you."

Jamie glanced at him, awed. "I never met a man with truer dreams than yours, Roland."

"An old man's dreams have little value. But you'll be tempted to stay here with us, Jamie Weston. It really doesn't matter to these people what sex you are. They would be disappointed, but would welcome you, anyway."

"I know."

"I would welcome you, too, but you're destined for other things. You must create a new rain dance with powerful medicine. Only take care, young one, or the medicine will be turned against you."

"I'll be careful." Jamie smiled, uncertain what any of that meant. But the water felt good, chill as it was, and she scrubbed her skin hard, removing a month's worth of grime. "Is there enough water for me to wash my hair?"

"Of course." Roland took the sponge from her, applied it to her back and shoulders. His hand slipped under her arm, brushed gently against her left nipple.

"That's fine," she said and firmly pushed him away, but the touch brought longings, momentarily sweet. The sensations were denied.

Wet and shivering, she dressed again in the same filthy clothes, then bent over the tub to wash her hair, with Roland using the bucket sparingly.

Dinner was ready when they returned to the main house. Carlos said grace, and Roland also, who thanked other gods for their blessings. The pretty dark-eyed sisters,

Consuela and Maria, fell all over themselves waiting on Jamie, which caused sly smiles from some of the adults, Roland included. Soon after the meal, the younger children were put to bed and the family went out to the plaza for its nightly entertainment.

A small fire was built in what had once been an ornamental fountain. Bright sparks spiraled upward in the smoke, scattering in the wind. Jamie, aware of the laughter and friendship around her, realized dully that she could never be a part of the love and closeness these good people shared. She stared into the flames and remembered.

Her own childhood had been happy enough before the drought. Will Weston had spent most of those years in distant parts of the world—wherever his work as a meteorologist took him. Sometimes there was an abundance of money, sometimes things were financially tight. Jamie's father had had little regard for budgets, whether huge government grants or simple family concerns, but they'd always gotten by.

Once, Jamie had hoped to be a writer of short stories and novels. Her teachers in school had encouraged her until the drought had ended those dreams. Her stories were never destined to be in print, but her vivid imagination had proven to be a valuable talent, one that provided the important things in life—food, water, and shelter. Now she was both author and actor, something she'd never dreamed possible before. Writers never really had the chance to watch the faces of their readers, never felt the energy that flows between audience and performer, or felt the giddy rush that comes with applause. Now that Jamie had, she could probably never go back to the written word.

Her best received tales were in the tradition of the *Arabian Nights*. Folks related to the arid desert backgrounds, to the fantasy and magic. They were sick of reality. Jamie's viewpoint characters were of all ages; her females, strong and brave, her males, intuitive and gentle when they needed to be. And always Jamie hid a little moral behind the action.

Except in the two days she'd spent at the Laguna settlement, she never once had had a chance to tell one of her tales. Instead, the first night she was asked over and over to relate the adventures of her own travels. They were hungry to know how the Eastern states fared, how others lived and survived. So she awed them with descriptions of the Great Lakes, those once huge inland bodies of fresh water, nearly gone now, sucked dry by the dying cities that lined their shores. In New York City, the remaining population clung more tenaciously to their old lifestyles. There were still cabs and muggings and theater and starvation, but no longer a housing shortage.

Inland, life was harsher, but on the whole, the people Jamie met were fairly open and willing to help one another. Bad people *did* exist. They always had, always would. She related several narrow escapes, once from a pack of domestic dogs gone wild. That time, she'd spent three long days in the limbs of a dead tree outside of Mobile, Alabama, where she found out the hard way that some dogs are very good climbers. All the members of the Laguna family were sympathetically aghast, except Roland, who laughed so hard he nearly choked. And Jamie knew why. Peeing from the treetop had proven a very dangerous and humiliating experience.

Roland was all too right about the moon eyes. This second night by the communal fire, Jamie found herself crushed between Maria and Consuela. She'd used her standard excuse, last night, explained gently the vow of celibacy that she'd taken, which wasn't altogether a lie. But it was obvious these kind folk were determined to give her a home here.

It was tempting. She'd been given water to bathe in, her hair was clean, and her belly full, but the tug of the guide stone was strong. Maria slipped a slender, work-hardened hand into Jamie's, and, flustered, Jamie pulled loose with a forced smile, trying not to offend.

Irene sat across the fire from them, accompanying herself on a guitar which had new strings, thanks to Carlos's trip to Navasota. She sang in Spanish, her voice lovely and wistful. A love song, Jamie felt certain by her expression. Ten adults clustered to the warmth of the flames and her voice. Jamie studied their faces, old and young, and touched the medicine bag at her neck, but Roland was right—she would not find what she was searching for here.

Carlos appeared in the firelight to lean down and whisper in Maria's ear, and she moved away so that he could sit beside Jamie, shoulder to shoulder.

"What do you think?" he asked quietly.

Jamie smiled. "Her voice is beautiful."

"Yes, it is, but I'm asking if you'll stay with us. There are too few of us, now. We have a lot to offer you."

"You do, but I'm sorry," the young woman murmured. "I can't. Tomorrow morning I'll have to leave. Only someone will have to show me the way back to the road."

"I'll take you in the truck."

The words had a slight edge to them—anger or disappointment. Jamie couldn't be sure.

II

On this particular morning as every morning, Lila Anne went to Mary's crib the moment she woke. The baby had to be changed first thing because she was prone to rashes. Mary still slept, her eyelids a deep purple against the tiny pale face, and it wasn't until Lila Anne picked her up that she noticed the baby wasn't breathing, that her little limbs were stiff.

"Aunt Nonnie!" the girl screamed and ran into the next room with the infant still clutched to her chest.

Her aunt sat up on the bed, half-asleep. She accepted the lifeless body from Lila Anne without comprehension, staring dazedly at Mary's face. Understanding made her eyes widen and fill with horror.

"What did you do?" the woman shrieked. "What did you do to her, you horrible awful girl?"

"Nothing," Lila Anne said in small voice, her world already crumbling. Mary had been her responsibility and the one thing she truly loved in her dreary, unhappy existence.

Choking on tears, she ran from the room and the house, with Aunt Nonnie screaming hateful curses after her. The cold morning air bit deep through her thin clothing, and a small amount of ice sparkled over the ground, the roofs of the outbuildings. In the distance, in the early sunshine, she could see the tops of the tallest buildings in Winona, but it was a dead place, now. Dead and deserted.

She glanced once behind her at the shabby house, hearing her aunt's muffled wails. There was nothing here for her now. It would've ended soon anyhow. When Bonner came to take Lila Anne, she was bound to lose little Mary. She'd decided a while ago to leave before that happened. There were glass jars of water and a very little food, stashed under the straw in the empty chicken coop. She went there now and gathered them with cold numb fingers, tying them around her waist by a piece of cord, then walked away as quickly as she could—toward Winona and the highway.

III

Trey knew in his first waking moment that he was in bad trouble. His shoulder was swollen and hot to the touch. Not from the slash—that seemed okay—but from the puncture wound he located by touch in the back of his shoulder. He'd failed to notice it last night over the pain and the blood, not that there was anything that could've been done, with its being out of sight and reach.

The mare blew, wet and noisy, somewhere off to his left, and he jumped. It was nearly midmorning by the angle of the sun, and despite the pain and feverishness, he began to pack their gear. The tiny spring was tapped one last time and gave water enough to satisfy the dun. Trey drank, too, as much as he could force down, in hopes of flushing the poisons from his system, then the mare was saddled and loaded down. Oddly enough, she took it all without her usual complaint, as if she were anxious to be away from this place.

He led her on foot down the mountainside toward the desert. Caution told him he'd best find help, that as quickly as the wound had festered there couldn't be much time, but already his thinking was fuzzy, and he continued to trudge south, still bent on his original plan. The mare nudged him once on the back of his bad shoulder, and the pain sent him to his knees, gasping.

The sun hit the meridian and started its descent. The far southern horizon seemed no closer, and Trey's steps had slowed, the sand dragging at his boots. In every direction, as far as he could see, there was nothing. Even the desert plant life had given up the ghost, leaving brittle skeletal remains to mark its passing. Finally Trey stopped the mare and used the last of his strength to climb into the saddle. Hunched in misery over the horn, he gave her her head.

IV

"Another day, Harry. If you want it, you'll wait."

Harry rubbed his mouth with the back of a hand, an agitated gesture. "My pass is only good for three."

"No problem. I'll call in an extension." Jeff plucked the receiver off the wall phone in the kitchen, and tapped the cradle several times. He flashed Harry an apologetic grin. "Then again, maybe I'll call it in later." The phone was replaced.

"But it's for certain?"

"Nothing's for certain around here, Harry. Except zero precipitation." Jeff began unloading packages from a cloth bag. "Fish for dinner for a change. Look, word has it there's a Canadian freighter docking tonight with med supplies. Including sodium Pentothal. If it shows, then I can get it early in the A.M. and pass it on to you and you'll be on your way."

"I'm about out of trade goods, Jeff. Hope there's enough."

"We're not talking black market, here," the chief of surgery said cheerfully. "We're talking outright theft."

"Jeff, I don't want you risking your head on this."

"Are you kidding? That shit's for lowlifes and dentists. We're so short on doctors that I could get away with murder. Sad to say, I probably do."

The fish were shoved under the broiler. Harry tried to lose the nervous energy that kept him tense. A few more hours was not so long to wait, if there was a chance to end

Kathreen Gilbert's suffering. She'd begged him to use the rifle, to put a bullet in her brain, and he couldn't do it, couldn't find the courage. But the gutless wonder would do it with drugs. It made him angry—angry that he couldn't save her, angry that he couldn't kill her, angry at what he considered a basic weakness.

"Hey, what's the matter, pal?"

Harry looked up, and realized he'd been grimacing. "Just worrying."

"That'll kill you quick." Jeff set a plate of broiled fish with several small, limp carrots in front of Harry. "I know the carrots'd probably taste better if I cooked them, but we need the vitamins intact."

Bitter, those orange roots, and pithy and chewy, but Harry ate them gratefully, along with the fish. They shared a few dried apricots for dessert, then vegetated in front of the TV till midnight, watching "Hunter" and "L.A. Law" reruns, and remembering how the world used to be just a few short years back.

V

Carlos had put Jamie back on the road early that morning. Despite his disappointment, he sent her off with a smile and food and water for the journey, wishing her well. She could always return, he told her when she thanked him for his kindness, then he was gone, followed by a dust cloud that hung motionless in the cold air long after the truck vanished from view.

She walked, slipping into the mindless, long stride that covered the miles. Some part of her was aware of everything around her, the light, the landscape, the black asphalt beneath her feet. But another part dreamed of a young girl, the daughter of a poor watermonger, who lived in a great desert city at the base of the mountain called Shandar. She envisioned crowded, dirty streets lined with artisans' booths. The girl's name was Roxalla, and her hair was long and fiery red. And she stood for hours in the hot sun selling cups of water to passersby. Until one day, a handsome pasha rode by. . . .

Over and over, the story ran through her mind, mutating, growing, until nearly everything was complete. She had no idea where it all came from; she never did. Some little thing would cue it, conscious or unconscious, and she'd be swept away into other words, other lives. It made her own life more bearable to have these waking dreams.

When the sun grew hot, she pulled her battered Braves baseball cap from the satchel, donned it and the sunglasses, and kept on, ignoring hunger and thirst. These were old friends, and she knew her limits, though she pushed them constantly. Better to go without now than later.

She crossed into Arizona just before dark, dog tired and starved. The land had gone barren again—more barren, rather. It took some searching to find enough wood to keep a small fire going all night. A light sleeper of necessity, she had no problem feeding the fire every hour or so. And somehow, after what she'd found along that Texas highway three days past, a nightlong campfire seemed prudent.

VI

Lila Anne hid out in Winona all day. Now that she'd finally run off, she realized she hadn't really thought about where she'd run to. Maybe to Phoenix to find her mother, as foolish as that sounded. But then she had only a vague notion of where Phoenix lay. Late in the afternoon, Bonner and her uncle came into town searching for her, shouting dire threats if she didn't come out; but she'd covered her tracks well and stayed hidden in the empty shelves of a supermarket. Bonner even walked right past her at one point.

Long after they'd left, she remained undecided, then finally, at dusk, lurking in shadows, she started east on the city streets. But dark fell quickly, and she ended up huddled in a clothing store on the outskirts of town. The front windows were broken out, but most of the clothes were still there, just dusty and faded. People were looking for food in the days before, not apparel. Lila Anne found a thick quilted jacket, a little large, and put it on, wondering briefly why Aunt Nonnie had never brought them to town.

All their clothes were next to rags. But, then, her aunt's good Christian soul abhorred thieving of any kind.

Lila Anne settled under a pile of frilly dresses in a back corner of the shop, determined to wait out the night, to survive it. Eyes clenched shut, she slowed her breathing so that nothing, absolutely nothing, would betray her to the shifting, changing darkness.

VII

Harry sat hunched down on the seat of the Jaguar in the predawn light once more. Only this time alone. Jeff had gone into the hospital nearly an hour ago, and Harry watched as first one truck backed up to the loading platform, then a second. Now two private police cars rolled silently into the parking lot; uniformed men got out and sauntered in through the emergency room entrance. Too casually for Harry.

He scrunched farther down in the seat. Then jumped a foot when Jeff knocked on his window, motioning him to roll it down.

"Take it and get the hell out of here." The young doctor handed him a 100-cc bottle.

"Why are the cops here?"

"Doesn't matter. Where's your scooter?"

"On the next block up."

"Good. I'll keep our policemen friends busy while you hightail it. Wait'll I get inside."

"Jeff—"

"Shut up and do it. I'll see you next time you head down."

"Thanks."

But Jeff was already heading back. Harry waited the moments it took the man to disappear inside, then slid out of the car and walked, as casually as he could, toward the road. No shouts of alarm followed him. Jeff's situation worried him, but so did the fact that he'd left his loaded cart alone on a city street for nearly an hour. Except the streets were empty, silent. Los Angeles no longer had a rush hour to deal with. That preternatural quiet was probably the eeriest thing of all.

The cart had not been touched, and Harry leaned down to unhook the trapdoor in the bottom, slipped the bottle, now wrapped in a sock, next to the Ruger, and sealed it back up again. He wasn't going to breathe easy until he was beyond the north gate and headed away. The scooter strained now under a full load, most of the weight in the gas cans stacked under the tarp.

The sun rose finally, but Laurel Canyon lay still in cold shadow. He slowed up enough to zip his battered leather jacket and eyed the movements along the streets he passed. Men with bundles of short sawn lumber loaded on their backs hawked their product in strident voices. Cookfires were already burning on the sidewalks. He caught a quick glimpse of a crowd of people clustered around a water truck, then noticed the gate up ahead.

He swung to the right and got in line. It took nearly two hours and one execution to make his way to the front. There was no ceremony to death in L.A., no gawking crowds, only the hapless folks trapped in line to watch. The gatekeepers did the deed after they dragged the prisoner, bound and gagged, to the chopping block. It took several blows with a wood axe to sever the head from the body.

So this is civilization, Harry thought bitterly. Like the rest, he'd watched against his will, fascinated by man's inhumanity to man. Afterward, every man, woman and child looked at one another with fear in their eyes. Everyone had something to hide, something that might possibly put them in the poor victim's place. Harry sweated despite the cold. He was most certainly the next likeliest candidate for the block.

"Pass," a huge black man demanded. A different fellow from the incoming gate.

Dumb, Harry handed the paper slip over.

"This expired yesterday, asshole."

Harry kept his voice clear, but mild. "If you'd please check your list, there should be a one-day extension called in by Dr. Jeff Cummings."

The man checked, then grunted. He worked alone on the outgoing side. The tarp was stripped back on the cart.

"Let me see your receipts for this stuff."

Harry handed him a small sheaf of papers. They were phony and real at the same time, all properly signed by friends of Jeff's who were willing to vouch for Harry. And the gatekeeper spent a good while checking the cart's contents against the receipts, then went into his small booth and made some calls. He seemed somehow disappointed when he returned. The papers were handed back, and Harry noticed that the drying blood on the man's hands had smeared the receipts. He'd been the one who climbed the wall and spiked the head. The body still lay leaking gore slowly into the dirt not ten feet from where they stood.

The chain link gate rolled aside and Harry saw freedom beyond it. He started the bike and headed toward the opening.

"Hey, you!" The gate man shouted suddenly.

Harry stopped the bike, despite every instinct that told him to run. He glanced back, hoping against hope that that sharp command had been intended for someone else. But no, the big man stalked after him.

"Ain't you the one that's doctoring in the outback?"

Harry nodded, tense.

"There's been a kid here for two days asking after you. Scrawny kid, 'bout yea high, with dirty blond hair. Check it out. I think he's pretty desperate."

Harry nodded again, some of the tension leeching away. This time no imperatives followed him through the gate. But the kid with the dirty blond hair appeared out of the crowd of ingoing traffic. He was dirty all over, perhaps ten, and only a touch above emaciation. Harry was afforded the barest glance, then he looked away.

Harry called to him, pulling near on the scooter. "You the one looking for a doctor?"

"Yes," the boy said, doubtful, his eyes searching Harry's face.

"If I don't look like a doctor, it's 'cause I'm not. But I'm the closest thing you'll find this side of the gate.

What's the problem, and I'll tell you whether I can help or not."

"It's my mom. She can't have her baby. It won't come out."

Christ. "Where you from? And how long has she been in labor?"

"Bakersfield. And it's four days now. Some people passing through from Oregon said you'd come to L.A. So I came."

Christ, again. "You're alone?"

"Yeah. I hitched a ride down."

Harry did not want to go to Bakersfield. He'd never liked the place *before* the drought. And the woman, four days in labor, could be dead by now. Then again . . .

"Climb on behind."

"We don't got any money."

"Climb on," Harry snapped.

The kid swung on behind, and wrapped bone-thin arms around Harry's waist as he put the scooter once more in gear.

VIII

All the next day Jamie walked steadily westward. The tale still spun in her mind, color and movement and light. It was nearly perfected, but would never be, not completely. With each telling it would change, however slightly. She'd donned the sunglasses against the drop of the sun, saw it grow huge and orange during its descent. Out of the wavering heat lines rising from the asphalt, a figure appeared in the distance, walking steadily toward her. The form shimmered ethereally, and Jamie wondered what this chance meeting might bring. Friend or foe?

But it clarified as it came—a young girl with long skirts and long hair fired red by the setting sun.

Without thinking she called out, "Roxalla!"

The girl stopped short, took two quick steps back.

"Wait!" Jamie cried. "Don't run. I won't hurt you."

"I wouldn't let you," the child said haughtily. "I'd scratch your eyes out. What did you call me?"

Jamie shook her head. "It doesn't matter. You reminded me of someone I ... know. My name's Jamie."

"I'm Lila Anne. Where are you going?"

"To California. Where're you headed?"

The girl hesitated. "I'm ... going to California, too."

"Then I think you're going the wrong way."

"Pretty dumb, huh?"

"Yep." Jamie moved toward her, and the child sidled away, the water bottles tied around her waist clinking. "You live around here? Where're your folks?"

Very natural suspicion edged Lila Anne's words. "My folks are dead."

"Tough break," Jamie said matter-of-factly. She started out, again. "Come on, I'll walk you home. You're much too young to be on the road."

Lila Anne refused to budge. "I won't go back."

"I don't care how bad it is, girl, it's not as bad as the road. Take my word for it."

There were buildings in the distance. Jamie, unthinking, dropped into her long stride. When she chanced to look back, Lila Anne was well behind, even at a trot. At least she was following. The dented green sign said this was Winona. Somebody had scratched the population out and put "0" with black felt pen.

She halted to wait for the girl. "Is there a shoe store in town?"

"Two or three," Lila Anne answered petulantly.

"Could you show me where? My boots are just about worn out."

"If you walk like this in new ones, you'll ruin your feet. There's a shoe repair shop right on the main street with everything you need to fix yours."

"You're pretty smart, kid. But my feet are tough, and I don't have time to learn the cobbler's trade."

"Can you drive?"

"As a matter of fact, I can."

"Then why don't you? There's cars all over."

"With batteries that are ten years dead among other problems."

"I know where there's one that'll work. If you take me along, I'll show you."

Jamie frowned. "Naw. Cars are too much trouble, and so're little kids."

"Suit yourself," Lila Anne snapped and walked back the way they'd come, back toward the highway.

Jamie watched her go without too much regret. A preteen female sidekick was the last thing she needed. The youngster would get tired, hungry, and scared and head home soon enough. She turned to check the storefronts and heard a sudden squeal.

Someone big had dodged out from between the buildings and caught Lila Anne by one thin arm. He now proceeded to jerk her back along the road.

"Hey!" Jamie shouted and ran after them.

The man swung around, burly and dark bearded. Lila Anne sank her teeth into his wrist, and he flung her away. She fell, tumbling across the pavement.

"You son of a bitch!" Jamie snarled.

"Stay out of it, boy. This is family. That girl's my wife, and I'll do as I please with her."

"I don't care what she is. You lay another hand on her, prick, and I'll cut it off. And I don't mean your hand."

The big man grinned. "Fancy her yourself, huh? Wanna fight for her?"

Jamie pulled the Buck knife. "Wanna die for her?"

He rushed her, too full of confidence in his size and meanness. She dodged left and slashed him along the right arm, opening his sleeve and his skin. He bellowed loudly and came at her again ready to grab her when she sidestepped. Only the knife switched hands. This time she nicked his left earlobe. That brought him to a confused halt.

"The next time I go for something vital." Jamie wiped the blood on her jeans and caught the knife by the blade. "I can throw even better. Want a demonstration?" She made a swift move, drawing the hand back.

The big man backpedaled down a sand-filled alley. "You ain't gonna get away with this, you shithead. I got rights."

"Fuck your rights!" she hollered after him, feeling a little childish. Then the tension drained away, and the nerves set in. Trembling slightly, she searched for Lila Anne, and found her lurking in a doorway.

"Are you all right?" Jamie asked her.

"I only broke one water bottle, but I skinned my elbow. I bet I don't hurt near as much as Bonner, though."

"Is he really your husband?"

The girl looked away. "My aunt and uncle are giving me to him. They say I'm not worth feeding."

"So, he's probably going to be back with reinforcements. Where's that car?"

"I'm coming?"

"Yes! Let's get a move on."

She was led down first one street and then another, and out into a residential area. In the garage of one shabby tract home, Lila Anne stripped back a canvas cover from a white '62 Cadillac. Jamie only knew the details because the child informed her of them. The thing looked new.

"Lester let me help him polish it. He never really drove it much, but he ran it a lot setting in the driveway to charge the battery. So I know it works. Here." Lila Anne got the hood up with a little help from Jamie. "It's got a deep cycle Die Hard battery. Lester said they were best." The engine was as spotless as the rest of the car.

"Where's Lester?"

"He died last Christmas." Lila Anne fell silent a moment. "He was really old, but he said Cloud was mine. That's what he called her. He said Cloud was mine as soon as I could reach the pedals. I know where the keys are."

"Good. Get them and let's get on the road."

Lila Anne dug through a can of nuts and bolts on a workbench and came up with a set of keys. "But we need to bring the hand pump and the gas cans." She pulled a long piece of pipe with a handle on one end down from a wall. "Caddies get lousy gas mileage. Lester made this so he could pump gas out of the big tanks underneath the gas stations. It's easy, once you get the lid off. Come on. I thought we were in a hurry?"

Jamie helped her load gas cans in the trunk. There were

other marvels packed there already, none of which meant much to Jamie, but the youngster cheerfully pointed out this and that; battery operated air compressor, flares, tools. Lester, bless his soul, had been a highly organized fellow. The length of pipe fit kitty-corner in the back of the car's roomy interior, and finally they were ready.

Jamie pushed the key into the ignition. The setup here was far different from Carlos's truck. No clutch. The gear shift on the steering column pointed to P. But there was an R, an N, a D and L, as well.

"So, turn it on," Lila Anna urged.

Jamie turned the key, and the car started instantly, rumbling with quiet power. "Did you ever see him drive it?"

"Sure."

"What do I do next?"

"You put it in reverse. I thought you knew how to drive?"

Reverse. R. Okay. Jamie backed the car down the drive and off the curb with a thud.

"You can't drive," Lila Anne accused.

"I can. I just haven't had much practice lately. And I've never driven a . . . a Caddie, at all."

"Oh-oh," the child said and hunkered down in her seat.

"Hey, it's not that bad." Then Jamie glanced in the rearview mirror. In fading evening light, two men marched purposefully up the street. Bonner was one. The other, of lighter build, carried a rifle. Panic struck.

"Lila Anne! Quick, what next?"

"D for drive. Hurry!"

She shifted and stomped the gas pedal at the same time. The rear tires shrieked and spun, and blue-black smoke billowed out. Even over the roar of the engine she heard the rifle shot. The mirror on the side of Jamie's door exploded into slivers of silver glass. Then the tires caught and they were slammed back into the soft upholstered seat, the vehicle roaring down the street slightly out of control.

"Which way?" Jamie cried.

"Go right. Here, here!"

They slid into the turn, and smacked up against the far curb, fishtailing back into the road.

"It's okay," Lila Anne said. "They can't catch us now. Slow down."

Jamie stepped on the brake pedal and threw them into the dash.

"It's got power brakes! Don't you know anything?"

"Maybe you should drive," Jamie snapped back.

"I would if I could reach the pedals and still see out the windshield. *You're* going to kill us."

"It's not my fault that you're so short. Jesus!" She was shaking all over now, but she put the car in motion again.

"You should never use the Lord's name in vain. If you do, you'll go to hell." Lila Anne sighed. "I already know I'm going there."

Jamie spared her a quick glance. "Good, we can go together. But first California. Which way to the highway?"

IX

Trey was only vaguely aware of the passing of time. Somewhere out on the desert, a great shimmering lake led him southward, promising water to slake his thirst, to cool his fevered body. The right arm was useless now. He'd managed to tuck the hand into the waist of his Levi's to keep it still as possible. Movement in the shoulder brought agony. Part of him wanted to turn the mare loose, so that he could lie in the sand and sleep, but the lake drew him on.

The dun convinced him at some point to pull the water bottles down and let her drink. And he drank also. With purpose, he could stay lucid for a time, and then it would be so clear to him, as if he watched himself from a distance, doing strange, unreasoning things. But somehow he had no control to stop them.

The sun went down again, and still the mare plodded on. Even in the night, the heat in his body continued, sapping his strength, fogging his mind. But he clung to the saddle horn, determined. There was someplace he needed to go, someplace he had to be, and it would come to him. If he just waited, it would come to him.

Chapter Four

CARLOS'S TRUCK HAD been cold and drafty and noisy—more than a little uncomfortable. The Caddie, on the other hand, soared. Unused to such power, Jamie drove clumsily at first, oversteering, overbraking. It took a while before Lila Anne finally settled, resigned to their fate, and even then she continued to cling to the armrest with an iron grip. Cloud swept up the steep grades without faltering. Jamie finally understood why the United States had been a nation of drivers. What godlike power this was.

The light faded, and a brief moment of panic ensued while she searched for whatever might turn on the headlights, finding windshield wipers and cigarette lighter instead. Lila Anne calmly leaned across to pull a knob. The twin beams swayed with the car, then steadied.

"Have you ever killed anyone with your knife?"

That mildly spoken question threw Jamie for a moment. She glanced sideways and saw the child deep in the shadows at the far end of the long bench seat.

"Yes," she said finally, unhappy with her own answer.

"Would you teach me?"

"Knives are a nasty means of defense, Lila Anne. They can cut both ways."

"But it's better than no defense at all," the girl said bitterly. "Teach me to fight with a knife, to throw it."

"That's just a matter of practice. But there's a real problem with throwing a blade. Essentially, you're disarming yourself."

"Then you carry two knives. Where's your other one?"

Jamie chuckled, shaking her head. "In my right boot. Only I don't think you're really the knife type, kiddo."

"Because I'm a girl?" The bitterness returned.

"No, that isn't it."

"I hate being a girl!" the child said with vehemence. "I hate being helpless and treated like a slave."

"We'll find you a good home somewhere along the way. I promise."

"You said I could come with you."

"I know. And you are . . . for a little while. But I've got something to do, and a child would just be in the way."

"Child!" Lila Anne snapped. "I've never been a child. And if you leave me anywhere, I'll run away. I'll cut all my hair off so no one will know I'm a girl, and I'll run away."

That last jolted Jamie, and she looked hard at Lila Anne for a moment. The car swerved slightly and forced her to put her eyes back on the road.

"That's your privilege," she said quietly.

A long silence followed, broken finally by muffled sobs. Jamie gritted her teeth, then relaxed.

"How about a quarterstaff for protection?"

"A quarter what?"

"A staff. A big long stick you can thump people's heads with. Like Robin Hood used."

"No, like Gandalf." The tears vanished. "And I'll carve magic runes in it."

Jamie sent her another sidelong glance. "You've read Tolkien?"

"When I was ten. But my uncle burned the books. Only it doesn't matter because I can't forget. They're all here inside my head."

A kindred soul. "Do you ever make up stories?"

"Sure, but they're not as good. Do you?"

"All the time. It's how I make a living. I'm a storyteller. Mind telling me why you're wiggling so much?"

Lila Anne groaned. "I gotta pee real bad."

"Why didn't you say so?" Jamie pulled the Caddie to the shoulder. "Well, go on."

"It's dark out there."

In the soft glow of the dash lights she saw the fear on the child's face.

"Just open the door and pee right there."

"In front of you?"

"I won't look, honest. Hurry it up."

The dome light winked on, and Jamie averted her eyes, smiling. An almost full moon rode the sky to the south, traveling west with them. She stared at its pocked face, momentarily mesmerized. The door swung shut again, and the light went out. Then something huge and winged passed across the lunar surface, occluding it, gone before Jamie was even certain she'd seen it.

"What kind of stories do you tell?" Lila Anne demanded.

"All kinds."

"Tell me one."

Jamie put Cloud back on the road. "I don't usually do it for free."

"It's not free. I'm letting you drive my car."

"Oh, yeah? Well, since you put it that way . . ." She gnawed her lower lip for a moment, then began. "In the city of Vell, at the foot of the great mountain Shandar, there once lived a young maiden, the only child of a poor watermonger—"

"What's a watermonger?"

"Someone who sells water."

"They don't have much water either? Like us?"

"Exactly. You want to hear this or not?"

"Go on. I'm listening."

Jamie turned her head away to hide her smile. Then a small hurt doused the pleasure. Best not to get attached to this bright youngster, they'd be parting company soon.

"Well?"

"Uh . . ." Jamie cleared her throat. "Right." And she began again, eyes on the sweep of the bright headlights over black pavement stretching endlessly before them.

II

Harry and the kid limped into Bakersfield at dusk after two hours spent broke down along the road. Clogged fuel line. Jeff's gallbladder-bartered gasoline wasn't too clean.

That in itself shouldn't have taken more than minutes to detect and remedy, except Harry was not a mechanic by choice, and he spent a good long time scratching his head before the possibility occurred to him. And that wasn't the end of it. The line clogged again. And again. Finally he had to remove the tank, empty the gas back into one of the jerry cans and filter the next load through one of his precious sterile gauze pads.

That did the trick, and stinking of gas, he brought them into town. Nasty neighborhood, Harry noted as they cruised through to the north. He rode with the rifle under his left knee now, in a homemade canvas scabbard. They caught only fleeting glimpses of the citizens of Bakersfield. Denizens, more like, seen in the shadows or rounding a corner. Shy folk and doubly dangerous in the twilight. Harry pushed the scooter to its limit, a rattling forty per.

The boy navigated, calling the turns, and, with the fading of the light, they found a ranch-style house in what must have been a wealthy area once. On a barren hill behind the tract, a lone rocking horse crude oil pump continued to nod slowly. Beside it, a turbine windmill spun. Harry could hear the whine from the street, even over the burble of the scooter's motor. He shut the bike down.

A light came on over the porch. Electricity. But the man that came out on the steps was as thin and ragged as the child that climbed down from the back of Harry's bike.

"Dad!"

The man walked in slow motion to meet them, and Harry noted the heaviness in his steps.

"She's dead," the father said dully, and tried to catch the boy in his arms.

"No!" The kid slammed past him, racing to the door.

"How long?" Harry asked.

The fellow focused on him then. "Just now, but there wasn't anything you could do. She was too far gone, too exhausted. God, she tried so hard." Light glinted on the tears that slid down his cheeks, and his hand shook as he wiped them away.

Harry threw himself in gear, tore back the tarp, and

found the medical bag, then rushed with it into the house. He could hear the child's wails and followed them to a back bedroom. The boy refused to move, and Harry smacked him aside, got the dead woman's belly exposed, and laid the stethoscope to the cooling skin. There couldn't be a chance in hell . . .

But there was. A faint, light fetal heartbeat, ticking the final seconds away. He grabbed the scalpel and made a careful incision, cursing under his breath. Maybe kinder to let it die. Hell. A big daughter in breech position, and well-developed, ready for life. He pulled the baby free, tied the cord quickly, and snipped it. How would they feed her if she survived? The bloody wax-coated skin was bluish, the infant limp in his hands. He cleared her mouth and throat. The eyes were half-open, glazed. He blew lightly to fill her lungs, knowing it was useless, but unable to give up. Again a breath, now massaging the limbs. Come on! Three minutes passed and nothing.

"It's too late," the husband said softly and laid a hand on his shoulder.

Harry shrugged it off, angry. He dried the baby with a rough towel, rubbing brusquely, stopping to fill the lungs again and again. On the last try she twitched, and her eyes closed. Head cradled, he brought her to his chest. With his jacket wrapped over her, he slapped her back gently, speaking encouragement with each tiny ragged breath she took.

Then she mewled, found her lungs, and began to lament in earnest. Harry felt a warmth spreading through his shirt. Hell! But nothing could touch the elation. Time and again, he'd been astounded by how strong the spark of life was in the newborn—of any species. Now the father grinned through his tears.

Harry laid the baby in his arms, wrapped in the towel.

"How are you going to manage to feed her?"

"I'll feed her," came a soft voice from the doorway.

A young woman, a toddler caught in one hand, entered. The son stood behind them, sorrow still strong in his face. They were all so very thin. The baby continued to cry.

"Give her to me." The woman uncovered one small

breast and brought the infant to it, guiding the nipple into her mouth. Fists balls, the baby gave a final squawk, then instinct took over.

Harry, suddenly tired, still took time to stitch the gaping wound in the dead mother's abdomen, then slipped the blankets up over her. He gathered up his gear and stuffed it back in the bag.

"You're not leaving?" the father said.

"Yes."

"But it's dark. It isn't safe around here after dark. You best stay till morning. Please. We don't have a lot, but you're welcome to whatever you want. It's the very least . . ."

Harry saw the boy still in the doorway; his eyes were on Harry, and there was nothing in them but pure hatred. Understandable, but painful all the same. He shook his head.

"Just tell me how to find Highway 99 from here."

He listened to the directions with half a mind. If he'd had the sense to strain the gas in the first place, he might have saved the woman. If he'd left L.A. the day before, like he'd planned. . . . If, if. The boy moved aside to let him pass and Harry paused, only the words wouldn't come. He went on out to the bike, tied the tarp down tight over the cart, and started the engine, ignoring the small silhouette against the porch light.

III

Trey walked with the sands shifting under his boots. His mother walked beside him, in the night, giving him hell about something.

"What!" he demanded finally. "What'd I do now?"

"Worthless idiot son! Turn around and go back to the Umatilla reservation. Let your uncles and aunts tend to you. Fool!"

"Too far," he muttered. "Too late."

"You want to die?"

"Anything to get you off my ass, woman!"

"Stupid fool. How did I raise such a fool of a son? You can't die yet. You've got something important to do."

"Yeah? What's that?"

Only before she could answer, something thudded against his bad shoulder, bowling him over. Red-hot pain stabbed through him. His mother screamed, a high wail of rage, and a cold wind beat against his fevered face. Through the delirium, he saw the arch of a great wing against the stars. Then the Oregon dun danced over him on her hind legs, ears flat to her skull, long teeth bared, squealing.

The rifle. It lay in his hands. Awkwardly, he levered a shell into the chamber and aimed it left-handed into the churning starless patch of sky above the mare's head. And pulled the trigger. For just an instant, by the light of the burning gases that burst from the muzzle, he saw a huge horned head with a hooked beak, then the wind drove sand into his eyes, and he buried his face in the good arm. The air grew still, at last. The mare stood near, chuffing anxiously.

"Get up!"

He moaned. "Mother, please."

"Get up, worthless child! It's not safe for you here. There's an arroyo a small way to the west. Go there."

Trey laughed till it hurt too much.

"You think this is funny?" the woman demanded.

"Mother, I'm sick, not crazy. You're an hallucination. There's no arroyo."

"You were always such a know-it-all. So die here, fool, and I'll nag you through eternity."

"I'm going, I'm going." Groaning, Trey used the rifle to pull himself upright.

The woman caught the mare's rope reins and drew her alongside.

"Mount. I'll lead the horse to this arroyo that doesn't exist," she said tartly.

"I don't think I can."

But her small hands came to support him, and he remembered her touch. It all seemed so real. Her fingers reached up to brush his face lightly, and he saw starlight on her cheeks.

"Don't cry, Mother."

"Fool! Do you think I'd cry over such as you?" She caught him when he started to slip off. "Some cowboy! See if you can stay on the horse just a little while longer."

IV

Flagstaff was a dead city. Jamie felt only relief over that. Here, the food riots had been really bad. The scattered bones along the highway were proof of that. Lila Anne had gone back to clutching the handgrip. When Jamie pulled off onto the surface streets, the girl's eyes widened. Under their tires, bones snapped like dry sticks.

"Don't stop here!"

"We better get gas while we can. There's not much ahead except mountains and desert."

In the glow of the headlights, they used a crowbar to pry the lid out of the asphalt at a 76 station, only the first tank held diesel fuel. The smell was different, Lila Anne pointed out, and the fluid slightly more viscous, oily. She'd been a very apt pupil of Lester's. The girl found another tank, and they tried again with better results. She fed the garden hose taped to the curved pump end into the Caddie's tank. Jamie cranked the little handle around and around. According to the gas gauge, they were only down a third, but it seemed to take forever before the girl finally shouted, "Enough!"

"Cold?" Jamie asked. The child's teeth were chattering.

"No." Her eyes roved the dark night that hemmed them in on all sides. "Thought I saw something moving."

"Then let's get out of here."

Jamie shook the last of the gas from the pipe and hose, but the fumes were still strong, and they drove off with the windows down.

"What did it look like?"

"There probably wasn't anything there. I see things—when it gets dark. Feel things. This place has a lot of angry ghosts. It's my vivid imagination. That's what Aunt Nonnie says."

"Give me a vivid imagination, anytime. They're valuable."

"Really?"

"Really."

Lila Anne settled back in the seat. "So. Got any more stories?"

"Lots."

"Well, let's hear 'em."

"Maybe later. It'd be nice if you got some sleep first. I'd like to drive straight through the night, if possible, and I think I may need your help to stay awake later on. Oh, there's beans and tortillas in the satchel if you're hungry."

"Boy, am I." The child began to dig through Jamie's few belongings. "The bowl leaked. The lid came loose a little."

Shit! "Be careful with it, okay."

"What's this?" Lila Anne held up a small slab of mottled rock.

"That's an Arkansas stone. A whetstone. I sharpen the knives with it."

"Got beans all over it."

"Great."

"Can we afford the water? I'll rinse it off."

"Later. Mind rolling some beans up in a tortilla and passing it over?"

Dutifully, the girl made Jamie's first, then made one for herself. The food disappeared all too soon.

"Guess we should save the rest for later," Lila Anne said wistfully.

"Good idea."

They drank sparingly, then Lila Anne stretched out as best she could on the seat. Jamie kept her eyes on the road. The highway led them down out of the mountains, into a wide dark basin dimly seen by faint moonlight. Cloud gathered speed, and Jamie tapped the brakes gently to slow their descent. Except for occasional rubble and the battered hulls of an auto or two, the pavement was clear. Still, it wouldn't be wise to go too quickly. Even with that thought in mind, the big Cadillac proved so powerful and smooth that Jamie found the speedometer needle edging the 70s, time and again.

A sign, loose on one corner and swinging in the wind,

told her that Kingman was fifty-three miles ahead. What had appeared to be the desert floor headed suddenly upward again. Regretfully, Jamie pressed the accelerator. Carlos had said that a steady, even pressure on the gas pedal gave the best mileage. But so far, the Caddie seemed to be much better on fuel consumption than the old pickup. She glanced at the gauges: oil temp, oil pressure, water temp, alternator. There was no way of knowing where the needles should rest, but they held firm for the most part. The water temperature climbed marginally on the uphill grades. Slowly Jamie allowed herself some faith in the vehicle.

Lila Anne slept all the way through Kingman and Needles, just across the California border. The great Mojave Desert stretched out before them, and Jamie slowed, leery of the sand drifts that had gathered in some places on the road over the years. A strange turn of fortune to be driving, not walking. But good fortune, when she considered the unending moonscape on either side of the road.

The young woman touched the medicine bag at her throat. There wasn't a moment now when she wasn't aware of its weight. She glanced down and found Lila Anne staring up at her, wide-awake, now.

"How old are you?" the girl asked suddenly.

"Twenty-five," she answered without thought.

"Lying's a sin, too," the child stated, sitting up.

"Go back to sleep."

"You don't even shave yet, do you?"

Her fingertips darted to Jamie's cheek, and Jamie flinched away.

"How old are you really? Sixteen? Seventeen?"

"Does it matter?" Jamie asked, an angry edge to her voice.

Lila Anne moved off along the seat. "I guess not. I only wondered."

"Well don't. It's none of your fuckin' business anyway."

"Potty-mouth," the girl muttered sullenly, then yawned.

Christ! First likely place, Jamie vowed mentally, *and out you go, kid.* The yawn proved contagious, and she blinked afterward, trying to clear her vision. The Caddie had drifted into the left-hand lane, not that anyone cared, but she brought it back to the right. The dash clock said 2:35 and she wondered if it was right. Time had lost all meaning years ago, except for the turning of endless dry seasons, the movement of day into night.

She called up an image of the road atlas in her mind. Highway 40 would end in Barstow. There might be gas there. Even with four full five-gallon cans in that wonderful deep trunk, the falling needle on the gas gauge bothered her. Still nearly half a tank. If it could be believed. She slowed to fifty-five, smiling. Mustn't exceed the speed limit.

Lila Anne had fallen back asleep, propped in her corner by the door. Thank God. For the next hundred miles, Jamie stared at the broken white line flashing toward her. She tried to find another story, but it wouldn't come. Too tired, too hungry. And the desert went on forever, broken only by a rare set of low sandstone mountains, weathered and worn nearly flat by the wind. Trying to cross the Mojave on foot would have been utterly foolhardy.

Waves of fine grit skirred across the pavement. Once, something flashed through the headlights, something large, moving fast, gone before she really saw it. *If* she'd even seen it. Barstow, forty miles. The gas gauge swam in her vision. Dangerously low. That slowed her even more. The moon dropped below the western horizon.

Lila Anne slept on, even when Jamie pulled into a Standard station and climbed out of the car. All four underground holding tanks were dry. So it was with the next station and the next. On the fourth try, in a cheapie station well off the highway, she got lucky. Working alone and with the Caddie's tank near empty, it took a long long time to fill. Hands nasty with gasoline, she searched the station for something to wipe them with. The headlight beams bouncing off the propped open, white enamel doors lit the bathrooms well enough. Too well, perhaps. In the men's room, she found the mummified remains of a man in a dusty three-piece suit, sitting back to a wall. The left side of his head had shattered outward, and he still clutched the pistol in a shriveled hand.

Carefully, Jamie took the gun and spun the cylinder. Five bullets unspent. His pockets proved empty. She wiped her hands on the suit coat, found a near-full roll of toilet paper in a stall, and went back out into the night, around the corner of the little building, to relieve herself.

Nearly 5:00 A.M. according to the green glow of the clock on the dash. Lila Anne finally stirred as Jamie got back into the car. The pistol was stashed under the seat, the toilet paper roll tossed in the back. Time to go, but first she checked the guide stone. Its pinpoint of blue light winked brightest and fastest when pointed northwest now. She didn't question its change of direction, only decided on how best to change hers. The weight of the cold glass brought a strange comfort, and filled her with longing for something as yet unimaginable. The stone was placed in a pocket, now. It would have to be checked more often.

"Hey, kid," Jamie said to the sleeping child. "I could use some conversation." She put the Caddie in gear and sent it out Highway 58 toward Bakersfield.

"Okay," Lila Anne murmured, still sleep drugged. She stretched and yawned, red-gold hair mussed and hanging in her eyes. "So where are we, and where're we headed?"

"Just left Barstow, California, headed toward Bakersfield."

"What's in Bakersfield?"

"Nothing that I know of. It's just on the way."

"To where?"

"Haven't found that out yet."

Lila Anne was quiet for a moment. "Okay. I don't mind, so long as I get to come along."

"I already told you, a kid would just . . ." Jamie's voice trailed off. Here was a young girl who'd never had any real love or kindness in her life, had never known her parents. No sense in being cruel. "My father was a meteorologist," she muttered and felt Lila Anne's curious stare.

"What's that?"

"A weatherman."

"How awful," the little girl responded immediately. "Aunt Nonnie told me about what happened to all the weathermen during the food riots."

Jamie nodded, mute. Like the messengers who brought ill tidings to ancient kings, the weathermen, both TV personality and scientist, were put to death by angry mobs of neighbors, friends, and sometimes even family. When all else had failed, they were sacrificed to placate angry gods, to call back the rain. Only that first taste of blood hadn't been nearly enough for the crowds. After that, a scrap of food or a drop of water had justified wholesale slaughter, and so the riots had started. The mob that had come to Jamie's house had been looking for Will Weston.

"Is that how your father died?" Lila Anne prompted her.

Jamie blinked and shook her head to clear it. "No. He just disappeared the night my brother and mother were murdered." These were not things she wanted to remember, let alone speak of, but the long drive and the exhaustion seemed to have loosened her tongue. "He told me to find the rain, to save the earth. Can you believe that? He gave me this ... guide stone."

"The thing with the little blue light?"

"You saw it?"

"Sure. You put it in your pocket." Lila Anne bounced suddenly on the seat. "But you know what this means? It means, we're on a quest—a quest to find the rain."

"No, *we're* not."

The girl ignored her. "This is great! It's just like *Lord of the Rings*. Did your dad say where the rain went?"

"No. But it's not here, not in this world."

"Well, that's pretty obvious. Do you know where to look?"

Jamie watched the highway rushing at her, heard the rumble of the Caddie's engine. "No."

"It's got to be in another dimension."

Lila Anne was capable of incredible leaps of logic and open to things far beyond her understanding. But then, she could read. Most children Jamie came in contact with were illiterate, mere survival being of greater importance to their parents.

She glanced at the little girl. "Have you ever seen a cloud?"

"Not that I remember," Lila Anne said.

"They're the most wonderful, beautiful things. And not just because they carry rain." Dreamy now, Jamie let her mind wander. "I remember the sky full of them, great white thunderheads pushed by the wind. They changed shapes as they moved. I used to lie in the grass, this deep green grass, on a hill near my home and watch them for hours. . . . There were mountains and valleys and castles and sailing ships. It seemed I could almost reach up and touch them. . . ."

"You're tired." Lila Anne stared at her now, eyes filled with concern. "Maybe we should stop and you can sleep."

"In a while."

Jamie glanced in the rearview mirror, saw rosy dawn spreading over a clear, empty, and monotonous sky.

V

The damn headlight was loose and the jiggling, jerking beam of light just about drove Harry nuts, but he kept on. The bitter cold had numbed his face and gloved hands a long while back. He'd cut across Wasco from 99 to 5 just above Bakersfield. Too many small towns along old 99, too many places to get waylaid. He wanted only to get back into the north country, where folks knew him and needed him. No one messed with the witch doctor, he was welcome in any settlement at any time.

Even on that long flat stretch of road, it took nearly half the night just to reach Sacramento, with its dark, convoluted freeway exchanges. None of the bigger cities in Northern California had survived, not even San Francisco. It had taken just one more nasty quake in the Bay Area to destroy their salt water–processing plant and convince the survivors to move on.

He left Sacramento far behind, made it to Red Bluff, and stopped to refuel, then sent the little bike puffing into the Trinity Alps past Redding. The sky was just lightening when at last he reached Weed. In that tiny deserted town, he sought out Kellerman's Garage, stashed the scooter and cart behind tall metal doors, and went to sleep curled up on a bed of old coveralls and shop rags.

VI

Morning brought a strange clarity of mind. The pain continued, but in some far distant place that Trey couldn't seem to connect with. He felt oddly light. To the west of the little arroyo they had sheltered in, Squaw Butte rose, and this was perplexing. By all rights, they should be well south. The Oregon dun stood saddled still, and he doled out the last of the water to her, drinking only a little himself, she being the more important member of the team.

With great care, he lashed the polyvinyl containers back behind the saddle. The right arm moved stiffly, and his grip was weak, but at least he had some use of it. South. He walked ahead, and she followed doglike on his heels. The sky above, the earth below, and he somewhere between, not quite here or there. It all made so much sense, now. The rich scent of crushed green grass filled his nostrils, bringing memories of spring. Hallucination, but he accepted it gladly.

The sun felt good, baking the cold from his body. Already heat rose in the distance, creating blue reflective nonexistent lakes. Far ahead, something appeared to rise out of the water—dark, crooked lines at first that came toward him, resolving finally into men, five of them in loose formation. Unsure, he halted, and the mare nudged him lightly from behind.

They came faster now, at a trot, one in the lead, the others strung out behind, and a sudden dread surged through him. He tested the cinch, then climbed on the mare, turned her in the opposite direction, and urged her into a lope. Ahead, a stretch of Highway 395 appeared, and he angled alongside it.

They followed easily, those dark shapes. The dun found a small burst of speed from somewhere. Trey pulled the rifle from the scabbard, throwing quick glances over his shoulder. The forms had shortened, as if they ran four-legged now. In the distance, in his state of mind, he might have mistaken them for men. But a pack of wild dogs would kill as easily, and they were gaining fast.

He stepped off the saddle, and the mare sat down, hind

feet tucked under her, sliding to a dead stop as any good cow pony should. With shaky hands, he pulled the latigo loose and stripped the saddle off, slipped the headstall free.

"Go on!" he shouted at her.

She only rolled her eyes, sides heaving. He struck her across the rump with the rifle barrel, and she took a great leap forward, running finally north and east out over the desert. Behind him, a howling began. He turned and sat on the ground, his knees used to steady his arms, then levered a shell into the Winchester's chamber and pulled the trigger. The motions were repeated over and over, until the rifle was empty. Still they came, all but one that had fallen to lie twitching in the dirt.

They were on him, too swift for his eyes to focus. Something struck him hard in the chest and knocked him flat, winded and wheezing. He got a brief impression of yellow eyes in a massive shaggy head before teeth closed over his throat.

"No!"

Not his voice. A long-fingered hand dragged the animal back, and angry blue eyes in a narrow face regarded him.

"The meat is poisoned. No good. Smell it?"

"Edilin is dead!"

"This I know."

"At least let us take the horse."

Trey struggled to rise and earned himself a kick to the side of the head that put him right back down in the dirt. Through tears of pain, he saw four naked men with shoulder-length hair standing over him now, all blue-eyed and fair.

"I claim first brother's right."

"So cut its throat and be done. As sick as it is, it cannot live much longer."

One of them squatted beside Trey, the sun flashing on a long curved blade that ended in a wicked point. The milky blue eyes bored into him, and the man's nostrils flared.

"Familiar scent," he grunted, with a glance back up at the others. "This is the one we could not find at the Wallen Ranch."

Trey's heart lurched, and he swallowed back hurt and fear. "Cannibal," he managed through gritted teeth.

The man with the knife grinned. "No. Cannibals eat their own, and we do not, man-thing. We are hunters. This world was ours long before your kind overran it. Now we only claim it back."

"Kill it!" someone snapped impatiently.

"When I please!" the one before him snarled, a guttural animal sound. "I want it to live for a while, yet."

Trey closed his eyes, sliding toward unconsciousness. Delirium, more impossible nightmares. He wondered vaguely why his mother wasn't also here to nag and berate. A stinging slap to the face brought him back. With effort, he focused on the man.

"What are you?" Trey whispered hoarsely.

The fellow grinned again, and a wide pink tongue lolled past overlong canines, dropped well below the bottom of the jaw, saliva dripping. The blue eyes shifted to yellow for just an instant and outright terror seized Trey finally. He rolled to the right, scrabbling for escape until a foot caught him in the bad shoulder. He screamed, and this time the agony mercifully put him out.

Chapter Five

SOUTHERN CALIFORNIA HAD traffic. Not much, just a slow steady trickle of crowded vehicles, bicycles, people on foot, mostly headed toward Los Angeles. A few headed away north—the direction in which the guide stone now led Jamie. But she decided to check Bakersfield out a little more closely in hopes of finding Lila Anne a home.

The cities that Jamie had passed through in Texas, New Mexico, and Arizona had all had a sterile, windblown emptiness about them. Bakersfield's streets were lived-in, dirty and squalid; the children and adults, bleak-eyed and filthy. Lila Anne deserved better.

But the town also offered the first open-air marketplace Jamie'd seen since New Orleans, and this was of some interest. They'd finished the last of the beans outside of Barstow, pouring them over brittle tortillas and relishing every bite. Now the next meal was very much on Jamie's mind. The Caddie caused heads to turn when she drove it into the center of the market and parked the vehicle where they could best keep an eye on it. They locked the car up, ignoring the small crowd that gathered to touch the wide fins, the hood ornament. Cloud was considerably dusty.

Lila Anne paused longingly before a stack of dented canned goods with faded labels, all well over ten years old, and some showing signs of internal pressure. Jamie shook her head and towed the red-haired girl down the sidewalk. They passed a table sporting cartons of cigarettes.

"Aren't these kinda stale, by now?" she asked the vender. He only shrugged.

The fresh foods were few and not all that fresh, but somewhere in the hills, people had water, enough for small gardens, even enough to raise a few scrawny chickens. One booth offered home-canned fruits and vegetables in glass mason jars. But the prices were steep. Jamie checked the seals carefully and then did some fast bargaining. For five gallons of their precious reserve gas, they took away two quart jars, one of plums, one of corn, and a slab of smoked dried fish.

In the car on the way out of town, they sampled the fish, and Jamie realized just how protein starved they were, but the rest was put away. With care, the food would last them two, perhaps three days. Between them, they still had well over a half gallon of water, and the Caddie held a half tank of gas.

Jamie sought out Interstate 5, some twenty miles west of Bakersfield, and turned north again. All around were gently rolling hills, devoid of life, and overhead, a sickly blue sky tinged brown with dirty air. Watching the sparse traffic that passed them going in the opposite direction, she felt a sudden foreboding, and soon learned how foolhardy her trade in Bakersfield had been. Every deserted gas station they stopped at along the way was dry, every storage tank empty. There were other stations, armed encampments with vehicles waiting to pay outrageous prices for fuel. Certainly, driving had great advantages over a long trip on foot, but there were great disadvantages, too.

Finally, Jamie gave up any hope of finding gas so close to civilization. It was a waste of time and fuel just to search. Best to drive on as far as they could and hope for better luck in the north. At the very worst, they'd end up on foot again. From then on, she drove carefully, but quickly, and what they had in the tank took them as far as Merced, where the last three jerry cans in the trunk were put to use.

Lila Anne provided the entertainment, now. Her tales were somewhat disorganized, but highly inventive, and she had a definite flair. Even with all the bright chatter, Jamie began to feel the strain of the long trip. She still hadn't slept, or even rested, and now the giddy sense of power that driving gave her wore thin.

Beyond Sacramento, with the Caddie tank at less than a quarter full, she resumed her search of the small towns along the road for gas. The hassle annoyed her—and her obvious addiction to the luxury of a car. But, she warned herself, it couldn't have lasted much longer anyway.

"I'm getting us nowhere," she said bitterly after the fifth try. "So you pick the next town and the next station."

"Try Red Bluff," Lila Anne said immediately.

"Neat trick, if we could do it, but I don't think we've got enough gas."

"Then we'll just have to walk."

Jamie sighed. "Yeah, that's what I figured."

They got as far as Orland, running on fumes, and Jamie let the Caddie coast into the first station they came across. Two of the big tanks were dry, the third so low that it was well out of reach.

"I'm a gas junkie," she muttered as she tore loose the section of garden hose on the hand pump and jammed it into the end of the pipe, then used some more of Lester's black electrician's tape to seal the connection. By damn, it worked. The gas had to be pumped into the jerry cans first, but was well worth the extra effort. They filled the car and all three cans, then headed up the highway.

No traffic now, hadn't been any since before Sacramento, which suited Jamie just fine. Not only did she like driving, she liked owning the whole road. But the Cadillac engine began to make strange noises when she stepped on the gas pedal, an odd rattling instead of the normal boost of power. Even so, it ran smoothly enough along the upper end of the Sacramento Valley. Almost directly ahead, towering over the small mountain ranges on either side, Mount Shasta rose into the early afternoon sky. No winter snow capped it, only gray stone and shadow. Still, it dominated the landscape, and Jamie found it difficult to look anywhere else.

"That's a magic place," Lila Anne said quietly, eyes trapped by the solitary mountain.

Jamie could only nod.

II

The sound of running water brought Trey around finally. But it was only the blood rushing in his ears, nothing more. He opened his eyes on a dizzying view. Beneath his feet, the sky fell away, deep and blue. Above his head, the earth hung low. Another glance skyward showed him the inverted top of a telephone pole. His ankles had been lashed together, then hooked over a lineman's iron foot peg. His wrists were likewise bound and fastened over his head to the base of the pole, which left him hanging, his back against the splintered, creosote-soaked wood, only inches from the ground. Not a happy situation.

But worst of all was the small pan from his gear, set before him on the ground, close enough that he could see the water glistening in it. The surface quivered, stirred by a hot dry breeze off the desert. Trey licked at his lips, and found his tongue too dry. For a while, he tried to work a foot loose from one of his boots, but the ropes were tight.

Any tug at the ones on his wrists brought searing pain to his shoulder.

Now he could smell the water, could smell the moisture the air sucked away, and wondered idly just how long it took to die of thirst. Too long, and that made him fight the ropes all the harder. Damn it, where was his mother? All night, she'd badgered him, helped him, and now he was left to face this all alone. Without much hope, he searched the upside-down horizon, and found only the saddle and his gear scattered in the dirt off to the left.

A big lizard with a long whip tail scrabbled over the reddish shale to the pan and helped itself to the water, tongue flickering.

"Hey," Trey snapped irritably. "That's mine. Get outta here."

The reptile gave him no notice, took its fill, and waddled off toward the road. Trey felt a little like the dog in the manger—if he couldn't have the water, he sure as hell didn't want anyone else to have it. Only there wasn't much he could do about it.

The blood continued to pound in his ears and his shoulder, and his head felt close to bursting with the pressure. Maybe he'd get lucky and die of an aneurysm first. Maybe he wouldn't. That thought made him groan and close his eyes.

III

"Stop the car!" Lila Anne cried.

Jamie hit the brakes without thinking, and they slid some twenty yards along the road.

"Jesus!" she growled.

"I saw my staff. Wait." The girl pushed open the Caddie door and trotted back down the shoulder, her long gray skirts fluttering around her ankles.

Jamie let the car roll back alongside her on the hill. The trees on either side were mostly dead, the evergreens and the oaks, the maples, the myrtles—all dead or dying. Lila Anne disappeared over an embankment, and Jamie felt a sudden fear, but the girl reappeared moments later, dragging a long pole.

"It's beautiful," Lila Anne said proudly.

"And twenty damn feet long. We can't carry that."

"So cut it shorter."

"With what?" Jamie groused, but put Cloud in park, and set the emergency brake. The staff had, after all, been her stupid idea in the first place.

The toolbox had a hacksaw and plenty of spare blades, none of which were meant for cutting wood, but it worked well enough. They measured the pole against Lila Anne first and cut it off a few inches above her head—because she still had some growing to do, according to her. The diameter on the narrow end was just right for her small hand and the wood, a pale reddish gold, was lightweight but strong and smooth.

"Good choice," Jamie praised her as they started out again, the staff stored on the backseat with the pump.

"Can I use your knife to carve it?"

Jamie hesitated. "I'll have to think about it. Neither of my blades are really made for whittling. I don't want you to lose any fingers."

"I'll be careful, honest."

"Later. Right now, I think we've got a problem." The young woman glanced at the dash gauges. "Cloud's been losing power. What does it mean when the oil pressure goes down and the water temperature goes up?"

"Trouble."

"That's what I thought."

"There's plenty of oil in the trunk. We should stop and check the level."

Jamie pulled into the little hamlet of Weed, only a couple of miles down the road. Just off the main drag, they found a small garage with the name Kellerman in faded red letters. She pulled into the little area in front of the two big metal doors, more as a joke than anything else, as if the mechanic, Mr. Kellerman himself, would step out to help them.

They opened the hood and checked the oil—way down below the add mark on the dipstick.

"No problem," Lila Anne said cheerfully. "We'll just put more in." She started for the trunk with the keys in hand.

"Child," Jamie said, following her, "if we put more in, it's going to all come back out. Unless we figure out where it's leaking from and stop it."

Lila Anne pursed her lips, then nodded. "You're right." She turned and considered one of the wide garage doors, then began to tug at the handle.

"What're you doing?"

"We're probably going to have to look under the engine, too. Maybe there's a floor jack and tools in here that we can use."

Screeching on its hinges, the door rose and Jamie put her shoulder under the edge, then pushed until it swung up and out of the way. Inside, in the dust and grime and dirt, sat a small motorcycle with a cart attached behind.

"We'll have to move it," Lila Anne said and stepped into the building. "I wonder who left this little trailer?" She pulled at the canvas cover.

"Hands off!" someone called from a shadowed doorway. A rifle barrel swung into the light.

"Hey!" Jamie called. "Take it easy, mister. Nobody's gonna steal anything."

"Damn straight." The fellow stepped into the light himself, wary, the rifle almost, but not quite, aimed at the young woman.

He was tallish and thin with rather long sandy blond hair touched at the temples by gray. He'd been sleeping back there, his gray eyes were still puffy and swollen, and Jamie couldn't decide how dangerous he might be. A knife throw against a rifle shot might just kill them both.

"Lila Anne," she said gently, her attention fixed on the stranger.

The child stepped back from the cart, her gaze also on the man, but for another reason.

"Do you know anything about cars?" the girl asked.

"Very little," he answered shortly.

"We got an oil leak and we've gotta fix it, 'cause we're on a quest."

"Sure you are." The fellow glanced at the Caddie. "That's what you're driving?"

"That's Cloud."

"That's a Sherman tank." He laughed humorlessly and edged over to his scooter. "Move your monster, and I'll get out of your way."

"But we need some help—it's a real important quest," Lila Anne went on, and Jamie wanted to strangle her. "We're gonna get the rain back."

Now his smile was genuine, and he raised his brows. "Quests are a bit out of my line." He swung a leg over the seat. "But good luck. You'll need it." The bike started up. "Move!" The rifle waved threateningly in Jamie's direction.

She backed around the front of the Caddie and got in, only Lila Anne still had the keys.

"Keys!" Jamie hollered, and the girl brought them.

With the Cadillac out of the way, the man pulled by and drove off down the street. Jamie put the car into the garage.

"Some people are so impolite," Lila Anne said sullenly.

"Will you lay off the quest shit? Don't be telling everybody my business."

"I only—"

"Look at this place. It's full of tools all right, but I don't know what any of them are for. Do you?"

Lila Anne stared at her feet, then looked up. "You're really tired. That's why you're so cranky."

Christ! "Let's just try to fix this monster and get back on the road."

IV

Harry shoved the rifle back under his knee and sent the scooter up Highway 97, which angled northeast off of 5. The fifty-odd miles to the Oregon border were spent in contemplation. They'd scared the hell out of him back there in Weed. Just a couple of dumb kids, but it was the last place he'd expected to see anyone. And the boy— maybe not so dumb, maybe dangerous.

Kellerman's had been a secure rest stop on many occasions. But not anymore, and that was a shame, because on the road, there were few enough places where you could let down your guard, where you could sleep deeply without fear. By the look of the light, he'd done a little too much sleeping in Weed. Afternoon of a short winter's day. No matter. It was less than two hundred miles to Bend. He felt desperate to get there and desperate to stay away. Mercy killing was killing all the same, and he hated killing, hated death. Get it over with, get Kathreen's suffering done with. And his suffering.

Klamath Falls was next on the road, a pretty little Oregon city once that lay at the southern tip of Upper Klamath Lake. The lake was not completely dry yet, a narrow marshy area lay at the center and a number of small families still lived in the outer edges of the city. He'd played witch doctor here on several occasions.

But on the outskirts of town, a tall blond man along the side of the road waved him down. Harry slowed with a quick visual search of the slender form for weapons. There was nothing in the man's hands and no sign of ambush, though that was always a possibility.

"Are you the doctor?" the guy called and stepped into the road to meet him.

"Sort of," Harry admitted. The man had a curious accent.

"You're Harry?"

"Right."

"The Nielsons said you would come this way. We have a brother hurt bad. Can you help?"

"Where?"

"In Lakeview, east of here."

Harry looked off to the north and felt a pang. "Climb on behind. Tell me the particulars."

"Particu . . . ?"

"Tell me how he got hurt and when."

As fair as he was, the guy was certainly hairy. His arms, bare from the elbow down, were covered with a thick blond mat. And when he grinned as he came to the bike, it looked like his teeth went all the way around his head.

"We are hunters. My brother was hurt this morning."

Harry put the scooter in gear, and it started out, groaning about the extra load.

"What is it? Broken bone, cut?"

"Yes, yes. We can pay, we can trade. Have a lot of good things."

Hell. Lakeview was a good four hours, a hundred miles, and there were a couple of nasty high passes to get over, to boot. Going up would be bad enough. Coming down with a heavily loaded cart pushing all the way—that could be trouble.

V

His mother had once explained to him a certain Native American philosophy concerning reality. Place a rock in the center of a circle, she'd said, and no matter where you stood on the circumference of the circle, the rock remained the same. The only thing that changed was your perspective. That rock was reality. Reality for Trey was a pan of water which, at this particular moment, had to be viewed upside down and that pissed him off.

The sun slipped finally behind the butte, and the sky under his feet darkened. He dozed again and found full night when he woke. Thirst had become a pain more acute than his shoulder. Now moonlight shivered on the surface of the water in the pan. The lizard had come back during the day—with numerous small relatives. That, plus evaporation, had lowered the water level by half. But he could still see it, still smell it.

"How did I raise such a fool?"

She stood beyond the pan of water, shaking her head sadly.

"Mother," he said. It came out as a croak. "Mother . . . I could use a little help. Get me down."

"I can't."

"But last night . . . The water. At least give me some water."

"You should have gone to the reservation."

"You're right. I'm an idiot. Just pick up the pan and bring it to me. Please."

"I can't."

"Mother, I'm dying here."

"I know." Her voice held such sadness that Trey felt a stab of fear. She continued, "You're not crazy, remember? I *am* only hallucination, child."

"You're paying me back for last night. All right, I deserve it. Only help me."

"Last night, you helped yourself—"

"No! I felt your touch, you led the mare . . . Mother?"

Empty air before him, cold moonlight. If he'd had the energy or the moisture to spare, he might have cried some. But he didn't. He only closed his eyes and slept.

VI

God, it was cold at five thousand feet. Harry took them over the Quartz Mountain pass and started the long, rough descent in the dark. Halfway down the grade, the road got suddenly brighter. A great dusty white beast of a car swayed past them. Harry looked up in time to see a head with streaming hair hanging out the passenger side window. The girl waved, and the Cadillac sped away to disappear around a curve.

Harry muttered an oath against the wind. He'd scorned the Sherman tank, but just who was freezing his ass off at twenty-five miles an hour now? The man behind him, who'd said his name was Ferlin (Swedish, Norwegian?), didn't seem to mind the cold or anything else.

"Go left," the guy shouted in Harry's ear when they finally reached Lakeview.

Harry went left, then left again. Ferlin's family apparently had taken up residence near the old Hunter's Hot Springs. They parked the scooter at the front door to a large rustic two-story building. There were outbuildings in back. Ferlin waited for him on the porch.

"Hello."

Startled, Harry spun at the voice behind him. By moonlight, it seemed Ferlin stood in two places at once. Another brother, maybe, just as tall, with the same long blond hair, same long face and wide mouth.

"I am Targin," this one said, with the same queer accent. "Thank you for coming so far. We'll make it worth your while."

"Let's see if I can be any help, first."

"You can. Please come in."

The inside of the house, lit by a single kerosene lamp, was pleasantly furnished and clean. The smell of roasting meat made Harry's mouth water, but under the cooking, the air was permeated with a faint musky animal odor that Harry disliked. A woman as handsome and pale as the brothers, and nearly as tall, greeted him. She wore heavy woolen skirts and braids circled her head, and she offered Harry a wide, toothy smile.

"He is back here," she murmured.

Ferlin followed, or maybe the other one, Targin. In a dark room, they brought him to a bed with a still form.

"I need light."

"Of course." The woman left.

"What happened?" Harry asked the shadow beside him.

"He's hurt."

"Right, I gathered that."

The lamp arrived, flickering, and Harry, staring down on the unconscious blond man in the bed, decided these folks must be quadruplets or quintuplets. He pulled back the covers.

"It's his leg," the one brother said. "We gave him something to make him sleep, because of the pain."

The bloody pant leg over one hairy thigh had been torn back and Harry removed the compress to uncover a neat hole in the flesh.

"This is a bullet wound."

Targin, he thought, nodded solemnly. "We were hunting."

Harry looked past him to another bed against another wall made visible now in the light. The body on that mattress was completely shrouded in sheets.

"Who's that?"

"Edilin's dead."

"Another hunting accident?"

"Hunting accident."

Better not ask for details. Harry busied himself with his medical bag, then checked the patient's vital signs. The heartbeat was slow and heavy, but steady.

"What did you give him?"

"Something to make him sleep."

"But what? I need to know if he's gonna stay under while I dig out the bullet. It's important that he doesn't move."

"He won't."

Harry took a deep breath. "Just to make sure, I want you to hold his ankle while I work."

The wound was on the inside of the thigh, angled toward the anterior, too damn close to the femoral artery. With extreme care and by the light of the one lamp, he probed for the bullet. Fresh dark blood welled sluggishly from the hole, and he used the clean soft cloths piled on the little table by the bed to dry the area over and over. Sweat beaded his forehead though the room was cold. Finally the hemostats—his best pair of mosquito forceps with their tiny curved beaks—touched something solid deep in the muscle. He worked the ends over the object gently and clamped the forceps closed, then with held breath drew the bullet slowly out. The flow of blood grew suddenly heavier, and for just a moment Harry believed the worst, that he'd nicked the artery, but the bleeding slowed almost immediately. He got the iodine from his bag.

"Here," the woman said from behind him. "Use this." She placed a small glass jar filled with a fine yellowish beige powder in his hand. "Golden root."

"Goldenseal?"

"Yes. Very strong medicine. Yours now. Keep it to help others."

Goldenseal was a folk remedy with reported miraculous healing properties, extremely rare and nearly impossible to get ahold of now. Harry opened the jar and sprinkled a pinch of the contents in the oozing wound. Blood and powder congealed immediately, turning a bright red-gold.

He turned to thank the woman, but only Targin remained. Harry covered the area with a couple of sterile 4 x 4s, then wrapped the thigh with gauze and tied it.

"He's going to have to stay off the leg for a while, at least a few days. And no hunting for a good deal longer."

Targin nodded, then grinned. "Very fine work, Dr. Harry."

"Thanks." Lord, he was a dentist, and those teeth still made him nervous.

The blond man moved suddenly, snapped a fingernail into the center of Harry's forehead so hard it stung.

"Ow!"

"You're a man with value, and now you're *tonwin*, one of ours. Protected."

Harry rubbed the sore spot, found a small lump under his fingertips. "Thanks. I think."

"You'll have dinner with us."

"Gee, that's really nice of you, but I can't—"

"You'll have dinner with us," Targin repeated firmly.

Resigned, Harry packed his things. All but the instruments he'd used. "If you've got enough water, I really need to clean these." He'd use chemical sterilization later—not nearly so good as an autoclave, but better than nothing.

"Plenty of water," his laconic host said and led him back out into the front of the house, then into the huge kitchen. The blond women busied herself at a wood-burning cookstove. The huge table was already set and already occupied by three blond men.

And the two kids from Kellerman's garage, Harry realized with mild shock. Small world.

"Hi!" the redhead called, obviously happy to see him.

"Thought you guys would be clear to Washington by now," Harry said brusquely and found the sink to lay his instruments in. "Or is the quest over already?"

The dark-haired youth with the very big knife at his belt flashed him a sour look.

"Cloud died," the little girl told Harry, with just a hint of sorrow. "We thought we fixed the oil leak, but we only made it worse."

"Tough break."

Harry found a seat at the table on the long bench next to the child. The teenage boy watched him, wary and distrustful.

"I'm Lila Anne," the girl said and offered Harry a grimy hand to shake. "That's Jamie."

"Harry," said Harry, ignoring the hand.

Food arrived, a great haunch of roasted meat on a platter and a pan filled with boiled potatoes. Harry's mouth watered painfully.

"Where on earth did you get potatoes?" he demanded.

The woman smiled as she set the dishes in the center of the table.

"I grow them near the hot springs. There is more." She brought two more filled pans, one with cooked carrots, one with beets. "You like? Yes?"

"Oh, yes!"

Targin—no, Ferlin stood up to carve the roast. The meat was a pale white-pink, thinly edged with crusty brown fat.

"Is this pork?" Harry asked as he held out his plate, marveling.

Ferlin displayed his teeth again. "Pork. Yes."

Harry searched fruitlessly for silverware. But the two brothers still seated were already shoveling the food into their enormous mouths with their hands. Oh, well, when in Rome . . . Actually Harry found he enjoyed the process of eating with his fingers, though his water cup got considerably greasy when he drank.

Heaping plates had been placed in front of Jamie and Lila Anne, but neither seemed to be eating much.

The tall blond woman reached across the table to pinch the back of the little girl's wrist. "You are much too thin. Eat!"

Lila Anne reluctantly pushed a carrot into her mouth. Weird kids, Harry decided, and tore a big bite from the slab of meat in his hands, almost snarling. That made him pause. Their hosts and hostess were noisy eaters and now, somehow, with all the smacking and tearing and chomping, dinner seemed more like feeding time at the zoo.

Suddenly Harry felt a little queasy, the rich fat curdled in his stomach. He dropped the meat back to his plate and concentrated on the carrots and potatoes.

"So, how'd you end up here?" Harry asked Lila Anne in a low voice, leaning close.

"We got invited to dinner. By one of the men. He found us just after the car broke down on the main road."

"Not too bright, accepting invitations from strangers."

"You're here."

"It's different. I'm a grown man and I came here to do some doctoring."

Lila Anne shrugged and murmured, "They seem nice enough, just . . . strange, maybe. I don't think Jamie likes it here though."

By Jamie's expression, he definitely didn't like it here. Harry was feeling the urge to be on his own way. Life, nowadays, presented bizarre little situations around every corner. But this particular situation was . . . Harry glanced around the shadowed kitchen and wondered if he ought to be afraid.

The brothers growled briefly over the last of the meat. It looked like Targin won. The sister cleared plates, and Harry stood up.

"Thanks for dinner, folks. I hate to eat and run."

Ferlin smiled. "You'll sleep here tonight, *tonwin* . . . friend."

"I really have to be going. . . ."

"You'll all sleep here tonight, where it's safe. There are things in the dark that you know nothing about. With us, you'll be protected."

Beside him, Lila Anne shifted uneasily.

"This little one," the sister said gently, "says you are a storyteller, Jamie. We like stories. Would you gift us with one?"

She leaned to take Harry's plate, and he noticed random coarse blond hairs on her handsome chin.

"Tell the story of Roxalla," Lila Anne prompted, and Jamie nodded, barely.

They repaired to the living room, where the dying fire on the huge hearth was built up again. Jamie began his tale, and Harry watched the child-like delight on the firelit faces around him and decided his earlier worries were unfounded. These were simply foreigners, odd but kind. And Jamie . . . The young man had an uncommon grace, telling his story as much through body language as with the rich warm voice that changed with each character, now feminine, now masculine. Even the narrator had a separate distinct voice. The hands fascinated Harry, long graceful fingers, yet sturdy, strong.

The tale was woven into a complex and colorful tapestry. There were goddesses and mortals, lovers and magic, danger and sorrow. And Death came to the sweethearts in the guise of a great wolf, Jamie said, "with eyes the color of thickening blood." Around them, the brothers murmured approval and appreciation.

Roxalla, the heroine, traded her memories of love for the life of her loved one and all seemed lost for a time. . . . Jamie's voice trailed off as the tale ended, and Harry blinked, fighting his way back to reality. Storytelling in the Pacific Northwest had made a resurgence over the last few years. In his travels, he'd been treated to a number of tales, but never to anything like this. The kid had a hell of a talent.

"Another!" Lila Anne pleaded, and the others joined her.

Dark eyes glittering, Jamie returned to his small stage in front of the fireplace. Harry smiled and settled back in his tattered old armchair.

Chapter Six

SOMETIME BEFORE DAWN, Harry woke alone and cold in the double bed. The kids were gone. They'd all been crowded under the covers on the one mattress in an extra bedroom, Lila Anne between them. Necessity made bedfellows of odd fellows. It hardly mattered, and it kept them warm. Only now they were gone.

He found the kerosene lamp by touch and lit it with an old paper match that took a while to strike. His fingers shook with the chill. Yes, their gear was gone, too; Jamie's pack and canteens and Lila Anne's silly stick that she called a staff. Might be a good time for Harry to likewise vanish before he got hung up again. The Blond Brothers were a little too enthusiastically friendly. Last night, the sister had even tried to drag Harry off to her own bed. Things had gotten a bit tense there for a time. He shuddered at the thought of sleeping with that handsome but bewhiskered amazon. Sorry, he just wasn't that hard up. Not yet, anyway.

The kids had gone out the window and left it wide open. No wonder the place was so damn cold. Harry collected his medical bag and climbed over the sill, treading as quietly as possible over the shingled porch roof, then jumped to the ground below. On impact with the earth, a jolt of electric pain shot through his legs. Shit!

The scooter had been stored in a small shed behind the house. He rolled it and the cart out, panting with exertion, and got them headed downhill on the dirt drive before starting the motor. Even so, it sounded overloud in the early morning hush. A thin gray light had arrived and overhead the stars faded. To the east, a faint pink glow began to spread up through the sky. Almost, he wished the sun wouldn't rise. In this pale dawn it was easy to remember the world as it had been, green and alive.

He turned left on the main road, Highway 395, and passed the white Caddie a mile or so down, sad and abandoned on the shoulder. A huge oil spot spread out from under the engine. This highway would bring him to 31, which angled back north and west toward Bend. Only at the junction—out there along the Albert Rim—he saw two small, early morning shadows trudging northeast. On foolish impulse, Harry went right where he needed to go left. All in all, it would only add another thirty or forty miles on the trip to go this way. It bothered him, though, how easily he could ignore Kathreen's suffering now that he had the means to end it.

"Mornin'," he called as he pulled alongside and slowed to match their pace.

Lila Anne, wild red hair floating out behind her in the chill breeze, had a big smile for him. Jamie refused even to acknowledge his presence.

"Hey!" he snapped at the boy. "Mind telling me just what the hell I've done to piss you off?" The kid kept walking, eyes straight ahead. "You know, most folks like me. I'm a real nice guy."

Lila Anne grinned at Jamie's back now.

"Was it the crack I made about your quest? If so, I'm sorry. I really *am* a nice guy, but I've got a big mouth." Harry glanced at the girl. "Lila Anne, if that damn stick . . . I mean, if your staff is getting heavy, you can put it in the cart. And if you want, you could ride behind me a while. Since we seem to be headed in the same direction. . . ."

The child looked doubtful. Harry slowed a little more, and Lila Anne dropped back to walk beside him, her staff thumping on the asphalt.

"So, is Jamie your brother?" he asked.

She shook her head. "Jamie . . . rescued me."

"From what?"

"It doesn't really matter, he just did."

"And he's really serious about this quest business?"

"We're going to get the rain back. Jamie's father was a weatherman, and he gave Jamie a stone to lead him to the rain."

"No kidding? So where'd it go—the rain?"

"It went," she leaned close and whispered conspiratorially, "into another dimension."

That made him smile. Hell, why not another dimension? Harry certainly couldn't offer a better explanation. And these two seemed determined to succeed where the best scientific minds on the planet had failed. Other children in other ages had followed similar visions. It saddened Harry to think these might be the children of the last age.

"Wanna ride?" he asked again, but it was Jamie he wanted most to talk to, to explore that bright dreamer's mind.

Lila Anne glanced at the youth stalking ahead and nodded, setting her stick on the tarp. She hiked her skirts up, slid on behind, and Harry sent the little bike with its heavily loaded cart rolling past the boy, saw the tight jaw, the anger in his face. Perhaps it was jealousy. Maybe Jamie didn't like the girl receiving attention from other men, although their relationship appeared siblinglike, and Lila Anne seemed a little young yet for anything else.

The boy could cover ground with those long legs, but Harry didn't pressure him overmuch and held the Riva at a slow, steady ten miles per. Lila Anne wrapped her thin arms in their padded jacket sleeves around his waist and hugged tight. It brought an odd paternal ache to his chest, and that made him wonder. The sun rose higher, the morning chill burned away, and Harry could see a great butte climbing skyward ahead.

"Stop!" Lila Anne shouted near his right ear.

Automatically, he braked. Behind them, Jamie broke into a run as Lila Anne scrambled away.

"No!" the boy cried. "Lila Anne!"

Now Harry saw just where the girl was headed. On a telephone pole along the road, a body dangled, hung upside down by its feet. Jamie caught Lila Anne on the soft shoulder of the road and towed her back.

"You've got to get him down," the child said angrily.

"He's dead, Lila Anne."

There was definitely the stink of death in the air. Harry, unhappy, left the bike idling and crossed the stretch of ochre ground to the pole. More incredible human cruelty to leave a man to die of thirst with a pan of water under his nose. Most of it had evaporated off, but a little of the precious liquid glinted in the light.

"Why?" Lila Anne asked, utter confusion in that single word.

"Maybe," Jamie muttered, "he did something bad and this was the punishment."

Harry squatted beside the man's head with its straight

black hair falling curtainlike below, and dared to touch the neck in search of a pulse he knew couldn't possibly be there. Only the skin was fired by a heat other than the sun's. Shit!

"He's alive." Harry turned on Jamie. "For God's sake, help me cut him down."

Gently he severed the rope on the wrists with his pocketknife, then steadied the body as Jamie reached for the ankles high overhead. Harry caught the limp form as it fell, and together, they laid him carefully in the dirt. The lips were swollen and cracked, the face puffy with pooling blood, but over all came the smell of necrotic tissue. And the feel of fever. Harry searched for the cause and found it, finally, after stripping the bloodstained shirt down over the young Indian man's arms. Below the right collarbone was a bad cut that had been cauterized and then festered anyway, but worse, there was a large dark puncture on the back of the same shoulder, where a hematoma had grown underneath the skin. Only the fluid inside felt too thick—abscessed. If so, it would have to be dealt with quickly, but first the dehydration.

Harry returned to the bike and shut it off, then pulled the tarp back on the cart and began rearranging things. He searched for a foil packet he'd found in a deserted veterinary supply store in Santa Rosa months ago. It was well past the expiration date, but might still be of help. He found the thing finally under a box of old sheets and pulled it out. Manufactured by Pfizer, it was meant for the treatment of scours—diarrhea—in young livestock. The main ingredients were potassium and electrolytes, with some backup vitamins. Harry hurriedly finished clearing a space along one side of the cart, then got Jamie to help him carry the unconscious man into the slot, setting him with his back propped against the low plywood wall. Lila Anne fussed in the background until Harry gave her something to do.

"Here," he snapped while he mixed some of the scours medicine with water in a chipped ceramic mug. "Feed him this, a tiny sip at a time or he'll choke. Rub his throat to make him swallow if you have to, but get every bit into him, then I'll fix more. Got that?"

Worried, her little hands fluttered a moment, then she took the cup and stood at the side of the cart, the man's head held steady in the crook of one arm while she tried to administer the fluid.

"You!" Harry growled at Jamie and shoved the medical bag in his hands. "You're going to help me drain this abscess."

He hooked a fresh No. 6 blade on a clean scalpel handle and swabbed the puncture with iodine. With the very first cut, a bright yellow-green pus exploded from the wound. The stench of dead flesh swept over him, unlike anything he'd ever smelled.

"Jesus!" Harry gasped.

Lila Anne, eyes wide, stoutly continued her ministrations. Beside him, Jamie covered his nose and mouth with one hand and turned away, gagging.

"There's a bottle of normal saline in a cardboard box at the back of the cart," Harry snapped at the boy. "Clear plastic quart bottle. Get it!"

He let the foul viscous fluid run down the outside of the cart to the ground. His own stomach rebelled. From the bag, he took a pair of his precious few sterile surgical gloves and donned them, then probed the cavity, pushing the man forward slightly—despite Lila Anne's complaints—so that the sunlight could show him as much of the interior as possible. This was not a normal abscess. Some sort of poison had been injected through the puncture, and the tissue damage was extensive.

If the poison had gone systemic, if there was gas gangrene, then Harry was wasting his time. By all rights, this man should already be dead. God, he hated what came next. With great care, the walls of the abscess were scraped clean, until fresh clean blood flowed. The trapezius muscle was the most affected. Luckily the shoulder blade had been missed. Bone abscesses were well beyond Harry's limited abilities.

He grabbed the bottle from Jamie, and filled a large syringe, then flushed the wound with normal saline. It should be packed with a treated gauze, which Harry didn't have. But the jar of goldenseal powder was right under his fingers and would have a better drying effect than antibiotic salve. He stripped off the gloves and dusted the wound with the powder, inside and out. At that, they got their first reaction from the patient. He jerked forward with a small mewl of pain, then slumped into unconsciousness again.

Lila Anne jumped away, and Harry caught the injured man across the chest, pulling him back.

"I hate to mention this," Jamie said from behind him. "But maybe you should hurry it up, doc. Whoever hung the guy up may just come back to check out their handiwork."

"Then help me finish, dammit."

The cut on the chest could wait. Together, clumsy with the team effort, they got the wound covered and taped and Harry immobilized the right arm, wrapping it against the patient's stomach with torn strips of sheet. Under his directions, Lila Anne had mixed more of the electrolytes with water and fed it.

While he repacked the cart, Harry debated an antibiotic. Injectables, once rehydrated, spoiled quickly without refrigeration, and Harry rarely got his hands on any. Oral penicillin would have to do. They'd just have to wait until the patient came around. *If* he came around.

With the load all lopsided and threatening to collapse, he started the scooter down the road again. The patient had been stretched out on his left side facing the one wall, then covered with blankets and some of the lighter boxes of medical supplies—just in case they ran into anyone along this barren stretch of countryside.

II

For Trey, at the moment, the world consisted entirely of pain, but somehow, retreat into the darkness had been barred. There was movement, not the slow rocking sway of the Oregon dun, but a rumbling under him and occasional jolts that brought agony. And voices dimly heard.

Then a sudden stillness. Gentle hands touched him,

shifting his position, and his head was cradled, a cup pressed to his lips. The liquid, nasty and bitter, still brought relief from thirst, and greedy, he swallowed too quickly, choking.

"Easy." A soft voice, young and feminine.

His eyes were crusted with a gummy material. He fought to open them and found a thin freckled face haloed with frizzy red hair near his own. Her concern and kindness were obvious, and she smiled, tilting the cup again.

"He's awake," she called.

Two more faces floated into his view peripherally, distorted. Beyond them, a fat yellow sun rode the sky. His choices of reality were few—this was death or hallucination. He tried to struggle in the young one's arms.

"No," someone said, and a hand pressed him back. "Don't move."

The cup returned, and he drank until it was dry, licking the last of the moisture from cracked lips. Then, exhausted, he closed his eyes and let the empty, silent darkness take him once more.

III

They reached Riley by late afternoon, and Harry had to make an unhappy choice. Jamie was determined to go east, and Bend lay in the opposite direction. They gathered around the injured passenger again while Lila Anne gave him the doctored water.

"I have to get to Bend, but I won't be there long." Harry watched Jamie's face. "If you'll come with me, then we can all continue this . . . quest of yours later."

"No one invited you," Jamie said coldly. "No one invited either of you."

Lila Anne, crouched in the clutter of the cart, looked up in dismay. "But I want to help."

"Help him." Jamie pointed at the man Lila Anne held. He'd come around again, dark eyes glittering with awareness.

"There's safety in numbers, kid," Harry offered. "The

drought's been going on for fifteen years now. What's a day or two matter at this point?"

The fellow in the cart got his left hand on the edge of the plywood and pulled himself upright despite Lila Anne's protests.

"Some . . . thing," he croaked, his voice all but gone. "At night. Big, winged." He slumped back, worn out by the effort, and Harry leaned over to better hear. "Danger. Wolves." The man clutched Harry's shirt front weakly. "Stick together."

Jamie smiled. "I'm going east. If you find me later, well enough. If you don't . . ." He shouldered his leather bag and walked away.

Lila Anne exploded from the cart, grabbed up her staff, and galloped after. Down the road a piece, she caught up with the boy. Only Jamie stopped and rounded on her, and, in low angry voices, they argued. When they were finished, the teenager headed off alone, and Lila Anne returned, head bowed, feet dragging.

Harry dared to put an arm around her. "It's okay. I know a family in Bend that would love to have you. And our friend in the cart does need you."

She pulled away. "His name is Trey."

So. "Come on. I want to get to Bend before dark. Since Trey seems to think this place isn't as empty as it looks."

IV

After she was certain they were gone, Jamie pulled the guide stone from her jeans' pocket. In the center of the glass a small speck lay suspended, winking a faint blue in the sunlight. Shadowed by the other hand, the glow grew stronger. She turned slowly around, watching the light blink.

Last night, the stone had pointed her almost due north. Now it glowed steadily and brightest when she faced east-southeast. The flickering had grown faster over the past couple of days, which brought an odd elation and a very sensible fear. The quest, as Lila Anne had called it, was about to begin. Jamie knew that with certainty.

There were other things that she knew, an understanding that lay just beneath her conscious thoughts and surfaced when she least expected it. The stone had brought her unerringly to the ones who were supposed to accompany her on this journey—a little girl, an outback doctor, and even Trey, who was the warrior of another tribe that Roland had spoken of.

So why had she turned her back and walked away from them? That was difficult to answer. Her father had said to be strong, and Jamie was. Since that night over ten years ago when she'd listened to her mother and Robbie die, and then been abandoned once more by Will Weston, Jamie had carefully cut herself off from the human feelings around her. Her disguise as a boy was always a good excuse, but it was more than that. Without attachments, there was no possibility of hurt. And no responsibility to anyone but Jamie. That could not be easily given up.

Harry presented the biggest problem, though. There were similarities in the features and mannerisms of the doctor and her father. Disconcerting to say the least. Except that after so many years, her memories might be faulty, and she could be seeing things that didn't exist. It was that strong attraction to Harry that repelled her most. Hell.

She followed the road into Burns. Empty streets, empty buildings. In a Rexall with blasted windows, she did some minor shopping, stuffing a new toothbrush and a plastic hairbrush in her bag, and the contents of a large dusty box of tampons wrapped in a brown paper sack. Playing the part of a boy didn't exempt her from certain biological functions, and by mental calculations one of those functions was due in a couple of weeks. She hated the hormonal changes that brought confusion and made her doubt every decision. Mostly it just pissed her off.

The satchel wasn't too heavy, even with the old revolver wrapped in a shirt. She'd stashed the two quart jars in Harry's cart. They'd find them easily enough. It hadn't been an entirely selfless act—she'd kept half the smoked fish for herself. She just didn't want to lug all that extra weight around.

Another smaller town lay ten miles to the south on Highway 78. The evening light was already beginning to fade from the sky, though. She could make it, but the young Indian's warning, added to her own memory of a thing found along a Texas highway, made her search out a comfortable place to rest instead.

V

Lila Anne did a little quiet crying. The noise of the motor scooter covered this lapse. With her aunt and uncle, tears were cause for severe, often brutal, punishment and to be avoided at all cost, but sometimes, she just couldn't help it. The misery and anger had to come out, like now.

She'd never see Jamie again. The adventure of a lifetime had been that close, and now there was nothing. She'd be left in the care of another family, kind or cruel, and for her the quest would end. The bike slowed and stopped.

"Time for another dose of electrolytes for our friend," Harry said. "Can you mix it yourself this time?"

She nodded, head down, and wiped her nose on the sleeve of her jacket.

Trey woke immediately when she slipped her right arm under his neck. He even managed a smile for her, and the smell of sickness wasn't nearly so bad now. His left hand found hers and helped guide the cup to his lips.

"Thank you," he muttered in a gravelly voice and squeezed her hand lightly.

"Give him these," Harry ordered, and dropped four white tablets into her palm, two fat ones, two small ones. The cup was refilled from a canteen and given back.

Trey had trouble swallowing the pills, but he did it. She wondered briefly about his odd name, wondered if maybe she'd heard wrong. His dark eyes closed, and his head lolled back.

"Hey, let's go!" Harry called, and when she climbed on behind him, "You'd make a good nurse, kid. Scratch that. You'd make a good doctor."

The praise lifted her mood somewhat, and she snugged up against him, trying not to think too much.

VI

A once lovely little town, Bend lay tucked along the border of the Deschutes National Forest, now as barren and destitute as the rest of the country. But not quite empty. A few families struggled for survival with a small, but steady, water supply.

The road was in bad shape, and the forty-mile trip had taken nearly three hours. It was full night by the time they arrived at the Gilberts'. Warm yellow lamplight glowed from the windows to the right of the porch and wood-smoke drifted from the chimney. Harry shut the bike down. A face peered through the lace curtains, then disappeared.

"Harry!" Craig Gilbert let the screen door bang closed behind him.

"Hiya, Craig." Harry crossed the brittle, dry yard. "Got some folks with me this time. One's pretty ill."

"Well, good Lord. Bring them in. Do you need help?"

" 'Fraid so."

Craig, tall and large boned and in his late forties, came to lift the patient up over the side of the cart and carry him all alone into the house. Craig was a strong man; he had even been a fat man once, only now the skin lay in empty folds at his jowls. Harry followed him, then noticed Lila Anne wasn't with them.

"Lila Anne?"

The girl looked up from where she stood on the far side of the scooter.

"Come on, it's cold. You'll like it, here. I promise."

The house was kept overwarm for Kathreen's sake. Craig laid their Indian patient gently on a long couch, pushing pillows under his head. Trey hadn't wakened. Harry glanced around. Under the big man's sole supervision, the house was kept neat and tidy.

"How is she?" Harry asked, a little knot forming in his gut.

"Getting weaker," Craig answered, eyes averted. "I can hardly keep anything down her, and she's so hungry all the time." Then he looked up, smiling. "She'll be happy to see you though. Hey, before I forget. Jerry Sims got back from Salem yesterday. Says they got a chicken pox epidemic going and could sure use you, pronto. And Julie Parsons' baby may have whooping cough."

Harry nodded, distracted. "I can head out tomorrow afternoon maybe." He caught sight of Lila Anne. "Oh, this is Lila Anne. All the way from Arizona, if you can imagine that."

"Hello there, young lady," Craig said in his basso profundo voice.

"Hello, Mr. Gilbert." The girl smiled vaguely and gazed at her feet.

"And the one on the couch is Trey. We found him along the road near Squaw Butte."

"Is he gonna be alright?"

"I'm beginning to think so. But you just never know. Is Kathreen awake?"

"Yes, I just carried her to bed. Go on back."

Harry left them there in the living room, following lamplight from an open bedroom door down the hall. On the threshold, he paused to steel himself. The flesh had almost completely left her bones. How life could go on in such a state was beyond him. The room smelled sweet, without the odor of lingering illness. Craig bathed and tended her with constant loving care. Even her auburn hair shone with a fresh-brushed luster. Not like his mother, whose hair had thinned and gone gray from the chemotherapy.

"Kathreen?"

"Harry?" She turned her head barely, and her eyes lighted. "I prayed you'd come back safely." Her fingers stroked a rosary laid on the blankets under hands too weak to move. "I couldn't die before I asked your forgiveness."

"That's not necessary—"

"Yes, it is." Her voice was a whisper. "What I asked of you was terrible and wrong. . . . The same as suicide. I was in danger of losing my immortal soul ... and asking you to give up yours. I'm so ashamed."

"Kathreen, I understand. If it'll make you feel better, I forgive you. And I know, God does."

"You're a sweet man," she murmured, tired.

"Can I give a listen?" he asked in order to change the subject.

"Of course."

He pulled the stethoscope from his jacket pocket and plugged his ears, then slipped the end under the lace front of her gown. The heartbeat was light and quick, not strong but steady. He slid it down farther under a shriveled breast and listened to her lungs. The bottom lobes were filling with fluid slowly, a little worse than last time. Antibiotics had staved off pneumonia for a while.

"How's the pain?" he asked, pocketing the stethoscope, then discarded his jacket in the hot stuffy air.

"Not too bad," she lied with a smile.

Now it was his turn to lie. He picked up one of the skeletal hands and took Craig's upright chair by the bed.

"I've brought another drug from Los Angeles. It just may help, but there's danger involved. You could die from it, Kathreen."

"I want whatever you feel is best, Harry." Those peaceful eyes offered love and trust.

"Craig has to know of the risks. It's his choice, too." Dear God, he wasn't sure he could do this. "I'll go talk with him."

"I heard a child's voice earlier."

Harry smiled. "Yes. Lila Anne. Would you like to meet her? She's an apprentice storyteller. Of sorts. I'll send her in."

He left the bedroom, sick at heart. Out front, Lila Anne was going through a bookcase with barely contained excitement. She looked up when Harry tapped her shoulder.

"There's a very kind lady who'd like to meet you. She's awfully sick, though."

"Are these her books?" Lila Anne asked.

Harry nodded. "She's too weak to hold a book now.

Maybe you could tell her a story, or even read to her, if you'd rather."

"All right."

Craig stood up from stoking the fire, but Harry passed him without a word, and headed outside to the cart. On his knees he pulled the bottom door open and found the sock with the bottle, then nearly dropped it. His hands shook. Get it over with, a small voice inside urged. And another voice, stronger, pinned him. You can't play God. It's every creature's destiny to live, suffer, and die in its own time. Harry rested an elbow on the rear gate of the cart and buried his face in his arm. Cold out here. His jacket was still on the foot of Kathreen's bed. Godlike, he was giving as well as taking away. Lila Anne would be the daughter the Gilberts could never have. Craig would love her like his own. It would all work out so neatly.

So why the hell was the ragged sleeve of his shirt getting wet?

VII

Jamie made herself comfortable in a hardware store after finding lanterns and shiny red kerosene cans, full. There was even an Aladdin blue flame kerosene heater tipped over in a storage room. She refilled and lit it, then adjusted the flame. A little warmth, a little light, and fish to eat. And a roof overhead. Somehow, that seemed most important.

Dust had formed small drifts on the worn tile floor. Jamie tossed faded jackets and sleeping bags in the dirt nearest the heater and made herself a nest of sorts, then ate the fish, savoring each flake. That, plus water, was enough to fool her stomach into thinking it was full, at least for a while. Sleep would be nice. She settled back, burying herself in the quilted material.

Only sleep refused to come. The wind came instead, whistling through the buildings, a cold dry desert breath that shook bits of paper and sagebrush loose, sent them skittering along the sidewalks. The scrabbling sounds made her edgy, but eventually she dozed.

And came bolt upright. Something walked the street outside, a sharp loud clopping and under it, around it, the sound of heavy breathing. That sent her in panic to a shadowed corner of the room, knife drawn. Except she had a weapon now that was far more deadly. She dived back to the lantern, caught up the satchel, and yanked the pistol free. Outside, silence.

Jamie caught her breath when steps started across the sidewalk, then aimed the gun and pulled the trigger just as a huge shape pushed in through the doorway. But the hammer fell on the empty chamber with a dull click, and she saw the enemy, the long narrow face and huge dark eyes. God! It was a horse.

The animal squeezed past the doorjamb and walked in as if it belonged.

"Hey!" she hollered when it caught the strap on one of her canteens and began to drag it away. The size of the creature scared her, but the loss of the water scared her more. Jamie made a grab and tore the strap from its teeth.

The horse jerked its head up, eyes rolling, then extended its neck and emitted a deep, "Huh, huh, huh." If you could attribute human expressions to an animal, this one's face was full of hope. Shit! The damn thing was begging.

"Look," she said, feeling stupid. "I'm really sorry, but I can't help you. It's every man . . . and animal for himself around here."

It came toward her, backing her into the wall, stepping into her bed and over. Terrified, she froze, head pressed to the fake wood paneling behind and felt a velvet-soft nose against her cheek. The creature lipped her gently, blowing gusts of warm breath in her face. Oh, Christ! She pushed it away with a hand.

"All right, dammit. But I know I'm going to regret this." Jamie searched behind one of the counters for something, anything that might hold water, and found a Day-Glo orange Frisbee. "This'll have to do. Back off, bub."

Foolishly, she collected the full canteen, the big one with the flannel sides, and began pouring the contents in small amounts into the plastic dish. The horse was a noisy drinker, and sounded something like a giant with a straw.

By the size of the creature, it would take far more water than she had to satisfy it. But when the canteen was empty, the animal moved a short distance away, lifted its tail, and deposited a small brown load on the floor.

"Not housebroken, huh?"

The horse cocked a back hoof, and its head drooped, eyes closing. Jamie returned to her nest, afraid that she'd somehow made a friend for life.

VIII

Harry stared into the flames, numb.

"It wasn't your fault," Lila Anne said quietly and wrapped her arms around his neck. "You did everything you could."

He didn't want her comfort, preferring to heap guilt and blame where it belonged, but, even in his own pain, realized the hurt he could cause by rejecting her. So he patted her arm before shrugging her away. A huge shadow passed in front of the fire. Craig stirred the embers and placed a small log in the center.

"It's over," the big man said, bewildered. "It's finally over."

"Craig—"

"No, Harry. You only meant to ease the pain, and you have. I'm grateful."

Harry drew a heavy breath. "About Lila Anne. And Trey . . ."

"It's fine. I'd love to have Lila Anne. And we'll take good care of the young man. Just leave the medicine. If he wants to stay on, he'll be welcome, too."

There. See? Everything neatly taken care of. This little part of the world had no need of Harry Roswell. He stirred, moving against a heavy current, and went out into the night to bring the things in from the cart—some penicillin, salve, and gauze pads. On the couch, Trey mumbled when Harry moved him, unwrapping the bandages. The abscess was draining heavily, the pads already fouled, and he threw them into the fire. When the goldenseal was applied, the young man hissed, suddenly wide-awake, and said, "Fuck!" in a loud clear voice, then apologized profusely.

"It's okay," Harry said and tended the wound on the front of the shoulder as well, then wrapped the guy up again, mummylike.

He seemed a nice enough kid, but accepting strangers, injured or otherwise, into your home was always a risk. Harry hoped he wasn't bringing Craig more trouble.

"Soup's on," Craig said, returning from the kitchen, a bowl in each hand. "Stone soup." He smiled. "Actually, it's turnip. I only use the stones for flavor."

Food held no interest for Harry, but he fed a bowlful to Trey. Lila Anne, seated at the dining room table, ate hers listlessly, her fingers touching a small book with red binding that Kathreen had given her. *Alice In Wonderland.* She'd be happy here. The house was full of books, fiction and nonfiction. Though, Harry supposed, nonfiction could be considered fiction for all the reality it held.

He knew now that he wouldn't be going east, wouldn't be looking for Jamie Weston. That'd been an impossible dream. This was all there was, all there'd ever be; drought, hardship, and death. No, he'd be going west into Salem, into the settlements that depended on him, needed him.

Chapter Seven

THE HORSE MADE noises in its sleep: sighs, wheezes, intestinal grumbles. All extremely irritating. Jamie turned this way and that on her bed. There seemed to be no position comfortable enough for her to relax and block out the external sounds. Finally she took the guide stone from her pocket and stared into it, letting the winking blue glow hypnotize her until a heavy, dreamless sleep came.

II

"Harry . . . Harry . . ."

He fought his way back to wakefulness, still drugged with emotional exhaustion.

"Harry, she's gone."

Craig squatted beside Harry where he lay buried in blankets on the living room floor, shaking his shoulder gently. Memory flooded back in an awful wave.

"Craig, I'm sorry—"

"Lila Anne's gone. I don't know when she left, but it had to be a while ago. Before light, I'm pretty sure."

"Lila Anne?"

"Harry, it's not safe for her out there alone. Not even in daylight. We've been losing people in the last week. Out on the roads. And some of the outer ranches have been hit."

"Huh?" Harry blinked, unable to focus his eyes and his mind at the same time.

"Cannibals, we're pretty certain."

Cannibals? Jesus Christ!

"She didn't take water," Craig continued. "Or food. And I don't even know which direction the poor girl went."

"I do," Harry said through his teeth. He climbed to his feet, caught up the Ruger from where it leaned against the wall. Trey had himself upright on the couch, wrapped in one of Craig's voluminous predrought shirts. "What the hell are you doing?" Harry demanded when the young man tried to rise.

"I'm coming with you."

"No fucking way, fella."

"Yes!"

Harry snarled, "Suit yourself," and opened the front door on bitter chill morning. He took the porch steps in two fast hops. Trey followed, slow and unsteady, and Harry shoved the rifle into its canvas scabbard before firing up the scooter, tempted to leave the young Indian. But he made it across the yard and slipped on behind Harry, finding a good hold with his free arm.

Harry kicked the bike into first and it started out, the motor bogging as always because it was cold and over-loaded.

"Cannibals!" he grated. "People using people for food. I can't believe it. There hasn't been any of that since the food riots." Harry searched the road ahead for some sign of Lila Anne.

"It may not be exactly cannibalism," Trey said, loud enough to be heard over the motor.

"Then what?"

"My parents were killed, cut up. But I don't think by anything human."

"You're still running a fever, pal. Shoulda stayed with Craig." That caused a long silence, and annoyed, Harry finally broke it. "All right, let's hear the rest." He turned the scooter down Highway 20, and headed east into the sun.

"We have—had a ranch out near Long Creek," the young man went on. "I was hunting water all day and came back and found my mother and stepfather butchered. I took off, scared, thinking the killers might come back. Then a few nights later, up in the Mulhuer National Forest, something grabbed me while I slept . . . something big and winged. It got me in the shoulder. That's when the fever started."

"A winged cannibal?" Harry demanded.

"No, damn it. I've only seen the winged thing at night. Just listen, I'm trying to get to the point. *They* caught me out on the desert later. Five men, at least that's what I thought. Only on foot they outran me, and I was on horse-back. And they ran on all fours part of the time. I'm sure of it. Like dogs . . . or wolves."

"But they didn't kill you?"

"No, they said the meat . . . *my* meat was poisoned."

"You were hallucinating," Harry said gently.

"Well, I sure as hell didn't hang myself upside down on that pole. I'd shot at them with the Winchester, and killed one, I think. They were pretty pissed about it."

A chill rippled through Harry. "What did they look like, these men?"

"Blond, every damn one of them. Long blond hair and blue eyes. And a whole lot of teeth."

Harry closed his eyes, then opened them quickly when the bike wandered. His gut knotted, and if it hadn't been empty, he might have been sick. Just what did they feed him the other night? He saw the roast clearly with its thin layer of fat, crispy and brown. Oh, Christ!

Where was Lila Anne? The road stretched on before them, empty.

III

"Get out of here!" Jamie swung her arms, and the horse stopped, head jerked high, bobbing. "Beat it!"

But when she turned and walked away, it came after, following on her heels. Hell, it was a free road, wide open. Certainly room enough for the two of them. But the damn thing scared her, huge, strong and treading on her shadow. She stopped again and swung around.

"Look. My stomach's empty and, right about now, a horseburger sounds awful good. You better beat it while you've still got a chance."

The animal had halted when she did, and Jamie shook her head. It was kind of pretty, she supposed, if you went in for horses—tan-colored, with chocolate brown legs and nose, but mostly a shaggy coat stretched over a rack of bones. It considered her, this time without any hope in those dark liquid eyes, then finally headed off in another direction, north through the town toward a series of dry rolling hills. Beyond them, mountains rose, stubbled with dying trees.

"Good riddance," Jamie muttered and felt lonely all of a sudden.

IV

They were a good way out, at least ten miles, and still no Lila Anne. Which seemed odd. She had to have left the house well before light, and if the previous night at the

Blond Brothers' was any indication, Lila Anne was really terrified of the dark.

"She's gone," Trey said into his right ear. "Poor kid, wandering around at night. It got her."

It. "Bullshit." But even Targin—or was it Ferlin?—had said there were things to fear in the night. The whole fucking world had gone nuts ten years ago, it hardly seemed possible or even fair for things to get any crazier.

"Hey!"

Trey pointed into the distance with his good arm and came dangerously close to falling off. Harry slowed. There she was, walking, skirts trapped against her legs by the wind, copper hair streaming back. They motored up beside her.

"Lila Anne!"

She kept on, staff thumping. Harry stopped the bike and dismounted, then trotted to catch up with her.

"Lila Anne, come on. It's time to go back."

"You lied," she snapped, still in motion.

"Huh?"

"Last night, you were talking about going west to Salem. You never planned to help Jamie."

"That's not true. It's just there're other people need me more." Harry, turned to face her, did a fast backward shuffle to keep ahead.

"So go on."

"There're other people need *you.* Craig needs you. Trey needs you."

"Jamie needs me."

Harry stopped dead in her path, forcing her to halt. "Jamie doesn't want your help. He made that pretty clear. You have a new home. Come on. Now." He tried to take her arm.

Quick, Lila Anne caught the staff in the middle and swung the high end at his head. Easy enough to dodge, only the other end came up suddenly on his blind side and caught him hard on the upper arm. Pain shot both ways at once, making his eyes water.

"Shit!"

She sidled away, her face contorted with sorrow. "I don't want to hurt you, Harry."

"It's a little too late for that." He tried to rub the feeling back into his hand. "We can't leave you out here alone."

"I can take care of myself."

"But you can't, Lila Anne. There're . . . some real nasty things roaming around."

"I'll go with her." Trey's voice came from behind him.

"Oh, that's great," Harry snapped. "You'll be a big help. For about ten minutes."

"Come on, Harry. At least we can help her find Jamie."

"Look, pal. You're the one that told me about a big bo-geyman with wings flying around in the night. And . . . other things during the day. There may not be a Jamie left to find." His own cruelty astounded him. Lila Anne's eyes filled with tears. "Ah, Christ!"

"You shouldn't use the Lord's name in vain," she said in a tiny voice.

"All right! We'll find Jamie. But if we run into blond, blue-eyed wolves along the way, don't blame me." Harry glanced back at Trey. "First things first. We've got to change your bandages."

Recuperative powers of the young. Or the healing powers of goldenseal. Harry wasn't sure where to lay the blame. The incision was already closing, and the drainage had slowed, but the abscess showed no signs of refilling. Trey, on the other hand, was still slightly feverish. He took the antibiotics and aspirins Harry gave him, and made no protest when Harry once more rearranged the cart to make room for him.

That's when Harry found the mason jars. *Craig?*

"Those are ours," Lila Anne said. "We traded for them in Bakersfield."

"Breakfast anyone?" Harry asked happily. He still had a small bag of dried apricots, but it would hardly feed three.

"So long as we save some for Jamie." Lila Anne caught his wrist in a surprisingly strong grip.

"You bet," he agreed, remembering the rap she'd dealt him with her stick.

It took a while to locate his only eating utensil, a battered wooden spoon, and they shared it around, however unsanitary. Corn and plums, a feast. But by unspoken agreement, they ate only a little and not just because of Jamie. There could be hungrier times ahead. Harry realized that, in a way, he'd gotten complacent knowing that, in each settlement he visited, his needs would be seen to. He never really went hungry or thirsty, never really suffered. He was thin, sure, but not so thin as Trey or Lila Anne. Or Jamie.

Trey had slipped back on the blankets in the cart, sound asleep. It'd taken everything he had just to stay upright this long. Harry closed the jars, wiped the spoon on his pants, and packed the lot away. The sun had some strength, now.

Lila Anne climbed on behind when he started the bike. The wind brought grit, and he regretted the loss of his goggles, but that was months ago, and the road could be viewed well enough with his eyes half-closed. Uneasy, he pushed the scooter, making it strain at the load. So where are you, Jamie? Still headed east? Still questing?

Still alive?

V

On the edge of town, Jamie checked the guide stone again. It flashed slowly as she turned in a complete circle, only this time, when her hand was pointed in a southwesterly direction, the flash didn't just speed up. The tiny light at the center of stone became an intense blue star, steady and unwinking. She tried once more, but there was no mistake. The easterly course it had set for her last night had changed. She stood on the edge of Burns, where Highway 20 would take her almost due east. Behind her 78 headed toward the southeast. But she remembered another smaller road, marked 205, that went south.

Jamie pulled the satchel up higher on one shoulder and started back into town. By day the buildings looked far more desolate and empty. On one street corner, buried in a mound of decaying trash, she could see white bones as dry as the desert. An empty-eyed skull watched her from the top of the heap. Funny, but she hadn't noticed it yesterday, even though the pile lay directly across from the sporting goods store.

The wind brought faded sheets of crumpled paper to skitter underfoot, and sand to bite into the backs of her legs. The hiss of the grains sliding over the broken asphalt made her glance repeatedly over her shoulder. Each side street along the way was checked until the right road presented itself. The stone was kept now in the palm of her hand and checked constantly, but the light grew bright and steady each time she faced south. A sense of urgency began to gnaw at her.

The highway led Jamie out of town along a barren strip of countryside. She dropped into her ground-covering stride, mind emptied of thought. A sign along the road said Frenchglen lay forty miles south, and that Malhuer Lake lay only ten miles ahead.

Bridges cut across what were once two fingers of the lake. She paused on the first to gaze down at the wide lake bottom. There were great fissures in the dried mud—large enough and deep enough to swallow trucks, by the looks of them. Some of the cracks had tipped the stanchions under the bridges and fractured the roadway in several places. Jamie continued on, ignoring the discomfort of heat and thirst.

With the sun high overhead, she paused to sip from her smaller canteen—the larger being empty thanks to the horse and her own stupidity. Hunger dug at her stomach, and a few small flakes of the dried fish were sucked on. There was little left of fish or water. And nowhere to ply her trade in exchange for life's necessities. Fear began to niggle at her, her rational mind overcoming the tug at her spirit. What if the guide stone were only a mad father's fantasy, leading her nowhere? Here in the desert, the point of no return might have already come and gone.

Once more, Jamie gazed into the glass and let its blue light bring a little peace and hope. However false those feelings might be, they brought comfort. There *was* something at the end of this trek, something worth fighting for. Worth dying for even. Rain. The light in the stone continued to brighten as she walked, and excitement came to mingle with the fear. She paused beside a narrow asphalt road that led away east. A small sign told her the town of Diamond lay in that direction.

But the guide stone led her off the main road and onto a dry creekbed on the left. The ground grew rugged and steep, and Jamie struggled up the inclines, then slid recklessly into stony ravines, feeling an ache in every joint. A rock wall rising up out of sight brought her to a halt. The glass was placed back in her pocket, and with fingertips and boot toes, she climbed laboriously to the top. There, another stone outcrop reached into the sky. The dry wind sucked away the sweat on her face, and she crouched, panting, to gather strength for this next ascent.

At the top, she found herself on a high sandstone plateau. Behind her to the south were mountains. To the north, in the distance, a paved road ribboned, west to east—it could only be the one that led to Diamond. Between the twisting highway and where she stood was a dirt road and a far gentler passage to the plateau. That brought a tired, breathless laugh.

Wearily, she retrieved the stone, then followed its icy blue light over the barren rocky soil toward the low range of mountains to the south. At a point where a deep arroyo cut into the earth, blocking her path, the stone's light flared suddenly, blindingly, and a beam of blue light shot skyward, bright even in the direct sunlight. Jamie sank down to squat on the edge of the ravine, the fingers of her left hand closed tight over the stone. The beam of light vanished. This was the end of her search, and the beginning.

She allowed herself a sparing drink from the canteen while considering what the next step in her journey might be. Below, the arroyo was in shadow. The sun had drifted westward but not by much, not enough to throw such dense black shade across the floor of the ravine. It was then she felt something behind her, eyes watching her, intent and unfriendly.

Slowly, Jamie turned, drawing her knife. Not ten yards away, a huge dog sat staring. Not a dog, she realized, but a wolf. The shoulders and head were massive, the eyes an odd sky blue. The fur, a mottled tan and gray, blended into the rocky background so well that had the wolf been much farther away, she couldn't have seen it. The animal's gaze shifted away for an instant, the eyes turning yellow and back to blue.

With a low growl, the wolf rose up, came off its forefeet, straightening. The shape changed, lengthened, stretched. Aghast, Jamie rose also, legs rubbery with exertion, knife blade flashing silver in the light. The gun lay buried in her satchel still, but was there time to find it? A naked man now, the creature stepped toward her, long blond hair windblown. This was one of the brothers from Hunter's Hot Spring.

"Storyteller," it said and smiled, but the eyes were calculating and cold.

"Stay away," Jamie warned.

The blond man took another long stride toward her, and she stepped back. The edge of the arroyo crumbled underfoot and she dropped into the depression, twisting and tumbling. Something caught in her side and brought sharp pain, then the knife flew out of her grip, but somehow she held on to the guide stone. Her head struck rock. Red light and agony fired into her skull simultaneously, then came a dark nothingness.

VI

"Hey!"

At Trey's shout, Harry slowed the bike and stopped it, glancing back. The young Indian sat upright in the cart now. His free arm was pointed toward a dusty side street of Burns.

"Do you see Jamie?"

"No," the kid called. "It's my damn horse." Clumsily, he climbed over the side of the little trailer. "She's heading down Highway 205."

"A horse?" Lila Anne repeated, awe in her voice as she climbed off the bike.

"I thought we were looking for Jamie." Harry shut the

motor off and strolled after Trey and Lila Anne. Sure enough, there was a scrawny tan horse trotting away down the asphalt, headed south.

Trey stuck two fingers in his mouth and let loose with a shrill whistle. The horse slowed and looked back, then continued on.

"She may have found water," Trey muttered. "We should follow her."

"Jamie's headed east," Harry reminded him.

"I know," the Indian said, "but we shouldn't pass up a chance like this. She doesn't look like much, but she's real good at sniffing out water."

"What's her name?" Lila Anne finally chimed in.

Absentmindedly, Trey glanced at the little girl. "She doesn't have one."

"Why not?"

"I don't know. She was my dad's horse, and he just called her the Oregon dun."

"I'll think up a good name for her," Lila Anne offered.

"Sure." Trey looked across at Harry. "Better make up our minds for us fast, Doc. She's halfway to Frenchglen, already."

Harry scratched his head. "Hell. What about Jamie?"

Lila Anne touched his sleeve. "Let's follow the horse for a while, then if she doesn't find water, we can come back and go east again. Water's important."

"Yeah, it is. All right, load up, people."

With some difficulty, Harry got the scooter and cart turned around, then felt foolish when he signaled for a left at the corner. He hadn't done that in a long time. The horse was a dark speck retreating down the highway, and Harry pushed the Riva to a shuddering thirty-five miles an hour. Then slowed it again when they reached the first bridge. Malheur Lake lay dry and broken below them and the road lay cracked and twisted before them. The horse, unmindful, trotted on ahead.

Twice, Lila Anne and Trey had to help him drag the scooter and cart over breaks in the asphalt. Ten miles past the lake they came to another road headed east with a sign announcing the town of Diamond only eight miles beyond the junction. Trey's horse had disappeared.

"We better go back," Harry said loudly.

Trey, in the cart, only nodded, eyes still searching the rugged horizon in all directions. Then he suddenly straightened.

"What the hell's that?"

Harry followed his gaze into the southeast. There against the hazy outline of a small mountain range, a bright glowing blue line disappeared into the sky. A laser of some sort? But who would have the kind of power necessary to create such a strong beam? He dragged his eyes away.

"We better head back to Burns."

Trey got to his knees, and leaned against the plywood side. "Aren't you even curious?"

"Not that curious. Let's go."

"*I* want to know what it is," Lila Anne insisted.

"We've wasted enough gas and enough time," Harry growled. "I said I'd help you find Jamie, not go gallivanting all over Oregon."

"What if it's a beacon?" Trey demanded. "Someone asking for help?"

"Jeez, you guys are driving me nuts!" Harry straddled the bike again, looking over his shoulder at the young man. "You know where the penicillin is? Take a couple, and shut up."

Lila Anne climbed on behind. "I'm hungry."

"Tough!" Harry snapped and started the Riva, then sent it down the road toward Diamond.

Soon enough, they came to a dirt road that led south up a long, steep grade. With misgivings, Harry followed the blue beam of light. The potholes were nasty and deep and the cart bottomed out continually. And a dry wind gusted up behind them, driving the dust in great clouds until they were all choking and miserable. At last, the road grew so steep, the Riva could only spin its little tire. Trey and Lila Anne got behind the cart and pushed and they proceeded in this fashion until the last grade brought them to the top. A long wide plateau stretched out into the distance.

"It's there!" Lila Anne cried. "See it?"

The beam of light streamed heavenward from the ground near the far end of the flat. But other than jumbles of stone scattered about, there was nothing—not a bush or a tree or anything—large enough to hide a laser. Harry shook his head while the others situated themselves, then drove the scooter slowly over the rough surface. The blue beam grew no larger as they approached; if anything, it grew smaller, more defined.

On the verge of an arroyo, Harry shut down the bike and dismounted. The light emanated from somewhere below. On the edge, he paused, gazing downward, and felt his heart give a great jump. Jamie lay among the shadowed rocks at the bottom, unmoving, one leg twisted under him, and from his left hand the blue light beamed.

"Ah, shit!" Harry squawked.

Lila Anne came up behind him to stare into the ravine. "Jamie!"

Harry grabbed her arm. "Get the medical bag. Hurry!" Then he flung himself over the edge, nearly losing his own footing and skinning an arm on a sharp stone on the way down. Shaking, he felt for a pulse in the wrist and found it, found blood, still glistening and fresh on the boy's face. Blood matted the hair just above the right eye. Gently Harry straightened the leg, feeling for breaks. Nothing. Above them, Lila Anne started carefully down the slope. At last, Harry touched the glass oval that lay in Jamie's palm, then picked it up. The light died abruptly. The thing was much too heavy for glass. He pushed it into a pocket for further investigation later and took the bag from Lila Anne.

"Is he dead?" she whimpered.

"No! Now stay out of the way until I'm finished."

"How is he?" Trey called from above.

"Alive," the little girl answered, then squatted beside Harry.

He felt the arms next and the neck, afraid to move the boy. The wound in the scalp over the eye was deep and there was considerable swelling. Good. Better the swelling be outward than inward. But by now, he felt certain Jamie had sustained a concussion, maybe even a fractured skull.

"Jamie," he said quietly, a hand on the boy's chin. "Jamie, wake up."

Nothing. Helpless, he stared down at his unconscious patient. How on earth were they going to get him out of the gully? Lila Anne continued an irritating whimper. Harry dug through the bag and pulled out the stethoscope, then unbuttoned the top of Jamie's loose shirt and slipped the mike underneath. At first the significance of the rounded flesh didn't truly register. More injuries? But these were very natural swellings, very nice ones, too. Ashamed, Harry jerked his hands back.

"What's wrong?" Lila Anne demanded.

"Nothing," he snarled, and rebuttoned the shirt. "We've got to find some way to get . . . him out of here. We've got to wake him up. There's a danger of coma."

"What's coma mean?"

"It means not waking up—sometimes for years, sometimes never. It's bad."

"Jamie!" Lila Anne practically shrieked, pushing past Harry. "Wake up! Now! Jamie!"

"Christ, Lila Anne!"

"You gotta find the rain. Wake up, Jamie!"

It was a shrill harsh tone, capable of waking the dead, and Harry saw Jamie's hand move, more of a twitch than anything else.

"Keep it up," he ordered.

"Jamie!"

The boy's . . . the woman's hand moved again, and her head rolled to the side, face contorting with pain.

"Jamie!"

Harry caught Lila Anne's arm. "That's enough." He leaned close to the young woman lying in the rocks. "Hey, kid. You've got to wake up. Open your eyes."

She did slowly, not quite able to focus on Harry standing over her.

"My head hurts," she whispered.

"I should guess so. It's got a knot the size of a coconut on it."

"There was a wolf, only it wasn't . . . I fell . . ."

Harry felt a chill. "Just relax. But don't go back to sleep. We'll get you out of here and someplace safe."

"Can't go. This is the place. . . ."

"What place?"

"To find the rain, stupid," Lila Anne snapped.

Jamie seemed to panic. "The stone. The guide stone. Where is it?"

"You mean this?" Harry pulled the thing from his pocket.

Not quite coordinated, Jamie reached for the glass, and he put it into her hand. At her touch, the blue light flared again, now shooting at an angle out of the ravine.

Lila Anne gasped. "It's beautiful, Jamie."

"Yeah," Harry agreed, "but what the hell is it?"

"I feel sick," Jamie muttered, paling.

Oh, no. Harry helped her turn slightly and watched her vomit a small amount of clear fluid into the sand. Definitely concussion. The stone slipped from lax fingers, and the light died. Harry pocketed it again.

"Kiddo, we've got to get you—get all of us—somewhere safe for the night. When you're feeling better, we'll come back."

"No!" Jamie managed, and was sick again, retching dryly. His eyes . . . *her* eyes, dammit, started to roll up into her head.

"Hey! Don't go out on us again. This is real important Jamie. Stay awake!"

"You've got lots of blankets," Lila Anne said. "We can build a fire here—"

"With what?" Harry asked. "Rocks don't burn real well."

"Me and Trey'll find wood."

"Trey and I," Jamie corrected her, voice hardly audible.

"Yeah, Trey and I. No problem."

"All right, fine. Get on it. The light's fading fast." As Lila Anne scrambled back up the slope, Harry pulled a piece of torn sheet from his bag, then, using water from Jamie's canteen, cleansed the head wound. It needed stitches, but a scar above the hairline would hardly show, and she was suffering enough as it was.

He had painkillers in the bag, too, but even without the nausea, they couldn't be risked. Already, Jamie was drifting off.

"Oh no, you don't," he said roughly and jiggled her until her eyes popped open. "Tell me . . ." He placed a gauze pad smeared with antibiotic salve over the wound. "How long have you been masquerading as a boy?"

Jamie stared at him, then looked away. "A long time. Did you . . . Did you tell the others?"

"No. I figure it's a patient-doctor confidence. Mind telling me why?"

"I don't feel up to it."

"Tough. It'll keep you awake. And me, too."

She almost smiled, but her hazel eyes grew bleak with more than the physical pain. "It was my dad's idea. He cut my hair the night my mom and brother were killed . . . during the riots. I was fourteen, then. He said it was safest for me as a boy, and he was right. Wasn't too difficult to pull off; I've always been a pretty good actor."

"You had me fooled," Harry admitted with a faint smile. "In fact, I found you attractive, and that made me wonder if my sexual preferences weren't changing. Had me worried there." He remembered in brief flashes, the wariness and hostility he'd felt toward the boy in the Weed garage, then later, the awe at that same boy's graceful fluid performance at Hunter's Hot Springs.

Jamie's hand clenched convulsively. "God! My head hurts."

"Easy, kid. The pain's just telling you you're alive. Keep talking." Harry deftly cleaned the blood from her face, finding several more abrasions. "Fourteen during the food riots . . . That makes you, what? Twenty-four?"

"Twenty-five. How old are you, Doc?"

"Ouch. Too close to forty for comfort." Harry settled back on his heels. "You know, somehow I've got to figure out how to get you up to the cart."

She stared up at him. "Did you see a wolf, or a man when you got here? Or am I just crazy?"

"Didn't see a thing but your blue laser. Only you're not crazy. Trey saw wolfmen, too, a day or so ago. Our blond, blue-eyed hosts, night before last, apparently have other-worldly talents. They're the ones that hung him on that telephone pole. But we've got other worries besides. Wolfmen during the day and something huge and winged at night."

"I know," Jamie murmured.

"You've seen it, too?"

"No, but I've seen what it leaves behind. These things don't belong here. They've come through from wherever the rain's gone. I'm sure of it."

"Believe it or not, that makes me feel a whole lot better. I need explanations, no matter how wild."

"I think I could get up that hill now. With some help."

"You sure?"

"No. But let's try."

"You're one tough kid." Thoughtlessly, impulsively, Harry leaned down and kissed her on the lips, then saw her go rigid. The anger on her face told him he'd done a very wrong thing.

"Don't ever do that again," she whispered.

"I'm sorry—"

"And get one thing straight, Harry. You're welcome to come along on this quest, but *I'm* running the show. Give me the guide stone."

He handed it over along with the knife he recovered from the arroyo, and watched in wonder as the stone lit with blue fire again. How did she do that? Jamie put the stone in a small leather pouch on a thong taken from a pocket and fumbled to tie it around her neck, hissing in pain. Harry helped. With an arm about her waist, he got her to her feet. She swayed, dizzy, and he glanced up the slope. This was never going to work. They needed a litter and ropes, and big strong men to haul on them.

Trey's face peered down at them. "Guess what, gang?"

"What?" Harry snapped.

"We've got a little extra horsepower here. Grab hold."

The end of a length of rough hemp rope from Harry's cart snaked down to them. Reluctantly, Harry wrapped a hand in it, and caught Jamie up against him. She submitted graciously.

"Ready?" Trey shouted.

"Ready!"

The slack on the rope tightened, and Harry braced himself with the two of them angled against the wall, walking slowly upward. If the rope went slack, they'd fall. Harry held his breath. But the pull was strong and steady, and carried them both up over the edge.

Trey stood proudly at the head of the skinny tan horse. Between them, Lila Anne and the young man had rigged a makeshift harness of rope around the animal's neck and chest. In Harry's arms, Jamie went suddenly limp, head lolling. Damn. He caught the young woman under the knees and lifted her.

"Lila Anne! Help me get h—im into the cart."

The girl rushed to straighten the blankets, and Trey, leaving his horse, came to hover worriedly.

"Sorry, pal," Harry told him. "But you just lost your bed."

Chapter Eight

THEY BUILT A fire in the fading light. Not a big one; the wood supply was sparse here on the plateau. Trey glanced around, nervous, feeling far too exposed in this high place. In the southeast, the Steens Mountains were a bare outline rising high against the evening sky. Where the little group had encamped was actually a large flat-topped foothill to the Steens. North, he could just pick out Squaw Butte, Dry Mountain, and Sugarloaf. Strange how such familiar surroundings could take on an ominous feel.

Trey had fashioned a halter of sorts for the mare, and

stood rubbing the dirt and dried sweat from her coat with a bit of cloth. The wind took the dust and feathered the dun's forelock and mane. She'd found water somewhere; her flanks filled out nicely. But tomorrow she'd be thirsty again, and they could follow her to the source. Content now, the Oregon dun submitted to his grooming, one hind foot cocked, ears flickering.

"She's really beautiful," Lila Anne said from behind him.

"You don't know much about horses, do you?"

"No, but I know a pretty one when I see it."

Trey laughed. "This is a nag, cow-hocked and ewe-necked. And ugly as sin."

"You're mean. She's pretty, and I'll bet she's real smart, too."

"Do you know how big horses' brains are?"

"No . . ."

"Well, they've sort of got two, both the size of a walnut, connected in between. It looks a little like a dumbbell. And that's what they are, dumbbells." Trey finished with the cloth and caught Lila Anne's arm. "Don't go behind her. She kicks. And stay away from the front, too. She bites."

"Probably because you say such nasty things about her," the little girl snapped. She pulled free and walked right up to the Oregon dun's head, began scratching the animal's jaw. "She deserves a nice name."

"Yeah? Like what?"

"I'm still thinking."

"Well, think about it over by the fire. It's getting dark." Trey slipped the rope halter off the mare's head and followed Lila Anne back to the cart. Harry was seated on the trailer tongue, head bent over the plywood side, talking. Trey snagged a spare blanket and pulled it around his shoulders against the icy wind.

"How's Jamie?" he asked.

"Okay." Harry stood up, groaning. "Mind keeping . . . him awake, while I heat up some of the broth from the corn. With luck it'll stay down, then we'll try some solid food."

"Sure." Trey took the doc's seat, got an upside-down view of the patient stretched out in Trey's old bed. Jamie's right cheek was purpled and swollen, visible even in the reflected, fluttering light from the fire. Blood had already soaked through the bandages on his head.

"Oh, man. You look like hell."

"Thanks," Jamie muttered. "You didn't look so hot either when we first found you."

Trey chuckled. "Well, the doc fixed me right up. See? I've even got the use of my arm." Pain shot into the shoulder when he raised his elbow. "Sort of. Get out of here!" he snarled at the Oregon dun, who had come to nose through the cart. The mare snorted and dodged away, insulted. Trey turned back to Jamie. "Hey, mind telling where you got that laser?"

"My father gave it to me. But it's not a laser."

"It sure as hell is. Only not like any ever made on this planet. Could I see it. Please?"

"Maybe some other time . . ."

"I just want to look. Harry says it's clear like glass, only heavier. I won't hurt the thing. Promise."

Jamie, lips pursed, tugged at a thong around his neck, and Trey took the small bag, admiring the beadwork. "Medicine pouch. Nice work. Yours?"

The boy nodded and brought himself pain for the effort. Trey dumped the little glass oval into his palm. It felt cool and warm at the same time, and very heavy.

"What makes it light up?"

"Me."

"Weird." Trey held it up to the firelight, and peered intently. "There's a tiny dark speck right in the center. Oh, and look at this. There're two wires, or hairs or something feeding out to the sides. You can hardly see them they're so thin."

"Here," Harry said as he returned to the cart. He handed Trey the chipped ceramic mug filled with hot corn liquid. "Feed Jamie this. Let me have the stone. I want to see those wires."

"No," Jamie said.

"Yes. Just take it easy, kid." Harry took the stone and began to rummage through some boxes in the cart.

"What's he doing?" Jamie demanded.

"Beats me. What're you doing, Harry?" Trey asked.

"Looking for my dental tools. I've got a couple of explorers in here."

"Explorers?"

"Small curved metal picks we use for dental exams. Dammit, feed that to the patient while it's still warm."

"Sure, sure." Trey maneuvered himself into a position to support Jamie's head and get the drink into him.

"Got 'em!" Harry said triumphantly.

Jamie gagged on the liquid. "Don't mess with it, Harry! You promised."

"*I* promised," Trey reminded the boy.

Harry squatted by the fire, the stone balanced on one knee. "I just want to see what happens . . . if I ground the connections . . . between these two wires."

It was like an explosion in a vacuum—soundless white light flashed over them in an outward-bound wave. The ground lurched suddenly under their feet, and Harry . . . Well, Harry, flying backward, followed the wave of light into the darkness beyond the campfire.

Trey's ears popped painfully. "Shit! Harry!" He left the cup in Jamie's hands and, half-blind, raced in the direction he'd seen the doc go. Somewhere behind him, Lila Anne was shrieking. Somewhere before him, he could hear Harry.

"Jesus H. Christ! I think I broke my ass. Ow!"

Trey had stumbled over something soft and gone down flailing. Grumbling, the two untangled themselves and limped back toward the fire. Jamie was up, staggering with the effort, head in hands.

"I found it!" Lila Anne cried, and picked something up from the bit of ground that Harry had so abruptly vacated moments before. "Look what it did to your explorer things." They were fused together, a welded distorted mass of stainless steel.

"If you've destroyed the guide stone, Harry, so help me . . ." Jamie snatched the glass from Lila Anne's fingers, but at the boy's touch, it came to life once more, and the blue beam, brighter than ever in the dark, soared toward the stars.

"Well," Harry announced, rubbing his tailbone, "it's electrical. Some kind of storage battery."

"Gee, Doc," Trey said, an arm around Jamie, helping him back to the cart, "I'm sure glad you found that out. That's real important."

"Just shut up and take some more penicillin."

"Thanks," Jamie whispered, and lay back on the blankets. He covered the stone with his fingers, dousing the light.

"You gonna be okay?"

"I have to be. Any time now, I may have to go through."

Trey hesitated. "Go through . . . what?"

"I'm not really sure. An opening of some kind. If I stay here, I'll find it. That much I know. All the earth's rain is going somewhere, and that's where I'm going."

"I guess that's where I'm going, too, then." Trey marveled at his own words. They had sort of popped out, without thought. "Lila Anne thinks the rain's gone to maybe another dimension. She's darn smart for a little kid."

"I noticed. But Trey, I really don't know where I'm going. It's nice of you to offer to come along, and I'm sure I could use the help, but we could all end up dead."

Trey smiled. "My mother used to say that we're all dying from the moment we're born. She used to say a lot of things, but I never really listened. Anyway, I should already be dead. I figure the three of you bought me some extra time, and I owe you." The young man settled on the trailer hitch again, long black hair whipped back by a gust of wind. "You know, I've never been anywhere. Salem, a couple of times. Big deal. But I always thought . . . that if I had the chance, I would've gone into space. Stupid, huh? A rancher's stepson, an Umatilla Indian no less, with dreams of going to Mars." He shrugged. "So now, I've got a chance to maybe really go someplace, and I'd be willing to bet it's someplace wet. I hope I'm invited."

In the flickering shadows, Jamie seemed to be looking

inward. Voice husky, he finally said, "Of course, you're invited."

Fear and elation rushed through Trey. "All right!"

II

Lila Anne stayed by the fire in the company of the Oregon dun and a surly Harry. She watched the man divide up the last of the food into four separate metal bowls. The horse tried to serve herself and earned a whack on the nose with the wooden spoon.

"Goddamn thing thinks it's a dog," Harry groused. He held out a bowl to Lila Anne with the spoon that probably had horse boogers on it now.

The girl accepted the bowl. "I'll use my fingers. Thanks."

"Suit yourself." Harry shrugged, and carried two more bowls across to the cart.

She ate watching the man, and decided she liked Harry Roswell a lot. He was quite handsome in a way, very heroic-looking, rugged and tanned, gentle but strong. As different from Bonner as a man could be. The sight of him brought a strange little flutter in her stomach—something besides hunger pains. Lila Anne forced her attention to the food, appreciating every small taste, though the plum juice had dribbled into the corn.

Harry returned to the fire to eat his dinner, his rifle across his lap, one eye on the darkness beyond the firelight. Lila Anne leaned forward to drop several more sticks into the flames, trying not to see the surrounding night. Harry would protect them. Harry would . . . She jumped when something touched her shoulder.

"Jamie wants to talk to you," Trey said quietly.

"Okay." She licked the last of her dinner from the bottom of the bowl and set it aside.

The short walk to the cart made her uneasy, but for the first time in her life, she was with people she truly trusted. Jamie's eyes were closed.

"Hi," Lila Anne said loudly. "You're not supposed to go to sleep, you know."

The boy blinked and managed a wry smile. "I was just resting."

"Did you throw up your dinner?"

"No."

"Good. You wanted to talk to me?"

Jamie licked his lips. "Yeah. This is the place where we'll be going through. Do you still want to come along?"

"Yes!"

"All right, but it'll probably be dangerous."

"I've got my staff."

"Right. Harry says you know how to use it, too." The boy chuckled. "Look, I don't know how long it'll take me to find the opening. I don't even know what it looks like. But you might be able to help me...."

"How?"

"You said you feel things in the dark, that you see things sometimes that aren't there in the light."

Lila Anne shivered. "If I notice anything, I'll tell you."

"Good."

"Only Jamie ... didn't they use lasers to cut things?"

"Yes, but the guide stone's laser doesn't."

"It doesn't cut anything here, but ... it might be like a key, too. It may make an opening for us. It's got a lot of power. Harry found that out. I'm real sure the stone isn't just a light."

Jamie mulled that over for a time. "Lila Anne, sometimes you amaze me. You make connections far better than most adults." He pulled himself upright in the cart. "Well, it won't hurt to try."

"Are you sure you feel good enough?"

"I'll manage."

Lila Anne returned to the two men huddled by the campfire. Even with her padded jacket on, she could feel the bite of the cold wind that made the flames flutter madly. Harry looked up, face bizarre with the dancing shadows.

"Jamie's going to try to make an opening," the girl announced.

"Now?" said Harry with a touch of alarm.

"He's just going to try. It may not work."

"What may not work?" Trey asked, his eyes aglitter in the dark.

"Using the guide stone to cut a way through."

"Are we ready for this?" Harry demanded. "Maybe we should wait till daylight."

Jamie entered the circle, moving slow, his satchel and canteen slung around his neck. He found a rock to sit on. "I don't want to wait."

"Well, hell. I hate to—excuse the expression—rain on anyone's parade," Harry said. "But I think this whole business is plain crazy. But just in case it isn't . . . make the hole big enough to take my cart through. With this accident-prone bunch, we're probably going to need it."

"I'll try." The boy opened his fingers, loosing the bright cobalt beacon into the sky. Carefully, he aimed the beam down toward the earth, drawing a slightly off-angle line up, then across, and finally back down.

"Nothing," Trey said with disappointment. The night was as it had been, solid and black.

But not for Lila Anne. "No, no! There's something there. I can see it."

"What an imagination," Harry growled.

There was a doorway, a depth to the darkness that hadn't been there earlier, but it was slowly filling in.

"There! See it," she snapped and pointed.

"Lila Anne, there's nothing there," Harry said. "This whole business is nuts. Jamie, go lie down before you fall down."

The boy stood up, swaying slightly, but instead of heading for the cart, he stepped toward the faint opening.

"Jamie!" Lila Anne cried as the youth vanished in the darkness.

"What the hell." Harry jumped to his feet, the rifle in his hands.

"Hurry!" The little girl darted after Jamie. "It's fading. The door's disappearing."

A nothingness enfolded her without physical sensation, only a feeling of resistance. Legs and arms grew leaden. Pressure filled her head, ears aching suddenly.

Then light, dazzling sunshine, and Lila Anne stumbled,

caught herself. Trey appeared in empty air beside her, an arm first, a leg, torso and head. He yelped when the light hit his eyes. Jamie squatted in the red dust close by.

"Where's Harry?" Lila Anne demanded, then staggered when the doctor plowed into her out of nowhere. He squinted and glanced around, the rifle still in his hand.

"Christ!" the doc snapped. "Look at that sky, for shit's sake. Look at this whole place. We're no damn better off than we were."

It was true. In every direction, arid, flat, and lifeless land rolled endlessly. The sun, suspended over the horizon in a cloudless pale green sky, was not their sun, but closer, fatter, red tinged.

"Harry!" Trey shouted and flung himself against the older man, throwing them both clear when a long nose appeared behind them. The mare came through, floundering as if snared in something thick and sticky. She struck the ground on her side, thrashing, and the air left her lungs with a great *whump!* Wheezing, the dun got hooves and legs under her and heaved herself upright, then shook the dust from her coat and stood panting.

"Now what, Einstein?" Harry demanded, picking himself out of the dirt. It wasn't entirely clear to whom he spoke.

But Jamie, swollen battered face pale in the daylight, gazed around in confusion. "I don't know . . ."

Harry opened his mouth again, then staggered a step and the color drained suddenly from his face, too. "Whoa, I feel really weird." He sat down in the dirt abruptly.

Lila Anne started toward him, and saw Trey grab a handful of the mare's mane to keep from falling. A wave of giddiness swept over her, the world spinning for a moment before it settled. But something had changed, something inside her was very different.

She hovered over Harry. "Are you all right?"

"I'm fine," he said in wonder. "This is great. Must be something in the air. More oxygen, maybe."

Trey peered over the dun's back at Jamie. "Do you feel it?"

"Feel what?" the boy asked.

"I don't know exactly. But it's nice. I feel really strong, really . . . powerful."

"I," said Jamie, "feel sick," and bent over to vomit corn and plums into the dust.

III

It took a long time to find her way back to the light, and then it was an unhappy return. Her head pounded to the beat of her heart, and almost, Jamie thought she'd dreamed it all, only the sky beyond the three heads crowded over her was a pale green. The color brought on another wave of nausea.

"Jesus, Jamie." Harry's voice. "What can I do? I don't have a goddamn Band-Aid here. My cart's on the other side."

"What could you do if you had the cart?" Jamie asked faintly.

"Nothing. Except make you more comfortable. At least we'd have blankets."

"It's too hot here, already," Lila Anne complained. "What we don't have is water."

"We didn't have much of that anyway," said Harry. "At least Jamie had the smarts to bring his canteen." There was only the barest hesitation before the *his*.

Jamie closed her eyes. "Sorry, but it isn't even a quarter full."

This brought a long worried silence which Trey broke finally. "I think we picked the wrong door. This one's got the tiger."

"What?" Lila Anne demanded, straightening.

"Old joke," Harry told her. "But no problem. Jamie, use the guide stone. Take us back home."

Jamie opened a stiff hand. Even unconscious, she'd gripped the glass so tightly that her fingers ached in counterpoint with her head. But now the stone lay lifeless in her palm.

"It's dead!" Lila Anne gasped.

"Help me stand," Jamie ordered, and felt them take her

arms, lifting. God! the pain. Drunk with it, she rotated slowly, the stone held out before her.

In the direction of the reddish sun hanging low near the horizon, the guide stone began to wink slowly, not blue but the same color as that awful green sky.

"I suppose that means we should go that way?" Harry said without enthusiasm. "I'll carry you."

"No, just lend me a shoulder to hang on."

"Two shoulders," Trey said stoutly and offered his good left one.

In that manner they trudged slowly over ochre dust toward the sun. Through the pain, Jamie observed this world, even more bleak and destitute than the one they had left. Had this place ever seen rain, or had it been robbed as well? Nothing organic existed here now. They had come from the dying to the dead, and this was Earth's fate if they failed.

Somewhere along the way, an uneasiness settled over Jamie. She found herself glancing continually around.

"What's up?" Harry asked finally.

She started to shake her head, but the pain stopped her. "I don't know. Feels like . . . like someone or something's following us."

The doc took a firmer grip on his rifle, and both he and Trey began to watch as well. Jamie allowed herself to relax a little. They shared the last of the water and continued on.

Hours might have passed. If so, the sun moved far more slowly in this world, setting or rising. She couldn't tell which. Perhaps they were near a pole, with the sun circling the horizon. This seemed to be the case, when Jamie checked the guide stone again. Now it pointed them somewhere to the right of that swollen red orb. Sometimes the horse wandered on ahead, sometimes it lagged behind. Lila Anne dragged her coat in the dirt and griped continually.

"I didn't get to bring my staff. I'm thirsty. I'm tired."

Jamie tried to ignore her, tried to ignore her own exhaustion and pain. Beside her, Trey paused momentarily, throwing their stride off.

"Do you see that?" he asked.

"What?" everyone demanded in chorus.

The red sun in her eyes, though not so bright as Earth's, dulled Jamie's vision as she searched the horizon.

"Straight ahead," Trey muttered. "It looks like ... a building of some sort."

Jamie forced herself to move slightly faster. The still, dry air burned in her lungs, and the pounding in her head quickened, but finally her eyes found Trey's building, right angles against the green sky, a low structure of the same dull ochre as the ground. Trey had to have the eyes of a hawk to have seen it so soon.

Lila Anne ran ahead, and the horse broke into a trot, kicking up little puffs of dust as it went. The distance was deceiving though. The building seemed almost to recede the longer they walked.

"Goddamn!" Harry bitched. But there, at last, was Lila Anne, hanging through a windowlike opening, waving her faded plum-colored jacket.

"Shade," she cried when finally they arrived. "It's cooler inside."

Harry stood gaping at black letters painted over the wide entrance, some in an Oriental script, some in a strange hieroglyphics. The English announced clearly, Shirrah. Under that, someone had scrawled, Summerland, in fat red letters with what looked to be lipstick. They stumbled inside and found two walls lined with stone benches under tall, open window apertures. Jamie sank down on one gratefully. Along another wall was a counter of sorts, with what might be a chalkboard hung above. The scribbles on it were smeared, but she could make out some Arabic numbers: 8.15, 12.45.

Harry collapsed beside Jamie, and began a breathless laughter that held a slight hysterical edge to it. "It's a fuckin' bus depot. I can't believe it—a fuckin' bus depot."

"If so, the buses stopped running a long time back." Trey dragged a finger through the thick dust on the counter.

Along the one remaining wall was a line of four boxes of a dull silver metal, something like the smaller freight containers used by airlines. Lila Anne was already wiping the dirt from the top of one.

"This one says 'The Guardian.' " She went on to the next. "And this one says 'The Physician.' Here's one for 'The Sorceress,' and the last one's marked 'The Sage.' " Eyes wide, she glanced at them. "There're four of us and four boxes."

"Coincidence," Harry said.

"But you're a physician. I'm the only girl, so I must be the sorceress. Jamie's the leader, so he's the sage. And that makes you," she pointed at Trey, "the guardian."

"They're probably empty," Trey told her.

But Lila Anne was already opening the box marked The Sorceress. "Oh, wow!" she whispered, and reached inside, pulling a familiar long wooden pole out from a container no more than two feet high. "It's my staff! But someone's carved runes all over it, and look, it's got a metal cap on the bottom." She leaned it against the wall, and reached in again. "Clothes." A long skirt with swirls of iridescent green on a black background appeared. A matching blouse was found, and a heavy cloak with gold tube beads sewn in mystical symbols. Shoes—soft moccasin-like footwear lined with sheepskin.

"What's wrong with this picture?" Trey said suddenly.

"What do you mean?" Harry asked.

"It looks like a Halloween costume, for shit's sake."

"What's Halloween?" Lila Anne demanded, but her eyes were on the clothing. "I'm going to put them on."

Harry looked bothered. "I wanna know how that staff came out of there. Look in yours, Trey." Then, when Trey shook his head, "What are you scared of? Go on and look. Pretend it's Christmas instead of Halloween."

Reluctantly, Trey pulled up the lid on The Guardian and stared.

"What?" Harry asked.

The young Indian reached in and pulled out what could only be a saddle. It had a high wooden front and back, the seat covered with soft blood red leather. The bridle followed, with wide straps and reins fringed with leather in the same red color.

"Any doubt who that belongs to?" Jamie asked.

"No. There's even brushes and currycombs."

"Is that it?" Harry finally stood and crossed to the boxes.

"No." Trey pulled a set of heavy saddlebags out, then unbuckled the flaps.

Now Jamie could no longer resist. She gathered near with Harry as Trey opened the bags. They were filled with small, round, olive drab pull-tab cans.

Harry held one up. "Army C rations, and the seals are still good! Shit! Instant coffee. Ham, rice pudding, fruit salad. Food, boys and girl! Oh, and look, little bottles of shampoo, cream rinse, tiny bar of soap, and a toothbrush—all courtesy of Hyatt Hotels. Jeez. See if you got any water in there."

"Nope. Look in yours."

The box marked The Physician was opened, and happily Harry produced a filled skin bag. "Water or wine. I almost hope it's wine." It was water. "Oh, well. There isn't much, but it's better than nothing." He handed it to Jamie. "Drink."

"I'm the guinea pig? Thanks." But she estimated what a fourth might be and drank. The skin did not grow emptier. Before she could comment on that though, Trey began pulling other items from his box.

A long wooden bow, unstrung. A quiver of arrows. And a slender sword in a fine leather scabbard.

"Shades of Robin Hood," Harry muttered, looking up from his box.

Trey wasn't through. Next came clothing; a black leather vestlike jerkin, fringed like the reins, a white shirt of a coarse material, with full sleeves, soft black leather boots and . . .

"Oh, no," Trey snapped. "No way. I'm not wearing panty hose." He held up the black knit tights.

"You don't have to wear any of it," Harry told him, finding a pair of deep green ones in his own box.

"Yes, you do," said Lila Anne from behind them, and they turned.

She had dressed in the sorceress's costume, and there

was no longer a young girl standing in the entrance. The skirt was flared at the bottom, the blouse billowy and full. She'd even donned the cloak and, standing there with the staff in one hand, her red hair flowing around her shoulders, the effect was anything but Halloweenish.

Jamie saw the look in Trey's eyes and smiled.

"Whoa, hot stuff," Harry muttered.

"You've gotta wear the clothes." Lila Anne tapped the staff lightly on the ground. "It's important."

"Why?" Trey asked, his eyes still fixed on her.

"Because we're on a quest."

Harry chuckled at Trey. "Well, what the hell. I will if you will. And you got the better outfit. Mauve is not my color, especially with forest green tights. I'll make a lot more patients sick than well with this color scheme."

"What else is in your box, Harry?" Jamie asked.

"Everything a doctor could want—in twelfth century Europe. Lots of herbs, goldenseal included, which is nice. Then there're rudimentary scalpels—all the better to bleed you with. And drills. I can take care of your headache with them. And, finally, some things very suspiciously like instruments of torture. Attention everyone. We will avoid injury and illness at all cost, because my malpractice insurance has obviously expired."

Grinning, Harry nudged Trey's elbow, and they took their clothes outside to dress.

"Open yours," Lila Anne said.

An odd revulsion filled Jamie. "No."

"You have to."

"I don't. I won't." She found the bench again and slumped onto it.

"Then I will." Lila Anne pulled up the lid on the Sage's box. "It's empty," she said with some disappointment. "Except for this." The girl—the Sorceress—pulled a long white envelope from the container. "It's addressed to you."

Jamie took the envelope. Her name had been printed on the front in ballpoint pen. Against her will, she opened it. The hurried cramped handwriting on the page within was her father's.

Jamie dearest,

There isn't much time, so this letter must be brief. If all has gone well then you are here with three brave comrades. This is not by accident, nor entirely by design. Something more than fate has brought all of you here.

If this sounds melodramatic, forgive me, but by now you've noticed that things are done just a bit differently in these parts. Your friends will need their new-found magic and all its trappings in order to serve you best, while you will have your wits alone to save the earth and your lives.

The guide stone is programmed to take you where you must go. Guard it with your life, because without it your quest is doomed. I will place along the way those things I feel will help you most. Other than this, your choices must be your own.

Don't waste precious time searching for me, baby. I'll have been dead for many years by the time you see this letter. Just remember how much I love you. Whatever happens, I'll know you tried your best.

Dad

"What's it say?"

Jamie looked up at Lila Anne, numb. "It's from my father. He left all this for us. I don't know how, but he did."

"Well?" demanded Harry from the doorway. He did what he assumed was a model's dainty turn, and despite the pain and sorrow, Jamie laughed. The doc's outfit was more of a tunic with a low, gathered waist. His buskins turned up on the end like a jester's, thankfully minus the bells. "Hey," he said, and reached out to drag Trey into view.

Trey's clothing was more like Lila Anne's—arresting. Still chuckling, Jamie felt a slight shiver ripple through her. His long black hair against the rough black leather gave Trey an almost frightening aspect, even without the weapons, which he'd left beside the trunk. The Guardian was meant to be a dark knight, dangerous. And his legs were rather shapely in a masculine way. Harry's weren't so bad either, Jamie decided.

"If the merriment at my expense is over," Harry said sourly, "let's see what Jamie's box coughed up. Where are your clothes?"

"He didn't get any," Lila Anne told him. "All he got was a letter from his dad."

"Unfair!" Harry cried, then did a double take. "A letter from his dad? Let's see it."

Jamie shook her head barely. "It's private."

"If it concerns all of us . . ."

"All he says is that he's left some things along our way that may help us. He doesn't say where the rain's gone, or how we're going to find it. The guide stone is all we've got to lead us."

"Who cares, I'm hungry." Lila Anne's voice was plaintive.

The Oregon dun, who had remained outside, put her head through a window now and did that hopeful little huh-huh-huh that Jamie had heard before.

"The horse needs food and water, too," she pointed out.

"Lots," Harry said, suddenly glum. "Hope she likes ham spread. "Did you check that magic box of yours for hay?"

"I didn't see any," Trey answered.

"Well look again."

Trey did, and grinning, came up with an armload of hay. At the sight of it, the mare tried to climb through the window. Shouting, the young man shooed her off, then threw the feed outside.

He returned to the benches where cans were being popped open. Jamie passed him some of his own to open. Harry produced plastic silverware from the saddlebags, and no one had anything to say for quite some time.

Chapter Nine

HARRY DECIDED NOT to let the little inconsistencies keep him from enjoying his meal. The water bag, passed around and around, never got any emptier. The saddlebags, dipped into again and again, remained bulging. While there were biblical precedents for this sort of thing, it couldn't go on forever, Harry cautioned himself. Still, they could take advantage of the situation while it lasted. Unless, of course, he woke back at Craig Gilbert's and found this all some vivid dream. At this point, he felt sure anything was possible.

He glanced at Jamie, still pale and drawn, seated a little way from him on the bench. She'd eaten very little. "Is your meal going to stay down this time?" he asked.

"So far, so good," the young woman muttered quietly.

"Sit tight. I've got bandages in the trunk. I can at least make you look, if not feel, more presentable. And all the herbs are labeled; there might be something for nausea."

Harry's box offered peppermint leaf and lemon grass "for disturbances of the stomach." There was also a teapot and a can of Sterno. And strike-anywhere wooden matches.

Lila Ann had her own box open.

"What's up, kid?" Harry asked her.

"I'm getting the book."

"Book?"

She held up a slender, hardbound volume. *"The Sorcerer's Primer In Staff Magic."* She pronounced primer like the paint. *"A Thousand and One Spells For the Beginner.* It's got a glossary of terms, too."

"What's the copyright date?" Harry grinned as the girl flipped the pages.

"Ummmm. Forty-three, eighty-one, whenever that was. Magician's Union Fifty-five, Ana . . . Analonaria. Is that a place?"

Harry shook his head. "Got me." He opened the Sterno and lit it, found a tripod for the teapot.

"It's got over a thousand pages," Lila Anne added.

"Right." Harry paused. "Let me see that."

She handed it over. Like the boxes, the waterskin, and the saddlebags, the book seemed to have endless pages, yet the covers when closed were less than an inch apart.

"Do me a favor, Lila Anne . . ." He passed the book back.

"What?"

"Don't try any of these spells just yet. We've got enough to deal with at the moment."

This made the girl unhappy, but she nodded. Harry retrieved the waterskin to fill the teapot, then set it on the tripod to heat. Trey took the skin next.

"I'm going to water the mare."

"Maybe you should saddle her up, too."

"None of us have had any sleep, yet."

Harry shrugged. "Do you feel like sleeping?"

"No . . ."

"Neither do I, even though I feel dog tired. But go ahead and ask the others. Personally, I'd rather get on the road, try and find some place with a decent sunless night to bed down in."

"I don't know," Trey muttered. "At least in the light you can see what's coming at you."

"Hey, day or night, you got your sword and bow."

Trey snorted. "Wonderful cliché—an Indian and his bow. I never shot one in my life, and I don't know shit about swords either."

"Well, you never know *what* you can do until you try. Maybe you can get in some practice along the way."

"I'll trade you both my weapons for your rifle."

"Sorry, think I'll hang on to that baby. It'll be out of ammo quick enough, then all I'll have is a club. God, I wish I'd had enough sense to grab the reloads." The little kettle began to whistle, and, distracted, Harry tried to figure out how to make tea without a bag.

II

Trey's box, which had been empty, now held a very familiar dented and sooty little pan. With the curry brushes, he carried the pan outside to the dun and, squatting beside her, began to empty the waterskin into it. She drank for a very long time—long enough to let Trey do some wondering.

Perhaps the boxes only produced what was needed, what you were thinking about at the moment. Of course, this didn't explain away black knit panty hose or most of the gear. And did they replicate things or collect them from somewhere else? There were labels in the clothes. Trey had checked, but they weren't in any known language. Not to him. They must have been purchased by somebody somewhere. Jamie's father? But how? Thinking too much, though, was going to drive him nuts.

Finished, the mare began to play in the pan, blowing water and snot into his face, and he stood up, grimacing, before taking the brushes to her shaggy coat. She hadn't left a single stem on the ground where he'd thrown the hay, and showed no signs of distress. Whoever or whatever had known enough not to offer up some rich fodder like alfalfa in the box, which could make a half-starved horse very sick.

She actually groaned with pleasure now as he brushed her. When the stiff bristles hit just the right spot, she'd stretch her neck out and wriggle her upper lip. Finally he returned to the entrance of the small building where the tack had been placed. Doglike, the mare followed him.

The bridle had a snaffle, and he'd never ridden her with a bit, only the hackamore, but she opened her mouth willingly enough for it. The saddle blankets were wool, of the same deep red as the leather, and spread back all the way over her hips, hiding the sharp angles of her bones. A wide crenated strap fastened under the tail, more for decoration than utility; another went across the chest. The saddle itself was lightweight, with its high wooden pommel and cantle, and the seat of quilted leather was well padded. The stirrups were iron, of the type found on English saddles, but he figured he could get used to them.

Her head snapped around when he tightened the leather girth, and her long yellow teeth glistened in the reddish sunlight. Trey bared his own in a grin. At least some things hadn't changed.

"I told you she was beautiful," Lila Anne said from just inside the door.

Trey allowed himself a little touch of pride. "I guess you were right."

And it was true—the Oregon dun was as different under her tack as Lila Anne was in her sorceress costume.

III

Lila Anne stepped back to let Trey past, stepped away again when he brought the saddlebags out. They seemed to be packing to go. While Jamie drank tea, Harry pushed plastic bags full of sticks and leaves into a large leather bag. He'd already put the heavier things on the bottom.

"You know," Trey called to the doc, "if you don't have room in your purse there, these saddlebags seem to work both ways. We could probably put Lila Anne's staff in them."

"Thanks, but I think this bag works the same way."

Lila Anne took her staff and herself outside, out of the way. She'd already studied the staff, but now she could admire it in the light. Intricate swirls and signs had been burned into it, then a clear finish had been painted overall, darkening the wood slightly, but it was her staff, the very one left behind at their camp on the plateau. All the small knots were in the right places, the narrow end chipped slightly where Jamie had sawn through.

The urge to open the book and try a spell was terribly strong, but Harry was right. Best not to dabble in unknown arts until they knew more about what they faced. Still . . . could a little magic hurt anything? She glanced at the others. Harry was busy with his packing. Trey tied the bow and quiver to the back of the saddle, slung the sword in its scabbard over the wide front end. But Jamie, head wrapped in a clean white bandage and drinking tea from a chipped ceramic cup, stared right at Lila Anne.

With a sigh, she walked back inside and sat beside the boy. Trey arrived at almost the same moment.

"Harry wants to head out. Be best if you rode the mare. Until you're feeling better."

Jamie shuddered visibly. "Thanks, I can walk."

"Don't be afraid," Lila Anne said. "She's really a very sweet horse."

"Not exactly," Trey contradicted. "But I'll be leading her, so you'll be fine. Honest."

"Your shoulder isn't completely healed either, Trey. You ride her. I'd really rather walk."

"The doctor says," Harry said from beside his box, *"you* ride."

"Shit," Jamie muttered.

"I wish I could ride her." Lila Anne smiled hopefully at Trey. "Maybe sometime, do you think. . . ?"

"Sure," the young man said, but his eyes were downcast. "Uh, Harry. Should we maybe bring our magic boxes along?"

"How?"

"I don't know. Maybe we could stuff them all into one and—"

"There's a slight problem," Harry cut in. "I already tried to pick mine up. Either it's bolted to the floor—and I don't see where—or it weighs about a ton. I don't think we're supposed to take them with us."

Lila Anne stood. "There's no sense in being greedy. We've got everything we need for a quest." She started for the door. "Are we ready? Let's go." Behind her, the rest finally shuffled into motion.

Trey helped Jamie up on the horse. The boy clutched the front of the saddle with white-knuckled hands. Harry milled around in confusion for a second.

"We need a little sage advice," he said after a moment. "Which way, boss?"

Jamie loosed a hand long enough to pull the stone from the medicine pouch. Trey led the mare in a tight circle until the green light began to blink once more. The sun had shifted much farther along the horizon, and now they traveled with it at their backs. Lila Anne felt light, buoyed. Her stomach was full, her thirst quenched, and what's more, there wasn't any reason to worry about the next meal, or the next. That was a freedom she'd never known in her short life. Questing just might possibly be a grand way to live.

IV

The rocking motion of the horse threatened to make her sick again, but everyone seemed so determined that she ride, Jamie kept her mouth shut and endured. At least the headache had lessened. Sleep would be nice, though. It was impossible to figure how long it had been since they'd left Earth. That in itself was a bizarre concept. None of them wore watches. They had little use in the real world anymore.

Trey walked close to the mare's head, muttering to her now and then—the horse, not Jamie. It'd taken Jamie a while to realize that. He looked very natural in the clothing now, though something seemed to be missing. A little triangular hat with a long narrow feather, Jamie decided finally, and resisted the urge to laugh.

The station disappeared behind them, and the landscape stretched boringly out to an endless horizon. She kept her eyes down as much as possible; the color of the sky did more drastic things to her stomach than the horse's plodding pace. The guide stone continued to wink jade, although the longer they walked, the quicker the flashes came. Sometime in the near future, they would expect her to take them elsewhere. After all, she was the Sage, the leader. Would the stone cut an opening in daylight? Ashamed, she felt anger at her father. If he could do this much, then why not more? He should have brought the rain back himself, instead of leaving the job to a daughter.

The mare sidled under her suddenly, dragging Trey sideways.

"Whoa, dammit!" he snapped. "What's the matter with you?"

"I saw something move," Lila Anne said, pointing off to their right.

Jamie remembered her earlier unease, lost in the excitement of their arrival at Shirrah station. All four of them searched the ochre ground now. Nothing.

"What an imagination," Harry snorted, then dodged out of the way when the mare swung quickly toward him, head high, eyes rolling.

"Get down," Trey said urgently to Jamie. "Hurry! I can't hold her."

Jamie tried, got a foot caught in one stirrup and nearly fell, then Harry was there to untangle and pull her free. Puffs of dust appeared on the air before them, and the mare backed away, squealing in anger and fear. Now Jamie saw them. Wolves, shaggy yellow-red beasts creeping toward them over the ground, nearly invisible against it.

Harry unslung his rifle, aimed and pulled the trigger in one smooth motion. But the weapon only clicked. "Shit!" He tried again and again, with the same results. The wolves slipped closer.

Trey had somehow managed to mount, but the dun swerved violently to the left, nearly dumping him. An unearthly howl rose wavering on the hot still air and was joined by others. One wolf, more aggressive, darted toward Lila Anne, and Harry stepped in its way. The rifle swung by the barrel caught the wolf across the nose, and sent the creature yelping back to its brothers. Another dived in, this time at the mare's heels. Instead of running in terror, she turned, ears flat to her skull in rage, and closed her teeth on the wolf's shoulder. But instantly there were two more at her hind legs.

Over the snarls and squalls, Harry shouted wordlessly at Jamie, then something struck her from behind and sent her tumbling. Harry's rifle swung over her to connect with another shaggy head. Somewhere beyond them, Lila Anne began to scream, and Jamie saw her strike futilely at an attacker with her staff. But Trey arrived suddenly with the mare, the sword swung high, left-handed. The silver arc of the blade fell across a furred shoulder, and the wolf's head separated from the torso, rolling to Lila Anne's feet. There were already two wolves lying dead in the dirt where they had harried the mare only moments before.

The young Indian's face was transformed, brutal and enraged. He was truly the Guardian now. The Oregon dun danced under him, and he guided her with his knees, the reins dangling loose on her neck, while he slashed with the sword. She responded to every cue as if man and horse were one. Another wolf was dispatched and another, until only one remained, spraddle-legged and panting, outside the circle of defenders. Trey and the mare halted before it.

The animal regarded them with yellow eyes, then turned toward Harry slowly.

"Why do you forbid us food, *tonwin?*" the animal said clearly in a guttural raspy voice. "We would have taken only what we needed, as is our right." Then, keening, it loped away and was quickly lost against the ochre ground.

Trey collapsed against the mare's neck, the arm with sword dangling, blood dripping from the blade. The dun's sides heaved, and her thick coat was matted with sweat. Harry rushed to support the Guardian with a hand.

"Trey—"

"What the fuck was that all about?" the young man demanded breathlessly, words muffled in the horse's mane.

"Tonwin?" Jamie picked herself up from the ground, and slapped dust from her clothes.

"Yeah, well," said Harry. "One of the Blond Brothers called me that after I took Trey's bullet out of another brother's leg."

Jamie stood close to the horse as Trey straightened finally. "I suppose that means you're supposed to throw one of us, now and again, to the wolves," she said.

"Harry!" Lila Anne snapped, joining them. "I'm going to start learning these spells right away. This is bullshit. If I've got any magic to protect us, then I'm damn well going to use it!"

In silence, the other three stared at her.

"What?" she glanced behind her.

"You said bullshit, Lila Anne. And damn," Harry said in awe.

The girl's face went blank momentarily, then she snapped testily, "Well, I can't imagine who I'd pick up foul language from." She smiled up at Trey. "You were wonderful. I didn't know you could use a sword."

"Neither did I. Had to use my left arm, though. The right shoulder still won't lift very high."

"Look, what you did—you killed all but one," Jamie pointed out, and saw a fleeting sorrow in the young Indian's dark eyes.

He started to slide the sword back into the scabbard and Harry laid a hand on his wrist.

"Better wipe the blood off first or you'll find it glued in the leather next time."

Lila Anne smiled at Harry next. "You were wonderful, too."

"Yeah, me and my club," Harry grunted. "No sense lugging the thing around if it's no good."

"Put it in the saddlebags," Trey advised.

Harry grinned. "I will. If only for the amazement value." He unbuckled one side of the bags. The rifle disappeared inside, as if dropping into a black hole. "Wonder if we'll ever find it again?"

"Look, I've got to walk the mare to cool her out before her muscles stiffen." Trey picked up the reins and nudged the horse with his heels. Harry went to study one of the corpses in the dust.

"Will there be more? Wolves?" Lila Anne asked Jamie, suddenly a little girl again, worried.

Jamie watched Trey move off. "If not wolves, then something else. I warned you, Lila Anne."

"I know."

"But I'm sure glad we've got Trey."

The girl drew a deep breath. "Me, too."

V

They trudged onward, all on foot now—the Oregon dun had expended her little reserve of energy. The toes of her hooves dragged in the dirt. Harry noticed that Jamie had fallen behind, and he dropped back beside her.

"Want to call a rest?" he asked.

She shook her head.

"You don't want to get separated from the rest of us. Could be dangerous."

"I'll keep up. Don't worry." She stared at him, perplexed. "Harry . . . these wolves didn't change. Why? They could talk."

"Got me." Harry cocked a brow, then spoke hesitantly this time. "No offense, Jamie, but I've decided you're crazy—with a psychosis so strong that it's sucked us all in. Of course, maybe *I've* invented all of you, all of this, instead. Except this is way beyond what I could imagine. It must be your dream. But . . ." He glanced away into the distance, "crazy as it is, it's still far preferable to reality, to all the thirst and hunger and sickness that I couldn't do anything about. So dream on, Jamie, as far and as long as you like. Just take me with you."

The young woman chuckled. "You're not making much sense, Harry."

"Yeah. You check the guide stone lately?"

Jamie opened her fingers and showed him a light flashing stronger and faster. "It's happening much quicker this time. There's a jump point somewhere close."

"A jump point . . ."

"I don't know what else to call them. Exits? Openings?"

"Jump's as good a definition as any." Harry dared to take Jamie's hand. "I may blow your cover, you know. I'm having a rough time saying he, instead of she. I don't see any reason to keep the truth from Trey and Lila Anne. We're all in this together."

"You have to." She jerked her hand away. "Don't, Harry. Don't do this. . . . Don't confuse me."

"Don't confuse *you?*"

Lila Anne dropped back with them, her staff in one

hand, the book open in the other. She'd finally removed the cloak and had risked putting it in Trey's saddlebags.

"I found out what *tonwin* means, Harry. It's here in the primer."

"Oh, yeah?"

"It's a Werelin term."

"What's a Werelin?"

" 'A breed of sentient chameleon wolf indigenous to Shirrah,' " Lila Anne read. "They're magical and mostly immune to staff magic, but I should be able to do a warding spell."

"You're picking this up pretty quick."

"That's because I'm exceptionally bright," the little girl said matter-of-factly. "Anyway, *tonwin* is a sort of brand the Werelin put on creatures they find useful. Loosely translated, it means friend."

Harry nodded. "I suppose that's better than enemy."

"Well, not really. It also means pet or property . . . as in livestock. As in food."

"Oh."

"How can they survive on this world?" Jamie asked. "There's nothing here."

Lila Anne turned a page. "They're the last species on this planet, and they've only made it because they can shift into other worlds. It says they colonized Earth back before we humans had evolved. Then we overpopulated and ran them out."

"Until recently," Harry observed. "That book seems like it's got a lot more than magic spells in it."

"Well, that's what's funny," the girl said. "Whatever I'm wondering about, the answer seems to be on the next page I turn."

"Find out what it's got to say about where and how we'll find the rain," Harry said abruptly.

Beside him, Lila Anne's brow furrowed. "That's weird."

"What's it say?"

"The words have gone all scrambled. See?" She shoved the pages under his nose.

The paper contained nothing but gibberish, now. Harry sighed. "It was worth a try."

Jamie began chuckling again.

"Are you guys coming or what?" Trey shouted from where he'd stopped well ahead of them with the mare.

They walked again. The light seemed to fade somewhat, and Harry looked back. The sun had actually dipped to the horizon, running the rim of the world, partially occluded now. It slipped farther down, and a few bright stars appeared directly overhead.

"What's this?" Trey asked. "Nighttime?"

Harry came to pace beside him, leery of the horse. "Probably as much night as it gets around here this time of year."

"Did anyone bring toilet paper?" Lila Anne arrived, her staff stumping along in the dirt.

"Check your purse, Harry." Trey grinned.

"Purse, my ass." Harry opened the pouch, found tissues in the impossible jumble. "This do?"

"Thanks." Lila Anne started to trot away.

"Hold it," Jamie hollered. "Stick close."

"Then everybody look the other way!" They did. "What do I do with the paper?"

"Bury it," said Harry. "We trashed our own world. No need to trash someone else's."

They waited patiently for her. The twilight deepened around them as they moved on. Harry caught Jamie checking the guide stone again, and found himself hoping for that bright beam of light that would take them someplace else. He was near exhaustion and knew the others could be no better off. And wherever they landed this next time, someone would have to stand watch while the others slept. That someone would be him, he decided after a good look at his weary companions.

"Bingo!" Trey cried, and Harry spun.

Jamie stood with the stone in her palm, a green pencil-thin light beaming toward the few stars. An unreasonable wave of relief washed through Harry. But at this point anywhere seemed more appealing than where they were. Anywhere, except home.

"Let's get it right, this time," he said irritably. "Don't leave anything behind, and for God's sake stick close. Lila

Anne, point the way, but let Trey take the mare through first. Then we'll land on her instead of the other way around. Jamie comes last, because . . . uh, he can hopefully cut another opening if the first one closes too soon. And, damn it, be ready to defend yourselves if need be."

Harry felt like a drill sergeant, but no one complained. Too damn tired.

But not tired enough. Trey eyed him thoughtfully, fighting a smile.

"What're you gonna do, Harry? Hit 'em with your purse?"

Jamie reached down carefully, pulled another knife from her boot, and offered it to Harry. "Take this." She had her other one already drawn. "Ready?"

VI

Trey rolled his right shoulder as he watched Jamie cut another doorway to somewhere. His left arm ached, but the right shoulder was worse. He couldn't ever remember being this tired, and yet his nerves were strung tight.

"Go!"

At Harry's command, Trey led the mare forward into the bit of darkness Lila Anne pointed out. The ground shifted under his boots, and both he and the Oregon dun staggered a step in deep white sand. They stood on the crest of a high dune in a world that seemed to be nothing more than an ocean of sand in any direction he looked. The wind had an icy bite to it, and while here the sky was a deep blue, the light from a distant small white sun had a constant dusky quality to it. Trey stared into the distance with dismay.

"Hey," Lila Anne muttered. "Move over." Then the landscape caught her gaze as well.

The young Indian led the mare to the side just as Harry came through. The doc stumbled over his curly-toed shoes and rolled, flailing down the side of the dune before Trey could react. Harry's loud and vivid curses followed him all the way to the bottom. Once there, he untangled himself and began to scramble clumsily up the steep incline.

Jamie arrived at last, knife in hand, tense, until he realized there was no enemy to face. By now, the doc had nearly finished the long climb back to the top, still cussing. He sat heavily at Lila Anne's feet and pulled his buskins off to empty them of sand. The girl brushed the grit from his hair, clucking sympathetically.

"Shit," he growled. "It gets worser and worser. I'm beginning to think there isn't a drop of water anywhere in the goddamn universe. And it's cold as a witch's tit in a brass bra here. If these drastic changes in temperature keep up, we're all gonna have pneumonia." Harry looked up at Lila Anne, whose teeth chattered. "Get your cloak out of the saddlebags, dammit. See if you can find any for the rest of us."

Trey helped her. The bags produced three long cloaks and Lila Anne's old purple jacket for Jamie.

"Why'd we come here?" Trey asked the boy as he handed the jacket over.

Jamie shook his head. "Don't know. But if we want to leave, we've got to go that way." He opened his hand to show the winking guide stone. The light had turned blue again. "That way" led out into the endless desert, a direction that seemed no different than any other in this place.

"I could use about twenty-four hours sleep, right now," Harry groused and kicked the sand. "But it's too cold here. With the windchill factor we could freeze. And so far, every world's been worse than the last."

"Look over there!" Lila Anne called. She pointed at the same area Jamie's stone had indicated.

"What is it?" Harry demanded.

"I don't know. Trey, can you see it?"

He could. "Looks like people; can't tell how many, but they've got a horse." An uneasiness slipped over him.

"Nomads, maybe?" Jamie muttered from beside him.

"Who cares," the doc said happily. "At least there's something alive in this sandbox besides us. Maybe we should check them out."

Now Trey felt a tiny rush of adrenaline. His hand found the sword hilt unconsciously. "Well, whoever or whatever they are, they're apparently in the way of where we need to go."

"Maybe," Harry eyed Trey's grip on his sword, "we should go around them."

Jamie nodded. "Good idea."

The group set off, following the dune top to the left. Trey, watchful, continued to lead the mare behind the others. The sand pulled at their feet and every step took double the effort, but the movement kept them warm. When the dune played out, they dropped finally into a valley and struggled up the far side. Once more on the crest of another dune, Trey searched the far horizon.

"Bad news, folks," he said. "They're matching us step for step."

"Shit," Harry snapped and collapsed in the sand. "I need some water."

Lila Anne sank down beside him with her book in her hands. She smiled when Trey brought the waterskin for the doc. Jamie only continued to stare at the shadowed forms in the distance.

"If they were friendlies," the boy said loudly against the whistle of the wind, "they wouldn't be pacing us."

Harry wiped water from his chin. "Yeah, except maybe they figure we're the ones who aren't friendly. Let's just duck down in the valleys going the other way. Maybe we can lose them by staying out of sight for a while."

Lila Anne held up her open book, the pages fluttering. "We can't lose them," she said, voice filled with worry. "This is a world called Reflection. Those people out there are us."

"What?" Harry demanded. "You mean that's a mirror image we're seeing?"

"Not exactly." The girl held a page to the light and read, " 'The images are a reflection of the soul, and while they have no life of their own, these creatures of the soul will steal the soul of their double. This world should be avoided at all cost.' "

Harry groaned. "Great! Now, they tell us. Does it say anything about how we can beat them or get by them?"

"Nope. I checked already. It only says we can't kill

them because they aren't alive, but that they'll die when we do."

"Jesus!" the doc snapped. "How in the hell did I let myself get talked into this? We've got to somehow commit suicide here and survive." He kicked at the sand, and it dribbled away down the slope.

Jamie said nothing, only continued to stare into his guide stone as if the answers would be there. For just an instant, the boy pressed the glass to his forehead, then suddenly stepped off the dune and slithered into the adjacent valley, headed where the stone pointed—straight toward their mirror images.

"Jamie!" Trey shouted, and saw the distant double of the boy advancing as well. "Come on!" he cried to the others and followed in Jamie's sandy path. The mare snorted and dragged back on the reins, then came after.

Damn. The kid could really move when he wanted to, long legs stretching to widen the lead he had over the others. At the top of the next rise, Trey saw his own double towing the horse behind him. Its moves weren't as exact as a true mirror image's would be, and there were physical differences, though the creature was still too far away to see clearly.

He could hear Lila Anne and Harry still in the rear. The doc was bitching. And scared. Trey could hear it in his voice. The young Indian loosened the sword in its scabbard. Maybe he couldn't kill the things, but chop them up small enough and they wouldn't be much of a problem.

"Jamie, wait!" he cried.

The boy kept on, and Trey could see the youth's double now. That nearly stopped him. The creature had no eyes, just dark empty holes in a face whose features were melted and warped. Jamie halted in the deep sand, just out of reach, and stood frozen. Trey's double came quickly toward him leading a horse. The animal, though also eyeless, did not look much different from the Oregon dun, but the dark-haired thing that was Trey in reverse terrified the young Indian. Its limbs were all bent wrong, the fingers were far too long, and its expression was a mask of hatred and rage. Trey drew the sword and so did his image.

Lila Anne came up behind him, and her double paused just in back of Trey's. The girl in long sorceress's skirts had dark holes for eyes, but, like the mare, seemed very much the same as the real Lila Anne. Harry's double, on the other hand, was horribly twisted, its face distorted with self-doubt.

"Now what?" the doc demanded, and his words were echoed by the thing standing opposite.

"Don't let them touch you," Lila Anne advised in stereo.

Jamie turned finally and looked at Trey. The young Indian felt a shock go through him. Jamie's eyes were wide, and he grinned, but it was a malicious feral turn of the lips. He jerked his knife from his belt.

"I should have never brought you along," he and his double snarled, and each jerked an arm back. The Buck knife flickered suddenly. Trey felt the blade graze the side of his neck as the knife sped by. But the creature across from him clutched at its throat. Something black poured from around the blade buried in the flesh. The Trey-thing slid to its crooked knees, then faded away.

"You tried to kill me, you bastard!" Trey cried and took a step toward Jamie.

"Wait!" Harry snagged his wrist.

Opposite them, the three remaining members of the mirror quest neither spoke nor moved.

"Quick," Jamie ordered Trey. "You don't have a double now. Take care of the others."

"They can't be killed," Lila Anne snapped, her eyes on the girl with a staff just like her own.

"By us. They can't be killed by us. But don't you see, they can kill each other. Don't anybody move just yet, except Trey. Trey, do it! Put the other sword in one of their hands and make it kill my double. Get the knife from its boot first."

Confused, the young Indian walked toward the silent image of Harry. He took up the sword from the sand and fit it into the Harry-thing's hand. Its skin was cool, almost plastic, and the touch of it disgusted him, but Trey forced the man to stumble over to Jamie's image, picked the knife from the boot top, then helped the creature push the long blade into the Jamie-creature's stomach. Black blood gushed from the wound. In wordless agony, the double of Jamie collapsed and vanished.

The boy grabbed the knife from Trey and had him help the image of Harry slaughter the horse with the sword. That was difficult, but worse yet was killing the eyeless Lila Anne. Jamie, with the knife in the girl's hand, stabbed the Harry-thing at the same moment.

"Shit!" Trey snarled when the sand was finally empty of doubles and rubbed his sweating hands on the black tights. "Shit!" He glared at Jamie. "I thought you were really going to kill me with that knife throw, asshole."

Jamie said nothing, only retrieved the knife in question and put it back in its sheath.

"He had to make it seem real," Lila Anne told the young Indian, "or the double would have missed, too." She turned to Jamie. "How did you know that would work?"

"Didn't. It was the only thing I could think of. Let's go. I'm sick of this place." He started away, following his stone.

"Yeah, well," Harry grunted. "I'm not so sure I want to see the next place."

Chapter Ten

JAMIE FOUND THE next jump point fairly quickly. The others dragged behind, exhausted. No one spoke, and Trey behaved coolly toward her. Understandable. If he had made the slightest move in the wrong direction, she would have killed him. At that moment in time, her actions had seemed logical and right, the goal being far more important then the lives it might take to achieve it. At this moment in time, the idea sickened her.

Now the others clustered around in the same order as the last time they'd gone through. She made the cuts neater this time and the opening good-sized. Lila Anne could still best see the doorway and sent Trey toward it, leading the horse. In the dim light Jamie watched them disappear, which offered up the bizarre image of half a horse walking through a window. Harry shooed Lila Anne through next, then with a quick glance over his shoulder at Jamie, he stepped out of existence.

Alone, panic threatened. The shadowy emptiness around her was suddenly filled with ghosts. Jamie fled out of it, taking a quick step down onto an unyielding surface. Bright white light flooded her vision, and noise—incredible noise filled her ears. Something thundered toward her, bleating loudly, and she crouched in confusion, knife ready, then a hand snagged her firmly by the neck of her shirt and jerked her back out of the way. Harry caught her shoulders to steady her.

The something rumbled by on three wheels, affording her a swift view of the driver's indignant face. As quickly as the vehicle passed, Trey's horse danced out into the street and scattered onlookers, her hooves clattering on the pavement. The young Indian fought for control without much success.

"Well!" someone snapped behind her. "What some folks'll do just to avoid paying their fare."

Jamie looked around at the small, rotund, and swarthy man behind the window of a building similar in shape and size to the one they'd arrived at on Shirrah. Beyond him, the benches were lined with people and luggage. Children played underfoot in the aisles. The sign over the entrance said, Analonaria Station 849, the name repeated in several languages.

She sheathed the knife slowly, staring up and down the road. Harry and Lila Anne were doing the same, eyes wide. There were skyscrapers here to rival the highest in New York City, with one-story hovels crowded between them, high-domed buildings and sweeping cathedral-like structures. Tiny open-fronted booths with canvas tops of bright-colored stripes were packed in everywhere. The narrow street was choked with traffic: motor vehicles, horse-drawn carts, and pedestrians of every shape and color. The odors of cooking foods mingled with the stink of raw sewage and heavy perfume. For Jamie, the noise was almost deafening after the silence of the sand world.

Trey was incurring the wrath of just about everyone. The Oregon dun knocked packages from arms and trod on the silk trains of brightly gowned ... men, Jamie decided. Many of them were bearded.

"Move on, move on!" a fellow in a white uniform and gold turban shouted at them as he directed the impossible tangle of traffic with gloved hands.

"Wait!" the swarthy man behind the counter cried, pointing an accusing finger. "Now I know them! It's the Terran Quest!"

Heads swiveled, dark eyes surveyed them, some curious, others with obvious distaste. Trey had finally swung onto the mare's back and fought her to a standstill with the reins. Jamie heard other voices now in the throng around them.

"It is. Those are the questers. There she is. The Sorceress ... the one that's said can bring the old man down."

She felt a tug at her sleeve.

"Sir? Excuse me, sir?" It was a boy, perhaps ten, bronze-skinned, in white pajamas, bowing continually as he spoke.

"What is it?" Jamie snapped, annoyed and flustered.

"My master would speak with you."

"Who?"

"He is Sim Chestel, Master of Nem, Lord of the Seven Isles."

A warm laughter followed this announcement, and Jamie followed the sound. A slender, swarthy young man with upswept mustaches, and wearing a gown of ivory silk, strolled toward them. Before Jamie could react, he kissed her lips gently, then dabbed delicately at his nostrils with a perfumed hanky.

"Welcome, travelers. Welcome to Hibib, the capital city of Analonaria. I am Sim Chestel, Master of hardly anything, and Lord of seven stepping-stones in a rather small puddle." He dabbed the hanky again to his nose. "I do, however, have a very nice villa on the outskirts of the city where weary adventurers might take their ease."

One by one, he kissed the others, the youngster chasing after him in an attempt to keep the hem of his master's gown off the filth in the roadway.

"It's not a long way, I promise you. But you," he placed an arm around Jamie, "could take us there more quickly, of course."

"How?"

"In your hand? The stone. Here, let me show you. Give it to me."

"No," she said sharply, gut instinct taking hold.

The young man's eyes clouded momentarily, then the smile returned, the handkerchief fluttering. "Foreigners. It's keyed to you only, sir, and would be of no use to me. But hold it then, only let me guide your hand."

Skillfully, Sim Chestel drew an invisible design in the air, his thin fingers wrapped around Jamie's wrist. The stone in her palm glimmered only the faintest blue light. Even so, a wooden gate appeared in the street. The little boy rushed to open it, revealing a shaggy carpet of green lawn that swept away to a multilevel building. There were living trees and bushes. A sweet breath of wind came through, moist and cool.

The temptation was strong, but wolves didn't always look like wolves. Beside Jamie, Harry seemed to be having the same thought. Only the Oregon dun had already made her decision. She wanted a bite of fresh green grass.

"Come, come," Sim Chestel said. "We mustn't hold up traffic any longer." He took Lila Anne's elbow and led her through after Trey and the horse. The little boy hopped along behind, with a handful of grimy ivory silk.

The lawn whispered underfoot; above there were masses of white puffy clouds against a deep blue sky. Lila Anne stood frozen, gaze trapped by those clouds. The mare tore hurried mouthfuls of grass while Trey pulled hard on the reins.

"Oh, let the poor thing eat," Sim said grandly. "It's that much less to mow."

"She'll get sick," the rider snapped, and dismounted.

"Bibi, bring the horsemaster. Quickly." Sim waved the little boy away. "Forget my hem, for goodness sake. Bring Calmus, now."

Bibi galloped off in the direction of a long, low building to the right of the main house. Sim Chestel continued on alone, turning back occasionally to speak, while kicking the train of his dress out of the way.

"This way, this way. Tea first, I think." He paused, inhaling deeply from his hanky. "No . . . baths first. Don't you agree?"

Harry grinned, ear to ear. "Soul sucking mirror images, wolf packs, and giant predatory birds, maybe . . . but this is the last thing I expected."

Jamie tried to swallow her unease as they passed under a wide canopy of vines onto a patio. The villa rose in landscaped tiers around them, white marble melded with granite. Behind them, Trey argued with a tall dark man, also turbaned, who had taken the mare's reins from him.

"I promise you, sir, she'll be well taken care of," the fellow said, gravely polite. "She'll get only the feed best suited to her present condition." He led the horse away.

"She bites!" Trey called after him, then, lips pursed, he met them on the patio.

Jamie had blocked out Sim Chestel's bubbling chatter, and now a strange rustling-hissing sound made her glance back. Rain, a gentle fall, showered down from the clouds. Her three companions watched, entranced.

Their host observed their awe. "Ah, yes. The weather mages are very skilled, hereabouts. But about those baths. Communal or individual?" He clapped his hands loudly, and Bibi, accompanied by several adults, came at the run. Sim glanced at his guests. "I'm sorry. I'm really not very up on American customs. You are American, right?"

"You got it, pal," Harry said.

"Then, do you bathe together?"

"Not if we can help it."

"Fine, fine. We have forty-three full baths and eighteen half-baths in the villa. Plenty of servants to assist. Bibi will have fresh garments brought ... or yours cleaned, if you prefer." Sim Chestel captured Lila Anne's hand. "Shall I assist your bath myself, dear Sorceress?"

The girl's cheeks colored.

"Like hell!" Trey pushed his way between them.

Sim smiled apologetically. "Forgive me, Guardian. Again, our customs differ. In this world, it is the lady's decision."

"And in our world, too," Lila Anne said, glaring at Trey. "Thanks for the offer, but I can wash myself."

She was led away by a servant girl no older than herself. Sim, after a graceful if distracted bow, flittered off in another direction, gliding across smooth red tiles and down a wide corridor with the shadow, Bibi, close behind. Three male servants of varying sizes and ages waited respectfully.

"I don't like this," Trey fretted. "They're separating us."

Harry scratched at a chin with several days' growth on it. "For a tub of water, I'll take the chance." He nodded at the attendants. "Someone—anyone—find me a bath, please."

"Lila Anne will be fine," Jamie murmured to Trey as she followed a little balding fellow in a long black coat away from the entry hall.

Her servant led her across an inner courtyard filled with fountains and plants in massive clay pots. Analonarian flora seemed earthlike, though perhaps the shapes of leaves and flowers differed. There were none she could put a name to, but it had been some time since she'd seen anything green and growing. The tiles underfoot were damp with rain. Corridors radiated into the rest of the villa through arched openings. Jamie climbed stairs, descended others feeling a twinge of panic. This place seemed larger inside than out, which was well within the realm of possibility, and it would be easy to get lost here.

Beauty and grace were in every direction she turned, yet

there was an overall shabbiness—as of wealth in leisurely decline. Her attendant paused before a final door and opened it on a bath of Roman proportions.

"Thank you," she said and stepped through, barring the fellow's entrance with an arm against the doorframe. "I can take it from here."

"Who will bathe you?"

"*I* will bathe me."

Distraught, the man wrung his hands. "Your clothes . . . Surely, you'll wish new apparel?"

"No, these are fine."

"At least let me have them cleaned, sir."

"I won't be that long."

"Oh, I'll have them clean in no time, sir. The laundry staff is very capable."

Give the guy a break, Jamie told herself. "What's your name?"

That seemed to shock him. "My name?"

"Yeah. I'm Jamie and you're . . . ?"

"Nelk, sir."

"Well, look, Nelk. I'm going to close the door, then I'll hand out the clothes. You do whatever you have to, only get them back quick. Okay?"

"Certainly, sir."

She closed the door in his face, then stripped. The jeans were so filthy they were stiff, and the flannel shirt had a number of bloodstains, not to mention the sweat stains and stink. They were held out through as narrow a crack as she could manage, embarrassed to let anyone else handle such foul-smelling clothes.

No lock on the damn door. But there was a chair that wedged nicely under the knob. The bathtub, a small swimming pool, hadn't been filled. Jamie turned and tugged on the one faucet handle, never really sure how she finally got it to run. The water gushed, warming quickly to a temperature just above body heat. While it filled, she used the john—a platform affair with constantly circulating water that a person had to squat over.

A full-length mirror gave her the bad news. Bloody bandage at an angle over the right eye, hair too long and stiff with oil and dirt, gaunt face and body covered with bruises, a very nasty one on the left rib cage. "Arggg!" she snarled at it.

The tub had filled. Water, water, everywhere. She fussed with the faucet and got it shut down, then stepped in. Oh, God, Harry was right. This had to be a dream.

II

Harry decided his own outfit, ugly green tights included, was preferable to the latest masculine fashions on Analonaria. Tunic and tights were whisked off to be cleaned while Harry allowed his back to be scrubbed, his face shaved, and his hair washed and trimmed. The bath soap smelled like jasmine with a twist of lime. Everything felt familiar and strange at the same time.

He dozed off twice in the warm water, and, with leaden arms and legs, finally climbed out of the huge tub. His attendant dried and dressed him like a child, fussing and twisting the material into place. Even the buskins and their little curly toes had been cleaned.

"What now?" Harry asked dully.

"Tea, sir. In the courtyard."

"Hope it isn't far."

He remembered nothing of the walk, moving dreamily over red ceramic floor tiles along wide corridors. The walls drifted away, finally, and lush green fernlike plants spilled into his path from pots. Water gurgled somewhere in the jungle. They arrived at an intimate table set for high tea. Sim Chestel lounged there with Lila Anne. The girl had a spoon in one hand, a half-melon in a bowl before her. She scooped some of the green flesh up and stood, carrying it to Harry's mouth.

"I've never tasted anything so wonderful in my life," she said.

"It's actually Terran. Honeydew." Sim smiled. "She's too young to remember it, but you're not, are you, Physician?"

Harry accepted the bite, the sweet, sweet taste producing bitter memories.

"Where are the others?" he asked.

"They'll be along soon. Do sit, Physician." Their host nodded, and a servant pulled a chair out for Harry. "Your Sorceress is truly beautiful. Such red hair is even rarer to us than to you." He reached out to rub his fingers in the silky strands. The girl, intent on her melon, failed to notice.

But Harry didn't like the glitter in the man's dark eyes. "Our . . . Guardian is hotheaded. You probably ought to keep your hands to yourself. Just a friendly warning."

"Forgive," Sim Chestel murmured. Tight-lipped, he poured tea into the cup in front of Harry. "Cakes, fruit?" This said with a graceful wave of a hand. "Please help yourself."

Jamie arrived, Trey soon after. Both had dark circles under their eyes, and Harry knew he had the same. Tea was poured all around, their host urging them to eat and drink.

"I won't keep your overlong," he said kindly. "I know you're tired, and you will need your rest if you're to enjoy tonight's celebration."

"What celebration?" asked Harry suspiciously.

"A small gathering only. No more than two thousand. I've sent the invitations already."

Trey set his teacup down with a sharp clink. "What the fuck is he talking about?"

"Fuck," Sim repeated. "Such a quaint euphemism. You must use it tonight. Everyone will love it."

Trey reached suddenly across the table and grabbed a handful of ivory gown. "Fuck you, asshole." The teapot toppled and spilled.

Jamie dragged Trey back. "Easy."

"We're not quaint little savages," Harry said carefully, "for you to show off to your friends. In fact, we should probably be on our way. Thanks for the hospitality."

They rose as one, even Sim Chestel.

"Wait, wait! Please, if I've offended somehow, I apologize. I know you're not savages . . . but you must understand. The prophecy harks back for millennia. Your coming was foretold, and I—Sim Chestel—was fated to be there at your arrival. Grant me this one night, please. Your lives will be miraculous, and I'll never be anything . . . but me." The handsome young face held pleading.

"What the fuck is he talking about?" Trey demanded once again.

Sim's eyes searched their faces. "The old man? You've come to destroy the old man."

"We're looking for rain, pal," Harry told him. "Our rain."

"Yes, yes. The old man took it. He's done it before to other worlds—those he feels aren't being reverent enough. But few have ever fought back. Mostly, they just dry up and die."

"What old man?" Lila Anne asked.

She sat back down, and slowly the others did, too.

Sim righted the teapot, clucking. "The creator of the universes. At least, he says he is, and none can gainsay him. He's been here far longer than the rest of us."

"Do you mean God?" The color had drained from Lila Anne's face.

"He calls himself that among other things. He says there was nothing except his self-awareness in the beginning, but that he wanted more than that so he made himself a hand to collect the emptiness. . . . He squeezed and squeezed until the mass grew so dense that it imploded and—"

"And then exploded," Harry muttered. "The Big Bang Theory. So we were prophesied?"

Sim nodded. "The old man himself said you would come. Well, that a quest would come against him. You aren't the first team." He smiled again. "They come along once in a while. You're the first in over . . . well, eight hundred of our years. No one's beaten the old man, yet. You see, it's a woman who destroys him because a woman carries life. So he lets no female at the citadel. He set the rules himself, cagey old man. But you might just make it. Anything's possible. That's one of his rules, too."

"Christ!" Trey snapped.

"One of the sons of God," Sim said, pleased with himself. "I've studied Earth a little. You have such diverse cultures, such quain—such simple outlooks on life. We have many Terrans on our world, on all the worlds. You adapt so well, so much better than the older races."

Harry glanced at Lila Anne and saw tears sliding silently down her freckled cheeks. "Lila Anne?"

"I won't," she said, voice quavering. "You can't make me. I won't help you kill God."

"But you're the Sorceress, darling." Sim took her small hands in his. "Don't you see? He expects it of you. It was his prophecy. Don't you suppose the creator of the universes gets bored, too? How terrible to be all-powerful. He needs a challenge. . . ."

"But I wanted to see my mother in heaven," the child sobbed. "I hoped I could go if I tried hard to be good."

Their host's handsome face went blank. "Heaven? Oh, heaven. I'd forgotten all about that. My dear, that's all just a stor—"

"Shut up!" Jamie cried. "Don't say anything more." Harry watched her wrap protective arms around the little girl's shoulders. "We'll rest now. I'll stay with Lila Anne. Harry, you room with Trey." She turned on Sim Chestel, Master of Nem, Lord of the Seven Isles. "We want adjoining rooms. We want our gear placed in them. All of it."

Sim worried the ends of his mustache. "You aren't going to leave before the party?"

"What?" Jamie snapped. "Skip out without paying the bill? You'll get your money's worth."

"Well, I hardly meant that."

Trey leaned down to smack imaginary dust from the man's shoulder. "I want to see my horse, first. Collect my sword."

Harry smothered a smile. Sim Chestel's beautiful, arrogant eyes were touched with fear, now.

III

"She's a wily one," the horsemaster said. "Gave my boy, Kener, a right good nip on the shoulder."

Trey leaned over the edge of the box stall door in a barn big enough to hold a football stadium. All around, there were sounds of horses, nickering, whinnying, shuffling. The Oregon dun had settled in the straw near the far wall, and refused to turn her head or acknowledge them in any way. She was likely offended by such imprisonment, never having been closed up in a stall in all her life. Now the mare expelled a great lungful of air with noisy disgust.

"Did she eat?"

"Oh, aye. A nice warm mash and some grass hay. Not too much. She's thin, but no thinner than the rest of you, I see." Calmus put a hand on the wall. "Beautiful markings on her legs. Never seen the like. Wouldn't care to trade her, would you? I've got a fine buckskin stallion, and she just might breed true. The Master of Nem fancies the unusual."

Trey shook his head. "You don't want to breed her. Her disposition is too foul."

The horsemaster laughed. "Just a matter of training, lad. We'd have her straightened out soon enough."

"Yeah, right." Trey moved away. He was almost tempted to let the guy try, and see where it got him. But there were harsh spade bits hanging along the walls, and a couple of other devices that looked like they just might break a horse's spirit as well as its body.

He found his saddle on a rack in the long breezeway. Nothing seemed to have been disturbed. The sword was taken back with him to the main house, the wide belt to the scabbard buckled around his waist. He kind of liked the feel of it now, and actually found himself swaggering a bit. A long gravel walk wound across the lawns, but Trey stuck to the grass. Would have been nice to stroll barefoot through it, but getting boots and tights off wasn't worth the bother.

The sky darkened again, and a light rain fell. He turned his face up to it, reveling in the wetness. Almost, he considered the possibility of staying here on Analonaria. If the others could be convinced . . . But no. Someone else's rain would never do. He wanted his own world green again, wet again, no matter the amount of insanity that might take.

IV

Lila Anne's tears had embarrassed her; they were childish and not befitting a Sorceress. With some amount of grace, she'd taken Harry's hand and allowed him to help her up from the table, then, Jamie close behind, they had followed a servant across the courtyard. Sim Chestel had called after them.

"Sleep well, my good questers."

They found the bedrooms across the hall from one another in some airy wing of the house. Harry, worried, hovered in the corridor, but Lila Anne managed a smile for him before Jamie closed the door to their room.

"Lila Anne—"

She looked down at her soft slippers. "I don't want to talk."

"Fine. Don't talk. Let me." Jamie sat on the edge of an enormous bed—one of two. "You mustn't believe all that nonsense Sim was spouting. He doesn't know any more about God than the rest of us. If there's some old man parading around and saying he's the Divine Creator, that doesn't necessarily make it so."

"Doesn't make it not so, either."

Jamie sighed. "Well, would you rather we went on without you? This quest may have been damned from the start, but so far, everything that's happened—no matter how frightening, how crazy—has felt right. Our world is dying, and if I have to arm wrestle God to get the rain back, I will."

"But we can't win. Don't you see?" Lila Anne collapsed beside the boy. "He's God, and we're only people."

"No, we're not. We're a team. You're the Sorceress, I'm the Sage."

The little girl smiled. "That's what you're being right now."

"Right now, I'm half-asleep. And I'd like to be all asleep, but I don't trust Sim Chestel."

"Oh, he's okay. But I can protect us." Lila Anne retrieved her staff from beside the door. "If this really works." She gripped the upper ring of symbols burned into the wood just as the book had instructed and closed her tear-swollen eyes, chanting, "To me, the powers of this place. I—I command you." Immediately, she felt the hair lift from her shoulders and knew a sudden fear. To call the powers was easy, to control them was dangerous. The air stirred overhead, and the wood under her hand grew icy. She kept her mind and intent clear, strong. "Obey me, now. Let nothing of ill intent . . . pass these marks. So mote it be!"

Jamie gasped, and Lila Anne opened her eyes. The tip of the staff burned with a gaseous green fire. Carefully, she slipped her hand down along the wood until the balance changed, the end dropping earthward. With the fiery tip, she drew an iridescent line along the floor beside the first bed, along the ends of both, and up to the wall on the far side of the second. Then, unsure of how to connect the lines, she stepped onto the mattress and continued up the wall and over, jumping to the first bed to close the ward.

"Open the door," she snapped imperiously, all caught up in the power of what she'd done.

Jamie jumped to obey, and crossed the hall to open the door to Harry and Trey's room without being asked. They were already sound asleep, and Lila Anne ended up stepping over them to complete the task. Amused, Jamie watched from the doorway.

"Some Guardian, huh? You didn't even wake him with a foot on his pillow."

"He's tired," Lila Anne said in Trey's defense. "Even a Guardian needs guarding now and then."

"How long does the spell last?" Jamie asked as he closed the door to their own bedroom once more.

"The book wasn't specific. It said only that a ward would last long enough for a good night's sleep."

"In this case, a good day's sleep. Can you turn the staff off, now?"

"Oh . . ." She closed her eyes again, seeing a ghost light on the insides of her lids. "With gratitude, I set the powers free. So mote it be!"

The light on the staff vanished, but the lines on the floor

remained, glowing faintly. Jamie pulled the heavy drapes over the tall windows, then fell on the far bed, burying his face in the pillows. Lila Anne laid the staff beside her on her own bed. Magic. Real magic as good as any Gandalf had made. I *am* a sorceress, she thought drowsily, and all her fears and worries drifted away . . . at least for a little while.

V

"Here they are!" Sim Chestel called over the heads of the multitude that milled in the courtyard, overflowed into the many corridors, and generally made forward progress in any direction nearly impossible. The party was already in full swing.

Jamie let Trey forge their way. Harry came next, with Lila Anne in tow. They'd disdained the party clothes their host had left in their rooms for them.

"I'm not ready for this," the doc grumbled.

"Food, wine for our guests of honor!" Sim cried.

How it would get to them was beyond Jamie. Someone stepped on her boot toe, apologizing in at least three different languages. Sim Chestel, in a gold sequin gown, caught her suddenly around the shoulders.

"This is our Sage," he announced. "And the Physician. The Guardian." He did not attempt to embrace Trey, whose hand rested on the hilt of his sword. "And our dear Sorceress." Lila Anne received a quick kiss before the Guardian could react.

The voices around them murmured appreciatively, and there were awed mentions of the girl's copper hair. Introductions began; someone poked a small cake into Jamie's mouth enthusiastically, and she nearly choked. Wine was pressed into her hand. Somehow the others had been whirled away in the crush of admirers.

"Well, they're thin, but sturdy," someone said behind her. "I think they've got a chance."

"Against the old man? I'll give you ten to one they never make it past Kynor."

"Done!" said the other and placed his wager.

Then another voice, a woman's, muttered loudly, "Their Sorceress is awfully young. Is she pregnant yet, do you think? And by which one?"

Offended for Lila Anne, Jamie turned and tried to find the speaker in the crowd, but it was impossible. At a tap on the shoulder, she turned again. A heavyset man in an orchid gown bowed as best he could in the crush.

"Joseph Glover, formerly of Chicago, Illinois. God, it's good to see another American." He pushed out a hand.

Jamie clasped it. "Jamie Weston, Madison, Wisconsin."

"Practically neighbors. How was the place last time you looked?"

"Which place?"

"The U.S.A., of course."

"Dry and dying," she said simply and felt a twinge at the sorrow on the man's face. "How long have you been here?"

"Nine years on Analonaria, but the time zones are really weird. Things happen a lot slower on Earth apparently because it's one of the rim worlds. The Great Lakes were drying up when I came through."

"How did you . . . come through?"

The fellow smiled, shaking his head. "I've never figured that out exactly. Went to sleep one night and woke up here. I've got friends who'd help me get back, but . . . well, this is better. You know?"

"Yeah."

There was some pushing and shoving, a shifting of the crowd. Joseph Glover rolled away on a swell, calling, "Hey! You gotta make it. You gotta save Earth."

Sim appeared to tow her in another direction. "I want you to meet some important people."

The important people had set up camp near one of the many buffet tables. Trey was there, ignoring the conversations around him while he helped himself to the food.

"Sim, dear," said a woman in a miniskirt, her legs painted even more than her face. "Is that the sword?"

"Oh, yes. You know it is, darling Ronda. Zwendal, forged by Galmar himself on Kynor over five thousand years ago. I recognized it immediately. It's the sign of a true quest."

The woman ran a slender, long-nailed finger along Trey's arm and leaned close to breathe in his face. "May I . . . touch your weapon?"

"Just exactly which of my weapons do you want to touch?" Trey asked sweetly.

Sim's rich laughter carried over the crowd. "Such a naughty Guardian. Better luck next time, Ronda. I want you to meet our Sage, anyway. He's far more amenable. This is the Lady Rondal of Nem, a royal fourth cousin of mine. And this is . . ."

Jamie tuned out. She'd realized that since their arrival, Sim Chestel had never once asked them their names, so why care about the names of his important people. She didn't return the bows, only nodded politely, answering questions in vague monosyllables. Lila Anne, pale and drawn, arrived with Harry at the table just as Sim went off in search of another group to introduce.

"I've had my ass pinched four times already," the doc groused, finding solace in a plateful of what might be potato salad. "Some old biddy went after Lila Anne with a knife."

"What?" Trey snarled, livid.

"She only wanted a lock of hair. I ran her off."

The young Indian relaxed a little. "What I want to know is how come all these people speak English?"

"They're polyglottal," Harry said with his mouth full. "They all speak a bunch of different languages. English happens to be all the rage, right now. Lucky for us. I barely made it through high school Spanish."

Sim, sequined gown shining, flowed toward them with his next group of VIPs. Harry groaned.

"They're all here," their host said, fawning. "This is the Sage, and this—"

"I've had enough," Jamie snapped rudely. "We've done our duty, as far as I'm concerned. We'll be leaving now."

Harry rolled his eyes.

"Don't be silly," Sim said. "The party's only just begun."

"Well, I've heard about your parties, bub." Harry set his plate down. "The last one went on for a month and a half, local time."

Sim waved his hands. "It hardly matters with the time zone differences whether you leave now or next year. You'll find you left Earth only moments ago."

"If the Sage says we're going," Trey said, "then we're going."

"I won't hear of it!" Now their host's hands fluttered in agitation. "My guests will never let you leave so soon."

Harry, retrieving his plate, said loudly. "There's an old Earth party game—perhaps you've heard of it? It's called a food fight." Every head in the place swiveled to look as he pushed the potato salad carefully into Sim's face. "Messy, but fun. The idea is to aim for the face. And anyone can play." Harry reloaded swiftly and fired a two-handed volley of custard at a heavyset matron on the other side of the buffet.

With a stiff smile, she replied in kind, only Harry ducked, and Sim got it, again. The man stood shocked, mustaches dripping white goo. In the sudden dead silence that followed, Jamie laughed. Instantly, joyfully, the crowd found ammunition and began to riot.

The questers took refuge under the table, Lila Anne's staff banging shins and tripping guests.

"Do we have everything?" Trey asked. They did—all but the Oregon dun. "Okay, gang. Follow me."

Harry wiped his hands off on someone's gown as they plowed through the party at a crouch. No one came away unscathed, though. Lila Anne picked cake from her hair when at last they made it to the lawns. All able-bodied partygoers were pushing their way into the house, attracted by the happy shrieks inside.

Chuckling, Jamie wiped something sticky from her cheek. "Well, Sim may have lost his guests of honor, but thanks to Harry, this party's gonna go down in history."

"Hell," said Trey. "The doc's probably started a new fad. These folks seem awful hard up for a good time. Let's get out of here before the food runs out."

VI

Trey took them to the barns, chiding Lila Anne when she continually stopped to peer into one stall and another and admire the horses. The mare was near the back of the building in the far left corridor, he remembered, a box stall on the right-hand side. The electrical lights were low, held at a kind of twilight, so the animals could rest.

"Hey, you," Trey called over the door when he'd found the dun at last.

"She needs a name," Lila Anne muttered for the hundredth time.

At her voice, the mare stirred, and, grunting, pushed herself upright, then ambled over. She ignored Trey altogether and lifted her nose to blow gently in the Sorceress's face. Lila Anne giggled. Irritated, Trey pulled a halter down from a hook beside the door and slipped it over the dun's head.

"Would you hurry it up?" Harry said with a nervous glance down the shadowed breezeway. "I want out of this place and off this planet."

Trey led the mare to the tack area and cross-tied her in the corridor. "Sim won't do anything. He's a wimp."

"Yeah, but he's rich. Rich people can afford to get other people to do their rough stuff."

Jamie had been quiet all this time, leaning against the wall, watching, listening. Now, the boy spoke. "I don't trust the man in the least, but if he causes us trouble, it won't be in any normal way."

"He's a sly bastard," Harry agreed ruefully.

Trey picked up the pace. The mare needed little grooming. She, too, had been bathed. He saddled her quickly, strapping the saddlebags and bow with quiver into place. The sword he wore at his right hip now, because the left arm was still more reliable. The mare's hooves were checked next. They'd been neatly trimmed. The bridle came last.

"Let's go," he snapped and towed the mare down the breezeway.

Jamie had his guide stone out, the blue light winking rapidly in the dark that greeted them beyond the barn.

"That way," the boy said and pointed toward the right across the grass. He had his knife at his belt, the battered leather satchel, as always, over one shoulder, and Lila Anne caught by an elbow.

Trey let them go ahead. Harry paced beside him, eyeing the dun and the night at their back. Two crescent moons, one above the other, shimmered in the sky at their left, throwing enough illumination to keep them out of trouble—enough to make the landscape shadowy and ominous.

"How much farther?" Harry called to the pair ahead.

Jamie turned his head, face faintly visible. "I don't know."

"Shit!" the doc muttered.

They crossed a paved roadway and followed the guide stone over the wide lawns of other houses, some lit, some dark. This was definitely the wealthier end of town. A dog bayed, and the dun danced a couple of steps, then settled.

"You should be riding her," Harry muttered.

"Why?"

"Because you can defend us better that way ... Guardian."

Sound logic. Trey mounted, the sword scabbard dragging over the mare's rump. She hunched her back suddenly and bogged her head, then made two stiff-legged bounces. Harry dashed to safety.

"Heads up!" Trey managed to call, and watched Jamie and Lila Anne scatter. The horse snapped into the air with a high squeal, and Trey, losing his stirrups, nearly lost his seat. "Bitch!" he snarled lovingly as she hit the ground and rose again, each peg-legged jump rattling his teeth.

"Ride 'em, cowboy!" Harry shouted, laughing.

Only it wasn't so damn funny anymore. The dun seemed determined to dump him. He collided with the high pommel and was jerked back hard. The iron stirrups flapped above his knees, and he realized then that they were striking the horse in the flanks. Shit! He caught the left rein in both hands and hauled on it with all his might until the mare's head bent around toward his knee. Now she was forced to make a tight spin. Lila Anne, foolishly brave, dashed in to grab the other rein. The dun dragged her several steps, then stopped dead, panting.

"It was the stirrups," the little girl said quickly. "They kept hitting her and scaring her. Please don't be mad."

"I'm not mad," Trey growled. Every joint in his body felt loose, and he'd bitten his tongue, tasting blood.

Harry, from a safe distance, grinned. "That was some riding."

"Poor girl," Lila Anne cooed, stroking the mare's nose.

"Hey," Jamie called. "Can we get moving in a forward direction, again?" He held up the stone, the light blinking faster. "It can't be far."

"And how far will it take us, this time?" Trey murmured under his breath, feeling a sudden strange homesickness for Earth's barren hills.

VII

The moons set, and Lila Anne made another green glow at the tip of her staff to light their way. They climbed steadily up a long slope, some dark shape beyond them, a mountain perhaps, rising sharply against the starry sky. The temperature dropped, and she retrieved her cloak from the saddlebags, finding the cloaks for Harry and Trey. Jamie took Lila Anne's faded purple jacket once more. Somehow, Jamie led them from world to world, and still kept himself separate from the magic.

Used to hunger and thirst and exhaustion, they kept moving. Lila Anne wanted to walk near the mare, but the animal would have nothing to do with the glowing staff. Harry didn't mind when she walked with him. He smiled at her, his face made ghoulish by the green light. She reached for his hand with her free one, and without hesitation, he clasped it. A strong grip, but kind. Harry was a healer of the heart as well as the body.

Only steps ahead, a thin blue line flashed outward to strobe the darkness. Jamie aimed it toward the ground as the rest gathered near.

"Same as last time?" he asked Harry.

"It's worked out pretty good."

Trey dismounted and stood at the mare's head while Jamie drew the opening. The horse followed the young Indian through willingly. Harry took Lila Anne's hand and led her across. This time, the drag at her body was stronger, and the staff flared and died in the emptiness between. Harry held tight, pulling her forward into the light. Only when she looked he was gone, and her hand clutched nothing but air.

She stood alone on a hillock in full sunlight. No Trey, no mare, no Harry. Behind was rolling meadow dotted with little copses of wind-shivered trees, before was an endless thick woods of small stunted oak and evergreen. The sky stretched away in all directions, deep blue with white clouds moving swiftly across it. So beautiful.

"Harry!" she called. "Jamie?"

Nothing, only a gust of wind to answer, lifting her hair and cloak. A sick fear swept through her. If they had gone elsewhere and she was here . . . then she might be trapped in this place forever. The staff. The book would tell her how to find her friends. Except the book was in Harry's pouch.

"Is this what you're looking for?"

She glanced back toward the meadows. A little bearded man, a very little bearded man in knee breeches and jerkin, stood at the foot of her knoll, a book held up to her. *Her* book. She grabbed it.

"Oh, thank you! Where did you find it?"

"Right here. That's how I figured it must be yours. But I'm afraid staff magic won't move you between worlds. You'll need a guide stone for that."

"How do you know all that?" she asked, suddenly suspicious.

"Your friends are here. They just shifted a little farther north. I wanted a chance to meet the Sorceress. Would you like some tea?"

"I'm sick of tea."

"A Coke then, or Pepsi. Diet, if you like, though I don't

advise it. You need to put on some weight. You're a growing girl, yet."

"Who *are* you?" Lila Anne demanded, but descended to
the meadow to stand over him.

"Who do I look like?" he asked and walked toward the
nearest stand of trees.

She followed, studying him. A round little man with
large hairy feet in leather sandals, short curly brown beard.

"You look," she said finally, "like a Hobbit."

"Oh, very good! I'm not, of course, but it's what I
wanted to look like. I thought that would put you most at
ease. Here we are."

Within the trees was another hillock. This one had a tiny
front door and two windows cut into the grassy slope.
There was also a clothesline strung low between two sap-
lings, with teeny tiny clothes pinned on it. The little man
offered her a stool beside a small table, then brought her
a red can that said Coke on it. She'd seen faded empty
ones scattered around Winona, of course, but had never
tasted the drink. This Coke was cold, and she fumbled
with the pull ring on the top. The flavor was almost sick-
eningly sweet, and the bubbles stung her tongue.

"Well, it's an acquired taste," said the little fellow as he
took the stool opposite.

"Where are we?"

"This is Kynor. A pleasant enough place if you like lots
of solitude. Of course, I require more solitude than even
Kynor has to offer. But," he leaned over the table, "I am
here for only one reason—to meet the enemy."

"Who?"

"You, dear child."

Lila Anne, hand gripped tight around the staff, stood up.

"No, no, no!" the fellow said hurriedly. "That was
meant literally. I only wanted to meet you, see what I'm
up against."

"You're not God," she snapped. "God's . . ."

He grinned. "What? Much bigger?"

"I don't know, but you're not Him. You're cheating, and
God wouldn't."

"How am I cheating?"

"You've done something with my friends, that's how!"

The fellow looked pained. "They're fine. A little worried about *you,* but fine. Sit down, dear, and let's have a pleasant talk. It's all I want. Ask me questions. That's allowed."

"You created the universe?" Lila Anne sat warily.

"Universes. Yes. Somewhat by accident. This was the first. I got better at it, later."

"So how come you gave all these different worlds magic, but not Earth?"

"Who says I didn't give Earth magic?"

"It doesn't have any."

"Oh yes it does, my dear. Everybody started out pretty much the same. It's your wretched human species that always refuses to accept reality, always wanting to make your own. Everything I've ever done for you, you've destroyed. Including the planet." His little arms waved in agitation. "So busy looking at the fine details, you miss the grand design." Then he noticed Lila Anne's distress. "Not you personally, child. I don't mean it that way."

She swallowed back tears. "Where's the rain?"

"Put safely by. Once Earth is sterile, I'll start again. The flood was a miserable failure." He looked into her eyes, searching. "Best for you, my dear, to find your friends, then choose a world somewhere, like this one, and settle down. Give up your quest. You can't possibly win. If you go against me, you'll die."

"Is there . . ." She stared at her slippers, then glanced up. "Is there at least a heaven?"

He shook his head slowly, face empty of expression. "No. Everything is recycled, of course. But what you are, your unique essence, will never be again. There's only one life for each of you, and that should be incentive enough to live it as best you can."

"Then it wouldn't do any good . . . to pray, to beg you to save Earth . . ."

"No. My mind is quite made up, and, as much as I've enjoyed our little chat, I really must get on about my business. And so should you." When Lila Anne stood, he reached up to take her hand and kissed it. "See that cut through the woods? Follow that, and you'll find your companions at the Kynor station. It was wonderful meeting you, but if I never see you again, I'll be very happy. Oh, don't forget your book. There's a pocket in the cloak to carry it. Take the soda, too. If you don't like it, give it to one of the others."

Chapter Eleven

"No," Jamie said again firmly, her anger barely in check, her fear carefully hidden.

The Guardian stormed, furious, around the small station, cloak billowing out behind him. Harry stood in a corner, eyes wide.

"You're not thinking straight, Trey." Jamie caught his arm as he swung by.

"She came through. Harry saw her. Then she ... she just ..."

"Moved," Harry finished for him.

Trey jerked free of Jamie's grasp to trap the Physician in his corner. "Think, Harry. Which way did she move?"

"Jesus! She just moved, zap, gone. I don't know where."

"Left or right, Harry? Up or down? Come on!"

Harry shook his head. "Right, I think. Maybe."

"Good enough." Trey started for the door, for the mare standing just outside.

"No!" Jamie said through her teeth. "Damn you, we stick together."

"You can't keep up on foot."

"And you can't desert us. You're the Guardian." Jamie paused, tilting her head slightly. "Listen," she ordered when Trey opened his mouth.

It came again, a murmured voice outside the station. Harry grinned, and Trey's frightening Guardian aspect faded abruptly.

"She's talking to my goddamn horse while we're in here having heart attacks." The young Indian leaned out the window. "Where the hell have you been?"

Jamie and Harry joined him.

Lila Anne held up a familiar red can. "Does anybody like this stuff? It's still kinda cold."

"Oh," Harry said wistfully. "Where'd you get that? Is there any more?"

"God gave it to me. And you'll have to ask Him." She passed the can to him.

Jamie felt a chill, and shrugged it off. "Met the old man, did you?"

The girl nodded wordlessly and glanced away.

"Well, come on," Trey demanded. "What'd he do? What'd he say?"

"He said . . ." Lila Anne started, then began to scratch the dun's neck. "He said we should give up, find a world we like, and stay there. Or we'll die. And we will, because he's God and we can't possibly win."

Trey headed for the door.

Lila Anne's eyes were bleak. "We'll be dead, and that's it. There's nothing after . . . no heaven. He told me."

"That's a relief," Harry said, eyeing the soda can with doubt. "That means there's no hell, either."

"There's nothing, Harry! Nothing! I won't see my mom; I won't see baby Mary. They're gone. Forever!"

The tears came finally, and Trey put strong arms around the child, holding her close.

"Maybe he was lying," he said softly.

"No." Lila Anne pushed him away, and Jamie saw a momentary hurt in Trey's face. "This life is all we've got, and I think we just oughta kick the old man's ass. Maybe we can't win, but I wanna do some real damage before we go."

"Whoa!" Harry hooted. "The Sorceress is pissed!"

Lila Anne crossed to the window, leaning across the sill toward Jamie.

"We have to slow down, find someplace safe to stay for a while. We need to rest and gather our strength. I need to study the magic, and Trey should learn to use the weapons. But you're the Sage. It's your decision."

"Sometimes, I think you're the Sage," Jamie said, smiling. "What do you think of Kynor? Will it suit your purpose?"

"I saw little deer on the way, other animals. They didn't seem afraid. *I* didn't feel scared, even though it's pretty dark down here under these . . . squashy trees."

Harry, listening in on the whole conversation, said, "Weird, huh? A six-foot-high forest. For what it's worth, I like this world."

"There're some meadows back that way." Lila Anne pointed off beyond the mare. "They're sunny and green. And there's a path."

Trey had been listening, too, and Jamie eyed the Guardian thoughtfully. "What do you think, Trey?"

He shrugged. "Seems safe enough, but we better keep watch. There's been nothing so far on this whole crazy ride that's been exactly what it seems." He brightened somewhat. "If there's deer, though, there's fresh meat."

"Oh, no there isn't!" Lila Anne snapped. "You're not going to hurt them."

Trey flashed her a wicked grin. "How else am I going to practice with my little bow and arrows, except on little deer?"

"You can practice on little trees."

"But little trees just stand there doing nothing."

"You better not hurt them, or I'll make you very sorry." Lila Anne thumped the staff and stalked away.

"Hurt which?" Trey called after her. "The trees or the deer?" He glanced at the others. "Does she mean it?"

"Probably," said Harry.

"Shit! I would really love some venison."

Harry pushed himself back from the sill. "Me, I'd rather stick to C rations, thank you very much."

II

With staff magic, the staff was obviously used as the focal point. The problem, Lila Anne decided, was not in the staff, then, but her own inability to direct the natural powers. Oh, sure, the warding spell had been simple enough, and the ethereal flashlight business. After that, though, the calls grew extremely complicated. The more magical energy desired, the more physical energy must be expended—in the calling and the controlling of the powers.

Remembering the spells was easy. She could call up a mental image of any page she wanted. Harry said she had a photographic memory. But so far, practical application evaded her. Too many pages were devoted to death spells, something she dared not practice here—couldn't practice, because they required the tapping of strong rage and hatred. She wasn't sure she was capable of finding those in herself, even under dire circumstances.

Feeling dismal, Lila Anne settled in the sweet grass and laid the staff across her knees. Behind her, two blue-and-white-striped canvas tents were pitched. Trey's saddlebags held no end of surprises. She tilted her head back and let the afternoon sun warm her face, let it glow orange through her eyelids.

"Hey, kid."

Trey's voice. She looked up into his angular features, the long black hair drifting around his high cheekbones in the breeze. He squatted beside her, the strung bow in one hand, the quiver in the other.

"How many arrows have I got in this?" he asked with a grin.

She glanced at the quiver. "Twelve."

"Now, how many?" He pulled one out.

"Eleven."

"You're not paying attention. Count again."

Lila Anne studied the feathered butts. "Twelve." Technically, the one in his hand made thirteen.

"Okay, watch closely." Trey drew another free.

"Still twelve," she said.

"Damn straight. But I've done this a hundred times, and I still can't see the switch. It's driving me nuts." He stood up, nocked an arrow, and drew the bowstring back slowly, gingerly. The arrow shot away in a high arc, white shaft and feathers visible against the blue sky, wobbling a bit. "Shit!" the young man muttered.

"What are you aiming at?" Lila Anne asked.

"Nothing," he answered. "Just going for distance right now, trying to get some strength back in this shoulder. But look what the damn fletching's doing." Trey turned his left wrist toward her. Dark purple bruises marked the skin.

"Ouch," she commiserated. "Are there gloves in the saddlebags?"

"Yeah, but they've got wide cuffs and the leather's thick. I can't feel anything when I wear them."

"So cut the fingers off the left one, and just use it. At least that'll protect your wrist."

"How'd you get so smart, kid?" His teeth glittered briefly in the light. "Better yet, how'd I get so dumb? How you doing with the staff?"

"Terrible." She refused to look at him now. "I can't do this. It's impossible for me to consciously harm another living creature. I can't do battle with anything, let alone God. You guys have got the wrong Sorceress."

"Well, I think it's a little late to look for another." Trey squatted beside her again, his hand closing on her wrist. "I should shoot a deer and make you help me gut it, so you can see what blood and death are really all about. So you can see how killing is beautiful in its own way."

"Stop it!" But his grip only tightened.

"We're predators, Lila Anne! We've always killed to stay alive. It's necessary and right. I can help you find that strength inside you. You and I have got to fight side by side. Everything depends on us."

The intensity in his voice, in his eyes, scared her, then somehow his arms were around her, his mouth pressing clumsily over hers. Memories of Bonner's foul kisses overwhelmed her. She jerked away and rammed the butt of the staff into Trey's stomach, knocking him back, then gave him a crack to the side of the head for good measure.

"Asshole," she said with supreme disgust.

He was folded over, clutching stomach and head. "I'm sorry," Trey muttered in a dull, muffled voice.

Lila Anne walked away, headed back to the tent she shared with Jamie, anger twisting in her belly. The mare, ranging free on the meadow, looked up as she passed.

"What was that?" the Sage asked quietly. He stood with the canvas door cover draped over a shoulder. "A lesson in self-defense?"

"Trey was trying to convince me that I could fight and kill if I had to."

"Did it work?"

She hated the amusement in the boy's voice. "It worked better than he planned, I think. What a fucking asshole!"

"You're developing quite a potty mouth, yourself," Jamie observed before stepping back to let her inside. "It's pretty obvious he's in love with you."

"Well, that's stupid!" Lila Anne snapped, and sent a quick glance out at the meadow. Trey, with his bow and quiver, was gone. "I'm way too young for him."

"Looked in a mirror lately?"

Lila Anne felt her cheeks warm. She *had* looked while they stayed at Sim Chestel's, and found herself both elated and frightened by what she saw. Her breasts were starting to fill out, the nipples tender now and then, and there was hair growing in odd new places. Of course, that meant hormones and hormones meant . . . Yuck! She didn't really want to deal with all that at the moment.

"What am I going to do?" She sat on one of the small folding chairs within the tent.

"About Trey?"

"No. About magic."

Jamie took a seat on the fat down sleeping bag that was his bed. "As far as magic goes, I'm afraid I've no sage advice."

"Most of it's so easy." Her fingers wrapped around the staff, Lila Anne let it drop forward a bit, the weight dragging against her arm. She almost felt herself part of the wood. The staff was never out of sight now, and rarely out of hand. "I said I needed practice, but the things I need to practice, I can't. See, the book says staff magic is a heavy kind—brutal and cruel. The staff isn't considered a lady's weapon. Most sorceresses use rings, jewelry of some sort, to focus their power." The girl took a deep breath. "I'm going to let you down when you need me most. I'm going to cause the whole quest to fail."

"I doubt it," Jamie said calmly. "We're all in the same boat here. None of us knows what's really expected of us or how we're going to react when it's finally time. I've got a strong feeling that that's what's going to save us." He lay back on the bag, hands under his head. "It's okay to question yourself, but don't carry it too far, kiddo."

"Sim said none of the quests have ever made it."

"Then we'll be the first."

III

It was twilight within the dwarf forest. A narrow creek wound its way around bared roots, white water rushing. Trey moved at a crouch beside the stream. He couldn't stand upright under the canopy of branches and finally he sat, back to the bole of a tiny perfect evergreen, bow with arrow nocked, across his lap. It'd taken a while for the heat to leave his face. The knot above his left temple would take much longer. Christ! What a fool he'd been, caught up in her nearness, grabbing her like that.

There was a dark side to him now that seemed harder and harder to control. He vaguely remembered the Trey Sweetwater of Earth, the young Umatilla man who'd discovered his mother's butchered corpse and run in terror. The Guardian would never run. The Guardian—

Movement. From eye to hand the information passed in lightning succession. He jerked the bow up and loosed the arrow before any conscious command was formed. Far down the bubbling creek, a dwarf deer leaped into the air, back arched, then hit the ground and managed two forward steps before its knees buckled. The little creature collapsed, a feathered white shaft deep in the chest just behind the left foreleg.

Joy and elation swelling, Trey went to the kill. A dark

liquid eye stared up at him, empty. But he refused to feel remorse for something he'd done all his life. Hunting came naturally to him and not because he was Indian. He was a rancher's son. His stepfather had always poached deer on their ranch, feeling that, like the cattle they raised, the animals that grazed on their property were rightfully theirs—in moderation, of course.

Trey used the sword to cut the throat, and caught the carcass up by the hind feet, letting the dangling head drip blood into the rocky soil beside the watercourse. The thing weighed no more than thirty pounds. If the saddlebags offered up no hunting knife, he'd borrow one of Jamie's to gut and skin it. Lila Anne would be angry, but he felt no remorse there either.

IV

Jamie woke full of dread and loathing, the dream images still strong. Her own empty-eyed double—the ugly reflection of her soul—continued to stare back at her in the darkness, mouth contorted in a lurid grin. She turned restlessly in the sleeping bag, listening to Lila Anne, each quiet shallow breath a testament to the girl's peaceful sleep. Jamie closed her eyes and forced the nightmare away, then let herself drift finally on Kynor's sweet night air.

A hand clamped hard over her mouth, and she grabbed the wrist and her knife at the same instant. Harry murmured in her ear just in time to keep the blade from his gut.

"I need to talk to you. . . ."

She rolled out from under the canvas where he'd pulled a peg loose. "You idiot! I nearly killed you."

"Shhhh!"

He motioned away into the meadow, and she paused, staring upward. Oh, what a sky. It hardly seemed possible for there to be so many stars in the universe. The nightmare grew distant, impossible to remember under such galactic splendor. Harry led her out into the field, away from the tents, then tugged her down beside him in the damp grass. Birds sang to one another in the forest, and the Physician's eyes glittered with starlight.

"What is it? Where's Trey?" Jamie demanded, suddenly irked.

"Already asleep. It's my watch." He pointed off toward the horizon. "See? When that big green star sets, it's your watch. It's a bitch without clocks."

"No, it's not. I don't miss them at all. What I'm missing is my sleep." She waited for him to offer some explanation. The silence went on and on. "Harry!"

"I'm sitting out here," he said finally, "going nuts—thinking about you."

With a muttered curse, she tried to rise, but he dragged her back down.

"It's late, the others are asleep. Who's going to know? Can't you loosen up just a little?" He trapped her hand, brought it to his mouth. In the dark, she felt his lips on her palm, his tongue sliding between the fingers, and it brought acute pain, desire.

"You son of a bitch," she groaned. "Stop it! What is it about this place that makes men so amorous?"

"Maybe it's the company?"

"Harry, this can't happen. We've got a good working relationship. Don't screw it up with sex." But her careful control was already slipping and that frightened her. "We're going to blow the whole quest. . . ."

"How? I'll never tell," he whispered in her ear. "We might not have many chances like this." He found her mouth with soft hungry lips, and his hands unbuttoned the worn shirt, then slipped inside.

"Harry," she said sternly, fighting the heat in her belly, already lost. There was something happening here, something beyond the moment. "This once. Never again."

The man halted. "If you're not into it . . . I'm not looking for a mercy fuck, lady." He was offended, angry. "I've got a good right hand and plenty of imagination. I just thought—"

"Oh, Harry, shut up. And take off those silly tights."

V

He spent Jamie's watch in the meadow with her, only they were extremely preoccupied and did very little watching. A clear case of dereliction of duty. But in the three days and nights spent on Kynor so far, there'd been no problems, no hint of danger.

In Kynor's sweet—if somewhat itchy—grasses, Harry decided he would willingly risk his life to be with Jamie anyway, even for just a little while. Shit. Near forty, and giddy as a school kid over a girl with an attitude and a very sharp knife. It didn't matter—at the moment she was soft and warm and willing, and he'd been in love with her even before he'd known she was female.

But the first color of dawn shattered the spell. The young woman pulled abruptly free of his embrace, and face turned aside, gathered her clothing. Slowly, Harry shrugged on his tunic, aware of a chill.

"You didn't mean it, did you? About never again."

Hazel eyes cool, she gazed at him, and that was answer enough. He struggled into his tights.

"Sorry, Harry. I can't afford weakness."

"You think I'm a weakness?"

"If I let you, yes."

"Great. Wham bam, thank you, sir." Harry found his curly-toed shoes and jammed them on his feet, then stood, straightening the little skirt around his hips. Jesus! Things had sure gotten ass-backwards lately. "You're still crazy, and none of this is real. Look at me, in a goddamn miniskirt."

"It's very becoming," Jamie said, fighting a smile.

"Yeah, well . . . go ahead and smirk, but you can't have your way with a guy, and act like nothing ever happened."

"Harry . . ."

But he was headed back toward the tents, angry at being angry. Trey met him at the flap of theirs, eyes puffy with sleep.

"What happened to you, Doc? Your hair's full of weeds and shit."

"None of your damn business," Harry snarled and pushed by him to crawl into his sleeping bag.

VI

Lila Anne spent the day in the meadow, her nose in the book. She was sick of magical incantations, and glossaries full of ridiculous trivia. Fiction would be nice; horror, mystery, romance—anything. But the thin volume refused to answer these wishes. Perhaps it felt fantasy should be enough.

"Want a ride?"

She glanced up, squinting at Trey, who stood with the late afternoon sun over one shoulder. The Oregon dun stood saddled beside him, ears flickering lazily, tail swishing flies.

"No, thank you," Lila Anne said carefully, though it was something she wanted very badly.

"God, you sure can hold a grudge."

"You killed a deer."

"And I ate it," he added sourly. "Harry and Jamie did, too. Didn't your uncle back in Arizona ever hunt?"

"Yes," she admitted. "And I never forgave *him,* either."

"Kinda hypocritical, aren't you?"

"Am not!"

"You eat the damn minced ham in the C rations. You think there's some hog walking around on a wooden leg?"

"Pigs are ugly," Lila Anne snapped.

"I rest my case." Trey led the mare away down the meadow. She heard the word, stubborn, muttered.

"Wait! Trey!" The book was flung down in the grass, the staff forgotten for the moment as she galloped after them, long skirts tripping her. "I wanna ride. Please."

He grinned down at her. "Get on. Wait. Other foot, dummy, unless you like riding in reverse." He helped her get the proper toe in the stirrup, then after a hesitation, put his hands around her waist and boosted her up into the saddle.

Terror gripped her. She had no idea how far away the ground would be.

"She won't buck me off, will she?"

"I'll catch you," the young man said with a chuckle.

Clutching the front of the saddle, she was led slowly to the far end of the meadow and back. The mare behaved herself perfectly, ears swiveled back to listen to Lila Anne's murmured praise. Now the girl wished the reins were in her hands, that she could ride as Trey did, a part of the animal, racing over the ground with the wind in her hair. Only there was a slight discomfort involved.

"Trey? My rear end hurts."

"Yeah, that happens."

"All the time?"

"No, just for a while. Here." He helped her down, only the meadow seemed to rock under her still. "Whoa." His hands steadied her. "A little more practice, and you'll be a regular Dale Evans."

"Who?"

A shout came from the tent area. Harry, waving his arms.

"Dinner, people!"

Trey groaned. "God, I hate it when the doc cooks."

Lila Anne gathered her things and left Trey to unsaddle the mare beside his tent. Harry flashed her a small smile while he stirred something in the sooty pan hung over the campfire. The smell did not encourage her appetite, and she wondered just what the doc had mixed together this time. Lunch had been regrettable—tapioca pudding with carrots. Harry seemed to think they needed a hot meal, now and then.

"Where's Jamie?" the girl asked, trying not to look at the contents of the pot.

Harry shrugged. "Around somewhere, I guess."

Avoiding dinner, Lila Anne decided, the kind of wise thing expected of a Sage. The mare followed Trey to the campfire. The young Indian dug a measure of crushed corn from the bottomless saddlebags and fed her, then accepted a paper plate from the doc. Lila Anne received hers doubtfully, grimacing when something mud-colored was heaped onto it. The first bite wasn't all that bad, though.

"I put—"

"Don't tell me what's in it, Harry!" Trey pleaded quickly.

Lila Anne sat and ate, watching the mare delicately pick bits of grain out of the trampled grass with her long rubbery lips. The animal was losing that skinny look. They all were. Food and rest were powerful curatives. Trey, as always in somber black leather, had his shirt sleeves rolled up and there were muscles in his forearms now. He noticed her stare and offered a tentative smile, but the glimmer of hope in his eyes made her look away.

Why did things have to be so complicated? Harry, dark blond hair touched with silver at the temples, searched the meadow and the trees. The Physician was kind and gentle, never demanding. But that only complicated things all the more.

Whatever Harry searched for, he didn't find. Instead, he took one of the small folding camp chairs and parked himself near Trey. He glared at the food on his plate, irritated somehow, then looked up.

"We've been here nearly a week, kids. You guys have plenty to do, but I'm getting mighty bored."

Trey put his plastic fork down. "You want to move on, Harry, it's okay by me. I'm ready."

"Lila Anne?"

"I'll never be ready, so it doesn't matter. But shouldn't the Sage be in on this?"

"In on what?" Jamie asked, arriving from the direction of the woods. He paused to give the mare a careful pat on a shoulder.

"Harry wants to leave here," Trey said.

"All right." The boy peered into the pot over the fire, gave a bare shake of his head, and found another chair. He pulled the guide stone from his medicine pouch and held it out to them on his right palm. The blue light pulsed steadily. "I've checked it every day, and there's been no change. But the route seems to head directly through the dwarf forest. I think we should wait till morning."

Harry expelled a heavy sigh, and Lila Anne took pity.

"Trey's never heard Jamie tell a story," she said gently, but that only seemed to upset the doc more.

Jamie shook his head. "Somehow fantasy doesn't feel very necessary in a place like this."

"Then give us some reality," Trey said. "Remind us of Earth; remind us just why the hell we're here."

Gazing into the evening sky beyond their heads, Jamie nodded finally.

VII

Harry suddenly had other things to do—important things. Anything to keep his eyes off Jamie. He rummaged in the tent for his Physician's bag, then rummaged in the bag, checking the contents for the hundredth time, but the young woman's voice followed him through the thin canvas. In a quiet dispassionate tone, she remembered drought and devastation, cloudless blue skies and death. Against his will, Harry listened to those oh-so-vivid descriptions of white bones scattered over the streets of empty cities. It grew dark in the tent.

He stepped back into the fading daylight, slipping the strap on the bag over his head and one shoulder. A tea of valerian and camomile would calm his nerves. The fire crackled behind Jamie and her hands moved, drawing sorrowful pictures in the air. Trey and Lila Anne watched mesmerized. The Oregon dun stood dozing near the tent, unaffected by any of it. Harry dragged his eyes from the storyteller, from the Sage imparting grim wisdom.

There were stars already, a few bright flecks against the arch of the sky. He wanted to be away from this pastoral world and its soporific influences. It was too perfect, too ideal—another of Jamie's psychotic dreams dragging them farther under. Jamie . . . Her voice brought an ache of desire.

The mare's high squeal snagged his attention, and he saw her thundering toward him, ears flat to her skull, neck snaking out, long teeth bared. He backed away first, confused, then realized with overpowering fear that some insane rage drove the horse.

"Harry!" Trey shouted. "No!"

But he'd already spun away on the ball of one foot,

fleeing into the meadow. A sudden wind buffeted him, churning the air, and too late he saw the feathered legs, the open claws that waited to receive him. A desperate twist to the side only made him fall, and the scaled feet scooped him up before he struck the ground. Wings beating the dusk, the creature surged upward. Long toes closed over his chest and legs, something sharp pressing into a thigh. The skin gave with an audible pop, and fiery pain seared through the leg.

Harry shrieked in despair, plucking at the claws that held him, only vaguely aware of the ground dropping swiftly away. The mare arrived beneath them, foam spilling from wide jaws. She reared, struck with front hoofs at empty air, teeth snapping futilely, then the dwarf forest fell far below, and the campfire became a small distant speck of light. The pain spread through his body now. The claw dug deeper. Harry closed his eyes and let the darkness come.

VIII

"Kill it!" Jamie screamed at him.

Trey held the bow, arrow nocked. "I could hit Harry! If I kill it, the fall will kill Harry!"

"He's dead, no matter what," Jamie cried in rage.

Trey drew and loosed. The arrow flew true, the white shaft burying itself in the feathered breast. The monster rising into the sky faltered, then steadied. Already another arrow was on its way and another. In quick succession, Trey let a half dozen go. All but two found the target, catching wing and breast—to no real effect. Far above them, Harry had ceased his struggles, dangling limp from the claws.

Lila Anne was there suddenly, the tip of her staff a deadly green. She stabbed it in the direction of the fleeing creature, and shouted garbled words. A great green bolt of lightning erupted from the end of the staff. Fire arced the wide distance, found the tip of a wing, and flames exploded. The monster curled, tumbling earthward, then, just above the trees, the wings unfolded again, and it soared low, a small dark form still clutched tight in its claws. Creature and prey skimmed the forest and disappeared beyond the horizon.

Trey in shrieking outrage, slung the quiver and bow over his shoulder and grabbed up the bridle from the saddle by the tent. Lila Anne had crumpled into the grass sobbing, the staff dark beside her. He raced past to catch the mare.

Only Jamie blocked his path. "No!"

"Fuck you! He's still alive."

"You can't follow him on horseback. He's good as dead, Trey. There's nothing we can do."

"I can damn well try!" the Guardian raged and tried to push by.

Jamie snagged an arm and held on. Trey backhanded the boy, a hard crack to the side of the face that drove him to his knees. The Guardian observed his own actions from a distance. There seemed little connection between mind and body, only a driving need for action. The dark madness seemed to flow between them, because Jamie put a hand on the knife at his side.

Trey, without a thought, drew the sword, razor blade hissing from the scabbard, and swung it high. All peripheral vision was gone, all sense of reality. The silver blade fell toward Jamie's exposed shoulder and connected instead with Lila Anne's wooden staff, which appeared in the air before them. Tiny green lightning sparked between the two weapons, and a shock jolted through Trey's arm.

"Go on," the little girl cried, voice tight. "Get on your horse and ride off. You're no good to us anyway. We don't need a Guardian who can't tell the difference between who he's supposed to kill and who he's supposed to guard."

Trey stared at the sword, then at the child, with growing horror. There were tears streaming down Lila Anne's cheeks. Beyond her, Jamie, still on his knees, also cried. The Guardian felt sobs tighten in his own throat and flung the sword into the darkness beyond the tents.

"Harry!" he wailed and collapsed in the grass.

Chapter Twelve

THE RIPPLING, WAVERING flames filled Jamie's vision. There was an internal numbness now, a sort of calm sorrow. They had grown too complacent, lulled by the quiet beauty of Kynor on every side. She remembered distantly the night in the meadow with Harry, when she'd given in to animal lust. This was cruel punishment for that lapse in judgment, only the wrong person had taken the brunt. And she'd been so cold to him after, building emotional walls that Harry could never have crossed. Her eyes filled with water again, and the flames blurred.

"It was a griffin," Lila Anne said dully, sitting beside her at the campfire.

Jamie, in as dull a voice, answered. "No. Griffins have the back end of a lion, I think."

"It had horns, though," the girl insisted. "Great huge horns."

Across the flames, Trey stirred, and Jamie's eyes refocused on him. The young man sat cross-legged, his face bloodless, eyes red rimmed. This was nearer the wounded, half-dead Trey they'd found dangling from a pole—what?—two weeks ago. But Jamie understood a little better now just what they dealt with. The Guardian was a completely different personality superimposed on the other when their need was greatest. A spell, a glamour, that Trey had no control over—so intense that Jamie had nearly succumbed to it herself.

Trey had hit her, and caught up in his outrage, she had stupidly reached for her knife. That, in turn, keyed him to pull the sword. Somehow, Jamie must find a way to help

Trey control the Guardian, because he was as much danger as asset in his present state.

"I should have listened when he wanted to leave . . ." she murmured.

"No," Lila Anne said. "It still would have happened."

"But maybe not to Harry." Jamie tried to let the pain go. "Let's leave now. We'll use the staff for light. Under the trees is probably safest, considering." She rose. "Let's break camp. Get the tents."

Trey climbed slowly to his feet. "Forget all this shit. Leave it behind."

"We can't," Lila Anne said quietly. "Harry said we shouldn't litter. Harry said—"

"Shut up!" Trey snarled. "Harry's gone. It doesn't matter what he said." But he headed for the nearest canvas wall and began pulling the pegs from the ground.

Jamie helped him fold the tents, each fold halving the size until they had two small packets that easily fit in the saddlebags. The mare was saddled next and loaded with weapons, waterskin, and bags. They would have to choose their way carefully under the dwarf trees, and Trey would not be able to ride her. Soon enough, the knoll held nothing but the dying fire and crushed grass. Jamie brought out the guide stone though she knew the direction already.

"This way." She led them toward the forest, back toward Kynor station.

II

In cold gray morning light, Harry woke to find himself alive. This didn't make him particularly happy. A great deal of pain was involved. His right leg throbbed with fire, and the heat had filled his head. Fever. He was caged still in the creature's claws, one of which also remained imbedded in his thigh, but worse, a quick glance downward proved him suspended out over the wall of a cliff that fell away into a dizzying fog-shrouded chasm.

"Oh, God," he groaned, knowing there'd be no help from that direction. A look back revealed a huge and very dead feathered body lying sprawled over the stone floor of a great vaulted eyrie. He counted four of Trey's white shafts—two high in the breast, one in a wing. The fourth had pierced the throat at an upward angle, causing eventual death by the looks of the sodden red feathers. Each beat of the creature's wide wings must have pumped more blood until, at the last, it had found its home and lain down to die.

"Good work," Harry muttered in praise of Trey.

A clicking, clattering, came from behind his head. He twisted, to his own grief, and saw the cause. A baby bird—about the size of a small compact car and sporting random tufts of down on its leathery skin—scrambled over the stone floor. It began to chirp hopefully, nudging along the feathered corpse, until it arrived at the brink of the ledge. There it teetered, eyeing Harry.

"One more step, you little fucker," Harry urged. "Come on. Elevator going down."

But the critter sat back hard on its rump and tottered away from the edge. The chirps grew plaintive. Baby wanted breakfast. Only breakfast was not about to be served if he could help it. Harry reached carefully along the snagged leg, found coagulated blood and the same ominous yellow-green pus that had been in Trey's abscess. Shit. The pain made him grit his teeth as he unhooked the leg from the claw.

More scrabbling, more unhappy chirps. There were two babies now. They wobbled around the parent bird, and Harry found something new to worry about. Was this mommy or daddy? Would the mate arrive soon to prepare breakfast? Except the children had discovered the torn throat, the dark blood, and proceeded to feed themselves, ripping strips of feathered flesh from the neck. A wave of nausea rushed through Harry and he looked away, but the long drop below only made the nausea worse.

The body shuddered under the feasting, and Harry grabbed for support. One hand bloody, his grip failed. He slipped through the claws and caught himself by the other hand just in time. Great, just great! Icy air blew up under his tunic as he dangled over the chasm, and the inevitable pull of gravity made everything that much more dire. With considerable effort, Harry got an elbow, then the knee of his good leg, over a long scaled toe. This took him by slow increments along the creature's limbs and finally to the floor opposite of where the babies fed.

Sprawled on the cold, hard ground, he checked the Physician's pouch. The flap had stayed tied. A modicum of good luck then. He called up a mental image of goldenseal powder, pushed a hand into the bag, and pulled the proper packet free.

"Physician, heal thyself," he grunted and dusted the long bloody tear high on the outside of the right thigh after pulling the edges of the wound open as wide as he could stand. It stung like fire, only the burning sensation grew quickly worse until he felt he would strangle on the pain. "Shit!"

Next he conjured a roll of gauze, but surgical tape refused to materialize. Stitches were needed. A friend had once sewn up her own finger after a hatchet accident—no anesthetic, just a sewing needle and thread. Harry closed his eyes. No thanks. He didn't have that kind of guts. The torn filthy tights were pushed down and gauze wound around and around the thigh. He would have liked to discard the tights altogether, only the Physician's pouch didn't do clothes, and Harry had no intention of letting it all hang out.

The Physician's pouch also didn't do food or water. More's the pity. But Harry had to try after a quick listen. The babies were still feeding. The sounds didn't help his stomach much. He concentrated, dredged up the memory of a shiny plastic package, small and rectangular, and dipped once more into the pouch. Nothing, just a packet of herbs.

"Come on," Harry argued. "Tiger's Milk. It's health food, high protein. I *need* it. Some Gatorade, too, if you please."

The pouch produced a little cardboard carton with a straw taped to it, and the candy bar. The baby birds, sated now, wobbled around to his side of the loft, beaks smeared with gore. Damn. They regarded him with bulbous opaque blue eyes, curious.

"Get away," he snarled.

With a happy croak, one flopped toward him. Somehow Harry got himself upright and, dragging the bad leg, scuttled to a far wall away from the ledge. Before the drought, when he was young and stupid, he'd done some free-climbing up sheer rock walls. Older, wiser, and damaged, there was no chance in hell of his climbing out of here, up or down. And eventually, he'd end up a meal.

He followed the wall around the back of the eyrie. The birds came along, chuckling and talking, looking for conversation and company. Harry found a long forked stick, which he employed alternately as a crutch and a club. At the very rear he also found an exit nearly buried behind a wide nest of sticks lined with soft feathers. No more than a hole, it would require a good deal of painful squirming to get through. A quick look showed nothing but darkness behind the wall, but this wasn't a natural break in the stone. Harry touched the faint chisel marks with cold numb fingertips, wondering.

One of the birds staggered into the nest, headed his way. He pushed the stick through first, reached into the perpetual night, and found empty air. Oh, well. Nothing ventured . . . One shoulder had to be forced past the opening first. His hips snagged, then the bad thigh. Cold sweat slicked his face, and he touched the floor below, ignoring the pain long enough to pull his feet free. Slowly, his eyes adjusted to the slight illumination coming from outside. Fingers discovered something off to his left, and he dragged it into the light. A saddle of some sort, long harness straps, soft leather seat, but small, as if for a child. Dusty. He considered the matter while eating the candy bar and drinking Gatorade.

Ahead, utter darkness and another opening. To where? The babies fussed and complained in their nest, blocking the light now and again. Harry dragged himself upright finally, and felt his way along the left wall to the black emptiness. Stairs, cut roughly in the rock, dropped at a steep angle into the belly of the mountain. Great. Just great. Stick once more employed as a crutch, he started down the narrow steps. The leg throbbed, and every jolt from the

left one made it worse. The left hand was kept on the wall
to steady and guide him.

Where would this lead him? He wondered briefly how
the others fared, wondered if they still lived—wondered if
he would ever see them again. Jamie. The stairs seemed to
be curving, spiraling down counterclockwise, endlessly.
The left leg grew weak and trembly from effort. The right
continued to hurt at so intense a level that it caused the
mind to almost give up on the pain. Short-circuited nerve
endings. Just as well.

He was forced to rest at some point, head leaned against
the cold wall, ragged breath sounding overloud on the still
air. But somewhere below, blind eyes detected faint light,
and encouraged, Harry pulled himself upright to start out
again. The light grew a little brighter, forming an odd pattern of luminous lines as he drew closer. The shock of
finding flat ground instead of another step staggered him
momentarily. The lines of light came from between un-
mortared stone bricks of differing sizes, all wedged in together.

Harry checked the tiny dark chamber around him. There
were no other openings. Leaning his forehead against the
low lintel, he peered through a horizontal crack into a
bright room beyond. Too narrow a field of vision to see
much—some candle flames, a tabletop. He used fingertips
to tug at the bricks, but they'd been set from the opposite
side, worked tightly into place. Finally, when no better solution would come to him, Harry turned and leaned his
shoulders back against the barricade, then pushed with the
rubbery strength of his one good leg.

Stone ground over stone, slowly, and slowly the bricks
tumbled away. Harry tumbled with them, off-balance, sliding backward into the well-lit room to lay stunned. But at
least with the right leg elevated on the pile of bricks, the
pain and throbbing lessened. For that much, he was grateful as he looked around. Hundreds of candles lined the
high round walls, so high that the ceiling seemed out of
sight.

"Dear me," said someone, and Harry turned his head
slightly. "A live Physician. This won't do at all."

Little man, large bearded head, and—Harry tipped his head back a bit farther—large bare feet covered with a thick mat of brown hair. Lila Anne had described them in great detail over the last week.

Harry stuck out a hand over his head, still flat on his back. "Harry I. Roswell, D.D.S. And you must be . . . God. Excuse me if I don't stand."

God ignored the proffered hand, faded blue eyes troubled. "What of my roc? What's happened to her?"

"Dead?" Harry said in a small voice. "But it wasn't my fault. I swear to—" Whoops. "I swear I didn't do it."

"Of course not!" the little fellow snapped. "No doubt it was that infernal Guardian of yours. How he managed to survive two of her attacks . . ." God's eyes narrowed, pinning Harry. "You, young man, are supposed to be dead. This does not bode well."

For me, thought Harry unhappily. *Give him some good news, then.* "The babies are fine. You could say, they've learned a new appreciation of their mother." Idiot!

The man only smiled. "Yes, well, your survival is easily enough remedied. The others already think you dead. They've been quite demoralized by it, I'm sure. And there's an eighty-six percent probability that another of your quest members lies dead even now by the hand of a companion."

"Who? Who's dead?" Harry asked, dread coloring the words.

"The Sage. Most quests never get beyond Kynor station anyway. You're the first ever to make it to the Citadel. But, then, you came by the back door, so to speak."

Harry refused the fear and sadness. Jamie had beat the odds often enough. The sharp corners of bricks pressing into his back began to hurt in counterpoint to the leg. Best to just get things over with.

"So, you're going to kill me, now. . . ."

"Nothing personal. I don't usually do these things directly. It won't hurt. I promise you."

"You're a real pal," Harry managed, steeling himself for oblivion.

"But tea first, I think. The least I can do is offer you a nice cup of tea."

Despite himself, Harry grinned hopefully. "Got any more Classic Cokes?"

III

All night long they wound their way through Kynor's forest, following the light of the guide stone. Lila Anne walked slightly ahead with her glowing staff. Trey kept himself to the rear with the mare, still ashamed and heartsick. And furious. The rage would not abate no matter how hard he tried. This failure could be laid directly at his feet. He alone had lost Harry. He alone had raised a sword against the Sage. Worse yet, the desire to kill still burned unchecked. The Guardian needed an enemy that would stand and fight. Combat, blood, and death were the only things he understood now.

"Trey?"

Jamie had dropped back to walk beside him while there was room in the narrow, dark corridors among the trees. He shuddered, thinking of what he'd nearly done to the boy.

"What was your mother like?"

"Why?" Trey asked, tone harsh, body taut.

"Do you remember her?"

"Of course!" But that gave him pause. Her name was lost to him for some reason. He could no longer call up an image of her in his mind.

"My mother," Jamie said quietly, "was beautiful and gentle. Her eyes were blue. I inherited my father's eyes, his temperament. But it's getting harder to remember now, who I was before all this happened. It's important to remember, Trey. You have to be the Guardian, but first be Trey Sweetwater."

Trey realized his hands were clenched into fists, the mare's reins cutting into his right palm. He forcibly loosened them.

"Trey Sweetwater," Jamie repeated. "A very prophetic name if we do manage to bring the rain home with us."

Memories flooded back, not all of them pleasant. Against his will, Trey found himself speaking. "Sweetwater was my mother's name. I never knew my real father. She had a terrible fight with her relatives. Either they never forgave her or she never forgave them, because she would never talk about it. I was born in a white man's hospital, raised by a white father. I have no idea who I really am."

A long silence came after. The trees crowded close and Jamie was forced to go on ahead. Vague flashes brought Trey memories of a moonlit woman with long dark hair, traveling beside him in the desert. She was beautiful and gentle, too. Unnoticed, the rage had slipped away, the soul had realigned itself—a harmony of sorts restored.

IV

Harry tried to decide which was best: to know the exact moment of your death or have it left to the whimsy of some dispassionate god. This had to be how death row inmates felt, though. Limping badly, the Physician paced the floor of his prison for the hundredth time. A seamless stone wall encircled him, no windows, no door, no furnishings. Crossing the center of it took approximately ten paces.

The little man hadn't been unkind. Not really. Harry'd been treated to two cans of Coke. God was a gregarious sort, doing most of the talking, firing pertinent questions now and then. Later, He'd taken Harry out on a wide terrace.

"What world is this?" Harry'd asked, gazing out over canyons and mountains blue with distance.

God said something.

"Pardon?"

God repeated Himself, and Harry still didn't catch it.

"Hardly matters," the little man said. He led Harry around the terrace to a staircase that dropped steeply into the depths. No guardrail, no nothing, just endless narrow stone steps. "This is the way they'll have to come. Not that they'll ever make it this far."

The quest. Nasty climb, easy to fall. Of course, Harry wouldn't be around then. God had politely reminded him of that fact all through tea and Coke.

"Hey, aren't you omnipotent, omniscient—all those omni words? Don't you know what's going to happen, what's happening everywhere right now?"

"Wouldn't that be a bore. Not to mention nerve-racking." The little guy searched Harry's face. "Well, are you ready?"

"Not really. How about showing me where the rain's stashed, first?" When God looked doubtful, Harry smiled, stalling for time. "Hey, I'll be dead. Where's the harm?"

That pleased God, no end. "I like you, Harry." He hooked a hand in the Physician's elbow. "I like your sense of humor. And you're not afraid to die."

With unfeigned confusion, Harry threw a quick glance over his shoulder, then tapped his own chest with a finger. "You talking to me?"

"Delightful!" God laughed. He tugged at His lower lip. "All right, Physician. I'll show you your rain. But it's going to cost you."

"What?" demanded Harry, suddenly sorry.

"I'll need some time to think about it, but your death will have to be most unique and amusing."

"Hey, you promised no pain."

God shrugged. "Your choice, Harry. You can die right here and now, instead."

Some choice. "Show me the rain."

They went back inside, down circling corridors to a chamber much larger than the one Harry had fallen into. Lots of candles. Couldn't God afford electricity? Some wall-to-wall carpeting? The little man opened a rough-hewn wooden cabinet.

"There. The small one on the far right."

Harry leaned close, peering at a small crystal cube about the size of lump of sugar on a middle shelf. "That's it? All of it?"

"Every drop. Of course, it's still filling. The rim stars are far slower. Time is not a particularly stable element. But eventually, Earth will be sterile. I can start again. It *is* a nice piece of property, good locale. And we do learn from our mistakes. Go ahead. You may touch it."

Harry picked the cube up. Felt like crystal, looked like crystal. Something blue sloshed around inside when he shook it.

"So? If someone wanted to . . . say . . . put the rain back on Earth, how would they go about it?"

"Are you a masochist, Harry? Because that information will cost you, too."

The cube was carefully replaced on its shelf. Dealing with God was like dealing with the devil. Expensive.

The little man looked suddenly bored. "This has all been interesting, but I'm rather busy." Harry's whole body tensed. "No, Physician. Not yet. But I won't make you wait long. Until later, then."

Next had come a slight dizziness, and Harry had found himself in this place, alone and still alive. For a while. The leg continued to throb, but he was too nervous to sit. Perhaps the bandages should be changed. He still had his pouch. But why bother? The infection wouldn't have time to kill him. Hell, shoulda just died when he had the chance. This waiting would give him an ulcer quick. And the Cokes had found his bladder finally.

"Hey! Where's the bathroom?" he shouted.

Anybody listening? Must be, because now there was a small portable camper toilet behind him. Harry used it gratefully. The label said, Larson Chemi-pot, Ft. Worth, Texas.

"Do something, Harry," he snarled quietly. "How about waking up, damn it."

He sat on the floor instead, bad leg stretched out before him, and began systematically emptying the medical pouch. The heap on the stones beside him grew higher and higher and still the pouch was full. Impressive, but nothing that would get him out of this spot. Some of the stuff was pretty bizarre, including a grand assortment of razor-sharp instruments. Suicide? He contemplated his wrists with their blue veins. No. No easy way out for Harry I. Roswell. Sure would piss God off, though. Unless, of course, He planned it that way. Arrggh!

Think. He reached into the pouch again. This was going to take some fancy bullshitting. Harry formed the image carefully in his mind, thinking: Necessary for redevelopment of hand-eye coordination after limb injury. He didn't think about the injured limb being a leg, otherwise the pouch would never go for it. Ha! His hand held a long box of artist's pastels, now.

So, if you don't have a room with a view, you make one. Or an exit. He hopped one-legged to the wall, and with the black crayon, drew himself a door, then added a doorknob as an afterthought. Only after a long wait, the wall remained solid. Oh, well. It was worth a try. Something to pass the time, anyway. Next a window. This he put some effort into, thinking first to draw mountains and such, only a cityscape seemed better. Skyscrapers went up in fanciful colors—he was already running low on black. The oily chalk made rainbows of his hands.

A table was drawn below the window, somewhat crudely. A vase full of brilliant yellow flowers was added. Not bad. Starting to feel like home. Another window, opposite the door, turned out to look into another room for some reason. Not a conscious choice. And now, he drew a shape, human—a neighbor perhaps. Slender man seen from the waist up, brown hair, green-brown eyes. This was weird. Harry had never shown any particular talent for art, but here he painstakingly drew each detail, using only the perfect colors to shade the skin, shadow the cheeks. For the first time, he was aware of depth, dimension, light source.

It's the fever, he decided, aware of the leg, the deep pounding of blood within it. Sad. His neighbor's eyes revealed such sorrow.

"Who are you?" Harry muttered and pushed himself away from the wall, hobbling to the center of the room. The eyes followed him. He stared back. So familiar that face. Who? The pastel was thrown away in an almost violent gesture.

"Hey!" he shouted into the room again. "Will you just fuckin' get it over with!"

V

Lila Anne was crying, little sobs of absolute misery, but she continued to walk, the staff held out to light the way. Jamie felt so helpless, hardly able to contain her own emotions. She focused on the stone in her hand. The tiny flash had strengthened, grown more rapid. Soon, they'd leave this godforsaken world. And Harry.

The blue light blurred.

"Jamie?" Lila Anne's voice was hoarse.

She stepped out of the woods to stand beside the little girl. Stars were scattered thickly overhead now, and under them a great dark plain flowed away endlessly. Danger. Exposure to the sky. But the guide stone winked urgently. Trey stopped on the verge, the mare halting behind him.

"Well?" he asked finally.

"It should be dawn in a couple of hours."

"I want to go now," Lila Anne murmured.

Jamie glanced at Trey. The young man's face was impassive, almost peaceful by starlight, but his eyes were shadowed.

"I won't let anything happen to us," he said gently, then turned to the mare and pushed a toe into a stirrup, pulling himself into the saddle.

Over the creak of leather, Jamie heard the sword drawn, saw light glisten on the steel, and felt a tiny dread, but she followed the horse into the open. Lila Anne stuck close, nervous, scanning the night sky constantly as they walked. Jamie watched only the guide stone, mesmerized by its flash, stumbling now and then on the uneven ground.

At last, the promised beam appeared. It rose slowly from the stone, then exploded outward in a burst of blue light. Wordlessly, the other two gathered near, Trey dismounting, while she cut the opening. Trey and the mare went first, lost in the thicker darkness of that doorway. Lila Anne went next. Jamie paused to look back.

"Harry!" she cried. "Good-bye!" And stepped through.

The passage was heavier this time, dragging at limbs, fighting the forward motion. Nearly exhausted, she staggered free into cool daylight under a cloudy sky. Trey, the mare, and Lila Anne stood beside a familiar little building. This one said Hypano, in several languages. But it was deserted, as were all the buildings around it up and down the long street.

"Our itinerary," Trey observed, "doesn't seem to hit many of the popular tourist traps. Where is everyone?"

"Moved away," Lila Anne said and walked into the station. "There's a box in here!"

Jamie, gaze wandering over the storefronts, caught a glimpse of something in a far doorway. White bones heaped in the shadows. Some of the citizens hadn't moved away. Now she studied the windows and alleys with care, wondering if they should be afraid.

"Jamie! It's for you, for the Sage. Come on."

Jamie stepped around the mare. "What?"

"Another letter. That's all."

She accepted the envelope and sat on a dusty bench in a corner, fingers trembling while she opened it and unfolded the single white page.

Jamie,

If you have made it this far, then there is still hope. Remember that. You have very likely lost the Physician, but the worst is yet to come. Within this envelope you will find a key to the guide stone, an added program. It will allow you to bypass the next two steps, leaving only the last two. Technically, you'll be cheating, but since the old man's been cheating all along, He can hardly cry foul.

Now comes the hardest part. Don't react in any way so as to alarm the others. On Morlin, the next world, there will be a concerted effort made against the Sorceress. You must let them kill her. You must sacrifice both the Sorceress and the Guardian.

The trembling grew suddenly worse. With difficulty, Jamie focused on the words.

It's the only way, baby. Once they're dead, the old man will believe another quest has failed. The Sage

alone has never been a threat, and He's paid you lit-
tle attention. You'll be able to change immediately to
your final destination—the Citadel. Strike quickly,
and true. Only a woman can destroy Him.

You'll know what to do. Despite the sorrow and
loss, you'll do what you need to in order to save your
world. The stone will take you home after. I can't help
you beyond this. Now it's time for me to pay my
debts. Good luck, baby.

Love, Dad

Tears threatened, and furious, she crumpled the page
into a tight ball.

"What's it say?" Trey demanded.

They were both there, standing over her, worried.

"It says I have to go on alone."

"Bullshit!" The Guardian made a snatch for the letter.

Jamie pulled her knee up on the bench and drove a boot
heel hard enough into his left hip to send him staggering
back. Lila Anne barred him with the staff.

"This is as far as either of you can go," Jamie told
them, voice somehow calm. "If you come with me, you'll
die."

"If we don't, *you'll* die," Lila Anne snapped. "I'm the
Sorceress. I'm the only one who can destroy the old man.
Everybody says so."

"Well, everybody's wrong then. I'll come back for you."

Trey was obviously fighting the urge to rage. "Have you
looked this place over closely? There's something very
wrong here. I don't want to be stranded on . . . on Hypano,
for God's sake."

"Jamie, please." Lila Anne leaned close. "What did
your father say that's got you so upset?"

Angry now, she got to her feet. "Just forget it. You want
to come along, fine. Only remember, I warned you.
There's something in this. Get it out for me." She handed
Trey the envelope, then took the guide stone from her
pocket.

"There's nothing . . . wait. Jeez, it's tiny." He dropped a miniscule pellet in her palm. "What the hell is that?"

"We're reprogramming the stone. It's going to hop us past the next two stops. There's only one more between here and the Citadel."

Trey nodded. "All right."

Jamie looked at the speck in her one hand and the stone in the other. How? There was already a speck at the center of the glass. She sat back down, set the guide stone on the bench beside her, then gently set the one speck on top of the other. Nothing happened. With a fingertip, she pressed it down, felt the pellet slowly sink into the glass. The reaction was immediate.

"Whoa!" Lila Anne cried.

Wire-thin laser beams in prismatic colors shot high, opening outward like flower petals. The lights wove and danced over their faces, over the walls, until finally they closed again, forming a single tight beam of brilliant purple.

"Does this mean we can leave right now?" Trey asked.

"Probably." Jamie eyed them. She could run . . . somewhere, anywhere. Cut an opening and get through before they found her. They had the gear. They could find somewhere safe and live well enough if she failed to beat the old man and make it back. Adam and Eve, maybe, by the looks of the place, but Trey certainly wouldn't mind.

Trey smiled at her now. "Oh no, you don't." He closed a hand tight over her upper arm.

Chapter Thirteen

HE STARTED A long mural to the left of the "door." It looked a lot like the kind once found in airport terminals back before the drought—the ones drawn by Mrs. Reilly's fourth grade class. Only it wasn't too long before the throb in his leg forced Harry to settle on the floor again, shoulders to the wall. Depressing. The whole situation depressed him, and the guy in the second window continued to watch sadly.

Death had become a nasty preoccupation, impossible to shake. Just what would it take to amuse God? He glanced up at the ceiling, maybe twelve feet overhead. No air registers. Perhaps that was it. Suffocation just might be amusing enough. Harry could wheeze and gasp and finally expire, his face all mottled blue and white with cyanosis. The thought alone caused pressure in his chest, a sudden breathlessness. Hell.

Best to be philosophical about the whole thing. Death, after all, was just a process. However it came, you merely suffered for a time, short or long, then had the rest of forever to not exist. Too bad. Harry'd always favored reincarnation, though why that should bring solace was beyond him now. You still lost the immediate you, had to start all over again. Hell.

The leg pounded and ached. A couple of items from his cart had ended up in the heap on the floor. Maybe the pain meds could be conjured. Or better yet, a lethal injection like he'd provided for Kathreen Gilbert. Dying in your sleep should be pleasant enough. Harry snagged the medical pouch's strap with a finger and pulled it to the wall. After asking for the 100-cc bottle Jeff had provided him in L.A., the bag gave him two aspirin and a little slip of paper that read: This bag not programmed for Class III or IV pharmaceuticals. Hell.

He swallowed the aspirin dry, and settled for the added misery of more goldenseal powder and a fresh wound dressing. And the man in the window continued to stare. Harry stared back, frustrated, the pain making him more than a little crazy.

"Hey!" he snapped finally to the air. "I could sure appreciate lying down someplace comfortable. Where's the goddamn bed?"

Despite the ill-advised curse, the room tilted instantaneously, and he was staring at the ceiling, a skimpy pillow under his head, a firm narrow mattress under his body. His stomach rocked a moment, then settled, and it suddenly occurred to him that the old man might not be answering these requests personally. This prison cell could very well work along the same principle as the boxes and saddlebags and his medical pouch. Easy enough to test.

He ordered up a sink with running water—verbally, when thinking didn't provide immediate results—to wash his chalk-smeared hands in. It winked into being on the edge of his vision, right under his second window. Groaning, he dragged himself to the elaborate little vanity, washed his hands with a bar of Dove, and glared into his neighbor's sorrowful face. Maybe he should scrub the figure off the wall. No, it was already too damn lonely here.

But a little thread of hope touched him. Unlike lemmings, most creatures preferred to survive. Well, dammit, so did Harry Roswell. If he could assume he was still in the Citadel, then somewhere nearby was a cabinet with Earth's rain. Best plan would be to get out, grab the cube, and meet Jamie and the others at the bottom of those stairs. Didn't matter if he made it or not. What mattered was trying.

"Give me a door," he demanded of the chamber. Nothing happened. "All right, then. I want a hole in the center of the floor and a ladder leading out of this place." Still nothing. Think, Harry! Trick the sucker like you do the bag. "Give me a . . . Black and Decker masonry saw with a twenty-four-inch industrial diamond blade." Might as well ask for the best.

The thing appeared immediately on the floor. With a grin, Harry hobbled to the saw. It was huge and heavy, and certainly secondhand merchandise, but it just might do to get through these walls. He caught up the three-prong plug.

"Electrical outlet, please." He searched the walls. Nothing. Not even behind the sink or the bed. Shit. His cell was beginning to look somewhat cluttered, now. There had to be a way to do this. Harry lugged the thirty pound saw to the vanity and eyed the window. Think, dammit! But thinking seemed to be getting more and more difficult, due to fever, infection, and pain. Fuck it. He found the medical pouch in the clutter, and conjured more aspirin and some heavy-duty amoxicillin capsules, then washed them down with water from the faucet.

"And while you're at it, plug this in." Chuckling, he pushed the electrical plug from the saw into the top of the bag, then went back to the bed and lay down, the leg propped with the folded pillow.

II

Despite Jamie's protests, Trey held on grimly and dragged him to his feet. There'd been something in the damn letter. Trey was tempted to take it by force, but the boy had already pushed the balled up paper into his satchel. Lila Anne hovered near the bench, as confused by Jamie's behavior as Trey was. They'd already lost Harry, and had no time for this shit. A team worked on trust. At the moment, all the trust was slipping away.

"Let go!" Jamie flared, but he didn't reach for his knife.

"We do this together, or we don't do it at all." Trey held tight.

"All right!"

Lila Anne caught the hand with the guide stone, covering the purple light. "Promise, Jamie. You have to promise."

The Sage glared up at Trey. "Sure. I promise to let you waste your lives."

Trey looked at Lila Anne and found her eyes on him, pretty, freckled face clouded with worry. They'd come so far. But the thought of losing Lila Anne scared him.

"This next stop's a bad one?" Trey returned his attention to Jamie.

The boy nodded. "Yes. And everything will be thrown at the Sorceress. Don't you understand? The old man will never let a woman near the Citadel. At least let me go first—scout out the situation. See what we're up against."

Tempting. But they'd gone far more blind into everything so far.

"No," he said finally. "Sorry. I just don't know if you'd come back, even if you could. At least we've had this much warning." Trey considered the mare standing just outside the wide entrance. "Let's work it this way. Me first, as usual. Only this time cut the opening higher, and I'll go through already mounted. Keep Lila Anne between us. You take the bow, Jamie."

"No," Lila Anne said sharply. "The Sage hasn't got any magic. Your weapons won't work for him."

"Shit!" Trey snarled. "Then the knife'll have to do." He stared at the little girl. "You're going to have to use that staff for real. Can you do it, Lila Anne? Can you kill?"

She paled visibly under the curtain of red hair. "I tried . . . for Harry. . . ." Her voice broke.

"I know." Trey wanted so desperately to offer her comfort, but he kept his tone harsh. "Can you do that again? For all of us?"

"I think so."

"Fire it up just before we go through."

"It'll go out in transition. The powers are different from world to world, I think."

"Well, look it up in the damn book. Make it quick." Trey turned on Jamie once more. "I'll worry about what's coming at us, you watch our tail. Lila Anne'll help with that, 'cause I want you to jump us out of there just as fast as you jump us in. If we're outmatched, our best bet is to run like hell."

Jamie only nodded, refusing to meet his gaze. Uneasy, Trey released the boy's arm and glanced at Lila Anne.

"What's the book say?"

"I can't carry a spell through. Takes approximately thirty seconds to complete a new one."

"Make it twenty, Sorceress."

"Yessir." She actually managed a smile for him, and that just about broke his heart.

Gruffly he snarled, "Let's go, people," and realized he sounded like Harry.

III

The slithering sound nearly gave Harry a heart attack. His fever-bright imagination produced some Godsent poisonous snake sliding toward him across the floor. He jerked upright on the bed and saw the electrical cord disappearing into the medical pouch. After a moment, it halted, wriggled once, and was still.

Hmm. Afraid to hope, he returned to the sink. A gentle tug on the cord proved it solidly connected—somewhere. Nothing to do but try the thing out. Harry took hold of the upper handgrip, lifted the masonry saw up from the floor, and hit the deadman's switch. The monster juddered to life in his hands, shrieking bloody murder.

But where to begin? Somewhere low would be best. The thing weighed a small ton. Only he followed another urge, climbed onto the vanity on his knees and steadied the saw against his left thigh. Even so, the pain in the right one made him grit his teeth. The blade was started again, pushed carefully into the far right-hand edge of his window. If the walls were more than a foot thick, he was fucked. Or he could call up a jackhammer. Now, that would cause some serious pain.

The chattering and screeching deafened him, and by the time the first cut was made, his arms had lost all feeling. Sweat covered his face. Self-destructively, he cut the upper edge next, mostly afraid to leave the worst till last. The saw had to be supported constantly and exactly or the blade would bind. He stood, now, straddling the sink, the saw braced against his good leg, the bad one taking far more weight than it could tolerate.

The third cut, up the left edge, wasn't plumb. His arms were rubber by then. In the back of his mind, he was aware that no wrath of God had fallen. Perhaps Harry Roswell was simply the mouse in the maze, diligently seeking the way out, only to find something far worse than cheese at the end. Or maybe the old man was too busy to notice. Hurry, Harry!

Lower lip caught firmly in his teeth, he ran the blade along the top edge of the vanity. Last cut. Shit, even if this worked, he wouldn't have the strength left to go anywhere. The sound died away, and it felt like someone had stuffed cotton in his ears. The masonry saw was laid carefully on the floor.

"Six-foot pry bar, one-inch steel, please," Harry muttered, unable to hear himself.

The steel bar arrived immediately, but it took a while before he could lift it. Heavy, sturdy, the thing had a wedge on one end and a rounded tamper on the other. He used it as a battering ram first, cracking the tamper all along the inside of the seam, then reversed the bar and slipped the wedge into the bottom right-hand cut. There was nothing to use as a fulcrum except the edge of the cut itself. It took his full weight and a couple of good bounces before something gave, then chunks of stone and grit exploded outward. The bar fell, taking Harry with it.

Shit. Was anything worth this? Only now there was a dark hole in the corner. His hand passed into emptiness on the other side. Encouraged, he doubled his effort, prying and beating sections of stone out of the window. The neighbor's solemn face was finally obliterated, and the last chunk of granite fell with a thud into the darkness beyond.

Harry dragged himself onto the vanity once more, and peered out his window. Only out was merely another in. He'd cut his way into another sealed chamber like his own. Defeat left him near to exhaustion and tears. Except in the faint light from his own wall-mounted candles, he could see a shrouded form on a cot against the far curve of the wall in the otherwise empty cell. Some other poor unfortunate like himself, waiting for doom, and—what?— dying finally of boredom? Old age, forgotten by his jailer?

Harry crawled through his window, then dragged his bad leg across the cell. A fine white silt covered the black plastic shroud, possibly from the masonry saw, but not likely. Even in a sealed chamber, time would eventually leave dust. He tugged the top back, more curious than afraid. No desiccated corpse here. The man that he'd drawn in his window lay still on the blankets, hands folded peacefully on his chest—short-cropped brown hair, narrow handsome face, dressed in worn jeans, a blue work shirt, and high-top tennies. Who? But memory nudged Harry abruptly. The features were coarser, heavier, but this was Jamie's father. It had to be—the similarities were too strong to ignore.

The hairs on Harry's arm bristled with static electricity when he reached out to press two fingers to the carotid artery in his neck. No pulse and the skin felt cool, but not cold. A hand held just above the nose could detect no respiration, but the arm, when lifted, moved loosely. Harry rolled the body on its side and pulled the shirttail out. No lividity either. The man was settled back in the blankets. Some sort of stasis field, Harry decided. Perhaps God kept trophies. This wouldn't be nearly so messy as taxidermy.

And then again, maybe his neighbor only slept like the dead. Too bad there were no princesses to kiss and wake the sleeper. But there was Harry, who might be able to provide something more substantial. He considered the problem thoughtfully, scratching the bristles on his unshaven chin. Magic, or its technological equivalent, seemed potent in these worlds. Unlike Trey and Lila Anne, Harry hadn't dealt with it much, hadn't even tried. But why couldn't he harness the powers, too? The Physician should be able to heal on more than one level. There had to be more to it than herbal teas and aspirins.

He laughed at himself for trying to rationalize something that couldn't possibly work. To hell with that, just get on with it, Harry. The sleeper's faded blue shirt was unbuttoned, spread open to expose the chest. What was it Lila Anne mumbled every time she did a calling?

"To—" Voice hoarse, he cleared it and tried again. "To me . . ." This was incredibly stupid. "To me, the powers of this place . . ." Immediately, the air stirred, prickling the hair all over his body. What next? "Uh . . . aid me in . . . Christ! Just help me jump-start this guy's heart. Okay?"

He slapped his palms together and began rubbing them rapidly in a circular motion as though they were the paddles of a defibrillator, then glanced at all the paramedics that weren't there."

"Clear!"

His hands, faintly green tinged now, were placed firmly

on the bare chest, and the jolt that slammed down through his arms caused the body on the cot to convulse violently and knocked Harry flat on his ass. Shit! He sat a moment on the cold stones, swallowing the pain, and straightened the bad leg, then somehow found his feet again. The man on the bed had his eyes open now, staring sightlessly at the ceiling.

"Hello," Harry said gently. "Anybody home?"

The not-quite-vacant eyes turned his way, and the lips formed a tiny smile. "Hello."

The Physician put out a hand. "Name's Harry Roswell."

Still the faint empty smile, but the fellow raised a hand to clasp Harry's. "Will Weston."

"Shit! I knew it!" Now Harry grinned. "You're Jamie's father."

The fellow's slightly perplexed expression disappeared abruptly, replaced by something close to fear.

"When am I?" Will Weston asked.

"Don't you mean where?"

"I know where, but when? Jamie . . . How old is Jamie?"

"Twenty-five the last I heard. But you want to tell me what's going on? How you got here?"

Jamie's father had other things on his mind, though. He swung his legs over the edge of the cot and sat up. "Who are you?"

"I told you—"

"No, damn it. Which one?"

"The Physician."

Weston groaned. "That's right. Only you're supposed to be dead."

"Yeah," Harry snapped. "That's what everybody keeps telling me."

"But then, I'm supposed to be dead, too." A low chuckle accompanied that statement. "We've got to get out of here."

"Yeah, right. But let's first have a little exchange of info. It's your turn to answer. Seems to me, you've been pulling the strings for this whole quest business from the get-go. How?"

"There's no time. You were lost on Kynor, right?"

Harry balked. "There's plenty of time, 'cause we're not going anywhere, bud. And it's not your turn to ask questions."

"Kynor?"

"Hell! All right. Yes, that's where I got grabbed."

"How long have you been locked up?"

"I don't know. . . . It's pretty damn hard to tell—the candles don't even burn down. Maybe a day, or a little more."

"Then Jamie'll be here soon, if she isn't already. We've got to help her."

"Look, I just expended considerable energy, and this is as far as I got. There's no quick way out of here."

Will Weston smiled again. "Do you have your bag, Physician?"

"It helped me get through the wall of my cell."

"Then the bag is there?" When Harry nodded, Weston started for the window. "Let's go."

Shit! Harry hobbled forward. At this point, he wanted nothing more than to lie down on the cot and sleep for the next thousand years. Except the old man was likely depending on that. Will Weston took pity and helped him through the window first.

"I think we're actually going to pull this off," the man murmured as he worked himself over the rubble and into Harry's cell. He eyed the masonry saw, then Harry with appreciation. "Not bad. You're my kinda guy, Harry."

"Yeah, well—"

"Save it for later, friend." Weston grabbed the medical pouch, pulled the electrical cord free, and pushed a foot into the bag.

"Hey!"

"Harry, trust me. This is the only way." His leg was in the pouch up to the knee, and now he worked the other foot in beside it. "Tight fit. Follow close, Physician. Soon as I'm in, you start. I'll help, so don't get spooked when you feel a hand on your ankle. Just remember . . ." The bag had swallowed the man to the waist already, "bring the strap in with you, otherwise we'll lose the medical pouch."

Harry, in numb amazement, watched him work an arm in and shrug the leather up higher. "We'll get lost in there."

"Not a chance. Trust me, Physician. Come on. Your turn." That last was muffled. The top of Jamie's father's head disappeared, and the pouch flopped over on the floor.

"Shit!" Harry caught the strap and shoved a curly-toed buskin into the bag.

IV

Jamie cut the opening right there in the dusty street before the Hypano station. She cut it high enough to take a man on horseback. The purple beam seemed stronger, the cuts actually visible to her even in the hazy sunlight. All that was required of her was intent.

Trey had his bow strung and slung over one shoulder, the quiver over the other. With a thin smile, he glanced back at them, then drew the sword and started the mare forward. Jamie drew her knife. Lila Anne walked behind the horse, her staff held in both hands.

No time for thought now, no time for worry or guilt. Pressure on her ears, a dragging at the limbs. The sunlight winked out behind her, and Jamie stepped into deep sand, floundering momentarily. Overhead, a solid gray cloud cover stretched from horizon to horizon. To the left, dark stone cliffs formed a jagged barrier. To the right, a winter-restless ocean the same color as the sky surged onto the black sands of a small crescent-shaped beach. Jumbles of massive porous black stones bounded the beach at either end. All this was noted in an instant. Trey and Lila Anne stood alone, unharmed.

"Keep awake, you two!" the young Indian snarled. "Cut us a door quick, Jamie. Lila Anne, light that damn staff." He had already slipped the sword back into the scabbard and sat with the bow in his hands, an arrow nocked and drawn.

Fingers trembling, Jamie fumbled to get the guide stone

turned in her hand and dropped the knife into the sand. Damn! She bent to retrieve it, felt something whistle by just over her head. What? But she knew. The plop in the water confirmed it. Trey swung the bow and loosed, returning the fire with one of his white shafts. The fletching sang the same high bird song the enemy arrow had.

"Hurry!" he screamed at Jamie.

Lila Anne's staff glowed green now, and she began a warding spell, leaving a pale glowing residue on the sand.

"Lila Anne, get behind me!" Trey faced directly away from the waves, eyes searching for a target in the natural rocky wall that hemmed them.

"No, I can do this!" The girl continued her drawing.

Another arrow hissed into the waves, and another struck the sand at the mare's feet. Trey let fly, three lightning shots. Someone or something screamed. Jamie, frozen, saw dark figures pouring along the beach from the far end.

"Behind you, Jamie!" Lila Anne's voice, ragged with fear.

Jamie turned and watched another group rush toward them from the other direction. Surrounded! She fumbled again, clumsy with panic, and this time lost the guide stone in the sand. She had never reacted to a tense situation this way before. Something else was happening here, some inner block that made it near impossible for her to function normally.

Trey wailed suddenly in helpless rage, and Jamie looked up. Lila Anne took two steps toward her, eyes wide, and collapsed, a dark arrow shaft deep in her side. The staff fell beside her, and its fire leeched into the sand. Trey, screaming, sent rapid fire, first on the right, then the left. Both groups of attackers lost their forward men, and the others, stumbling over them, slowed, more cautious now. Soldiers, Jamie thought, flesh and blood and mortal, and bristling with weapons.

She'd recovered the stone, but to cut an opening was beyond her. She slipped to her knees beside the fallen Sorceress, horrified. The mare arrived, dancing in agitation, sand churning around her hooves. Trey dropped down next to Jamie.

"Get us the fuck out of here!" he hissed, and gathered Lila Anne up in his arms, careful of the arrow. The girl's head lolled back, lifelessly. "Now! Damn you, before they're on us."

There were only moments until the soldiers would arrive. A lone sniper continued to launch arrows from behind them without much precision. Jamie faced the waves, white foam rolling endlessly over the shingle, and released the purple beam in the air. Beside her, the mare squealed and lashed out with a hind foot. A long bloody groove appeared across one buckskin hip.

Intent! They could go nowhere unless Jamie turned her attention to the task. Despite the shouting on either side, she closed her eyes and drew a deep breath. The purple light played across the inside of her eyelids. She made the cuts, ragged ones because of the shaking, then turned on Trey.

"Go!" she said with urgency and pocketed the stone.

The young Indian took a step toward the opening, grunted suddenly, and went to one knee, then struggled back upright with Lila Anne still in his arms. All the color had drained from his face.

"Get the staff," he ordered breathlessly, and pushed past Jamie.

She saw the arrow then, buried beneath his right shoulder blade, just as he disappeared through the opening. The Oregon dun charged after him, and Jamie made a quick dive for the staff, snatching it up. A great curved blade descended in her peripheral vision on the left. She flung the staff up to block the stroke and drove a boot toe into the heavyset man's unprotected crotch. He doubled over, and she fetched him a blow to the side of the head with the Sorceress's staff.

Friendly fire caught the next hapless soldier as he closed on her, the arrow driving downward through the hollow of his throat. But the others had arrived. Jamie spun, clumsy in the sand, and fled through the fading exit.

V

The smothering sensation nearly panicked him, then a hand closed on his left ankle and pulled. Something went *pop!* and Harry, feeling very much like a cork from a bottle, shot suddenly downward. His stomach stayed somewhere near his throat during the whole wild ride—which reminded him of the giant water slides they'd had in Southern California back when there was water.

Will Weston broke Harry's fall at the bottom. The air left their lungs noisily.

"Get off!" Jamie's father grunted finally.

In considerable pain, the Physician rolled to the side and clanged against a metal wall. Odd lumps poked him here and there. There was darkness above, with pinpoints of dim light that were not stars. Harry found the upper rim of the wall and pulled himself up. Will Weston was already climbing out of the large bin—one in a long row of them.

"Where are we?" Harry muttered, glancing around. Great metal shelves rose into the dark on either side.

"This is the small items central warehouse," Weston answered.

"Small items?"

"The stuff you pull from that bag of tricks of yours. You've got the thing, right?"

Harry held up the medical pouch. It was inside out. "It all comes from here?"

"Where did you think it came from?"

"Hell, I don't know ... but not from a warehouse. I guess I thought it was magic."

"It is, Physician. By whatever name you want to call it, magic is the stuff that binds the universes together." Will Weston glanced around as he spoke. "On Earth, we just like to explain everything away, define it and redefine it. A combustion engine works on the principle of exploding gases that drive the pistons, right? Bullshit. It's magic, and we don't have the slightest idea of how it all really works." The man pointed down the wide corridor to their right. "We've gotta go this way."

Harry followed him, slowed by the bad leg. A horn

blared behind them, and they hustled to the side to let a small three-wheeled cart towing a chain of bins down the row go past. There was no one driving. Will Weston talked as he walked.

"I worked here below the Citadel for about four years. Put in their first computer system. Hell of a job, but what a challenge. We're talking computers set up in series. Ended up with a system the size of Rhode Island. Imagine that if you can."

Harry couldn't. He'd noticed people now—mostly little God-sized guys stocking the shelves, riding little cherry picker cranes.

"All this stuff just goes out free?" he asked finally.

"Oh, no. All guild members pay an initial user's fee for their tools of the trade. A carpenter pays a good deal less than, say, a physician. Then there's a monthly itemized bill, but it's reasonable. The old man's not greedy."

"Shit," Harry said. "My bill's gonna be a doozy."

"No, the old man foots the quests. Which is only fair, considering that you end up paying with your lives. The bastard." Weston turned a corner and headed left along another aisle. "You're a little slow on that leg. Let's catch a ride."

He stopped beside a train of bins and spoke with the fellow in the nearby crane, not in English. Harry listened, more than a little awed by Will Weston.

"Hop in," the man said a moment later and disconnected the three-wheeled car. Harry climbed onto the passenger seat and Will settled beside him. They putt-putted off down the aisle.

"Want to tell me now? About how you set this quest thing up?"

Weston laughed. "That's a long story, but I'll give you the abbreviated version. Hold on." He swung the car in a tight right turn. "All my brilliant scientific associates on Earth thought I'd gone nuts when I tried to tell them what I'd found—a hole in the atmosphere about two miles above eastern Oregon that was siphoning off the moisture. So I rented a Cessna and checked it out myself."

"You're a pilot, too?"

"I'm a meteorologist, Harry. Things above the earth concern me." The man threw him a quick boyish grin. "So I checked it out. And got sucked in. Now *that* was a helluva ride. The Cessna didn't survive the landing at the Citadel. I did. Barely."

"You're lucky you didn't end up floating around in an extremely small crystal cube."

"He showed you that? Not for free, I'll bet."

"Not for free," Harry agreed.

"Well, anyway, the old man was pretty kind considering—hell of a chess player. I made myself useful, and ended up doing the computer system. That's when I realized there just might be a way to beat God at his own game. He'd been pulling this quest business for millennia, but had it set up so he couldn't really lose. Of course, I promised him a quest to end all quests, one with some real risks involved. The little bastard went for it." Jamie's father sent the cart into another tight turn. "Information, Harry—the most priceless thing in the universes. Now, I had the computers to tell me all I needed to know. I hand-picked the Terran Quest."

"Bullshit!"

"And you thought it was random?" Weston shook his head. "All in the computers—personality files, genetics. These folks are gamblers, but I'm not. I want that deck stacked. The choices for Physician were narrow. At least, the drought was going to narrow it down quick. I had to pick probable survivors. Your friend, Jeffery Cummings, he was on the list, technically a far better surgeon that you would've ever been if your mother hadn't died. But Cummings lacked imagination, Harry, and courage—some things you've got plenty of."

Harry stared at him uncomprehending.

"Who ended up as Guardian?"

"Trey Sweetwater."

"The Indian kid from Oregon? Good choice. I knew Jamie would pull it all together. And the Sorceress?"

"Lila Anne . . . I don't know her last name."

Will shook his head. "I don't recognize her from my list, but wild cards were taken into account. The Sorceress and the Guardian were always expendable. Jamie's programming left as little to chance as possible."

"Brainwashed? You brainwashed her?"

"Nasty word, Harry. And highly illegal. More like conditioned. Hedging the bet. Jamie had to keep up the masquerade as a boy. You had to know the truth, of course, but if anyone else had known, if the word had somehow slipped out, it would have meant failure. On these quests, the Sage is really nothing more than a psychologist, and the old man doesn't pay him much attention. Jamie, as a boy, can get into the Citadel and fulfill the old man's prophecy before he ever figures out what happened. Maybe. For all the work I've put into it, there's still a fifty-six percent chance of failure."

"What do you mean, *I* had to know the truth?" Harry asked quietly.

"For the baby, Physician. Jamie has to be pregnant in order to destroy the old man." Weston slowed the cart and stared at Harry. "You did . . . ? I mean, Jamie would have known when the time was right."

"Yeah," Harry snapped. "Your plan worked that much." He swallowed his anger. A baby. "You said there's a fifty-six percent chance of failure still. Is there anything we can do to save them?"

"The quest, maybe. The Guardian and the Sorceress, no. Against saving Earth, their lives mean nothing. That goes for you and Jamie, too."

Cold son of a bitch, Harry thought, and noticed how Will hadn't included himself on the list of expendables. "You know, Weston, I'm not so sure I like you." He eased his leg into a better position.

Jamie's father only laughed again. "That's fine, Physician. Tell you what. If you and I survived this whole mess, we can step outside and settle the account. But I warn you . . . I'll kick your ass clear to Nebraska."

Somehow, Harry didn't doubt it.

"Will Weston!"

The words boomed hollowly, and Harry looked ahead. Banks of monitors stretched along a wall in the distance with dozens—no hundreds—of short, squashy people in chairs before them. A man, at least eight feet tall and bone skinny, strode toward them through the shadows.

Weston halted the car and jumped out. "Gregory!" They met there between the racks, and Gregory grabbed Will Weston up like a child, hugging him.

"Shit, boy!" The giant dropped his burden. "I haven't seen you in a good thousand years. I heard you pissed the old man off."

"Sure did. Gonna piss him off some more, pretty soon, if I'm lucky. Where's Roger?"

Gregory's dark eyes saddened and he shook his head. "Will, Roger died a long time ago. We doubled his life span, but . . . you earth-type humans are too short-lived to be worth anything."

"Yeah, well," Weston shrugged, "we also evolve quicker too, which sort of evens things out. Otherwise you bozos wouldn't have computers. Which reminds me, I need some time on the mainframe."

"Sure."

"How's the system holding up?"

"We're making do, but the quality isn't near as good as Earth's." The giant took note of Harry, sitting in the car, listening. "Hail, Physician!" His long stride brought him close. The smile on his narrow, sallow face seemed genuine. "Glad to see you're still alive. You helped finance my next vacation."

"Yeah?"

"That bit on Analonaria at the party. Sim Chestel doesn't let go of houseguests readily. Everyone figured the quest would be hung up for at least a year. I put my money on a month. But you did it in one day! You're one gutsy little fella." A huge hand smacked Harry on the shoulder.

"I had help," Harry said, wincing.

Will had wandered to the monitors and commandeered a chair and a keyboard. Harry climbed out of the car and limped after Gregory, wondering just what in the hell was going on. Someone kindly moved so the Physician could sit. The symbols flashing across the monitor screen in front of him meant nothing.

"At least it's almost over," Gregory said gently, kindly, from beside him. "No more worries, no more pain."

"What do you mean?" Harry demanded. A cold dread filled him.

"You don't know?"

"Tell me. Please."

"Your Sage got them farther than any quest before, right to the foot of the Citadel stairs. You should be very proud." Gregory reached down to touch the keys. The glowing symbols slowed. "But the Sorceress is dead and the Guardian dying, and the Sage can't possibly go against the old man alone."

Harry, his throat suddenly constricted, looked up into the giant's compassionate face. "I have to be with them."

"Impossible."

"Gregory!" Weston abandoned his monitor. "We need a ride inside the Citadel, quick."

"Will, it's not permitted. You're not even a member of the quest. Outside interference is strictly forbidden."

"For an old friend?"

"The old man'll have my ass, Will. I like my job. I like my life."

Will Weston grabbed Harry's arm and jerked him to his feet. "Come on. There's got to be more than one way to get to the Citadel."

Chapter Fourteen

THEY HAD COME from one gray world into another. Bleak, colorless granite spires rose on all sides, with sheer rock walls to hem them in. Heartsick, Jamie dropped the staff and squatted beside Trey. He sat with his left shoulder propped against a high slab of stone near the foot of a great winding staircase. Blood, nearly as black as the leather jerkin, flowed sluggishly from around the arrow in his back. Lila Anne, beyond help, lay pale and still across his lap. Jamie's unshed tears threatened to strangle her.

"Take the sword," Trey whispered with blood-rimmed lips.

"It won't do any good," Jamie told him. "I don't have any magic."

"Doesn't matter." The young Indian's voice grew faint. "The blade's still sharp. Go . . ."

The Oregon dun, her hooves clattering on the solid rock floor of the box canyon, raced to a far wall, spun, and charged back.

"No!" Jamie cried and flung out her hands for fear the mare would trample them by accident. "No!"

The animal slid to a halt only inches away. Her long neck extended, nostrils fluttering, and she reached out to lip Trey's hair.

"Trey," Jamie said softly. "Trey . . ."

No answer. The young man's eyes were fixed unseeing on Lila Anne's face, and his labored breathing had ceased. Jamie gave in to the tears at last. But not for long.

She bent close to kiss the Sorceress's white cheek, and the Guardian's. "I love you," she murmured, then unbuckled the belt and scabbard from around Trey's waist and pulled them gently free. His blood coated her hands. Jamie stood, strapping on the sword. The weight of it brought cold comfort, but one touch of the hilt brought a surge of violent emotions. And strength. Trey had somehow gifted her with his magic as well.

She took up the staff and experienced a similar, though gentler, wave of energy. They were with her, now and always—her lost companions. Their magical aspects and memories were hers now, mixed with the sorrow. In sudden outrage, Jamie grasped the staff with both hands and shook it over her head, screaming defiance at the unseen Citadel. It was lost beyond the top of the steps, where they vanished into the clouds.

"I am the Guardian, now, you bastard!" she bellowed. *"And* the Sorceress! And I'm going to beat you, old man!"

Her words thundered through the canyon, slammed back from the stone walls, over and over. She started for the bottommost step, and found the mare, ears flat, teeth bared, blocking her way.

"Get out of here!" Jamie swung the staff and struck the horse on one hip. Green sparks exploded from the tip. The Oregon dun flinched under the blow but refused to move. "Get!" She struck again, harder. The animal squealed in pain, but stood firm. Jamie swung again, this time aiming for the head—and caught herself. A bitter, certain knowledge came.

"I'm sorry! I'm so sorry." Jamie reached out a trembling hand to stroke the mare's sweat-soaked neck.

She understood finally. All along there'd been an unrecognized fifth member of this quest. Her hand still on the dun's neck, Jamie studied the staircase. The narrow steps rose steeply, twisting and turning as they went. No guardrail. To climb them on foot would be terrifying, but to take them on horseback—

No. The remaining two members of the quest must finish it together. The staff was too clumsy to ride with, but Jamie resisted storing it in the saddlebags. A fleeting clear thought came to her, the vision of a printed page—another gift from Lila Anne. She caught the pole in the center and began to turn it end over end, slowly at first, gaining momentum until it whirled like a baton. Green fire showered in the air, and before her the spinning wheel began to shrink until, at last, she held only a wand, its runes and designs burned into the wood with perfect tiny detail.

Jamie tucked it into the sleeve of her ragged shirt, then stuck her left boot toe into an iron stirrup. The mare turned to watch her with a critical eye. The gentle push off with the other foot came almost naturally, and she swung into the saddle, Trey's remembered confidence to guide her. Every move seemed familiar, right. She gathered the reins, let her heels drop, and found her point of balance over the animal's shoulders. So easy.

"I'm not afraid," Jamie said in wonder, but that was short-lived.

At a gentle nudge of the young woman's heels, the mare

launched herself up the staircase. Jamie leaned forward, hands snugged to the horse's neck, her chin in the short black mane. Every great leap took them higher, and though the mare scrabbled for purchase on the stone, she never broke stride, never faltered, not even on the turns. The world fell away with breathtaking speed, and it seemed as though they were flying—free of the earth. Jamie urged the dun on, her anger and sorrow driving them both.

II

"Harry! Let's go!" Will Weston released the Physician's arm and strode angrily away, down a wide shadowy aisle with full shelves towering over him.

The cavernous warehouse echoed the words, but Harry stood unmoving. He looked up at Gregory. The slender giant's shoulders were slumped, his long face filled with distress.

"Please, Gregory. You've got to help us."

"Physician, it's just not permitted."

"I'm a part of the quest, dammit!" Harry grabbed the man's fleshless arm. "I have a right to be with them—to die with them."

Gregory's expression softened. "That's true enough."

"Harry!" Will shouted again.

But Harry shouted back, "Weston, he's going to send us to the Citadel!"

"Just you, Physician," Gregory said hastily.

"Both," Harry commanded. He clutched the medical pouch tightly. Jamie's father returned at a trot, teeth flashing in the dim light.

The giant produced a familiar glass stone. Only this one had a strong purple beam.

"To the Citadel," Will said again.

Gregory shook his head. "To the foot of the stairs. Take it or leave it. This is going to show up on my personal bill, as it is."

"Wait." Harry drew a deep breath. "Has any quest ever gotten so close to the Citadel?"

"No. Never," the giant said.

"Gregory, maybe you ought to lay another wager—everything you can get your hands on—against the old man."

"You don't really think you've got a chance?" Gregory laughed.

Harry managed a smile. "We've got more than a chance. We've got Jamie."

"All right, Physician!" Will cried and slapped Harry's shoulder. "Let's go."

The giant cut a doorway directly around them, and thick darkness enfolded Harry's body. He put a foot down on solid stone, fighting the disorientation. Unperturbed, Will Weston continued to speak.

"The stairs will take us some time, but it can't be helped. If we're lucky, Jamie won't have started up them yet."

Gray stone walls came into focus, sharp angles and shadows in every direction. This was the Citadel's world all right.

"Damn! She's already gone," Will said from somewhere behind him. "Harry, the stairs . . . With your bad leg, it's going to take us forever to climb them."

But Harry had seen the dark shapes against a nearby slab of stone. No . . . He stumbled toward them, swallowing back sick fear, then went to his knees on the hard ground, despite the agony that shot through the leg.

"We don't have time for anything else," Jamie's father snapped urgently.

They had died in each other's arms. Harry closed Trey's empty eyes. Tears hot on his cheeks, he dug frantically in the medical bag and found a scalpel. The material of Lila Anne's skirt was cut away around the arrow, the wooden shaft cut off close to the wound.

Will Weston squatted beside him. "Are you crazy? You can't help them. It's Jamie who needs us."

Silent, Harry made a small incision to either side of the arrow. There was little blood. The child had died quickly, the arrow deep in a kidney.

"You *are* crazy," Weston grunted as the Physician

pulled a pair of hemostats from the bag and probed for the arrowhead. "Death. The ultimate anesthesia. This won't hurt a bit, right?" His fingers dug into Harry's arm. "We don't have time for an autopsy."

Harry, without thought, let go of the instrument and drove a fist into Will Weston's mouth. The solid connection produced a loud crack of sound and sent pain shooting through Harry's hand all the way to his elbow. Weston's head snapped sideways. He sat down heavily, legs sprawled out before him.

"Christ, Harry," Jamie's father mumbled and dabbed a fingertip at the bright red blood on his lips.

The Physician ignored him, and finished removing the arrow from Lila Anne's side. Goldenseal was dusted into the child's wound, then, with gut suture and needle, he repaired as much of the vessel and tissue damage as he could. The knuckles on his right hand were already beginning to swell. There might even be broken bones, but it didn't matter. He began on Trey next. Here the arrow had pierced the lung and congealing blood soaked the young Indian's clothing. Water dripped continually from Harry's chin while he worked—not sweat, he realized, but tears.

At some point he glanced around and discovered Will Weston gone. Far up the staircase a tiny dark spot moved, visible against the lighter stone. Harry would follow soon, but not just yet. Trembling, he settled Trey's body back against the stone, nestled Lila Anne's head in the young man's lap again, aware of the cooling lifeless flesh.

A strange voice began to chant, "Lazarus rose from the dead, Lazarus rose from the dead." *His* voice. But in this crazy dream anything was possible. Anything. He had to believe that. "To me, the powers of this place." The internal stirring came, the hairs prickling all over his body. He held his hands out before him. "Help me. Please. Help me heal them." A faint green nimbus outlined his fingers. "So mote it be!" He clapped his hands together, rubbing them in a circular motion and envisioned Lila Anne, her lips turned up in that same shy sweet smile that he'd seen a thousand times. Now the hands were slipped under her blouse and pressed to the girl's small chest.

No jolt of energy slammed through him this time. Instead the power seemed to bleed away, leaving him drained and sick. He tried again, this time on Trey, and got the same results. The only thing he'd healed was his own broken hand, the pain and purple swelling gone from the knuckles. The infected leg, though, was only slightly improved, slightly less painful.

Defeat left him bitter and determined. He stood over the bodies. Jamie had gone to face the old man and so would he. Harry slipped the strap of the medical pouch over his shoulder and mounted the first step, leaving irrevocable death behind.

III

Thick clouds closed around them for a short time, then they broke through into open sky. The mare's breathing grew labored, but she continued those long forward leaps. Jamie urged her on with fierce whispers and reveled in the tremendous animal energy transmitting through the reins to her hands and heart.

Close now, the Citadel rose, sunlight flaring on stone parapet and tower, turning them to gold—a mountainous keep cut from living rock. The Oregon dun took one last lunge and flung herself onto a broad empty terrace. In slow motion, she stagged forward, then her legs gave way, and she fell to her knees. Shocked, Jamie stepped from the saddle.

The mare toppled and lay groaning, her neck white with lather, her nostrils wide and pink-tinged, fighting for air. "No!" Jamie cried. "Get up! Damn you, get up!" She dragged at the reins, filled with a horrible guilt. Trey would never have pushed the horse so hard, demanded so much. "Up!" she shouted, desperate. Soon the animal's muscles would stiffen, and she would die in agony, another casualty of the quest, leaving the Sage all alone.

Jamie pulled the wand from her sleeve and called on the Sorceress's powers. At the first touch of the little stick, brilliant green sparks exploded, and the mare jerked. Jamie prodded her again and again, until the animal finally flat-

tened her ears to her skull and bared ugly yellow teeth.
Squealing in outrage, she managed to get front hooves out
before her, then heaved herself upright and stumbled after
Jamie, intent on doing her damage.

"That's better," the Sage laughed, relieved, and dodged
the open jaws easily.

She led the mare in circles on the wide terrace to cool
her and wondered about the silence. Where was the old
man? What was he doing? Watching, waiting, perhaps. Or
even out about other business. The mare's legs grew
steadier, but she'd slowed. Jamie poked her again from behind and had to avoid a back hoof that lashed suddenly
out.

"Bitch," she said lovingly, then pain and memory washed
through her, and the losses seemed overwhelming.

IV

Trey Sweetwater had a very strange dream. He dreamed
that he was dead. He dreamed that he floated above a gray
stone floor and saw Harry crouched over the Guardian's
body. Only Harry was also dead, and Trey wasn't the
Guardian anymore. That memory came clearly. He'd
passed the sword and the power to Jamie and then let go
of all the pain and heartache at last. Lila Anne was gone,
and he had no desire to live without her. So this couldn't
be a dream, after all, but the emptiness of death.

"Trey?" The gentle child's voice came as a whisper in
that vast emptiness. "Trey, please come back. Don't leave
me here alone."

He considered those words and the sobs that came after
them. A long silence followed while he searched for some
means to answer, and finally sucked in a ragged lungful of
air. The pain in his chest was suddenly there again, but not
nearly so bad as before. Trey opened his eyes.

Lila Anne peered closely at him, her pale freckled face
stained with tears.

"Oh, Trey," she murmured and wrapped small arms
around his neck. Somehow he found the strength to use his
own arms to hold her tight.

"You're alive," he said in wonder.

Under his chin, the little girl's head bobbed. *"We're alive. Harry did it. He was here, but he left. I think he went to the Citadel to help Jamie."*

"We'd better go, too."

Lila Anne pulled away to sit before him. "My staff's gone, Trey. And your sword. I can't feel the magic anymore."

Neither could he—it was an odd empty feeling. "Jamie's got them. But she still may need us."

That brought a smile to the girl's thin lips, then she leaned forward quickly and pressed her mouth to Trey's, a timid, yet lingering kiss that left the young Indian breathless.

"Lila Anne . . ."

"We better hurry."

V

This time, the Oregon dun refused to follow, and Jamie paused at the wide, dark opening in the Citadel's wall. The mare had returned to the top of the staircase to pace restlessly along the terrace railing, ears pricked, eyes gazing into the clouds below. She tossed her head and neighed—a great ear-shattering whinny.

"Hey! I'm going this way, pal," Jamie called to her one last time, in hopes the horse would change her mind.

But the mare ignored her, and Jamie passed alone into the dim corridor that circled downward into the belly of the castle. There were no doorways in this hall, no exits, only the one possible route and, despite no visible source, the level of light remained the same—faint, eerie.

At some point, a distant metallic clattering came to her. It grew louder the deeper into the Citadel she walked. She drew the sword and donned the Guardian's aspect, alert, aggressive. Just around the next curve warm yellow candlelight flowed from open double doors and into the corridor. The clattering continued. Jamie stood to the side and peered into an enormous round chamber. Candles by the hundreds lined the stone walls in rusty brackets. There were rough-hewn chairs and tables, cabinets and cupboards, all of them child-sized. A little man in a tarnished breastplate pranced among the furniture with what looked like a pot turned upside down on his head. A short sword in one hand, he jousted with a hat rack that was also decked out in pots and pans. These fell from the hooks and crashed to the floor with every blow. Chortling, the fellow crawled onto a bench and replaced them, only to begin another attack.

Jamie frowned. Could this be the old man? The thief of rain?

"Hello," she yelled over the racket.

The little fellow jumped, the hat rack fell, and the din of its collision with the ground faded slowly from the room. He snatched the pot from his head, obviously embarrassed.

"Who are you?" he demanded.

"I'm what's left of the Terran Quest. Are you the old man?"

The little guy looked at the sword in Jamie's hand, and his pale eyes narrowed. "You can't be the Guardian. The Guardian is dead."

"Yes," Jamie agreed sadly. "But I'll kill you with his weapon, anyway."

"Ha! I remember you now—you're only the Sage, and the Sage has no powers. He's a thinker, not a fighter."

"Then I think I'll kill you, old man. Where's our rain?"

"Oh, it's here." Bravely he waddled closer, a bearded dwarf with large, hairy feet. The short sword was set aside, and the breastplate rattled as he unbuckled it. "Before we do battle though, we'll have some tea."

"No thanks. I'm in kind of a hurry."

"Come now. I have sodas, or beer, if you like. It isn't polite to decline an invitation from God."

Jamie's jaw tightened. "You may have fooled Lila Anne, and the rest of the yokels, with that bullshit, but you're not God. I think you're just a little guy with a big ego and a fairly good idea of how the universe works."

"You are truly the Sage," the old man said, a touch of awe in his dry smile. "But whatever I may be, you'd best humor me, because I *do* have your rain." He turned away.

"Now, would you like some Earl Grey, or perhaps something stronger? I even have an excellent Analonarian brandy."

His pleasant, friendly manner offended Jamie. "You killed my friends, you bastard. I won't drink with you."

"I didn't kill them." The little man's voice betrayed hurt and sorrow. "It was the wretched quest. You should never have attempted it. I warned her—that poor little girl. I told her she would die, that you'd all die." There were actual tears in his eyes, and they evoked a great sadness in Jamie. "So pretty, so young. All of them lost, and you left alone without hope. How can you bear it?"

She couldn't. Grief nearly doubled her over. The old man rushed to her aid, clucking sympathetically. His hand closed on her arm—the one that held the Guardian's sword. Then the grip turned to steel. She gasped. His fingers dug deep into muscle and found nerve. The weapon fell from her numb hand, and with incredible strength, he flung her over the top of a table and into the wall. She struck on the point of her left shoulder and heard it pop from the socket. Gravity jerked her immediately to the floor to lie stunned, waiting for the air to return to her lungs.

"Such a disappointment," the old man snapped from somewhere beyond her field of vision. "Gullible fools, all of you. The Terran Quest came farther than any, and I had such hopes of an interesting game. . . . But it was only bumbling dumb luck that got you here. If you'd shown some proper manners, we could have avoided all this unpleasantness. A cup of tea, a little conversation—was that so much to ask? I would have let you die with your Physician, but I'm too angry, now. What are you doing?"

Jamie had turned painfully and gotten her knees under her. What was he saying about Harry? The old man came around the fallen table, Trey's sword in his hands. It took only the barest push from his bare foot to upset her again.

"I'm curious," he said almost gently, "as to why you bothered to come here. Only the female of your species can create and carry life, and therefore take mine. I thought that particular rule had a nice ironic touch to it, and only fair, considering the quests would be pitted against the Supreme Being." The old man shook his head. "So you see, without the Sorceress there was never any chance of your succeeding. This seems to be a peculiar Terran trait, to strive even in a hopeless situation. Stubborn, destructive, and witless—more Terran traits. We'll be well rid of your lot." He leaned close. "If I'm not God, how is it I can destroy whole worlds? Except for the one self-endowed weakness, I'm immortal."

"No," Jamie gasped. "You're not."

The old man placed the sword point against her injured shoulder. "You're not in nearly enough pain." He shoved the blade into the flesh and into the separated joint.

She didn't scream, refusing him that much satisfaction, but a red-gray mist flowed over her eyes. Hearing and sight dimmed. The little fellow chortled happily as he pulled back.

"This is wonderful, so personal. I really must do it more often." He brandished the weapon over his head, managed a short-legged strut across the chamber.

The angry, demanding voice in Jamie's head was her own. *Use the staff, use it now.* She fumbled in her sleeve and found the wand, slick with blood, then got her legs under her once more. With the wall for support, she pushed herself into an upright position.

"What?" cried the old man and laughed. "Up so soon? Perhaps more surgery is in order." But his amusement died when he saw the wand. "You can't use that any more than you could use the sword, you don't have the power."

"To me," Jamie muttered, "the powers of this place." Green fire flared instantly, and she spun the stick in her fingers, then in her hand as the wheel grew larger and heavier, the glow brighter.

"Impossible!" the little fellow shrieked, and tried to rush her, but the spinning fire held him back. "To me, the powers!" he cried and set the Guardian's sword afire, too.

The blade drove through the whirling staff, seeking Jamie's heart. Sword and wood connected, the combined energies erupted, and jade flames roiled into the high stone ceiling. The old man staggered back, disbelief still plain on his bearded face.

Jamie clutched the staff tightly, one-handed, and called up the necessary fury, the rage. So easy, too easy. The words from Lila Anne's book were whispered with venom, then, "Die, you bastard," she added and loosed the bolt.

It arced across the chamber. The old man flung up the sword to parry the blow and, deflected, the jagged green lightning arced into a far wall instead. The stone exploded, showering them with flying debris. A chunk of rock struck Jamie a glancing blow off the bad shoulder and drove her back to her knees. The pain!

"Jamie!" someone screamed, a remembered voice, vague with time and distance, but achingly familiar.

A quick look up showed her a ball of green light rushing toward her. She swung the staff only just in time to bat it back in the old man's direction. He ducked and the globe hit the wall behind his head. Another great smoking hole appeared in the stone. This time, the little fellow got the worst of the fallout.

He straighted, eyes huge. "Who are you?" he screamed in rage. "What are you?"

"Tell him, Jamie!"

That voice again. She searched through the smoke and dust for the doorway and found it, found the tall man standing there.

"Old man!" the voice called. "I want you to meet my daughter, Jamie, and she carries what she needs to beat you."

The stunned silence was both theirs. Jamie dragged herself up again though her legs wobbled.

"Daddy?"

"Yes, baby."

"Will Weston!" the old man screeched. "What have you done?"

"Brought you the means of your destruction. Your very own prophecy is about to be fulfilled."

"I should never have listened to you. I should have killed you that first day." The little fellow turned away from Jamie. "But it's not too late to do it now." He swept the sword up, aimed at Will Weston now.

No time to call up a spell. Jamie let the staff fall against the wall, jerked the Buck knife from its sheath and threw in one smooth motion. The long blade struck the old man in the back. He squalled and crumpled to the floor. With the help of the staff, she somehow got across the floor to kick the Guardian's sword away from the little man's reaching fingers. Will Weston caught her when she started to collapse.

"Easy does it."

His arms were strong around her, bringing pain to the shoulder. She pushed him away, her business not yet complete.

"No! You can't!" the old man cried. "Please. I'll give you back your rain. I'll give you anything you ask, only let me live." He looked at Will. "Help me. I saved you once. I treated you well."

"You used me—like you use everyone," Jamie's father said coldly.

Anger flared in the old man's eyes. "You *can't* destroy me. If I die, you die. I'm God! I created everything. I'm the dreamer and you're the dreamed. Kill me and the universes cease to exist."

Jamie began to mutter a final incantation, began to draw the energy necessary to complete it, but Will put out a hand.

"What if he's telling the truth?"

"He's not."

"But—"

Will Weston's next words were lost behind the old man's screams. Jamie brought the butt of the staff down with all her might on the dwarf's head. The skull burst open, green fire pouring across the floor and then over the body, consuming it. Nothing remained. She sagged against the staff. The act of revenge left her empty and exhausted.

Beside her Will Weston stirred. "We're still here," he said in amazement and inhaled noisily.

Jamie turned away from him.

"Baby? Let me see what I can do with that arm."

"No," she said dully. "I don't want your help."

"Jamie, please—"

"I let them die, because you said I had to. I killed my friends."

"I told you why that had to be."

"Well, Weston," came another familiar voice from the doorway. "Since the job of God is now apparently open, maybe you should apply."

"Harry." Jamie saw him standing there, unshaven, dirty dark blond hair even more silver at the temples, a dour smile on his thin face, and she burst into tears. "Oh, Harry!"

"You're a mess, kid. But never fear, the doc is here." He got her to a tiny, dwarf-sized chair. While Harry worked, she touched his hair with her good right hand, touched his cheek and chin to convince herself that he was really there. He smiled at her, rubbing his hands together, calling his own healing powers, and, with a gentle warm touch, maneuvered the shoulder back into the socket. Immediately the pain lessened. The story of his being brought to the Citadel, of finding her father in an adjacent cell was told with the same dry humor she'd come to expect from Harry Roswell. And had thought lost forever.

"I really don't have this down, yet," the doc apologized, when stitches were needed for the sword wound. His voice grew hoarse while he related his discovery of the Sorceress and Guardian, recounted his inability to help them. Jamie noticed tears welling in the tired gray eyes.

Will had gone exploring and returned. "Harry, I hope you remember where the old man stashed the rain, because we forgot to ask. And this is beside the point, but can anyone explain to me why there's a horse up by the stairs?"

"It was the Guardian's," Harry said softly, expression bleak. He stood up. "The rain's in the cabinet by that hole in the wall."

"Which cube?" Jamie's father peered into the shelves.

"Middle shelf, far right."

"I don't want to touch anything until you take a look. We can't make any mistakes on this or we'll end up hauling the wrong one back with us. Be just like the old man to fill some of these with something nasty, like methane or chlorine."

"Well, hell," Harry groused, then cupped Jamie's chin in his hand and smiled down at her. "My hero," he whispered and kissed the top of her head, pulling the tattered shirt back over the freshly bandaged shoulder. He crossed the chamber to the cabinet.

The two men studied the shelves for a time. Harry shook his head. "I'm sure it's this one."

"That's the left, Physician. Not the right."

"Yeah, but it was more frosted, sort of etched. That one on the right's too clear." Harry picked something tiny from the cabinet, held it up to the light and shook it. "This is the one."

"Give it to me," Will demanded.

"I wanna show the thing to Jamie." Harry shouldered the taller man out of the way, and promptly tripped over a little table. He fumbled frantically for a moment before the cube shot straight up out of his fingers.

Jamie's father made a desperate dive along the trajectory. He landed under it, sliding on his belly across the floor, hands cupped before him. The cube, tumbling, hit the stone flagging a foot to the right, bounced high in the air, and landed in Jamie's lap.

"Christ, Harry!" Will Weston snarled, face white. "Do you realize the kind of pressure we're dealing with? If that thing had cracked—" He snatched the cube from Jamie's fingers, inspected it briefly, then pocketed it. "It's time for you to take us out of here, young lady. Get out the guide stone."

She stared up at him, remembering those things about her father that had been selectively forgotten by the little girl she'd once been—his harsh impatience, his need for absolute power over every situation.

"We can't leave yet," Jamie said, with a glance to Harry.

"We can and will," Weston snapped. "It'll take us straight back to Earth now, right from here."

"No," she said. "I've got to get Trey and Lila Anne. They're going home too. And the mare."

"Jamie," her father started, then stopped. His jaw at the temple worked slowly, and he swallowed whatever else he had to say. "All right. Let's make it quick."

She rejected Harry's help as well as Will's, and collected her knife, the Guardian's sword, and the Sorceress's staff, then, under her own power, made the long, slow climb to the surface of the Citadel. The sunlight had shifted, the shadows changed and, beside the staircase, the Oregon dun stood statue-still, muscles taut, ears and eyes intent on something below. Jamie followed her gaze.

Black silk flapped in a stiff breeze, long red hair streamed across a pale white face. Trey climbed the steps behind Lila Anne.

"Harry!" Jamie screamed at the top of her lungs. She leaned over the terrace railing.

The Sorceress raised a hand to wave, and the wind gusted suddenly. Jamie caught her breath as the little girl lost her balance, but Trey's sure hands caught her around the waist. Legs somehow braced on the narrow stairs, he steadied her against the cross-draft, then they came on together.

Jamie hadn't noticed Harry's arrival or her father's, until Will muttered, "Physician, you've just been elevated to miracle worker."

As Lila Anne stepped onto the terrace, Harry grabbed her up and hugged her, careful of the wound in her side. The mare greeted Trey first with a bump of her nose, then caught the black leather of his sleeve in her teeth and jerked hard.

"Bitch!"

"She loves you," Jamie said softly.

Trey snorted. "She's hungry." He looked around. "Did we miss everything? Who's he?"

"That's my dad."

"The provider of magic boxes . . ."

"Trey. It was all my fault." Jamie studied the young man's face, still not entirely sure she believed what she saw. "I knew you'd die. And I still let it happen."

"Is this a confession or an apology?"

"I don't know. . . ."

"Just tell me, did you beat the old man and get the rain?"

"Yes, thanks to your magic and Lila Anne's."

Trey stroked the mare's soft nose. "That's all that really matters."

"This is yours." Jamie unbuckled the sword belt and held it out. The young man made no move to take it.

"The quest is over," he said simply.

Jamie pushed the belt in his hand. "Maybe, but knowing this bunch, we'll always need a guardian."

Was it magic that brought the light back to Trey's dark eyes now, or just the thought of being needed? He strapped on the sword, shoulders straightening.

"You're sure you're all right?" Harry was saying as he followed Lila Anne across the terrace. "I should take a look." But she had other things on her mind.

"Did you kill God?" she asked Jamie, face blanched against the tangled riot of carroty hair.

Jamie shook her head. "No. I killed a nasty old man who liked people to think he was God. But he wasn't."

"How do you know?"

"He was a sorcerer, Lila Anne, incredibly powerful, but that's all. God can't be killed. He's everything and everywhere. I know for a while I didn't believe there could even be a God, not after all the horrible things that happened. But then He gave me a miracle to prove that He does exist."

"What miracle?" the child demanded.

"Two miracles," Jamie said and hugged Lila Anne, then Trey with one arm.

"How about me?" Harry asked. "Don't I deserve a hug?"

He didn't wait for an answer, or a hug. In front of everyone, the man pulled Jamie close and kissed her—a long, wet kiss that was anything but brotherly. Jamie rolled her eyes in Trey's direction. His jaw had dropped, but Lila Anne was grinning.

"I knew it," she cried.

Will Weston tapped Harry's shoulder. "Just what are your intentions toward my daughter?"

"Your *what?*" Trey demanded.

Lila Anne gave him a gentle push. "Jamie's a girl. *I* already knew."

"You never," Harry snapped, turning the Sage loose finally.

"Did so! I saw those . . ." She eyed the three men uneasily, "things . . . in your satchel, Jamie. When we were staying at Kynor. But I already had an idea. Sort of."

"What things?" Harry demanded.

Jamie smiled at the girl. "Tampons." She handed the girl the carved pole which had been leaning against the rail. "The Guardian has his sword back. I think our Sorceress needs her staff."

"Wait a minute," Trey said. "I don't understand why . . ."

"Because," Lila Anne told him, "only a female could kill the old man. And the Sorceress would never be allowed at the Citadel. But the Sage . . ."

Will Weston finished the sentence for her. "The Sage was never even a consideration for the old man because he thought he'd already destroyed the only female. Jamie couldn't tell anyone. The more people that knew she was a girl, the more danger of the old man finding out."

"And just how the hell did *you* get here?" Trey turned a dark speculating gaze on Jamie's father.

"Harry can tell you most of that story later. First, I think the earth's been dry long enough, don't you?" Will nodded toward Jamie. "If the Sage will cut us a door, we can go home."

"Will it take us back to Oregon?" Lila Anne asked with a glance at Trey.

Weston nodded. "It'll take us anywhere we want to go."

"Anywhere?" Harry grinned. "I know just the place. . . ."

Chapter Fifteen

HARRY STEPPED OUT of the dark air and onto a fine Oriental rug. A Chippendale table of heavy oak bumped his hip.

"Jeff!" he hollered at the top of his lungs, in hopes that the doctor was home, then gave the massive dining table a push. "Jeff!" There were footsteps on the kitchen tiles.

Jeff Cummings paused in the entrance to flick on the lights. His eyes grew wide. "Harry? How—"

"No time to talk. Help me move the table off to the side." The carpet kept rucking under the table legs.

"Harry! What in the hell are you doing?"

"In a minute! Help me, dammit. We need some space here and quick!"

Between them, they got the table and chairs against one wall, just in time. Trey stepped into the room, and Harry watched Jeff's confusion turn to outright disbelief, watched him collapse in one of the chairs. The mare came next. Head and shoulders appeared first, and she gracefully set small hooves on the thick rug. The rest of her arrived, and suddenly the dining room was crowded.

"Should have aimed for the backyard," Harry muttered. But that wouldn't have been nearly as dramatic or as much fun.

Jamie and Lila Anne came through, then Will Weston, all of them milling in the tight area. Jeff was startled into life finally.

"The horse . . ." he managed, though his voice cracked. "The horse goes outside. Please!"

Too late. Nervous in such tight quarters, the mare raised her tail, and a little pile of manure hit the carpet.

"Sorry about that," Trey said gently. "I'll clean it up in a minute. Which way is out?"

"Here, through the kitchen." Jeff led the young man with his animal to the door and turned the patio lights on for them. The dun got her nose into a plate of carrots on the counter, got the slender wilted roots into her mouth before Trey could stop her. The dish shattered on the tiles.

Jeff caught Harry's elbow immediately after and towed him into the hall.

"Who *are* these people? How did they do that? And what in the hell are you wearing?"

"You forgot to ask, 'Where did you come from?' "

"Harry, for Christ's sake! What's going on?"

"You wouldn't believe it if I told you. Let me ask *you* a question. When did I leave here?"

Jeff stared. "Four days ago."

"Son of a bitch. I spent the first night in Weed, then a night at the Blond Brothers' and one at Craig's. The fourth night—this night—we left the planet. If we zipped back to Oregon right now, I wonder whether we'd run into ourselves leaving?" The Physician cocked his head, eyes on his friend. "Is that even possible?"

"Harry!" Jeff's exasperation was plain. "What in the hell are you talking about? Everything I've seen so far is impossible."

Harry grinned. "Buddy, take my word for it—*anything's* possible. We got the rain back. Everything's going to be fine now. Soon as we figure out how to turn it loose."

"I'm starved," Lila Anne said from the doorway to the dining room. "Dying can make a girl real hungry." She thumped her staff for emphasis, regal in her tattered Sorceress's gown.

"So? Go get the saddlebags from Trey. He's out back." Harry glanced at Jeff. "Oh, this is Lila Anne." But the girl had already disappeared. "Hungry, Jeff? For once you can eat as much as you like."

"Sorry, Harry," Will Weston said, taking Lila Anne's place in the entry, "but that's the last of the food. The rim worlds aren't set up for that kind of magic yet."

"Magic?" Jeff echoed. "Rim worlds?"

Harry leaned against the wall, finally aware of his exhaustion. "Well, I guess we'll have to eat what we've got and worry about tomorrow, tomorrow. Will Weston ... this is Jeff Cummings. Dr. Jeff Cummings."

"Good to meet you, finally," Will said and abruptly vanished into the dining room.

"The kid with the horse is Trey," Harry continued. "Found him up in Oregon. Found all the team members there about a thousand years ago, feels like. It's only been a couple of weeks, but God, I'm tired."

Jeff only continued to stare at him, dumb. Lila Anne returned with the heavy saddlebags over one shoulder. She eyed Jeff with regret.

"The mare ate your garden. Sorry. But there's plenty here for all of us."

"Harry!" Will's voice came to him from the dining room. "It's Jamie!"

Jamie. Harry repelled from the wall and pushed past Jeff. In the dining room, the young woman sat on one of the chairs beside the table. Will stood over her.

"I'm all right," she insisted, but there was a greenish cast to her skin. "Harry, the guide stone—" She held the glass oval up on her palm. No light shone from it.

"The battery's dead," her father said. He reached to take the stone. "I should keep it. You don't really need the thing anymore."

Jamie's hand closed over the glass tightly. "Maybe, but it's mine." She looked up at Harry. "Look, there's no need to fuss. I'm just tired ... a little sick to my stomach."

"Let me see," Jeff demanded. "I'm a real doctor." He flashed Harry a brief smile. "No offense, pal."

"None taken," Harry managed. "But she's got some recent medical history you should know about—a concussion about two weeks ago, I'd say, then just an hour or so ago, a dislocated shoulder and a sword wound in the same place. Oh, and she's—"

"Sword wound! Jesus, you people are driving me nuts," Jeff growled, but gently peeled Jamie's bloodstained shirt off the shoulder and opened the bandage. "Nice stitches,

Harry. I think she's just a little shocky. Best get her to bed where she can rest. The guest room."

"No," Jamie said firmly.

Harry took her hand. "Then how about a couch? We can all eat in the living room. Or the den. Jeff's got a TV."

"A TV?" Lila Anne's face filled with wonder. "A real TV that works?"

"Earth magic," Will Weston said sourly.

But Harry could see nothing wrong in that. "A real TV with real reruns."

"What's a rerun?"

"For you they won't be reruns," Jeff guaranteed the girl. He looked over the motley group crowded into his rearranged and somewhat soiled dining room. "If you're all careful with the water, there should be enough for everyone to shower. And I'll bet I can dig up some clothes, too. Not that they'll fit, but you'll get yourselves arrested walking around L.A. in those outfits. Harry, my friend, yours is downright embarrassing."

Lila Anne giggled as Harry sadly admired the numerous tears and runs in his green tights. "Yeah, well, where we just came from they were all the latest rage." He glanced up. "So! We eat, we bathe, we sleep for a year, then we officially end the quest. Right? Somebody tell Trey it's time for chow."

II

Whatever Harry might have hoped for, things didn't work out quite as he planned. Yes, he had a room to share alone with Jamie, a bed to share with her, though Will Weston had looked properly offended by that. Harry didn't care. Just having her warm beside him brought a happiness so intense it was almost pain. But within moments of settling, the young woman fell sound asleep, and that was best, considering what she'd been through. They hadn't discussed her pregnancy, but he felt it would be best to let Jamie bring up the subject. With Jeff's help, the doc had re-dressed the quest members' wounds, including his own, but they all needed time to rest, to heal. Somehow, that didn't seem likely yet.

Will Weston was in a rush to loose the rain. But with the guide stone dead, it looked like they were on foot. Too bad. The Physician would have appreciated a lift back to Oregon and his medical cart. It was a hell of a long walk. Even if it started raining tomorrow, there'd still be a need for a witch doctor in the outlying areas for years to come.

Harry shifted carefully into a more comfortable position for his leg. As exhausted as he was, he couldn't seem to sleep. The quest played over and over in his mind like a badly edited movie, worlds and characters all out of sync. Jeff had cornered him finally after a dinner of C rations, demanding the details, and everything Harry related sounded impossibly stupid while sitting here in the real world. Will had the cube to show for all their effort, but even that seemed impossible—a good deal of the planet's moisture caught up in a tiny piece of crystal. Crazy, all of it.

Jamie stirred in the clean sheets, mumbling, then molded herself to his body. Content, he closed his eyes and slept at last.

III

Trey slept lightly, the sword and bow on the floor beside his makeshift bed. He'd ended up on the couch in the den and had spent a long time staring at the ceiling before finally drifting off. The mare had settled well enough in the backyard after demolishing their poor host's veggie garden. Trey had left her tearing mouthfuls of years-dead lawn. The nutritional value of that would be nil, but it kept her busy and happy.

But something was still wrong, something Trey couldn't quite pin down. In this world without any tangible magic—as Will insisted—Trey still felt the strong impulses of the Guardian. Why? The earth was safe, its water soon restored. The quest was over, Jamie's father insisted. Trey turned uneasily in the blankets, then came wide-awake at the tiny squeak of a hinge on the door. His fingers found the sword hilt.

"Trey?"

At the whisper, he allowed himself to relax. "What?"

Lila Anne, a small shadowy form, moved into the room. "I don't want to be all by myself." She paused beside the couch. "Can I sleep with you?"

"No," he said quickly with a rush of sudden panic. He wore only a tee shirt, being too thin in the shanks to support Jeff's old boxer shorts. The thing he most wanted—and didn't want—was Lila Anne under the covers with him. "There's no room."

"My bed's huge. You could stay with me. Please." She sat on the edge of the couch and leaned against him, trembling. "It's cold."

Trey doubted the cold had anything to do with the shivering, but he opened the blankets to let her slip in. The girl sighed and snuggled close. He could feel her warm breath on his cheek.

"Do you remember dying?" she asked quietly.

Trey closed his eyes. "Yes."

"It wasn't so bad, not really," the child murmured. "I'm not afraid of death, anymore." Her fingertips stroked his jaw. "And I'm not afraid of love, either. I want you to kiss me."

"No, Lila Anne!" The thought terrified him.

A long hurt silence followed. "I thought . . . that you . . . that we could . . ."

"No. It'd be wrong. You're just a little girl."

"I've never been a little girl," she snapped, insulted. "I'm almost thirteen—old enough to be married off."

"You're still too young."

"So, how old are you?"

"Almost twenty. Much too old for you."

"You are not! Bonner was forty-six."

"Bonner was an asshole, and so were your aunt and uncle for promising you to him. And I was just as big an asshole for hitting on you before. But you seemed so . . . grown-up."

"I am grown-up." Lila Anne took a handful of the

young man's freshly washed hair and tugged his face to hers. The trembling had stopped, and she pressed her mouth over his in a clumsy kiss. There was fire behind it—a fire he very nearly succumbed to.

"No!" He gasped and pushed her away roughly. "Please, Lila Anne."

"I thought you loved me."

"I do," Trey muttered. "I love you too much. You may be grown-up in a lot of ways, but physically your body is still developing. You could get pregnant, for God's sake."

"I think that would be wonderful. I want a baby of my own—our own."

"Lila Anne, you're only twelve."

In the dark, she leaned close again. "So how long do I have to wait before I'm old enough?"

"I only know about livestock," Trey told her, embarrassed. "You'll have to ask Harry. He's the people doctor."

"Okay. I'll ask him. But if Harry says it's all right, then can we?"

"Jesus! I hope you're not going to be disappointed."

"How can I be? I've never . . . you know . . ."

"Neither have I," the young Indian admitted unhappily.

Lila Anne laughed. "But that's great, because then I can't disappoint you either." She crawled back under the blankets with him, and folded his arms across her chest. "Tomorrow we'll put the rain back and everything will be perfect. . . . I love you so much, Trey Sweetwater."

The Guardian kissed the top of her head and tried not to worry.

IV

"Last can, folks. Pork and beans. What am I bid?" Harry waved the little olive drab container in the air. All he got was a chorus of groans, even from Jeff.

They had gathered for a very early breakfast in the kitchen. The empty C ration cans lay scattered over the nook, and the empty saddlebags lay on the floor at their feet. Harry noticed curiously that Lila Anne sat with her stool pushed close to Trey's. She took his hand now and again while they ate.

"It's almost six," Jeff said with a glance at his wrist watch. "I gotta go. Got a hysterectomy at seven-thirty."

Will Weston caught the surgeon's sleeve when he stood. "We've got more serious business to take care of first. It's a matter of planetary survival."

Jeff smiled. "Your rain cube, right? Look. You're all welcome to stay here today, but the neighbors are going to start asking questions about that horse pretty soon. Questions will bring the authorities, and that's the last thing we want."

"I can't be bothered about what people think about a damn horse." Will kept his grip on the doctor's arm. "I want to know if there are planes still in use here."

"A few are kept ready at L.A. International." Jeff's smile had faded. "But you'll never get access to them. This is a police state. Ask Harry, he'll tell you. You're here without passes, and unless that guide stone thing can get you out, leaving the city alive is going to be your biggest problem. Paranoia is the rule in Los Angeles, my friend."

All eyes were suddenly on Jamie, who had dressed in her own grubby jeans and one of Jeff's oversized gray sweatshirts. Slowly she pulled the stone from a pocket. The clear glass oval lay lightless and dead in her palm.

Will shook his head impatiently. "The old man's dead, and the quest magic all used up. I told you, we're on our own. The only reason I let Harry bring us here was because there's some semblance of technology left. The cube has to be launched from the highest place. And that means a plane."

"Well, good luck," Jeff muttered. "Only please don't mention my name when they haul you off to the block. Harry, I hope you can get through to this guy, 'cause I'd hate to lose you." He nodded at the group. "Real nice meeting you all. If by any chance it starts to rain, I guess I'll know who to thank."

Jeffrey Cummings, M.D., and obvious skeptic, let him-

self out into the garage from the kitchen door. They heard
his car start, rumbling quietly through the walls a moment.

"What's the quickest route to L.A. International?" Will
demanded in the silence that followed.

With pleasure Harry saw Trey and Lila Anne exchange
a look, then turn to Jamie—they were still a team. The
young woman turned to Harry.

"Is there a high mountain somewhere close by?" she
asked.

"Mount Wilson's pretty good-sized and closest, but it's
beyond the wall."

"Wait a minute!" Will snapped. "I'm taking it up in a
plane. It's the only way."

"Jamie's the Sage," Lila Anne said gently. "She de-
cides."

"Whoa, kids. The quest is over." Jamie's father rapped
on the breakfast nook with his knuckles. "You did it, you
won. Now we're back in the real world, and it's up to me
to finish things. Tossing the cube off the tallest mountain
around isn't going to make it. We need a drastic drop in
atmospheric pressure to release the rain."

Trey shifted on his stool. Jeff's clothes hung on him, but
the sword was strapped around his waist. "*Is* the quest
over?" he asked his companions.

"Not quite yet," Harry replied. "And I think the team
needs to have a private meeting."

Will frowned. "Hey. Remember me? I'm the one who
made it possible for you to beat the old man."

"Thanks, Daddy," Jamie said, polite but firm, "but we
do need some privacy."

With reluctance, Will Weston stood up. "All right. But
think about this—how do you figure to get us out of the
city, oh, wise and wonderful Sage? I could fly us out."

"*All* of us?" Lila Anne asked.

"All—" Will started and caught himself. "Not the damn
horse. The horse is on its own." He looked them over. "So
have your little talk. Then we'll get back to business."
Jamie's father strode out the door to the patio, obviously
annoyed.

"What's wrong?" Jamie asked, her gaze on Harry.

The Physician shrugged, trying to gather his thoughts. Something was indeed wrong. But what? He felt Lila Anne's hand on his arm and wondered briefly at the sense of comfort it brought.

Harry pursed his lips. "Your father seems awfully determined to get the cube opened quick." That sounded fairly lame. "I mean, how does he know that it's going to take low pressure to set it off?"

"Well," Jamie answered, "he spent a lot more time at the Citadel than we did. Plus he's a meteorologist. And a genius. That's pretty obvious."

"Yes," Harry admitted, remembering Will Weston and his computer system the size of Rhode Island. "But we need to think this through ourselves—very carefully. There's something that's bothered me all along, but I was hoping we'd find a way to just reverse the siphoning effect." He studied the three young faces before him. "*I'm* not a genius, but it seems to me that, despite all the magic involved, there are still a few physical laws to be considered. Almost fifteen years of the earth's airborne moisture is trapped inside that piece of crystal. That's a hell of a lot of water. What's going to happen when it finally opens?" Harry paused.

"It's gonna rain," Lila Anne said.

"And how," Trey added uneasily.

"Right!" Harry licked his lips. "So take it a step farther. It's likely that an incredibly dense cloud cover will blanket the planet—fifteen year's worth—thicker than anything a nuclear winter would have produced." He'd lost Trey and Lila Anne with that last comment, but Jamie might remember those dire threats of a nuclear holocaust in the time before the drought. "So it's raining like hell, and it's for sure flooding. We're talking about hitching a ride on Noah's ark."

The Sorceress's face showed a dawning alarm; Trey looked worried.

"But there's worse," Harry went on. "Now, the sunlight can't get through to warm the planet. It gets cold—so cold the rain turns to snow, the water to ice. If anyone's survived the floods, they're faced with another ice age." He sat down. "Of course, I could be wrong. Someone please tell me I'm wrong."

Jamie drew a deep breath. "I don't think you're wrong, Harry. But what can we do?"

"The first thing is to get that cube away from your father, just in case."

"In case of what?" Lila Anne demanded.

Trey put a hand on the hilt of his sword. "In case he's working for the old man. Maybe the old man isn't really dead."

"No," Jamie snapped. "I destroyed him. I killed the little bastard."

"That's one of the things that's been bothering me," Harry muttered. "The old man's dead, long live the old man."

Jamie stared at him. "What?"

"When I first found you at the Citadel, I told your dad that he should apply for the old man's job. I was joking, only now maybe it isn't so funny. Consciously or not, I think your father has assumed the old man's aspect." He looked at the faces of his friends. "Just as we assumed the aspects of our quest personas. The old man isn't dead, after all, and he's still playing the game."

"Oh dear God," Jamie said, fatigue in her voice. "Then there's really no way to beat him."

Harry shook his head. "Technically we already have. If we take the cube back, Earth'll at least be safe from another flood."

"How?" the Sage whispered. "He won't give up until our world is ruined." A single tear spilled from the corner of her left eye. "We won, but we lost. And I thought all I wanted was to see a cloud in the sky."

Her despair swept through Harry, and the others felt it, too. They were all so connected to one another now. Lila Anne pressed close to Jamie's knees. Being the tiniest member of the quest, and totally unsuited for Jeff's wardrobe, she'd had to don her Sorceress's gown again.

"We can't quit either. We've still got each other. And the magic," she said softly.

Trey nodded. "I don't care what Will Weston says, the

magic's here. Just point me out an ass to kick, Jamie, and I'll do it."

That brought a lopsided smile to the young woman's lips. She straightened on her seat. "Go get my father . . . or whoever he is. Get Will. If he won't give us the cube, you've got my permission to kick his ass."

Grinning, the Guardian went out the patio door. Harry gazed out the windows. The winter sun had risen while they talked, the world outside was now washed with a cold reddish light. There were shingled rooftops and the naked branches of dead trees seen beyond Jeff's high wooden fence to the west. The real world, Will Weston had called it. In moments, Trey returned alone from the barren backyard.

"He's gone."

"Shit!" Harry snarled. "We've gotta track him down quick."

"So, he's headed for L.A. International airport, right?" Trey offered. "We'll catch him there. Let's go!"

"Slow down." The doc studied the floor. "LAX is huge, and getting there on foot . . . This is one of the ritziest areas in the city, we'll be picked up immediately."

"Then we'll steal a car," Trey snapped. "That shouldn't be so difficult."

Harry laughed drily. "Believe me, there's a very good reason why Los Angeles is crime-free, now. Let me think a sec." He stared at Jamie. The young woman was quiet, thoughts elsewhere. "Let me see the guide stone, Jamie."

One brow arched, she pulled the lifeless stone once more from her jeans' pocket and handed it over.

"It's dead," Lila Anne pointed out.

"No," the doc replied. "To be precise, the battery's dead. So I'm gonna recharge it."

"How?" the little girl demanded.

The Guardian looked skeptical. "Jesus, Harry. Remember what happened the last time you messed with it—the night we first went through to Shirrah?"

"Yeah, well . . ." That was painfully hard to forget. But now it was time to concentrate on being the Physician, time to test their theory that the magic wasn't gone. Harry closed his eyes and muttered the words under his breath. "To me . . ." The response was slow, but it came finally, a vague internal prickling sensation, and he wondered if it was only his vivid imagination. Eyes open, now, the Physician continued to mouth the incantation, eyes on his hands. A faint green nimbus formed around the fingers.

"Harry!" Lila Anne cried. "It's working!"

"Stand clear, kids."

Seated on the stool, Harry balanced the stone on one knee, and carefully touched the first fingertip of each hand to the point where the tiny wires exited the glass. The discharge slammed through him with twice the power it had when he'd given Weston the whammy. Every muscle in his body went rigid for just an instant, then he found himself sprawled on the kitchen tiles with Jamie supporting his head.

"Ow," he whispered. There were plate shards and silverware and overturned stools scattered around him.

"You idiot!" Jamie snapped.

"Here it is." Lila Anne recovered the stone from the debris. "Still looks dead, Harry." She held the guide stone out to him.

"Give it to Jamie," he said, his voice cracking.

At the young woman's touch, a brilliant purple beam of light shot into the ceiling.

"That's it! Let's get a move on." Trey grabbed Harry's arm and pulled him up.

Lila Anne glanced around. "We can't leave Jeff's place in a mess. It's not nice."

"We're in a hurry," Harry said. "Jeff'll understand. I hope. Jamie, cut us a door."

"What about the mare?" This, too, from the Sorceress, who seemed more intent on the details.

"She's safest here."

"No," Jamie said without hesitation. "No one stays behind. The Oregon dun is a member of the quest." She had already shouldered the black satchel that she'd carted from world to world all along.

"Hell," growled Harry, and shouldered his own medical

pouch. "Saddle her, Trey, and make it quick. Everybody outside."

The mare, of course, decided they'd all come to play "catch-me-if-you-can." She raced around the huge backyard, tail high, snorting and blowing. Five minutes of that and Harry was ready to kill her.

"Do something," he snarled at Trey. "Or so help me, we're leaving her."

At those words, the horse stopped dead in her tracks and opened her mouth wide for the bit. A short while later, she was saddled and ready. Lila Anne handed Trey the empty saddlebags, smiling, then her face went blank.

"My staff!" she cried with wide-eyed shock. "I almost forgot my staff. Wait!" The girl fled back into the house.

Harry waited impatiently until she'd returned. "All right, Jamie. Cut us a door."

"To where? I've never been to the L.A. airport."

"No problem. There's no automatic program running, anymore. Remember what Will told me? I just had to envision Jeff's dining room, and keep a hand on the stone while you made the cuts. So all you need to do is concentrate on your dad. That should take us right to him, wherever he is." Jamie looked doubtful. "Give it a try, dammit!"

"Jamie!"

At Trey's shout, they all turned. The young Indian pointed away to the east where the edge of a fat red morning sun had just cleared the peak of Jeff's roof. Above that, a tiny wisp of pink floated in a pale blue sky.

"What is it?" Lila Anne asked in awe.

"A cloud!" Harry whooped. "It's the beginnings of a cloud!"

The little girl stood frozen, one hand curled around her staff. "Does that mean Will's already broken the cube?"

"No!" Harry grabbed Jamie and gave her a quick, tight hug that made her wince. "Oh, sorry—your shoulder." He caught Lila Anne in a similar though gentler embrace, then released her. "It means, my dear, that the cube is no longer filling. It means the earth is making its own rain again." He sobered abruptly. "It also means that it might be safest not to open the cube at all and just let the planet heal itself with the water it's got left."

Trey, the mare's reins in one hand, growled, "Then let's get Weston before it's too late."

Jamie nodded, and Harry watched her make the cuts neatly, in short smooth strokes, covering the beams with a fingertip at the end of each glowing line—far more sure of herself than the first time she'd used the guide stone. The Physician started toward the faint wavering doorway, but glowering, Trey barred the way. With his bow and quiver slung over one shoulder, the young Indian drew the sword and led the mare through first. The Guardian's aspect radiated power and strength.

Will Weston had lied. The quest wasn't over; their magical aspects had followed them here. Filled with the wonder of it now, Harry offered the Sorceress a smile and a small courtly bow, and let her go next, then took Jamie's left hand. Together, they stepped out of Jeff's backyard and onto smooth black asphalt.

Harry found himself clustered with the Terran Quest under the blue-gray backswept wing of a monster jet. There were rockets attached to the underside, and Harry noted the wide rectangular scoops—navy aircraft. F-14, he thought, though his memories were hazy. Whatever it was, the Oregon dun was not happy about being so close. She sidled away, towing Trey with her.

Here where they stood, Harry realized after peering around, were a half-dozen such planes in a tight group. Beyond the jets in every direction, the asphalt, which rolled away to distant walls, was dotted with aircraft, large and small, military and commercial. The stench of kerosene and aviation gas hung in the air. Light poured in through an open, faraway door that rose several stories high. He gazed up and saw a remote ceiling with metal beams far above him. They were inside a gigantic hangar.

"Well," said Will Weston as he appeared around the nose of the craft. "What took you so long? I was beginning to worry." He wore a light blue flight suit, a little short in the leg, and carried a helmet under his arm.

"Daddy," Jamie said sharply when the man turned and

put a foot on the bottom rung of the ladder leading to the cockpit. "Give me the cube."

At the sound of a double metallic click, her father paused. Harry glanced behind and saw a revolver in the young woman's hand, the barrel pointed at Will's back. Where the hell had that come from?

Weston swung slowly around, hazel eyes on his daughter. "Baby, you're taking this quest thing far too seriously. You're not the Sage anymore. You don't have any supernatural wisdom to help you understand what's going on. You have to trust me. I'm the only one who can save Earth now."

"No," Jamie said, and her hand shook slightly. "The earth is already safe. It's started making clouds."

"If you open the cube," Harry added, "you'll destroy the world, not save it."

"Ah, Harry." Will grinned. "Physics was never your strong suit. You're going to strain that poor little brain of yours trying to figure all this out. So don't bother."

The doc swallowed his anger and put out a hand to warn Trey back. "Weston, we can't let you do this. You've got to give us the cube."

"No. I won't give it to you. But, tell you what, Harry, you can try to take it." Will's grin never altered. "Remember back in the warehouse, I told you if we survived, you and I could step outside and settle things? This is as good a place as any." The tall man gazed past Harry to Jamie. "You don't want my daughter to shoot me and be riddled with guilt all her life. Not to mention, there's a slight possibility she'll hit the cube, too. What a mess that would make."

"Put the gun away," Harry snapped without taking his eyes off Weston. Behind him, the hammer clicked again.

"Just you and me, Harry," Will said. "I don't want to worry about your Guardian carving me up from behind with that oversized kitchen knife of his."

"Trey."

"Jesus, Doc! Let me have him. It's *my* job. I'll get the fucking cube back."

Harry considered that with care and shook his head.

"Stay out of it, Trey." If Will were indeed the old man, and this was another round of the game, then Jamie might be the only one who could defeat him. Harry wanted first try, though. "Jamie, if I lose, shoot the asshole."

"Hey, that's cheat—" Will started.

Harry caught him in the midriff with the top of his head and slammed the tall man back against the metal ladder. The air whooshed from Weston's lungs, and he doubled over. *Ha!* the doc thought, then felt the man's knee collide with his nose. Sharp pain replaced exultation, but he hung on doggedly, smearing blood all over the front of Weston's flight suit. They grappled for a moment, searching for handholds, legs braced, grunting, then toppled and rolled under the fuselage of the jet. Over the rushing in his ears, Harry could hear the team's shouts, could hear the clatter of the mare's hooves on the asphalt.

He had an arm around Weston's neck now, the wrist caught tight in his other hand, only Weston had Harry in the same damn headlock, and they'd effectively neutralized each other for the time being.

"I'm gonna kick your ass to Nebraska," Will growled breathlessly. "Just like I promised."

Harry panted, "You're the genius. So how come . . . you haven't figured out that this is . . . a suicide mission."

"I . . . don't know what . . . you're talking about." Weston gave Harry's neck a good wrench, and Harry returned the favor as best he could. With a great deal of thumping, they rolled out on the far side of the jet.

On the last roll, the doc managed to twist his head far enough to sink his teeth deep into Will's exposed wrist. A mistake. Weston snarled in rage. The arm around Harry's neck loosened suddenly, and a fist drove hard into his left temple. Harry lost his hold on Will altogether.

"That," said Jamie's father from far away, "is also for the sucker punch you landed by the Citadel stairs."

The guy had a long memory and a strong sense of justice. Harry groaned. The blood taste was strong, Will's mixed with his own, and red lights swam in his vision.

"You're an asshole, Weston," he muttered, his pounding head resting on asphalt. "*I'm* an asshole. I should have known it was no accident when I found you in the cell next to mine."

At Harry's feet, Jamie's father hauled himself to his knees. He inspected the bite marks, then looked at Harry. "Yeah?"

"You planned this all along," the doc said carefully, levering himself into a sitting position. His temple throbbed, and he had to struggle to get the words straight. "You were just using us as a way to take over the Citadel."

"Maybe you aren't so dumb after all, Physician." Something flickered in Weston's eyes. "Oh, it all started with good intentions, but my priorities changed when I realized just what the stakes were."

The Oregon dun gave an angry squeal. Harry saw Jamie standing with Lila Anne and Trey just beyond the wingtip. They were silent now, trying to hear the low voices. "I think you're still missing something important here," he said to Weston. "How high do you have to take the cube?"

"Fifty thousand feet should do it."

"Is the cockpit pressurized?"

"Hell, no."

"You've still got that cube in your pocket, and you're gonna take it up to fifty thousand feet. I bet that thing's gonna blow with the force of a small hydrogen bomb. Where does that leave you, genius?"

That irritating boyish grin returned, and Will Weston chuckled. "I've got the old man's guide stone now—*my* guide stone. How do you think I got here so fast? All I have to do is set the jet in a steep climb, then I step right off the planet. No problem."

"Will, you can't do this."

"Oh, I have to. I can't let the Terran Quest have it all. Otherwise, every fast gun'll be at the gates of heaven looking to challenge my divinity."

"But you're not God, damn it!"

"Hey, I'm the closest thing to it you'll ever meet. You'll be fine though, just stick with Jamie. Remember? God: the Father, the Daughter, and the Holy Ghost." Will's grin broadened. "But first, I think I'll finish beating the crap out of you." He swung at Harry's head again.

The doc fell back, and Will's fist sailed harmlessly by. Harry jerked a knee to his chest, then planted one of Jeff's borrowed loafers in Weston's handsome face.

"Halt!" The word was shouted through a bullhorn and continued to boom through the hangar. "Nobody move!"

Everybody moved, milling in sudden confusion. Trey fought the mare for control, and the others scattered before her frantic lunges. Jamie dragged Harry to his feet.

"Halt!" A weapon discharged, but the shot, like the voice, came from every direction. The sound of many boots racing over the asphalt joined the echoes.

"Where's Weston?" Trey cried.

A low whine began that soon spiraled into the wail of turbines. Black exhaust poured from the F-14's afterburners, and, slowly, the jet's nose rolled around to point at the open hangar doors. Harry made a grab for the ladder as the craft taxied by, then dragged himself up the rungs. Weston, face lost behind an oxygen mask, peered down at him. Hydraulics hummed, and the canopy snapped closed.

"Harry!"

Jamie's shout, heard barely over the rumble of the engines, made the doc pause. He had a high view of the hangar now and could see a small troop of men in cammies running toward the moving jet from the far entrance. There were two jeeps out in front with three soldiers apiece; one in each vehicle clung to the handles of a single large caliber machine gun mounted in back. L.A.'s paramilitary—the keepers of these jets. But why? Harry gritted his teeth. It had to be ultimate paranoia and something more. Big weapons meant big power over the other city-states that had so far survived the drought.

Angry, the doc reached up and pounded on the high-impact Plexiglas of the F-14's canopy. He had no time to worry about Los Angeles's plans to make war on its neighbors. Weston turned his helmeted head. He gave Harry a wave and a thumbs up. The jet rolled quickly toward the troop of soldiers and the open hangar doors. No more shots had been fired, probably for fear of damaging the fighter jets.

"Harry!" The voice was Trey's this time. He'd mounted

the horse and had her at a run, angled in tight to the jet's fuselage. "Jump!"

You're crazy, the doc thought, but another glance at the advancing army convinced him he better try. He swung one leg out over the mare's rump and let go of the ladder. The horse veered away from the aircraft just as Harry landed behind the saddle. Her back hunched suddenly, and she bounced twice, two jolting plunges that sent the doc's teeth together hard. Harry grabbed Trey, and they both nearly came off.

A long, grinding shriek overpowered the rumble of the engines. Harry risked a glance back. The double doors were slowly closing. Will Weston goosed the throttle on the jet and the craft surged forward, gaining speed. The jeeps tried to block him, then dodged aside at the last possible moment. The pilot wasn't going to stop.

The mare slid to a halt near Jamie and Lila Anne.

"Use the staff," Trey cried to the little girl. "You've got to stop him!"

"No!" Harry snarled, and somehow slid off the mare without getting trampled. "We'll blow ourselves to hell, if you do." He turned to Jamie. "Get us out of here before those guards arrive."

"Where?"

"I don't fucking care, just do it!"

The young woman pushed the pistol into the waist of her jeans and dug out the guide stone. There were tears on her cheeks. Someone shouted, "Halt!" again, close enough to be heard without the bullhorn. Jamie cut a doorway, her hand a little shaky. Harry pushed Lila Anne through first, and screamed at Trey, who had turned the mare to face the enemy, bow in hand. The Indian youth launched several arrows before he finally obeyed, leaping down to drag the horse behind him over the threshold.

"Go, Jamie!" Harry yelled, and when she refused, grabbed her hand to tow her across.

Trey sent another quick pair of arrows back into the hangar as the opening faded. Now a cold winter wind tugged at them, gritty and dry, and bright Oregon sunlight dimmed their sight momentarily. Harry's cart and scooter stood on the rocky ground before them. There was very little dust on it. After all, they'd only left it here last night.

Chapter Sixteen

LILA ANNE LEANED on her staff and watched Trey doctor the doctor. Poor Harry, perched on one of the cart tires, was a mess. He held the medical supplies rummaged from his gear in his lap and handed them, as needed, to the Guardian. The doc's nose still bled some, and Trey very gently straightened the cartilage and put strips of tape over it, then plugged the nostrils with cotton. Jamie, on the far side of the cart, kept glancing at the sky. Her eyes glistened and Lila Anne, who had only the vaguest memories of her mother, wondered what it would be like to lose a father, than find him, and lose him again.

"Shit!" Harry hissed.

"It's your own damn fault," Trey grunted, and dabbed antiseptic lotion on a cut in the hair over Harry's temple. "If you'd let me take the bastard, we'd have the cube, now."

"You couldn't have done any better." Harry's voice was thick and nasal.

"The hell I couldn't!"

"Oh, stop arguing!" Lila Anne wailed, sick of the whole business. She thumped the staff and felt her own anger flow through the wood. The runes turned icy under her fingers.

"We better decide what to do," Jamie said quietly. Her first words since their arrival.

Harry nodded and winced at the same time. "When the cube goes off, Earth may get real inhospitable, real fast. I say we settle on Kynor. Despite my unscheduled flight out of there, I kinda liked the place."

"Or we could go party with Sim," Trey added. "I'll bet we're really celebrities by now."

Disgusted, Lila Anne listened to them. "You're giving up?"

Harry shrugged. "We'll wait around and see what happens." He squinted at the sun. "I'm actually hoping I'm wrong. The cube might open and, sweet as you please, give us a nice spring shower. But we better be prepared for the worst." The doc looked at Jamie. "Where to, Sage?"

"What about all the people that have nowhere to go?" Lila Anne demanded. "You said it might flood."

"I know." Harry studied his feet. "But did you notice all the firepower in that hangar? Nine-tenths of the world dies off and the last tenth is still hoarding enough weapons to wipe each other out a hundred times. Maybe the old man was right. Maybe it'd be better just to start all over from scratch."

Jamie came around the tailgate, the guide stone streaming purple light through her fingers. She held it out to Harry.

"What?" he asked, confused.

"Pick a place, and I'll send you," Jamie said. "Only I can't go. This is my home."

Lila Anne nodded. "It's mine, too. I'm staying." She felt Trey's eyes on her and wondered, briefly, if she were being foolish. The young man moved to stand over her, and she lifted her chin defiantly.

"You'll have to count me out too, Harry," Trey said. He brushed Lila Anne's hair from her face, then bent to kiss her cheek lightly.

"Hell!" Harry groused. "You'll change your tunes when the water's up to your asses."

The mare squealed suddenly, and for an instant, the sky was filled with white light. Lila Anne gasped and saw the barren mountains to the south undulate, an impossible rolling motion that sent clouds of dust high in the air. Underfoot, the ground surged, and the girl staggered. Trey caught her in his arms. The Oregon dun, the whites of her eyes showing, stood spraddle-legged in an effort to stay upright.

Lila Anne looked skyward again as the ground ceased to roll. Glowing red streamers of light shot toward the north and were sucked violently back. In the blink of an eye it was night, the heavens black and starless. A distant roar began.

"What is it?" she shouted over the unending thunder.

"Rain!" Harry shouted back just as the first drops struck her.

An icy deluge arrived, pounding them to their knees. Trey shielded Lila Anne as best he could, but the air had turned to water. She covered her nose, fighting for breath. Somehow, Harry dragged the tarp off the cart, and they huddled under it, deaf and blind. Shivering with the cold, Lila Anne ran her fingers over the staff in the mud beside her. She called up an image of a page in the long lost primer. With some minor changes in the wording, there was a chance she could use a warding spell to protect them.

"Hey!" Trey shouted when she pulled loose and started to back out into the downpour.

She paused. "Wait here!" Earth's powers responded immediately to her summons, and muttering, she demanded their help. The tip of the staff was touched with a unique blue-green fire now, and the girl pushed it into the mud, then began to draw the lines. The mare stood, nose down and trembling, beyond the cart. Lila Anne changed the pattern of her drawing to include the animal and the cart. The rain clogged her nose and throat, choking her, but she forced herself on, and the fiery line followed her. Trey, from the edge of the tarp, watched. At last, she had circled back to the beginning and closed the ward.

The Sorceress stepped inside and struck the butt of the staff to the ground with a splash. "So mote it be!"

The air cleared, the thunderous roar muted by the spell. Aqua light from the staff lit the area, reflected back by the water that sheeted over the invisible walls that Lila Anne had created. Slowly, the others climbed out from under the tarp.

"The bastard really did it," Harry snarled through gritted teeth. "Shit!" With disgust, he viewed his cart filled with water. Some of the boxes floated on top. "We can't stay here. Not unless we figure a way to build our own ark." Beyond the ward, the rocky ground was under several inches of water already.

Trey shuddered. "I'm freezing. Let's go to Sim's and dry off. At least there we'll have plenty of time to think things out, maybe come up with a plan."

"I told you you'd change your mind quick," Harry grunted. He glanced across the muddy ground. "Jamie?"

The young woman had her back to them, her gaze on the downpour beyond the ward. Lila Anne felt a surge of guilt and put a hand on Jamie's wet shoulder.

"I'm sorry about your dad."

Jamie sighed. "He's a jerk. He was always a brilliant jerk. He drove my poor mother crazy. It's just easier to ignore those kinds of things when you're little." She turned. "But we've got a bigger problem to deal with at the moment."

"Trey says—"

"I heard. I think we can spare a few more minutes in real time, though. I want to see if the guide stone can offer a solution." The young woman pulled her stone free and pressed it to her forehead with the light beam pointed inward. The glass flashed white, then died. Jamie's hazel eyes grew troubled. "Lila Anne, you loaned me your magic once. Do you think you could trust me with it again?"

Dread made the Sorceress's heart thud in her chest. "Yes. Only last time I was dead. I'm not sure it's something I can just hand over, but I'll try."

"You should know," Jamie said with a glance down, "the staff may be lost. For good."

"Oh." The dread turned to outright fear. Lila Anne forced a smile. This wasn't a spell she'd have found in the book, but she felt certain she could do it. "Put your hand on the staff over mine." Jamie's fingers curled over hers, and Lila Anne drew a deep breath. The powers were already there, glowing; she had no need to call them. The girl stared into the soft fire and imagined what must be done, then murmured, "I do give and endow this magic to my sister, the Sage, to use as she will. Take it." Lila Anne pulled her hand out from under Jamie's.

The light flickered and died. In the darkness, the Sorceress found the staff and retrieved it.

"Sorry," she said, lighting the tip once more. "Guess I have to be dead."

"Just what the hell are you trying to accomplish?" Harry demanded.

"Harry, shut up and let me think." Jamie considered the glowing aqua fire. "When I had the staff, I turned it into a wand, Lila Anne. Can you do that?"

"A wand? Sure, the spell was in the book." Lila Anne took a few steps back.

The staff was heavy as she began to turn it end over end, her hands at the center for balance. The fire showered in turquoise sparks from the tip, creating a glowing circle in the air. The circle began to shrink and the heaviness disappeared. The little girl held up a tiny stick to Jamie. "Okay?"

"Perfect," Jamie said. "Trey, I need an arrow. Harry, find me some of that waterproof medical tape."

Harry balked. "What in hell are you doing?"

"I don't really know."

"Bullshit!" the slender man snapped.

"Harry . . ." Jamie drew a deep breath of icy air. "The guide stone is more than just a key." When he opened his mouth, she cut him off. "I have to try this. It may not work, but let me run with it." She pulled the guide stone from her pocket, and its purple beam joined the fire of the wand, stabbing into the darkness beyond the ward, where the rain continued to pour.

"This is the last arrow," Trey said as he handed it over to Jamie who now sat cross-legged on the rocky, muddy ground.

Harry handed her a little metal holder of white surgical tape that dripped water. "Now what're you doing with the stone?"

"Programming it . . . I think," Jamie muttered and stared

into the glass for a moment, then placed the stone to her forehead again.

Lila Anne gave Harry a worried look, and the man shrugged. Finally, the Sage set the stone on her knee and tore a strip of tape from the roll. Lila Anne held the wand as it was fastened to the shaft of the arrow, but when Jamie began to tape the guide stone to the point, Harry squatted beside her and grabbed her wrist.

"That's our only way out of here, lady. You're not thinking of having Trey send the stone on a trip, are you?"

Jamie jerked her wrist free. "Yes!"

"No way," the doc snapped and reached for the arrow. The purple beam died at his touch.

"Harry," Lila Anne said carefully. "We need to trust the Sage."

Jamie stared at up the doc. "Don't interfere, Harry. Please."

The man's face, awash with the eerie aqua light, was filled with doubt and fear. "We could die here. We could drown."

"I know," Jamie said unhappily, and held out her hand. Harry gave back the guide stone, and it flared to life again. She taped it to the arrowhead, and murmured, "So mote it be . . ." When Jamie let go of it, the thin purple beam continued to glow, and so did the wand. She handed the arrow to Trey. "Send it."

"Where?" the young man asked.

"Straight up."

Trey looked doubtful. "The arrow's off-balance with all this shit taped to it. And in this downpour, it won't go very far."

"Just do it!"

The Guardian took the bow from the mare's saddle and nocked the arrow. His teeth chattered from the cold, and he gritted them, then drew the bowstring back as far as he could, the arrow pointed into the blackness high above them. He loosed it. The arrow sped screaming upward, and they watched the purple and aqua lights race into the sky and disappear.

For a long moment nothing happened. The Terran Quest stared into the night.

"Nice try," said Harry finally, his voice heavy with disappointment. "Maybe we'll get lucky and find the stone out there somewhere."

"Harry!" Lila Anne cried and pointed. High above them came an explosion of dazzling rainbow colors, then light streamed through the clouds. To the north, blue sky showed briefly before the storm closed over it again. But now there was a twilight glow over the world, and the roar of the rain let up slowly until it had dwindled to a quiet, gentle shower.

With a shout, Trey gave Jamie a sudden hug, then wrapped his arms around Lila Anne to hold her tight.

"What happened?" Harry demanded. "What did you do?"

Jamie smiled. "I think we've just shared our rain with Shirrah. At least that's what I was trying for. They need it even more than we do." She rubbed her face with her hands, wearily. "It's going to rain here for weeks and weeks, but I think we can handle it."

"I've lost my staff, then," Lila Anne murmured, and felt tears threaten. "It's in Shirrah, and we can't get there, now."

Trey, his arms still around her, leaned close to her ear. "Have you looked in the cart?"

"No. Why?"

"Do it." He released her.

She saw it then, the narrow wooden end of her staff poking up over one corner with Harry's junk piled all over the rest of the length. "But how . . . ?"

Trey grinned. "It's been there all along."

"The runes are gone," she said in wonder, dragging the pole out.

"No," the young Indian said. "You just haven't carved them into it, yet."

"You're right!" Then she paused, confused. "Now, wait a minute. That means . . ."

"Don't think about it too hard," Trey advised. "It'll just drive you nuts." .

Lila Anne stared at the Guardian. "Then we really do still have our magic, don't we?"

"We won it," Jamie told her. "The Terran Quest succeeded, so our aspects won't be passed on. And now we know that there's always been magic on Earth, that we can use it. I think that's almost as great a gift as the rain."

"Earth needs all the help it can get," Harry added. "Things weren't going so hot for this planet even before the drought."

The Oregon dun snorted and sidled close to Trey.

"Watch the toes," he snapped and pulled Lila Anne aside to protect her.

"She's scared. There's something out there," the girl said, and searched the wide wet plateau that stretched away all around them. "There!" She pointed a finger to the north, where she'd seen movement in the rain among the rocks and boulders.

Wolves, four of them, the same mottled color as the stones. They drew near, growing more distinct, then raised up on back legs and flowed into human form. The Blond Brothers. Trey, with a growl, drew his sword and stepped forward.

"No," Jamie said quickly. "They can't get past the ward. Let them come close if they will."

The rain plastered the long blond hair to the creatures' skulls, darkening it. Wide mouths grinning, they stopped just short of the glowing line. One held up a hand.

"*Tonwin,*" he said to Harry. "We've felt the powers here. You are truly a man of great value. You've won your rain back."

Jamie answered him. "Harry has even greater value. He's shared this rain with your world. You may return to it now."

"But why?" the speaker said, and his grin widened. "We are happy in this place. The hunting is good." The man's eyes drifted to Trey who gripped his sword tighter.

"No," Jamie told the creature firmly. "You are not welcome on Earth. If you stay, the Guardian will kill you all, just as he killed your brothers here and on Shirrah. There are other worlds to hunt, even your own in time, when the grasses grow again."

"This was our world before humankind took it from us."

"But it's no longer yours." Harry put a hand on Trey's shoulder. "If you stay, you'll die. Believe me. You have to go home."

"The ward will fade in time," another brother grunted.

The first brother sniffed the air. "True, but that one is the Guardian now. He bears the sword, Zwendal, and is even more dangerous than he once was." The blond man turned toward Jamie. "Storyteller, once you pleased us with your tales. We will hunt other worlds for now, but keep our memory in your stories—tell mankind that there are other brave hunters in the universes. Tell them that one day we may return."

Jamie nodded slowly. "You've always been in our stories in one form or another. We won't forget you."

"And you, *tonwin.*" The brother eyed Harry. "Remember, you are ours. Always."

The creature's blue eyes flashed yellow and his face shifted, the bones lengthening. He dropped to all fours and trotted away through the curtain of rain. The others followed him.

"Can we trust them?" Trey asked, his eyes on the retreating forms, his hand still on the hilt of the sword.

Jamie took a deep breath. "Probably. Otherwise, Guardian, you'll have to kill them." She paused, face draining suddenly of color, then turned away to vomit onto the wet ground.

"Whoa!" Harry cried. He caught her around the shoulders and helped her to the cart. "What happened?"

"I'm okay," the young woman said, voice strained, as she sat on the tire.

"This has all been tough for you," the doc snapped anxiously. "You've got to take it easy."

"It's no big deal. I was throwing up at Jeff's, too."

"For God's sake, why didn't you tell me?" Harry splashed around in the cart and came up with his stethoscope. He let the water run out of it before pressing the end to Jamie's chest under her sodden shirt.

"Because it was no big deal. Ow!" the young woman yelped. "Take it easy with that thing. My breasts are a little tender."

Harry nodded. "Of course they are. It's the upsurge in hormones. Causes the vomiting, too."

The Sage, still a little greenish, glanced up. "What hormones?"

"Pregnancy hormones."

Lila Anne squealed, "Jamie's gonna have a baby?"

Jamie's face went from green to white. "You mean . . ."

"You mean you didn't know?" the doc asked.

"No."

Harry watched her expression closely. The young woman not only hadn't known, but the information now didn't please her.

"I assumed you knew," he muttered. "Only a woman could kill the old man, but she had to be carrying life. Will said that you knew when the time was right. So, I thought . . . It's only been days. I'm sure there are herbs that . . . could terminate the pregnancy. Or we can go back to L.A. and let Jeff take care of it." Why did those words cause him so much pain?

Jamie blinked as if wakening, then turned her gaze on the man kneeling in the mud beside her. "Oh, Harry." She smiled and the warmth of it touched her eyes. "A baby conceived on Kynor will have to be just about the most special child ever born on Earth. Do you think it'll have dual citizenship?"

Relief swept through Harry, and he hugged her. Everything was suddenly right with the world. Rain. He looked past her out over the plateau, then gazed up into the smoke-gray clouds driven past on the wind. A baby. The wonder of it all filled him with hope. Even the desert would bloom again, live again, before settling back into the cycle nature had intended. Oh, the world would take decades to recover, maybe even centuries to overcome what these fifteen years of drought had done, but it hardly mattered. Harry Roswell would still be needed as a doctor here in the outback. And Jamie could tell her wonderful stories wherever they went, then, when the baby was due, they could stay a while in some small village. . . .

He searched the young woman's beautiful face. Her short-cropped hair formed a shaggy dark frame for cheek and jaw. She was a wanderer, strong, and self-reliant. Perhaps life with a country doctor would be too tame to hold her long—even with a baby. But he couldn't worry about that until the time came. Harry leaned forward to kiss her and bumped his broken nose.

"Ow!"

"Harry," Jamie laughed, "you're such a klutz."

Lila Anne basked in the happiness and felt Trey's arms fold around her once more, warm and secure. She tilted her head back to stare up into his face.

"I know what her name is now," she said softly.

He smiled down. "Whose name?"

"The Oregon dun's."

"Took you long enough. So what is it?"

"Lady Rain."

"Awfully pretty name," Trey growled, "for such an ugly horse. Hey! Lady Rain."

But the mare wasn't so ugly anymore. Feed and water had filled her out, hard work had muscled her hindquarters, widened her chest. Now she turned a glittering eye on Trey Sweetwater and bared long yellow teeth.

"Bitch," Lila Anne said lovingly.

RETURN TO AMBER...

THE ONE *REAL* WORLD, OF WHICH ALL OTHERS, INCLUDING EARTH, ARE BUT SHADOWS

ROGER ZELAZNY

The Triumphant conclusion of the Amber novels

PRINCE OF CHAOS   75502-5/$4.99 US/$5.99 Can

The Classic Amber Series

NINE PRINCES IN AMBER 01430-0/$4.50 US/$5.50 Can
THE GUNS OF AVALON   00083-0/$4.99 US/$5.99 Can
SIGN OF THE UNICORN   00031-9/$4.99 US/$5.99 Can
THE HAND OF OBERON   01664-8/$4.99 US/$5.99 Can
THE COURTS OF CHAOS 47175-2/$4.99 US/$5.99 Can
BLOOD OF AMBER   89636-2/$4.99 US/$5.99 Can
TRUMPS OF DOOM   89635-4/$3.95 US/$4.95 Can
SIGN OF CHAOS   89637-0/$3.95 US/$4.95 Can
KNIGHT OF SHADOWS   75501-7/$3.95 US/$4.95 Can

Magic... Mystery... Revelations
Welcome to
THE FANTASTICAL
WORLD OF AMBER!

ROGER ZELAZNY'S
VISUAL GUIDE to
CASTLE
AMBER

by Roger Zelazny and Neil Randall
75566-1/$10.00 US/$12.00 Can

AN AVON TRADE PAPERBACK

Tour Castle Amber—
through vivid illustrations, detailed floor plans,
cutaway drawings, and page after page
of never-before-revealed information!